PARADISE HIGH

Paradise High

a novel by
WILLIAM HENNING

SUNNYSIDE BOOKS
A Division of Monitor Lizard Enterprises
Bangkok

Published by Sunnyside Books LLC in Austin, Texas. For all inquiries, please contact the publisher via email at sunnysidebooksllc@yahoo.com

Cover design by Rafael Andres

ISBN: 978-1-7346122-0-2

10 9 8 7 6 5 4 3 2 1

*For my old man, who's having
a good laugh somewhere, no doubt.*

The ancient sage Hung Li-Kuh Yak descended from the mountainside NOT to proclaim the coming of a new breed of man, as his predecessor had done, but to profess a more elementary wisdom. "If you start playing with your dick," he spoke, "you're only going to make it harder on yourself." And with that, the result of a lifetime of meditation, the diminutive monk hiked up the folds of his burnt orange robe, so as not to trip on the drapery, and returned into seclusion, which is probably where he belonged...

I.

ND UNLIKE MARLEY, Grouse Boozer was only late: to begin with.

He'd left earlier that afternoon on a mission to the Indian Reservation liquor store, and I was beginning to worry the tribal authorities had spotted him for a fake and hauled his ass off to a wigwam someplace, given him twenty-five cents for a phone call, and taken away his car keys, in which case we'd all have been in a pinch since Grouse probably would have done something stupid, like use the quarter to order Chinese food in his cell instead of calling one of us. And we'd still be waiting for our beer.

I wondered again if I should have gone with him.

Grouse had called me at home mid-morning. I was dozing through church when the phone rang. I remember rolling over groggily and picking up the receiver, groaning something in what must have sounded like tongue-tied Swahili. In a nonsensical dream, I'd been watching as a young man in ancient Pompeii was flash-frozen in volcanic ash and then pawned off as a slave statue for the tomb of Pope Julius II. At the sound of Grouse's voice, I snapped into the present, but the bizarre set of mental images persisted.

The window blinds permitted a dull slab of light, indicating another gray afternoon, as they had forecast, and I'd already microwaved my underwear once that day. When I begged off Grouse's invitation to join him on his errands, he gave me an earful, but we soon hung up, and I promptly reassumed a semi-fetal, semi-comatose position, burrowing myself into the sofa cushions, dry humping a pillow, snuggling the blanket up under my chin, and thanking the goddess of mercy I wasn't outside.

The snow was still glittering down.

Grouse didn't gamble, so it was unlikely he'd stumbled across a blackjack dealer who couldn't bust or a simulcast jockey whose recent cheeseburger binge had gone unreported on the tip sheets. Although, that said, casinos have a funny way of holding a kid upside down by his ankles and shaking the ATM card out of his pockets.

I bunched up the sleeve of my jacket to check the time. It was 4:33 in the afternoon. The day wouldn't have been any quieter if you were wearing earplugs. The sun was already well into its descent, sending another one into the books, and it was a Sunday, like I mentioned, although nobody was keeping score. We were on winter vacation—"Christmas Break" having been purged from our lexicon by the sensitivity committee—and all the days somehow belonged together.

A city snowplow reached the four-way intersection opposite the park, turned the corner, and went roaring past with its steel shovel grinding against the frozen asphalt, blasting a half-pipe of dirty slush and wet snow onto the front yards across the street. As the truck continued down a tunnel of naked elm trees in the distance, the jarring noise faded steadily until it was as soft as a parachute landing.

The silence returned and the snowflakes accumulated, and the whole frosty scene called to mind the practical joke where you leave the restaurant saltshaker partially unscrewed, causing the next guy to dump a pile of sodium chloride onto his pork and dumplings.

In our case, there in the frozen suburban hinterlands of the upper Midwest, God was heaping an awful lot of salt onto our pork and dumplings. Christ, it was snowing like one of New York City's tickertape parades.

And some flakes were as fat as Communion wafers.

I huddled against the orange brick exterior of the warming house, flicking a cheap plastic lighter at a cigarette cupped in my hands, but the flame wouldn't catch. And if you've ever taken a long, slow drag on a cigarette that wasn't quite lit, well, it was beginning to feel like the preamble to *that* kind of night.

Then at last in the distance, through a slanting trajectory of snowfall, Grouse Boozer's old pickup truck, adorned in fog lights and CB tentacles, drew closer like an alien land rover on reconnaissance. On its approach, the truck fishtailed down a small frozen embankment, past the chain-link backstop on the baseball diamond, and glided to a halt next to me.

The windshield was snowed over except for two half-circular areas where the wipers had brushed it away. Grouse's window was cracked open, like he was smoking, but only country music came out.

I looked in. "What's up, Low Flyer?"

"What's up, yourself," Grouse answered. "And see how the fuck you like it."

He cackled, reaching over, and turned down the music, something about whiskey bent and hell bound. Then he held a finger to his lips and nodded toward the CB radio. Picking up the transmitter, he pressed the button, saying, "I'll tell you cocksucker eighteen-wheelers on North 169 one more time: Get out of the *goddamn* left lane!"

A redneck voice came back at him:

"Where *yew* at, boy? If I find out which *ve-hickle* you're driving, I'm gonna run you off this frozen road!"

Grouse smiled, revealing a plug of tobacco in his lower gums. He flipped the power knob to leave the trucker fuming and killed the ignition. I kicked a hunk of frozen sludge off the underside of the truck and asked him what the hell had taken him so long.

"The Injuns were having customer appreciation day," he replied, "and I couldn't leave without chatting it up for a while with the owner lady."

Grouse reached behind the passenger's seat, retrieving a brown paper bag that was saturated with grease.

"Nachos?" he said.

No thanks, I laughed.

In the truck's bed were two untapped kegs of beer collecting frost, part of the day's haul, along with a half-dozen liquor boxes filled with various spirits and wine bottles piled up on the back seat.

"The old gal wouldn't let me leave until her husband came back," Grouse explained. "She said he wanted to shake hands with me, which is understandable, I guess, since I am their 'most valuable customer.'"

He gestured the quotation marks with his fingers and told me what had happened. Apparently, the woman's husband—"Injun Willie," Grouse called him—was out playing pull-tabs at Dewey's Bait & Tavern but was due back any minute, the lady promised, as long as Willie hadn't driven the car into a ditch or soiled his pants again. He had left the liquor store earlier with a bottle of cinnamon-flavored schnapps, she said.

Grouse suggested maybe Willie had ducked into a bingo parlor to shake hands with a slot machine, to which she replied, in a heavy Minnesota accent, which Grouse now parodied, "He'd better not have, unless he wants me to use pieces of him for *ice-fishing bait!*"

Grouse editorialized: "When she laughed at what she'd said, her nicotine-stained teeth looked like half-popped popcorn kernels."

So Grouse killed time inside the liquor store eating free hot dogs, pacing the aisles reading booze labels, watching the local news on an old antennae television. When snowmobile drivers came in looking for "something to warm the innards," the bells attached to the door would jingle, announcing their presence. Each time someone entered the store, Grouse and the lady owner turned their heads toward the door, expecting it to be Willie.

When Willie finally arrived, polluted drunk after all, and began waving a finger in Grouse's face, telling him not to "mess with Willie, because Willie is the Golden Boy," slurring his speech, stinking of cheap booze and rotten luck, the old lady let Willie have it—and this was Grouse's cue to begin sidestepping toward the exit.

Somebody, playing a practical joke on poor Willie, had even tied a yellow cape around his neck.

Just as Grouse pushed open the door to leave, Willie got down on his hands and knees behind the cash register and began praying feverishly into the trash can.

"You looking for your knife down there, Willie?" Grouse asked him, trying to be funny. Willie wrenched his spine and let fly a second time. "Jesus, Willie, you okay?"

Willie looked up from the floor with bloodshot eyes, his hands wrapped around the corners of the wastebasket, and he pointed an unsteady finger in Grouse's direction. "Of course I'm okay, you son of a bitch," he growled. "I'm the Golden Bo—" But he had no sooner started on the last syllable than another projectile stream of cinnamon-flavored regurgitation departed Willie's stomach, this time destined for the old lady's shoes.

The woman was still hitting Willie with a broom when Grouse slipped out into the night. My buddy shook his head now and chuckled, evidently grateful for a live audience after the lonesome forty-five-minute drive. As he laughed, a thin scar revealed itself beside his left eye, the enduring memento of a childhood sledding accident in which he'd slammed face-first into a telephone pole at the bottom of Morningside Hill.

"And I take it Nathan Hooper was a hit?" I said.

"Bo, it could be a photo of Oprah Winfrey and Lucky Star Liquors wouldn't care."

Grouse leaned over and locked the fake driver's license in his glove box. Then he looked at me curiously and added, "It's a good thing they can't tell us honkies apart."

I kicked one of the hubcaps on Grouse's truck.

"Nice wheels," I said.

Grouse got out and slammed the door.

"Five hundred bucks," he said, shaking his head. "I'll send you the bill, asshole."

He spat a gob of brown tobacco juice onto the snow bank and sighed as a way of changing subjects.

"Anyway, how many guys are here?" he said.

"I don't know," I said. "Maybe fifteen or twenty."

As he crouched down to re-tie one of his duck boots, the floodlights above the hockey rink snapped on, bathing the ice in crisp, brilliant light, and shining with such singular intensity that the surrounding fields and sledding hill, home to the ice ramp known locally as Devil's Hard-On, remained cloaked in shadows. Earlier that afternoon, a soot-colored cloud had spread across the sky like a cheap rug, and now not even a sliver of moonlight pierced through it. From up there on the clouds, I imagined, the hockey rink must have looked like a hospital operating table: sterile and without shadows.

Then the warming house door banged shut and an irascible witch mother came stomping around the corner of the brick building, jerking on the outstretched arms of two heavily bundled toddlers, who were tripping over their bootlaces as they skidded toward a powder-blue minivan.

The woman cast a scornful glance at Grouse and me.

"Hi," said Grouse, holding up a hand. "How's it going?"

The woman grumbled something under her breath about "lack of conscience" as she jammed her key into the door and filed away the urchins.

It occurred to me that earmuffs had possibly failed to shield her children's virginal ears from the foul discourse of our degenerate friends. It wouldn't have been the first time.

She gave us another seething stare and shook her head.

Grouse looked at me and shrugged.

"It's probably hormonal," he said.

The woman slammed her door shut, producing a hollow "whump" that was promptly muffled by the woolly dunes of fresh snowfall. The minivan's engine wheezed as the vehicle slithered up the frozen embankment into the elementary school parking lot, which led out to the main road. Its glowing red taillights soon disappeared, and the way I saw it, good riddance: the evening's nagging motherly influence was gone.

I walked around to the passenger side of Grouse's truck and opened the door. His basset hound, riding shotgun, gazed up at me with heavy, bloodshot eyes, dejected, it seemed, by the indignity of being made to watch the world drift past through a frosted side window. The dog was named "Gump Worsley" after the legendary Minnesota North Stars goaltender who had played without a helmet and who once famously remarked, "My face is my mask."

In one of the great ironies of modern times, Gump Worsley was a deaf basset hound, born with a pair of aesthetic ears. The detail might have frightened off some prospective owners. Indeed, Grouse knew of the "factory defect" when he'd brought the dog home from the pound. In a textbook "hard sell," the local pound manager had warned Grouse that if he didn't take the dog, "it's probably headed for the ugly injection."

Thus, with an unexpected ethical weight on his shoulders, Grouse sized up the hound a bit more intently, observing it there on the vet's table like a bronze sculpture in the round. Grouse reasoned to himself that although the dog couldn't hear, it did have two sympathetic eyes—and in those lovely, melancholy eyes, Grouse thought he detected a soul.

"I'll take him," he said.

And, of course, the dog never knew of the divine intervention that had spared its life.

As dogs go, Gump Worsley held a fairly sophisticated world-view. During one leisurely summertime stroll through our old neighborhood, Grouse and his dog happened upon a snarling German pincher bitch that charged across her lawn and lunged at the ill-protected basset hound. The attacking dog's leash, like you see in the cartoons, tightened to the stake just as she got within striking distance, and the chain yanked her up around the neck, forcing her onto her hind legs, barking and snarling and showing a mouth full of broken-glass teeth.

The basset hound just stared off impartially down the wide, tree-lined residential avenue, seemingly oblivious of the looming peril. Gump Worsley sniffed at the lilac breeze with what Grouse later described as a "habitual air of regal nonchalance" but then slyly cocked his head to one side—*knowingly*, Grouse insisted—and gave subtle recognition to his attacker as he lifted a hind leg and pissed on the other dog's boulevard.

Like I said, a poetic worldview.

At the warming house entrance, Grouse heaved open the thick steel door, allowing his dog to navigate around a portable charcoal grill that was wedged in the jamb. I hung back momentarily underneath the yellow lights outside as Grouse made his public entrance.

He gave a loud greeting to the gathering inside the warm room, followed by a blunt warning: "If anyone feeds beers to my dog again, I'll—" But I missed the back end of his threat as the door slammed against the grill.

The squat, weathered-brick building wasn't much bigger than a two-car garage. Inside, an old rotary phone jingled like a city newsroom's, pinewood benches ran along three walls, and an old stone drinking fountain in front of the furnace room produced water so thick with lead you almost literally had to chew it.

The first thing you generally noticed upon entering the warming house was its peculiar stench, which had nestled into the hard sponge floor over many years of neglect. To my refined nostrils—I considered myself a sommelier of this particular brand of stink—the scent combined the less offensive notes of body odor, skunky beer, urine, and a hint of wintergreen snuff, all feebly masked by a cheap industrial mopping soap.

You wouldn't want your girlfriend to roll around in it before a date, but actually it was a smell you could grow fond of.

Back near the bathroom was a small office with a few hooks on the walls, an industrial desk with no drawers, and a tattered old love seat that was something of a rite-of-passage for those of us who'd brought girls back there. I was in the club, but I won't tell you who with. It's too goddamn embarrassing.

Anyhow, spirits were high that night, and the place was alive with laughter and ribald conversation. There was no music, no television, no video games: it was just the sort of old-fashioned high school pre-party you always sort of took for granted at seventeen, thinking, because you didn't know any better, that life would never require you to mature past that stage—or refrain from using colorful words like "twat."

"That twat," Grouse said at one point. "I hate those private school douche bags."

On the floor, a Bunsen burner, lifted from the high school science lab, had been jerry-rigged into a mini stovetop, on top of which a pot of eggnog was simmering. Peter O'Leary tended half-heartedly to the "holiday cheer" from his spot on the ragged easy chair next to the door, occasionally poking at the saucepan with a hockey stick. He was also watching the charcoal grill, and from what I could gather, he'd drawn the short end of the stick as far as responsibilities went.

"O'Leary!" Grouse announced, rather loudly. "I have a story you're going to love."

He succeeded at capturing the whole room's attention.

Grouse told us he'd stopped at Buckley's News & Tobacco to buy some "see-gars" before driving out to Mdewakanton country. Buckley's was a time warp, a place that had somehow avoided extinction without evolving, a strip-mall storefront that smelled like cedar wood and old comic books, and had turned its only real profits, we assumed, in the late-1980s when they hustled elementary school kids like us out of our hard-earned baseball card money.

As we grew older, we learned that the store also did a bustling business in the pornographic magazine trade, which was set in a back corner of the shop, fortified behind a pair of creaking, swinging doors, and guarded by a handwritten sign pleading: "Adults only, *please!*"

Grouse told us he had decided to "take a gander" at the new edition of *Lil' Shavers*, his "favorite periodical," which had reached newsstands that week. As he flipped through the glossy photographs with his back to the door, a few times it would creak open, meaning someone had entered, and creak again, meaning they'd left.

"I got lured in by this fascinating letter," Grouse said, "from a high school girl whose teacher makes her stay after class under the guise of extra tutoring. They were discussing the Battle of the Bulge, I think, when all of a sudden, in a sinister turn of events, the teacher pulls a shaving razor out of his desk drawer and whispers all horny-like to the girl, 'C'mon, Kelly. Don't you know that pubes are for puberty?'"

There was a ripple of laughter in the warming house, but Grouse hadn't reached his punch line. He said it was right then he felt someone bump into him.

"I turned around, and there was Mr. O'Leary," said Grouse, "thumbing through *The Plumbers' Almanac!*"

O'Leary blushed.

Grouse went on: "Your dad forced a smile and winked at me. He said, 'I won't tell anyone if you won't, Ryan,' and he walked out."

Grouse roared in tyrannical laughter and others followed.

The truth was that Grouse had long been exposed as someone who told stories in the way they were best meant to be remembered—which didn't necessarily translate into *how they actually happened*. Plus, he and O'Leary were involved in a tiff, as my mother would say, and so I don't think anybody would have been surprised to learn that the story about O'Leary's father was a total fabrication. Indeed, Grouse knew how to rile an adversary, and public defamation usually did the trick.

Their feud had begun the previous summer when O'Leary—a fun-loving practical joker by nature—concealed a gas station ham-and-cheese sandwich under the hood of Grouse's truck, causing the air-conditioning system in the ensuing days to blow rotten wafts of industrial-grade pork scent into the cab.

Grouse retaliated by stuffing a rack of barbecued pork ribs above the hard-foam ceiling tiles in O'Leary's basement, where they quickly decayed and began to stink like a rotting marinated corpse. To make matters worse, the source went undiscovered for days.

O'Leary, declaring that Grouse had gone too far, then slipped the phrase "eating a dick" into Grouse's final term paper for American literature class. Of course, Grouse didn't know about the addition until after he turned in the paper, when Mr. Jenkins called him on the telephone at home and quoted to him the section that read: "…which was of little concern to the philandering Benjamin Franklin who, eating a dick, alluded to some of his wilder escapades in his autobiography."

The fact that Grouse now implicated O'Leary's father as a fan of beaver magazines did little to quell their duel. But it did cause the room to rumble in laughter like a pack of hyenas with a joy buzzer.

Andy Morton reclined on a metal folding chair in front of the furnace room with a physics textbook fanned open across his lap. He was wearing a red insulated nylon jacket with "Rink Attendant" stenciled on the back in white letters, and he represented the authority by which we'd "reserved" the public ice rink that night. When he got caught snickering at Grouse's antics, he unwittingly became the next victim.

"Morty, you child molester," Grouse belched. "How the hell are you?"

Naturally, it was a rhetorical question.

Eluding his inquisitor's gaze, Morty slurped from a plastic bottle of hyper-caffeinated artificial-citrus soda pop, scratched nervously behind his ear, and forced a grin. After the spectacle of Grouse's entrance, and the public dressing down of O'Leary's father, Morty was smart enough to know that a response wasn't necessary.

But just when it appeared as though he would escape the pillory, a tape ball, set in motion by a hockey stick, whizzed across the room and ricocheted off Henry Beach's midsection, causing Henry to buckle at the knees and slump to the floor.

A voice denigrated the whimpering victim: "You pussy!"

Unable to contain himself, Morty thrust a finger into the air and proclaimed: "From the Latin-derived word 'pusillanimous!'" He laughed to signal his little joke, and then, finding himself unintentionally in the spotlight, he nervously slurped at his soft drink to keep his giggles from cascading into an uncontrollable outburst.

"Morty, how do you know all this stuff?" asked O'Leary, no doubt eager to shift the conversation further away from his father's smut habit. O'Leary flipped a sirloin on the grill, and I watched as thin strips of smoke disappeared out the door.

Andy shrugged and admitted to a peculiar hobby: he read dictionaries for pleasure. In fact, he told us, he'd spent the previous summer in Oxford, England, editing a college version of the wordbook. The pursuit no doubt impressed the Harvard folks, who'd granted him admission to their freshman class the coming autumn. Few of us were surprised.

I once saw Morty walking around Lake Harriett reading Joyce at arm-length. He was known to say things like, "I haven't read much Dostoevsky lately," which, of course, is the smart guy's way of saying, "Who the *hell* is Dostoevsky?" But he wasn't pretentious. In fact, the opposite: he was good-natured to a fault. Hell, if Morty made eye contact with a passing dog on the sidewalk, he would nod politely and smile hello.

But the problem now was that Morty kept talking.

"Can you imagine how cool it would be to own the complete version of the Oxford English Dictionary?" he wondered aloud.

"A lot of people think owning a Harley-Davidson would be cool," someone replied.

"Do you know how many volumes are in it?" Morty asked.

No one did.

"Thirty or more. With etymologies for every word."

"It means you could look up the derivation of any word," said Morty, pausing to suppress an eager grin. "Like 'derivation,' for example."

It was here that Grouse interjected on behalf of the room.

"Morty, is your girlfriend nice to you?"

"Why?" Morty replied.

Smart people always answer tough questions with questions.

"Because it seems like you might need some advice."

"Well, it sounds like a loaded question in that case."

"So what?"

"So what's your advice?"

"Never lose the upper hand in a relationship," Grouse said. "There, that's it. It's as simple as that. I'd just hate to see you find yourself in the dog house someday."

"Fair enough," said Morty, nodding appreciatively. "And here's some advice for you then: When in doubt, obfuscate."

"What does that mean?"

"Look it up," Morty said, grinning like an alligator.

Henry, the tape ball victim, was still whimpering on the floor. Peter O'Leary had moved behind him and now hoisted Henry up by his armpits, bouncing him up and down on his butt like he was playing a game with a baby. Awakening from his pain, Henry seemed embarrassed by the gesture.

"Stop," he laughed. "What the hell are you doing?"

"I'm making sure your testes don't ascend," O'Leary said.

"Well, cut it out."

Henry shook free of the nonsense, scampering away on all

fours to his duffel bag, from inside which he retrieved a jock strap with a built-in hard-plastic nut cup that he promptly pulled over his kelly-green sweat pants as insurance against potential future assaults.

His lower lip protruded like a cash register, swollen by a pinch of snuff in his lower gums. A handful of wet tobacco flecks stuck to his lips and chin.

"Hey, Boozer, did you get the booze?" he said to Grouse. Henry's tone was still bitter, evidently owing to the lingering discomfort of his injury.

"First of all—" Grouse answered forcefully, breaking into giggles before he could finish his reply. "Jesus, Henry, you look like you just went down on Pigpen's sister. You've got shit all over your face and lips."

Hardening his glare, Grouse added, "Second, I'm not your goddamn maid, so put some ice on your nuts and calm down a minute. I got everything I said I would, but that doesn't mean you're *entitled* to it. In fact, you might want to start kissing my ass—or at least adopting a more pleasant tone—unless you'd rather stay sober all night."

Grouse's voice issued with the force of a thrusting pitchfork, steel-like and indifferent, all muscle and ribcage. His cement-blue eyes were impenetrable. The truth was, he had bought everything requested of him. He'd even jotted notes on the back of an envelope so he wouldn't forget anything. He'd spent the morning on the phone with the girls, whose requests were quirky, maybe even annoying, asking for things like "a bottle of Mayfly Estates, 1994, the merlot."

The backseat of his truck was like a well-stocked bar, he told us, with a few handles of rail bourbon, a pint of vodka, root beer schnapps, gin, tequila, dark rum, Sangria wine, bottles of wine for the girls, boxes of boxed wine for the less discriminating, jugs of Fezziwig's Cider, and a handle of The Famous Grouse, finest Scotch whisky, for himself—all that, plus the two beer kegs and whatever people brought on their own.

It promised to be some kind of night.

The old rotary phone jingled, and, trying to be funny, I cupped the side of my mouth with one hand and hollered, *"I'm not here!"*
Nobody laughed.

O'Leary answered the phone. It was Duce Babyk calling from his car phone to share some good news. After listening to what Duce had to say, O'Leary covered the mouthpiece with his palm and announced: "Some of Heather's church friends are coming to the party tonight, but I don't think you guys will like them too much. All they want to do, apparently, is take off their shirts and give head."

Feigning disgust, Henry Beach moaned. "You mean, they don't even want to *talk* or anything?" The line was rewarded with laughter, and so, emboldened, Henry added: "Tell Duce I'm bringing a duffel bag full of prophylactics."

O'Leary spoke into the phone:

"Hey Duce, Henry said your stepmom's water just broke, so you should get over here as quickly as you can." He winked at Henry. "Yeah, it's a carnival of clowns and strippers here, and the alcohol just arrived so hurry up."

He hung up the phone.

Most of us were already well acquainted with Heather's "church friends." Among our pals, they were known affectionately as "Bobbin'" Robyn and "Blowie" Chloe, for obvious reasons. The duo (trio if you counted Heather) possessed remarkably loose morals, although I'm not passing judgment in saying that. In fact, at the risk of offending a fragile reader or two, I think it's worth briefly noting some of their finer qualities as human beings, since these girls advanced their genetic agendas with a certain endearing charm and ingenuity.

Robyn White liked to hum the Star Spangled Banner while performing fellatio—a true patriot, in my estimation—and she had achieved notoriety for publicly declaring her refusal to "take it in the butt" before she was married. She was saving that special act for holy matrimony, she said, a gift for her future husband on their wedding night. Chloe Brooks, on the other hand, only "took it in the butt," using the contrarian reasoning that she wanted to preserve her "real virginity" for that special someone with whom she would share a lifetime.

"It sounds like you, Henry," Grouse had joked.

And Heather Flynn, who was on the birth-control pill but always made her lovers wear a condom anyway, refused to allow any boy to—*ahem!*—finish inside of her (even inside the rubber) because she was saving that sacred act—of being an orgasm reciprocator, if you will, or of sharing the intimate conclusion to the Big Wiggle—for making babies or perhaps simply for consummating her "true" love.

Peter O'Leary, I think, was the one who commented on the troubled state of raising daughters in the modern age, saying, "What must those girls' parents think?"

To which I replied: "Girls like that don't have parents. They're spawned in little petri dishes. Seriously, I cringe on behalf of any loving father who is forced to endure the cheap horror of raising a slutty teenage daughter."

Spitting tobacco juice into a pop can, Henry Beach eyed me with a sloppy grin. "What about you, Billy? Any fathers out there justified in their fears tonight? In other words, are you finally ready to give Julianne a recital?"

A "recital" was the opposite of an "extraction," and Julianne Caswell had been jokingly dubbed my "eleven-teen-year-old" girlfriend because she was only a freshman.

But self-deprecation had its limits, I felt, especially when the taunt came from someone like Henry. And so, instead of a direct reply, I lobbed a mortar back at him: "Henry, shouldn't you be more concerned about possibly becoming our only friend to 'shoot the moon' in high school, sexually speaking, and go wire-to-wire without ever scoring a chick?"

Henry was so bad with girls, I joked, that if he were a porn star he would probably double-knot his shoes.

"And didn't you rent *Eraserhead* on Valentine's Day last year, the one and only night in your life you were absolutely *guaranteed* to score?"

Henry's eyes glossed over, as though I'd touched a nerve and touched it too hard. But he wasn't going to cry. No, Henry was tougher than that. If nothing else, he was resilient to these sorts of insults, like an oft-beaten field mule. Instead, he opted for another line of attack—on my flank.

"You'd better be careful, Billy. After your birthday next week, you could find yourself behind bars in Stillwater for what you're planning to do."

"And maybe you could tell us something else, while you're at it," he added. "Did Julianne's parents need to sign a permission slip before she could go out with you?"

The one-liner drew a singular, inflated outburst of laughter from Grouse, who, I knew, was only trying to bait me. Turning toward him for my reply, I said, "Don't laugh too hard. You wouldn't want to get another hemorrhoid."

The line got scant laughs, but it had cleared the runway, and so I stood up and tried again. I felt myself unfurling a self-conscious grin as I said to Henry: "All right, man, you got me. You know our career surveys came back? Well, it turns out I'm supposed to be the candy man." Then, crooning in a creepy, saccharine tone, and grinding my hips suggestively, I sang out: "*Stir it with love… and make your world taste sweet!*"

That joke didn't set the crowd on fire either, but a few comrades chuckled, and it managed to divert their attention. O'Leary, who was standing near the drinking fountain, asked a vaguely probing question over the murmurs and laughter.

"Hey Billy, is Julianne a Hebe?" he said.

"Yeah, I think she's half-Greek," I said.

"But, I mean, is she Jewish?"

"I don't think so. Why?"

"Naw, for some reason I thought she was."

And so went my brief stint in the public stocks, the tax each of us in that room was occasionally forced to pay simply for being a card-carrying member of the herd. Inwardly, I congratulated myself for having evaded Henry's inquiry, but his question still lingered in my mind, as it had been for some time.

In a melodramatic usage of italics, I silently asked myself: *Would tonight finally be the night my little pussycat got what was coming to her?*

Morty normally ran with a different crowd, but he and I were old pals from the student newspaper, *Solstice*, where we worked as senior editors under the guidance of Miss Florence Fogey, a white-haired, hunch-backed English composition teacher and strict grammarian who was part of a dying but priceless breed—which is to say she hailed from an era ("prelapsarian," she joked) in which kids would be far less likely to walk into a classroom with a young blonde teacher up front chewing bubble gum who would ask the class to "Call me Jenny."

Miss Fogey, by comparison, was a cigar-chomping drill sergeant. A staff writer at the newspaper once used too many exclamation points to express excitement ("The Sadie Hawkins Dance was so much fun!!"), but the only thing they excited was Miss Fogey, who scolded the young writer, informing her in a gruff, joyless tone that exclamation points "ought to remain the property of little girls and their stickers."

"Use them sparingly," Fogey continued. "The *words*, not the punctuation, should deliver your passion."

Miss Fogey's weary voice sometimes reminded you of your grandmother waking up from a nap, but that didn't mean she always offered gentle criticisms. Occasionally, her orthopedic shoes would be laced up too tight, or she'd catch a whiff of her own rosewater and formaldehyde perfume, and she'd tell you what she really thought.

"This is the worst sentence I've ever read," she said to me once. "And I'm not saying that to be critical."

I laughed. "How are you saying it then?"

On another of my early drafts, Miss Fogey had covered the margins in red ink. Her pen left actual physical grooves in the paper, indicating the depth of her exasperation with my sloppy prose. Reaching the bottom, she re-wrote the final paragraph entirely and then dragged her pen up through the middle of the page, all the way to the top, where she scrawled in capital letters, "THIS IS BULLSHIT!"

Apparently, she'd found an appropriate time for an exclamation point.

When I asked what she meant, Miss Fogey snarled.

"Take this out to the parking lot and back your car over it a few times," she said.

She was staring about three feet over my head. "This stinks."

"What's the matter with it?" I asked.

"Tighten it up," she barked. "Tighten it up, goddamn it. Here—" she thrust a paperback copy of something by Hemingway at me. "Go develop a bullshit detector, and don't come back until you've cleaned up this mess."

Then, the teachable moment passed, Miss Fogey cracked a wry smile and in her gentle voice added, "Don't try to write *anything* after you read F. Scott Fitzgerald."

She chuckled at her little joke and said, "Lord knows how many young writers *he's* screwed up."

I always assumed that when Fogey eventually retired she would settle down to expire underneath a pile of Dickens, and that would be that.

The old girl was a rallying point in my friendship with Morty, and the three of us had lunch reservations later that week at the Minneapolis Woman's Club. Morty and I wanted to thank Miss Fogey for writing our college recommendation letters. We had pitched in fifty dollars each and bought her an autographed copy of *Of Mice and Men* by John Steinbeck (signed by John Malkovich).

Incidentally, the night before our warming house gathering, I had played in a semi-momentous varsity ice hockey game. As a distinguished letterman (the worst player on the state's best team),

I had also penned an "inside scoop" for the newspaper. Miss Fogey had finally showed some mercy with her red pen. Perhaps she figured the teachable moments had all passed now, and that a kid might benefit from heading off to college with some confidence.

The story I'd filed, under the byline George Plimpton, ran like this:

If you've ever sat in a warm bath in the middle of a cold winter and pulled the plug and just sat there while all the warm water sinks down the drain, and the cold air starts licking at your skin, then you'd know how I felt sitting on the splintered wooden bench in my damp, cold equipment, staring up at the nine state championship banners hanging from the ceiling. I could tell myself that even though I was only an understudy for a supporting role, I ought to take comfort in association. At least I had that going for me—that, and a front row seat for the biggest game of the year.

Our opponent, the mighty Beltrami Bears, hailed from Minnesota's north woods, up there between Lake Wobegon and southern Manitoba, and their team was basically the same group of guys we'd slipped past the previous year to win the state tournament, 1–0, in front of 17,000 screaming fans in St. Paul.

The rematch pitted No. 1 versus No. 2 in the current statewide rankings, causing a hockey spectacle in a hockey state, and pointing every rink rat with a conversion van toward Willard Arena.

An esteemed sportswriter once observed that a procession of hockey players walking in their equipment looks like an army marching on stilts. As we made our way through the bowels of the arena, the crowd's gigantic presence was palpable, like a deep vibration—an almost dreamlike cacophony of muffled clangs and jumbled voices.

When we reached the tunnel's final turn and a toothless kid in a youth jersey cried out, "Here they come!" we accelerated to a trot and were damn near galloping by the time we popped knuckles with our assistant coach and burst through the gate onto the ice, plunging between two columns of cheerleaders on figure skates.

The student band erupted into our school fight song, and the horseshoe of home-crowd fans rose to encourage our entrance. On my third lap around the rink, I banged my stick on the glass in front of our student section, eliciting a tribal, orgasmic roar.

Then the Bears came piling onto the ice, greeted with the thundering approval of cowbells and bean shakers. Their goalie, in scuffed leather leg pads stuffed with deer hair, was first onto the stage, followed by a collection of country bumpkins with bleached hair and rat-tail mullets that flapped out the backs of their helmets.

They dumped two goals on us right away, the result of furious hustle and pent-up determination, and we quickly found ourselves off balance, nursing a sense of ill fate. We hadn't even broken a sweat.

Beltrami's third goal, which came in the first minute of the second period, drained our spirits completely.

Desperate for a swing in momentum, we began to play like goons. When Dominik "Duce" Babyk, Jr. throttled Beltrami's assistant captain along the sideboards and was called for checking-from-behind—a two-minute minor plus a ten-minute unsportsmanlike conduct— Coach Kinnard enlisted me to serve the minor penalty.

Note: When the referee's arm went into the air signaling a penalty, a chorus of "boos" rang out from our student section, and after some choice words for the referee, Grouse Boozer led our classmates in chanting: "*The ref beats his wife! The ref beats his wife!*"

"I cremated that guy, huh?" said Babyk when I joined him in the penalty box.

"Jesus, I thought maybe you'd caught him fondling your sister," I joked.

He ignored me, unclasping his chinstrap and stretching his legs, preparing for an extended stint in purgatory.

"We've got to energize this crowd," he said, surveying the arena over his shoulders. "I've never seen this place so full."

"Yeah, I'm stealing my fifteen seconds on stage when I bust out of here," I said.

The game was half over and I hadn't played a single shift.

"Good for you, Bo," said Duce. "Good for goddamn you."

When the two-minute penalty expired and the game official opened the penalty-box door, I could feel myself breathing heavily. There was a struggle for the puck in our defensive zone, and I skated hard in that direction, ignoring calls from our bench. One of our defensemen suddenly gained control of the puck and spotted me circling above the blue line. He slid the puck up the center of the ice, splitting two Beltrami defensemen.

I caught the pass on the tape of my stick and turned up ice with full momentum and nobody within four or five strides. At the blue line, I looked up to see how the goaltender was playing me. He'd come pretty far out of his crease to cut off my angle, so I didn't want to shoot from the outside. I skated hard until I reached the middle of the zone and then went into my move.

Faking to my backhand, I leaned that way to sell the fake, causing the goalie to pivot off-balance toward his glove side. Then I quickly brought the puck back to my forehand, and, with the goalie lunging across the crease, I snapped a quick shot aimed for the opening in the lower corner. Ping!

The puck ricocheted off the pipe and took an awkward hop over my stick while I swiped at the second chance like a soused Mexican at a piñata party. I planted my skate blades, sending a cloud of ice shavings into the air, but my angle wasn't good enough for another shot. A Beltrami defenseman slammed into me, knocking me to the ice, and the puck wound up underneath the pile.

When the referee blew the whistle, Coach Kinnard sent out a fresh line, and I sauntered over to our bench, soaking up the final moments of near glory. Straddling the boards, collecting my breath, I looked up into the stands. My dad gave me a thumbs-up. I cocked my head, as if to say, "What the hell," and he nodded effusively, smiling.

At the far end of the bench, Peter O'Leary leaned forward and said, "Hey, Billy, were you going for the triple deke?"

"That's right. I came up one short, I guess."

Meanwhile, the referee dropped the puck, and Beltrami sprung a forward out of their zone, catching our defensemen on the proverbial steps of city hall with their pants down. The Beltrami defenseman sailed a long pass to the floating wing, who caught the puck in stride and converted on his breakaway attempt, shooting between a gaping five-hole. We were down 0-4, and the game was helplessly out of reach.

A more intriguing sidebar didn't find its way into print.

During the second intermission, the mood in our locker room had turned downright morose, and so I ducked out of there, lumbering down the sponge-floored hallway past the Zamboni garage—which, incidentally, reeked like a puddle of reindeer piss—to the medical trainer's area behind one of the goals, where I found Duce Babyk slouched against a vending machine, sipping twenty-five-cent coffee from a styrofoam cup. I caught the tail end of his conversation with Elliott Sturgeon, the dirtball junior varsity student manager.

"Do you understand what I'm saying?" said Duce, as Elliott edged toward the double-doors leading into the stands.

Elliott turned half around, with a loopy, punch-drunk grin on his face and his hands stuffed deep into the pockets of his army surplus jacket. With his gaze fixed somewhere vaguely in the middle distance, he replied, "Yeah, man. I got you."

"All right, then."

Elliott exited, and the doors clasped shut behind him.

Duce sipped his coffee, convulsing with small laughter, and bent forward to watch through the window as Elliott plodded up the cement stairs. "Did you see that guy?"

I tried to get another glimpse of him, but all I could see were his camouflage pants and grimy black motorcycle boots. "What happened?"

"Jesus, man. You talk about stony-baloney."

"What do you mean?"

Duce arched his eyebrows.

"What do I mean?" he echoed. "I mean those guys are fucking catatonic up there."

My lips drew back in an irrepressible grin, as I finally comprehended what he meant. Ever since Elliott had taken over as the junior varsity student manager, the team's post-game rituals had evolved into "heavily medicated" affairs, first under the numbing influence of pharmaceutical opioids and now, apparently, courtesy of good, old-fashioned reefer.

The JV had been equally humiliated that afternoon, losing 0-6, and after their coach finished delivering his post-game eulogy, Elliott bolted the locker room doors shut and handed off pre-rolled, elephantine joints to the underclassmen as they entered the showers. Apparently, all seventeen players plus Elliott had gotten as stoned as Old Testament harlots.

As we skated our warm-up laps before the third period, I gazed into the student section in the bleachers, surveying the two rows of bleary-eyed student-athletes as they slobbered on their liquid cheese nachos, masticating as if they'd been jabbed with bovine tranquillizers.

After a few more laps, Duce and I eyed them together.

"Do you see those jackals?" I said.

"Christ," sighed Duce. "I wish I was up there."

As we skated past them a final time, the student section rose en masse and began stomping on the wooden benches like a thundering herd of wildebeest. Those in the front row banged their fists on the glass, and their wild cheers filled the arena. They seemed determined to inspire a dramatic comeback.

I fist-pumped toward the crowd and said to Duce, "Let's be heroes."

"Hey, that's the spirit," he said. "Let's do it."

Alas, a comeback wasn't in the cards. In high school hockey parlance, we "got embarrassed" in the final period, as Beltrami set up a neutral-zone trap that repeatedly foiled our attempts to advance the puck into their zone.

With some curiosity, however, I noticed that whenever Duce was on the ice our student section filled the arena with resonant "*Boos!*" or rather, what sounded like boos, but which, in fact, was the deep bellowing of his name: "*Duuuuce!*" At the end of each shift, he climbed back onto our bench and the séance ended.

As time ticked down, their cheers grew more insistent, and by the final minutes our fans were producing a sort of sustained primitive wail to cheer him on.

Finally, we pushed into Beltrami's defensive zone. O'Leary controlled the puck along the sideboards and flicked a pass across the ice to Duce, who one-timed a snapshot into the goaltender's leg pads.

"*Ohhh!*" our student section groaned, as the goalie fell to the ice and smothered the puck. Our bench stood up and leaned over the boards to watch the final minute.

With less than twenty seconds remaining, O'Leary dug the puck out of the corner and was curling out toward the net when our entire student section—every goddamn one of them, I swear—began to stab frantic fingers at the blue line, screaming: "*You've got Babyk! You've got Babyk!*"

O'Leary looked up and slid the puck through traffic to Duce, who had a clear sightline to the goal. He wound up and fired a muscular slap shot that exploded off his stick, travelling sixty-four feet in an instant, untouched, into the twining in the upper corner of the net.

Judging by our fans' reaction, you might have thought we'd just defeated the Soviets at the height of the Cold War. Our student section piled on top of each other in a riotous orgy, hopping up and down, arms flailing, jumbo-sized sodas splashing in the air. In the middle of it all, an American flag tied to a hockey stick was being waved vigorously.

Duce turned toward the crowd and thrust his arms outward in a mock crucifixion pose, receiving his linemates in a celebratory embrace. Our school band struck up the fight song, trying to give the moment as much emotion as it appeared to deserve. Duce raced over to the glass in front of the band and conducted them with his gloves on.

But with just twelve seconds remaining in the game, and our

team trailing by an impossible three-goal deficit, the rest of the arena was perhaps understandably mystified.

When the celebration ended and the referee dropped the puck at center ice and time expired—we lost—a brawny, flat-topped North Woods student on the opposite side of the arena stood up and waved his arms toward the scoreboard, taunting our classmates as he laughed with apple-red cheeks.

"Eat shit, you *fuckin'* cherry-nibblers!" he hollered.

Grouse clambered into the aisle and darted up a few stairs before turning around and belting out, across the ice: "Hey, asshole! Kiss my ass!"

Now, Grouse wasn't necessarily attracted to violence, and he wasn't provocative merely in order to pick fights, but he usually ended up brawling simply because he took pleasure in running his mouth. Physical conflict was only necessary, he said, because he couldn't restrain his vocal chords. Boredom drove him to it, in other words.

"Confrontation keeps your blood from coagulating in the veins," he once philosophized.

To his credit, Grouse never retreated from a fight, even when his opponent was built like the Iron Sheik. So when the Beltrami lumberjack raised his arms in the universal gesture of inviting a rumble, Grouse turned without hesitation and bounded up the stairs leading to the back of the arena, where he and our classmates met a hostile North Woods gang dressed in checkered flannel shirts and wool gas station caps.

The scene could have inspired a Shel Silverstein poem: "The hicks from the sticks versus rich city pricks."

As the two delegations squared off, Grouse quickly noticed a "mangled looking" girl standing beside the broad-shouldered woodsman. Her close proximity to him indicated she might be his girlfriend, although her letter jacket hailed from another suburban high school. Retelling the story later, Grouse said her gaping, slack-jawed stare looked "half-retarded or something," but he couldn't quite place what was wrong with her.

"I thought maybe she had fallen out of her crib as a baby and landed on her lips," he said.

The lumberjack flexed his neck muscles.

"Do you have a problem?" he said.

"No," said Grouse, "but she isn't much to look at."

The woodsman bunched up his flannel shirtsleeves and hunched his shoulders forward, assuming a more aggressive posture—similar to a macaque monkey before it attacks a group of schoolchildren. Then the northerner clucked his neck a few times, like he'd seen tough guys do in 1980s action movies, and cracked his finger knuckles.

Goldy Lindenheimer, our behemoth buddy, leaned down and set a massive paw on Grouse's shoulder. "What are you doing, Ryan? That guy is twice your size."

"Bullshit," Grouse said. "That fucker is malnourished."

Standing well over six feet tall, with broad wood-chopping shoulders and a nutcracker's jaw, the guy wasn't a bantamweight either. "Malnourished" might not have been the unanimous adjective, but Goldy giggled and let it go.

Grouse was leering at the guy and his homely girlfriend when all of a sudden, he later said, "like when a dragonfly hits you between the eyes on a jet ski," it occurred to him why the girl's expression bothered him so much.

Grouse eased into a half-smirk as he addressed his burly adversary with fresh confidence. "If you want," he said, matter-of-factly, "I can recommend an orthodontist for your girlfriend."

That was all it took. The other side charged, and all hell broke loose. Grouse tangled with the lumberjack, and the two exchanged a flurry of reckless, unguided punches, although neither fighter, I'm told, got in any clean blows. That was the version I heard from Goldy Lindenheimer anyway.

"Oh, bullshit," Grouse later contended. "I gave that hick a serious shiner."

From what I heard, Grouse knotted his arm around the

lumberjack's head and the two toppled to the floor, where they clutched and wriggled, seeking to land a knockout punch from an impossible angle. The rest of the melee resembled an old-time, bench-clearing hockey brawl, wherein some swung their fists, others grabbed handfuls of jersey, and the rest just stood off to the side and chatted with the enemy.

Goldy Lindenheimer recused himself from the contest, owing to an unfair size advantage and to his desire to remain "clean" in the eyes of college football scouts. Thus, he became the official fight historian. He estimated that less than ninety seconds passed before local law enforcement arrived.

That was apparently how long it took for the police officers to set down their coffee cups and say, "Excuse me for a minute" to the city councilmen with whom they were discussing their Christmas bonuses.

A female officer with a dark mane of hair tied in a ponytail yanked Grouse out of the pile by his belt loops and jerked him off to one side. In the less crowded standing-room-only section, she employed the "straight arm-bar takedown maneuver" to pin Grouse jaw-first against the concrete floor.

"That was unnecessary," he said to her.

In the locker room, recounting the story for the umpteenth time, Grouse told us: "Honestly, she hurt me worse than Grizzly Adams did."

The cop mashed Grouse's face against the floor while keeping his arms pinned behind his back. "Do you see this badge?" she demanded, with frothy spittle on her lips. "It gives me the *power* to take control of situations like this and restore order."

Grouse winced.

"Do you understand me?"

"Get off me, please. I'm not going anywhere."

"Do you want me to call your parents?"

"Go ahead."

The officer then demonstrated a textbook application of maintaining total physical control as she used one of her elbows to force Grouse's neck and face against the floor while, with her free hand, she slipped handcuffs around his wrists, which he'd offered freely behind his back.

"Ma'am, I think you're taking this a bit too seriously," said Grouse.

She yanked him up by the metal bracelets and pushed him against a wall. "If you continue to act insubordinately, I'll charge you with resisting arrest." She tightened her grip on his arm. "Would you like that?"

Grouse didn't respond.

"That's it, we're going to city hall," the cop said.

Clutching his elbow like a bird of prey, she led Grouse past the radio announcer's booth on the far end of the arena, continuing past a group of concerned parents. Grouse smiled as his little parade went by, hoping to convey reassurances about his unseemly predicament. "Hello, Mr. Buckley... Mr. O'Leary... Hi, Mrs. Lindenheimer," he said.

"Are you okay, Ryan?" my dad asked him.

"Sure, no problem. We're just going to have a little chat."

"Is this your son?" the cop asked my dad.

"No, he's a family friend. Is there something I can do?"

The cop didn't reply. She was listening to the radio on her shirt collar. The other officers were calling for backup. The policewoman led Grouse into the heated foyer, past the concession stands, which always reeked of fake-buttery popcorn and instant coffee, to the arena management office.

Officer Lindquist rapped on the glass door, and Larry Snodgrass, the arena manager, pushed it open.

"This is one of the instigators of the fight," she said. "Can you detain him for me while I return to provide support?"

"Sure thing, Connie," said Larry Snodgrass.

The officer removed the handcuffs in case they were needed back at the "fracas" (her word), and Larry told Grouse to sit and wait in an empty office. A couple of minutes ticked past on the wall clock. Larry checked his wristwatch before stepping into the corridor to see if any other excitement was brewing.

Throngs of fans were pressing toward the exits, and Grouse couldn't believe his luck. With Larry's back briefly turned to him, Grouse stood up and plunged through the Emergency Exit doors, racing down the stairwell to freedom. By the time Larry noticed his captive was missing, it was too late.

Our team bus got snared in heavy post-game traffic outside the arena. Through the front windshield, a procession of red brake lights was stacked up like an utterly hopeless rush-hour commute in a snowstorm. The diesel engine groaned as the bus plodded forward, inch-by-inch. Our driver, a college kid who evidently had better things to do with his Saturday night, finally radioed for a police escort, and when the squad car arrived on the shoulder, its swirling red and blue lights punctured the calm darkness inside the bus. Reflexively, I held up my hand to shield my dilated pupils from the nauseating strobe lights. The police car guided us onto the shoulder, past some cones, and around the clogged traffic.

Back at the high school, I peeled off my cool, damp long underwear and hung my gear inside my locker. Then I wrapped a towel around my waist. The cement floor was cold on the bottoms of my feet. My only reward for sitting on the bench all night was this hot shower, and somehow I felt like I deserved it.

I stopped at the urinal and relieved myself of what felt like an interminably long piss. It was as though none of the water I'd consumed on the bench had been sweated out. O'Leary was rinsing his hands in the sink. Nobody said much. Like actors in mourning, we observed an almost ritualistic silence. Eyeing me in the mirror, O'Leary said quietly, "Don't forget to flush."

Defective plumbing caused water to spray out horizontally from the metal pipes above the urinal whenever someone pulled the lever, and so when I turned to walk away I leaned across the tiled wall and flushed it from a distance. Water burst out sideways, arching down onto the floor, and O'Leary smiled over his shoulder as he returned to his locker.

In the communal showers, I turned on three showerheads and aimed them for a cross-section on the floor. The water came out immediately hot, and steam quickly gathered like fog. I could see that Duce had been summoned to Coach Kinnard's office, which was visible through a large plate-glass window on the locker room's far wall. Coach Kinnard sat on a chair with one leg crossed over another, his finger touching his temple. Duce, who was standing with his back to me, shrugged his shoulders and shook his head. I couldn't hear what they were saying.

Nobody else showered at the high school. Most guys just changed into their street clothes and went home. I closed my eyes and let the hot water pound against my neck and shoulders. The warmth encouraged the blood back into my extremities. My fingertips regained their feeling, my toes stopped burning, and my penis returned to something of an acceptable shape and size. I allowed my mind to wander.

Several times, I wondered if our team might have rallied and perhaps even won the game if I hadn't missed on the breakaway in the second period. One inch to the right, and we'd have been trailing by only two goals with half a game to play—a far more reasonable deficit.

It didn't matter, I kept telling myself. I should let it go.

"What happened?"

Duce had entered the showers. He glanced toward the office, where the lights had been switched off, and reached for the handle to turn on another showerhead. After adjusting the heat, he leaned in and drenched his hair, slicking it back with his hand, and then plugged a nostril with one of his fingers and blew out sharply to empty his nose.

"Nothing," he said. "Coach just wanted to share some of his typically brilliant observations about our loyal fan base."

"What about them?"

He rinsed the snot off his hands in the shower.

"Well, he accused me of 'exciting the crowd,' whatever the

hell that means. I don't know what his problem is. And he kept calling me 'maestro' for conducting the band. '*Eh, do we really need a maestro more than a hockey player?*' Fuck him. To be honest, it sounded like he was arguing *against* a vocal home crowd, if you can you believe that."

Duce snorted, forcing more snot into the back of his throat, and then coughed a wad of greenish-brown effluence onto the floor, where it stuck to the tiles momentarily before a tiny rivulet carried it down the drain.

"He kept referring to my 'super' fan club and asked why nobody else has as many 'super' fans as I do," Duce said. "He honestly reminded me of a jealous girlfriend."

I didn't say anything. I just stood there listening to the white noise of the showers, which sounded like a million crickets chirping at once. On one hand, I understood Coach Kinnard's skepticism: I'd also noted the oddly enthusiastic way our friends had cheered in the third period.

But to me it felt like a practical joke—and an hour later in the showers it seemed downright trivial. They had cheered for less obvious reasons, I was sure.

"You should have told him you're the people's champion," I finally said. "The varsity hockey captain who moonlights as the leader of a proletariat movement."

Duce offered a half-smile, faintly supportive of my weak attempt at humor, but evaded my eyes.

"Yeah, something like that," he said.

Then he lathered liquid soap in his hands and rubbed it across his chest and shoulders, and reloaded with another massive dollop for his nuts. Truth be told, Duce's dick wasn't all that big, but he had a pair of nuts on him like a Third World golden retriever. Well, the detail isn't really important except that it seems like such a good metaphor for his character.

He was presently lathering himself with such vigor that I felt compelled to comment:

"What the hell are you doing?"

"I'm soaping my nuts."

"Well, Jesus," I said. "Calm down, man."

He ignored me and carried on with his feverish scrubbing, while the showers roared like tropical monsoon rains. The warm water battered my chest, and the steam pried open my bronchioles, easing my breathing. I rubbed my eyes with my knuckles, and when I blinked them open Duce was looking off toward the coach's office with a contemplative scowl, as if trying to decide whether he wanted to tell me something more.

Then he eased into a semi-guilty smile and said, "Hell, I don't know why I'm being so cagey. You'll hear about it anyway, so I ought to just come out and say it. The truth is this: I *was* responsible for riling up the crowd before the third period. I made our pals an offer they couldn't refuse, and they stayed to cheer on their benefactor, so to speak."

Duce laughed to signal his sarcasm.

"You know Dom and Sharon flew down to Kirsten Springs this morning?" he said.

Those were his parents.

"That's right," I said.

Duce raked his fingernails through his matted hair.

"So I thought we might enjoy a little soiree while they're gone. A little post-Christmas, pre-New Year's Eve, dreidel-take-all holiday celebration."

"Now you're talking," I said, forcing a grin. "So what's the secret?"

He shook his head.

"Naw, I dunno. I was still in denial mode, I guess. Before the third period, I told Henry I'd host an all-night *blitzkrieg* if I put one on the scoreboard, with booze and *whore's da-hoovers* on the house. I told him to spread the word. I figured it'd keep our friends from going home early."

I recalled his conversation with Elliott in the trainer's area, but frankly I wasn't sure Elliott was capable of delivering on the details in his compromised mental state. He might have promised a cotton candy machine and a petting zoo.

To relate the obvious: what Duce had done was arrogant and self-aggrandizing, but it was also undeniably original. I had to grant him that. Nobody else I knew could have dreamed up such a scheme with a straight face and pulled it off. But then something about it gave me pause.

"Wait," I said, nagged by this sudden doubt, "what if you didn't score?"

This caused Duce to grimace, as if I'd somehow missed the point, but then he just grinned the sort of grin he was famous for—like he had just swiped your wallet without you knowing it—and he replied, "Fuck you. I scored."

Which, of course, was true.

I turned off the showers and reached for my threadbare green towel, which was hanging on a nearby hook. Still dripping wet, Duce put his arms through a white, waffle-textured robe and stuffed his feet into an old pair of hotel slippers. He tramped off toward his locker down a far aisle.

"So tomorrow's the big one," he called out, "the one they've been warning us about. Eat plenty of vitamins tonight and rest your liver, old sport."

"Sounds like a plan," I said.

He slung his white robe over a row of green-painted metal lockers. "And get a big sleep," he said.

"I've got nothing tomorrow, except maybe church in the morning," I said.

Duce laughed scornfully.

"I'll tell you what, Billy Bo," he said. "You can forget about church tomorrow because we're going to get you fixed up with a whole new type of religion."

Outside the high school, Grouse's pickup truck was idling underneath an expired street lamp. As Duce and I pushed open the glass double-doors, we were promptly walloped by a gust of frozen wind. The air was colder than the inside of a metal lunchbox that had been left overnight in the freezer. Christ, it was too cold even for the dogs to bark. Duce and I raced in short, choppy strides down the icy sidewalk.

"Shotgun!" he called over his shoulder.

"Son of a bitch!" I shouted, nearly slipping on the ice in my disappointment. When we reached the truck, I squeezed between the doorframe and the front seat, and as I lowered myself onto the bench in back my tailbone crunched against a roll of hockey tape. The pain leapt up my spine like it had been set in motion by a carnival strongman's sledgehammer.

"Damn it," I groaned, pulling the tape out from underneath me. But as I propped up my butt, my knee banged against the hard plastic seatback, which also hurt, and I complained bitterly: "*Cheese and fudge and rice!*"

"It's better than the bed," Duce pointed out, "which is where we'd put Henry."

"It's also better than the back of a hearse," Grouse noted.

"Yeah, you're both right."

I adjusted myself and the pain subsided as the endorphins let loose. "Speaking of hearses, Babyk, I've been meaning to ask how your new vegan lifestyle is treating you?"

"Good, good," he said, grinning wolfishly over his shoulder. "I had a hummus bagel sandwich and three strips of extra-crispy bacon for breakfast."

I laughed. "You're such a humanitarian."

The week before Christmas break, our biology class had dissected fetal pigs in a laboratory experiment that provoked outrage among several of our classmates, who called it "twisted" and "unconscionable" and refused to participate. Queenie Selby, one of our good female pals, had led a vocal opposition.

"It's sick," she complained. "Just stop and think about it for a minute."

"Come on, Queenie," sneered Duce. "Even Michelangelo saw value in dissection. As an artist and kindred spirit, you of all people should be able to appreciate that."

"Those were dead people!" Queenie exclaimed.

"Well, do you think the piglets are sleeping when we slice them open?"

"*Dee-uce*," Queenie drawled in her native Texas accent. "They're ripped from their mother's wombs so that a bunch of half-asleep teenagers can casually poke through their guts. We're not medical students. We're not even biology majors. How does dissecting animals benefit any of us, really?"

"It's science."

"Now you're on a slippery slope," Queenie said.

Duce proved her right on all counts. When he received his laboratory tray containing a fetal pig, he play-acted like he was sodomizing the animal with his scalpel, chuckling as he narrated to himself: "You like that, don't you, you porky little slut?"

Queenie didn't find it funny.

When Duce elevated the shock value of his joke, sneaking the animal's heart out of the lab into the classroom, carrying it with a pair of forceps, and depositing it inside Mrs. Eichmann's desk, Queenie ratted on him. Our biology teacher tried to force a confession out of Duce, but he had stolen another heart from Henry's pig unwittingly and offered it as proof of his innocence.

But Duce had no sooner cleared himself of that trap than he dug himself an even deeper hole. Out of nowhere, it seemed—in a bid for laughs, I guess—he asked Mrs. Eichmann whether she had "dissected any fetal Jews during graduate school."

The question was meant as a joke, I suppose, and a handful of kids laughed at the outrageousness of the suggestion, but the off-color line got him suspended from school for a week.

His dad had to meet privately with the principal, Mr. Vaughn, in order for Duce to avoid missing two hockey games during his suspension, as school policy normally dictated.

Duce cursed the girls for snitching on him about the heart, and like all aspiring Mafioso he vowed revenge. "I'm going to make those dippy broads swim with the fishes," he warned.

From the back seat of Grouse's truck, I patted Duce on the

shoulder. "God damn, Babyk," I said, with laughter in my voice. "When I spend too much time with you, I start feeling like I'm liable to catch second-hand depression."

Duce tried to turn around, but the seat belt prevented him. "My shrink tells me I'm bi-polar without the upside," he said, trying to be funny, I think.

"So you're depressed?"

"Fuck you, I'm not depressed."

Grouse turned up the radio to drown out our bickering and pointed his truck onto the highway ramp that led toward downtown Minneapolis, where we would soon find ourselves in the freewheeling warehouse district, surrounded by sleazy tit bars, live peep shows, low-rent dildo parlors, and other intellectual hangouts that were open all night.

The girl working the cash register at Tuna's Broken Heart Club—previously known as Tuna's Frolicking Nymphs until Tuna Lorenzo, the proprietor, filed for bankruptcy and went through corporate restructuring—dangled a knee-high red leather boot off the barstool in a slouched posture that I immediately recognized as a mark of terminal boredom.

Standing beside her, a bald-headed, goateed bouncer with obscenely large trapezoid and bicep muscles cracked a lame joke ("…and I was like, 'That's a *stupid* question!'"), and the pair of co-workers giggled. They could have been working in an all-night pancake house for all they seemed to care.

I handed the bouncer a fake ID. It was state-issued with my picture on it, but it said I was twenty-one years old. Grouse and Duce, who presented their real IDs, were only eighteen. The bouncer didn't seem to notice the discrepancy, or he didn't care. As Duce handed the girl a twenty-dollar bill to pay his cover charge, a voice boomed out from our periphery:

"Boys!"

It was Tuna, the owner, with an unlit cigarette between his lips and reading glasses dangling from his neck on a lanyard. He had spotted us from a stool at the end of the bar where he kept watch on both stages, alternating between what were no doubt filthy, pornographic musings and slobbering on a bacon cheeseburger. His denim jacket had mustard stains on the collar.

Approaching us, he spread his arms, beaming like a pedophile on a playground, and said, "Welcome to Tuna Town!" He turned to the cashier and, like a hip older brother, said: "These guys are with me, Summer. VIP all the way."

"Up to you, Tuna," replied Summer indifferently, returning Duce his bank note.

Stanley "Tuna" Lorenzo—degenerate smut peddler and former felonious jailbird (something tax-related)—was a long-shot childhood role model, but in fact he had been a steady fixture in our lives for nearly eight years, ever since he'd coached Grouse's and my fourth grade youth football team.

When Tuna got paroled, the judge had sentenced him to one hundred hours of community service and approved his bid to serve the time as a volunteer coach, Tuna having played some college ball at St. Olaf.

Our offense would huddle around Coach Tuna, who wore a navy-blue mesh cap pulled down low over his eyes as he flipped through the playbook. Before showing us the call, Tuna—who would invariably be chewing a stick of spearmint gum to mask the cigarette he'd smoked while we were on defense—would ask, "Anybody got any dirty jokes?" Somebody might tell one, and then we'd get our play call.

Now, with his push-broom black moustache and tinted reading glasses, he looked every bit the part of the man who had opened Tuna's Strip Joint in the early-1980s, slept on a cot in the back office nearly every night since, barely understood financial accounting, and whose idea of value-added innovation, besides occasionally changing the establishment's name, was adding an aquarium along one wall, stocked with—what else?—a school of baby-sized tuna fish.

As we followed Tuna to the VIP section, Grouse nodded

toward the fish tank and said to Duce, "Want to go for a swim?"

Tuna laughed, but he wasn't in on the joke. The line referred to a night the previous summer when a group of our pals had been chewing on cigars and sipping whiskey out by Babyk's swimming pool, and Grouse floated the idea that we drive across town to the new Arthur Foyer Zoo, where we could tailgate in the parking lot and then go swimming with the dolphins and feed beers to the Sichuan takin.

Bolstered by a stiff drink, Duce seconded the motion, and after a brief jeering for the rest of us, those two set off, armed with a twelve-pack of beers, a warm alcohol buzz, and the reassuring confidence that comes from knowing you're about to do something illegal—but not *that* illegal—and gain surefire admittance to high school immortality.

As the story gets told, those two scaled the chain-link zoo fence and ducked behind the great ape house, scurrying along one of the brick paths through the shadows. One beer can, half loaded, was hurled at the takin, an inter-bred-looking part-ox, part-cow from the Himalayas. The beer can's impact caused the gold-fleeced animal to release a horrific "*mooooo!*" and Grouse cackled every time he related that part of the story. He would be disappointed if I left it out of the official record here.

Arriving at the marine exhibit, the young trespassers heard that irksome, motherly voice of conscience that spoke without words. Or perhaps it was the coyotes howling on the northern trail. They both chuckled sheepishly for a moment as they realized they might not actually be prepared to follow through with their plan.

But as Duce conceded a final giggle, Grouse pulled his shirt over his head and unbuckled his shorts, saying, "Fuck it, I came for a swim." He climbed over the guardrail, stepped across a garden of wood chips, and sat on the glass edge of the pool in his birthday suit.

He said to Duce, "You'd better wait a minute. If one of these bastards bites me, you'll be glad you went second."

Duce nodded, his shoes still tied, and Grouse fell backwards, Navy Seals-style, into the tank.

Duce quickly decided he hadn't come all that way to be remembered as the "other guy" in the history books, and so he removed his shirt and was emptying one last beer down his throat when a flashlight shone in his eyes.

Grouse, meanwhile, was enjoying a deep, refreshing dive and pondering why, after the age of about five or six years old, people so often forget the innocent pleasures of skinny-dipping. That the dolphins paid him little attention after his initial overtures didn't bother him. "It was just so pleasant feeling my bare nuts glide through the water," he later said.

But as he was streamline kicking past the underwater viewing areas, something peculiar caught his attention. Behind the thick glass, he noticed light beams slashing through the darkness. As he propelled himself past a second window, he saw the same thing. He went up for a breath and called out to Duce.

"Hey, Babyk!" he said, treading water. "This is fantastic. They love me."

"Who loves you?" a gruff voice replied. "The children?" Grouse didn't have a chance to respond before the security guard added, in a shout, "Out, *now!*"

The lights he'd seen, it turned out, belonged to the flashlights of young children who were participating in "The Magic of Sleeping Underwater Night," a special zoo event in which kindergartners brought their sleeping bags to the underwater viewing areas to "sleep" with the dolphins. Grouse had unwittingly become the highlight of their evening.

To avoid a host of unflattering charges—trespassing, public intoxication, exposing oneself to minors, among others—both families became Zoo Benefactors at the $25,000 level. Duce's dad knew some of the zoo's board members—and the St. Paul police chief, it turned out—through the local Good Old Boys network, and the board and authorities agreed to chalk up the episode as "boyish indiscretion."

Tuna giggled hearing the story recalled and then released the type of phlegm cough that only heavy smokers can produce. He doubled over and hacked dryly, like a wishbone had gotten wedged in his trachea.

"I thought you were giving up those things, Coach," I said.

"I did." Tuna frowned. "I quit last weekend, flushed my last pack down the toilet Saturday night. But in the middle of the night, the damnedest thing happened. I woke up to take a leak, and two of them hadn't gone down. They were floating right there in the bowl."

Tuna shook his head mournfully.

"Well, I fished them out," he confessed, "and dried them off on the radiator and smoked them the next morning with breakfast."

It was a fitting anecdote for old Tuna, whose whole life, it seemed, had been one long attempt at vice control. When we were eleven and Tuna deemed we were old enough for "grown-up truths," he confided to us that he'd learned how to roll joints while he was in prison—although he wasn't rolling them to smoke pot but to smoke cigarettes, which were tough to come by in the Stillwater State Prison. He made the "little darlings" by stuffing dried loose tobacco into pages of Bible paper. For some reason, it was easier to smuggle in tobacco that way. Go figure. But that was Tuna, anyhow, a scrapper all the way.

"How does King's Corner sound?"

Tuna gestured toward a gaudy purple faux-velvet sofa and throne framing a black cocktail table. We would be a dollar's throw from the club-level stage, Tuna told us, where all of his "hand-selected starlets" performed.

"This is good, Tuna," said Duce. "We'll take it from here."

Tuna clapped five stubby fingers on my shoulder, kneading the muscle, and despite his intentions, which were probably fine, I didn't like thinking where those five stubby fingers had been. I noted to myself that he obviously hadn't been to the "good touch, bad touch" seminar yet.

Then, for no particular reason, he laughed, the way good-natured people do when they get nervous, and coughed like he'd swallowed his cigarette.

Tuna adjusted the fat gold ring on his middle finger and smiled at us reassuringly. He told us to enjoy ourselves, and if we needed anything we could have "the butler" hunt him down. He would be taking care of some paperwork in his office.

"I'll send some A-leaguers over to keep you boys company," Tuna said with a wink.

We thanked him again as he left.

"Oh, and one more thing," said Tuna, spinning around on his heels. "We're serving Cornish game hen tomorrow for lunch, and it's usually pretty popular, so if you're interested, you might want to get here early."

Then he added, "And if you want to arrange a private room liaison with one of the girls, so you can squeeze her tits, don't be shy. I won't tell your parents."

As he walked away I could hear him coughing up a fury.

Peering through a lingering haze of cigarette smoke and candy-colored party fog, I watched as the working girls hustled the room for clients. Their faces were caked in cheap foundation and heavy makeup, their bodies clad in tacky erotic uniforms. The past casts a long shadow, I thought, while neon light casts no shadow at all. Strip joints felt to me like a biological absurdity, and for some reason they made me think of chimpanzees: "So this is evolution, huh?"

Concealed behind tinted doors in seedy downtown commercial zones and populated by the sort of men you'd been taught to avoid, the strip joint reflected society's successful stigmatization campaign. The result—this stage, these girls, the shadowy patrons—was the compromise grudgingly reached by all sides.

"Some of them are like dimes," Grouse was saying to a loner drinking club soda at a table next to ours. "There's almost nothing there. Those have always been my favorite. Then there are ones, especially if they're a few shades darker, which have these little pinky fingers poking out of them. I don't like those as much, to be honest, but they're sort of interesting. I mean it seems like the bigger they get, the smaller the pinky fingers. I don't understand why, but you almost never see the 'ronis with something popping out of them, except maybe something akin to a ball bearing."

The other guy stared back blankly.

"What kind of nipples do you like?" Grouse asked him.

For serious participants, the idea was to gawk and ogle, and then return home as speedily as possible, trying to preserve the sweet memory of what you'd seen: *Ah, the ripe undercarriage of a community college demi-whore!*

Shortly after we arrived, a chubby girl in pink leggings and a leotard approached our table and plopped down on the arm of Grouse's chair. She was working. She had to.

"How are you gentlemen tonight?" she asked, smiling limply. "Are you ready to get crazy?"

There wasn't much confidence in her pitched and confused-sounding falsetto voice, but the girl seemed determined to make a buck. I might argue on her behalf that male social mores had devolved into an unfair game of herd-like checks and balances. By that, I mean our pack mentality wouldn't permit even token consideration of the girl, in spite of the fact that independent of such artificial social pressures, each of us would have gladly "gone hogging" and hardly have even looked at it as such.

Instead, the three of us exchanged glances that confirmed our disinterest, and Grouse said: "You know, I can sometimes work up a fetish for girls like you but not tonight. I think we just want to talk with each other for a while."

It was as close as Grouse came to flattery.

"What?" the girl said.

"Listen," Grouse added, "you might be a tad portly, but you're not too much woman for me. That's all I'm saying. It's my friends I'm thinking about."

And then, not for the first time, I'm sure, the dejected girl slung her tiny purse over her shoulder, climbed down from

Grouse's chair, and waddled away from our table in search of greener pastures.

Alas, she'd picked a profession where Darwinian selection meets capitalism. The incident reminded me of a poster in our biology classroom that read, and I'll paraphrase: "Every morning a gazelle wakes up in Africa, and it needs to be faster than the slowest lion, or it will die. At the same time, a lion wakes up, and it needs to be faster than the slowest gazelle, or it will die. Either way, when the sun comes up, you'd better haul ass."

So onward she went toward slower gazelles.

Our waitress introduced herself as "Xerxes." She wore a crisply starched, loose-fitting Oxford shirt and red thong underwear, like she'd met a businessman over the noon-hour and left in a hurry in some of his clothes. She clutched a note pad across her chest and pointed at us with her pen as she took our orders. She had a zipped-up, serious look about her, with a bony, aquiline nose and squinty little eyes. She gave the distinct impression she was fed up with something.

"What can I get you to drink?" she asked, mechanically.

"Bring me a Pig's Eye," said Duce, slouching and looking off.

"I'm sorry, we don't serve alcohol since the Broken Heart Club is fully nude."

Duce raised his eyebrows in sarcastic puzzlement.

"Okay, how about a ginger ale?" he said, dryly.

Grouse straightened in his chair.

"Hey, I've got an idea," he said, leaning forward. "Why don't you join us for a couple of cocktails?"

Xerxes strained to make her sullen expression appear more disinterested.

"Sorry, but I'm working, and like I *just* told you guys, we don't serve cocktails. Do you understand me?"

"All right, well how about a dance then?"

"I'm a waitress, not a dancer."

"Okay, then. How about just a peek?"

"A peek of what?"

"Behind the magic curtain."

He gestured at her red underwear.

"I'm sorry, but technically I'm not allowed to move my T-bar."

Like circus monkeys in a room full of nitrous oxide, the three of us erupted in wild, uncontrollable laughter, and it was several long moments, punctuated by gasps and more giggles, before Duce was able to collect himself enough to force out the words: "What did you call it?"

"My T-bar," she repeated, to deflated chuckles.

"Phew." Duce wiped his eyes. "That's a good one."

Parodying the dryness of a financial accountant, he said, "Technically, we can't amortize the third-quarter losses without subsequently adjusting our previous returns."

"Oh, what the hell," Grouse said, "bring us a round of ginger ales. We're living on the edge tonight."

Underneath the table, he tapped my knee with a flask full of whiskey.

After we had loosened up on some bootlegged cocktails, a saucy bimbo came over who appealed to all three of us even though—or perhaps *because*—she had a cliché stripper look about her: peroxide-blonde hair, store-bought C-cups, and a worn-out groin that looked like a dog had used it for a chew toy.

Duce reached into his wallet and told the girl he'd give her a hundred bucks to "show us what you've got." She had a cheap smile and a husky smoker's voice. She wasn't much older than we were, but she moved like a pro.

She wriggled out of her satin shorts and then crossed her arms in front of her chest, bringing her shirt up over her head. Then she pulled down her crotchless black lace underwear, unclasped her bra, and climbed onto the cocktail table, assuming the ready position. The three of us leaned in for a closer look, like we were trying to fix a television together or something. She straddled our drinks and leaned her head back toward the ceiling.

As soon as she'd begun her routine, Duce quietly dug into his jeans pocket and pulled out a small laser pointer attached to a key chain.

"Good morning, class," he said softly, barely audible over the thumping music. He aimed the laser above the unsuspecting girl's private parts and drew a small circle, keeping a straight face as he whispered discreetly out of the corner of his mouth.

"This is what we call the *mons pubis*," he said authoritatively.

With the laser, he drew a vertical line down the middle of the girl's genitals, and formed two ovals, clearly delineating each side. Grouse had another name for what Duce was showing us, but Duce insisted on proper nomenclature.

"The *labia minora*," he said, "and, of course, the crowd favorite, *labia majora*."

Grouse and I choked on muffled laughter. The girl started bouncing now, simulating copulation, and squeezed on her breasts, moaning as though climax was inevitable. Then, throwing us all for a loop, she transitioned to a slow gyration, which appeared to irritate Duce since it complicated his demonstration.

He pointed his laser at the middle of the girl's swaying genitals, attempting several times before finally succeeding at identifying our focal point with a tight circle.

"The clitoral hood," he said. "Okay?"

Then, to the girl: "Hey toots, how about doggy style?"

The girl batted open her eyes, as though she had emerged from a deep meditation, but rolled over mechanically and obliged. I wondered where she'd been imagining she was. Now, she was essentially mooning us from close range, and with the laser Duce highlighted the area between her anus and vagina.

"Ah, yes," he said admiringly. "The sacred perineum."

Now, I can't imagine there are too many college anatomy courses in which the male students sit hunched over their boners while their professor uses a rudimentary laser pointer to highlight the finer features of a clean-shaven, eighteen-year-old potential nymphomaniac who smells like baby oil.

We were all getting along fabulously until Tuna, with typical Tuna timing, tiptoed up behind us and just hovered there, his lurking presence dissolving our little congress like an ill-timed, mixed company fart. When the girl noticed her boss standing there, she sped through to her grand finale, and as she gathered her clothes afterward, Tuna maneuvered through the chairs and sat down next to her, groping her a little bit and slobbering a kiss on her cheek. She smiled insincerely at Duce and scuttled away to find other clients.

Tuna nodded approvingly as he watched her walk off.

"I forgot to tell you boys one thing," he said. "Come see me before you leave so I can validate your parking ticket."

"Yeah, okay," said Duce, with obvious irritation in his voice. "Thanks, Tuna."

Duce turned to Grouse.

"Do you mind buying some booze and other supplies tomorrow if I give you money?" he said.

"Are you guys having a party?" Tuna interjected.

"Naw," said Duce, "just something low-key."

"Okay, well, remember, I can send a few girls if you want."

"Thanks, Tuna."

Tuna smiled.

"Or topless maids for morning cleanup," he added.

Duce's eyes brightened.

"I might take you up on that, Tuna," he said.

Tuna wheezed as he pulled himself up to his feet.

"Or, if you guys need a place to party, you can always party at my place."

"Yeah, thanks, Tuna."

"Anytime you want," Tuna said. "As long as I can get a little *stink finger.*"

And he laughed extra hard, to let us know he was joking.

Our postures froze.

"Sure thing, Coach," I said. "High school girls will love you."

"Well, now," said Tuna, stuffing his hands into his pockets, "I don't know about that. Maybe one or two would be curious what it's like being with an *experienced* man."

And he winked at Duce.

Then Tuna added, "Anyway, last thing, for your party: I've got some IV bags in my office if you guys want them. Nothing rips a bad hangover like an intravenous saline drip. My buddy Todd, who's a pediatrician, whenever he goes up north for the weekend, always tosses one over the coat hanger on the ride home on Sunday to sober up for on-call duty."

"Fortunately, none of us is on-call this week," I said.

Duce, running his fingers through his receding widow's peaks, changed topics with this: "Say, Mr. Lorenzo, what do you think is better for hair loss: Rogaine or Propecia?"

When we had first met Duce in middle school, his hair was already thinning at the crown, but now he looked like a fraterni-ty-house stoner, with wispy black hair that was all but transparent at his temples. Tuna's brother Ricko owned a barbershop in one of the northern suburbs, and Tuna fancied himself an expert by association.

"Well, now," Tuna started, "Ricko says to shampoo your hair only once a week. He says your head's natural oils are ideal for preventing hair loss. He says that's why homeless people so often have such thick hair. Did you ever notice that?"

We hadn't noticed that, no.

"But if you want the honest-to-god truth," Tuna added in a more fraternal tone, "don't waste your money on either of them. If I was your age and going bald, I'd just save up and buy myself a Corvette. That's all these girls care about anyway."

Still later in the evening, each of us was engaged in conversa-tion with a different female. I overheard Duce ask his girl to the prom. Grouse was talking to a fried-blonde in her mid-thirties who had an awful pair of fake udders, the kind that left a zipper scar underneath the nipple and made you wonder whether her surgeon was cross-eyed.

"I'm sorry," Grouse told her, "but pigtails and a plaid skirt, outside of the San Fernando Valley, don't knock off nearly as many years as you might hope."

The girl frowned a pair of unnaturally swollen lips.

"You smell nice, though," he added.

"Really?" The girl blushed. "You're sweet."

It was that familiar stripper scent, *Eu de Slut*, the standard-issue industry fragrance they all seemed to wear. It smelled like a cross between the candy-sweet mist of a disco fog machine and a hooker's dirty-hot pheromones.

"But then again you've given birth. I can see your C-section," he said, stealing away the compliment. "So that's another strike against you."

"That's why I got breast implants!" she exclaimed.

"Woman, you're swimming against a strong current."

I laughed a few minutes later when I overheard Grouse telling her about a "show" he'd seen on the Mexican border while he was on a church mission trip to Tijuana in middle school. He had snuck out one night and gone to a local bar, he told her, where a Mexican woman stuck a banana into her crotch, spun a little break-dancing move on the floor, and snapped open her thighs, firing the missile-shaped projectile into the crowd.

"Oh my god!" the stripper at Tuna's gasped. "So that was part of her *act?*"

"No, no," said Grouse, with a wave of his hand. "That was part of her charm. For her act, she made love to a donkey."

Meanwhile, I was ready to put my girl on a high-dose SSRI and start charging her by the hour. She sat there and rattled off a whole litany of discontents, starting with how her mother was a former stripper who had convinced her to try the work while she "still had it" since the money was so good. The girl's lipstick was the color of a freshly waxed Pontiac.

"Fucking money," she sighed.

"Why don't you get a job at the mall?" I asked her.

"Because the money sucks."

"So what are you complaining about?"

"Just this," she said, gesturing all around her.

"Me?" I laughed.

"You, yeah. Everyone. Here, you want to see it? Look."

She pulled aside her shorts, showing me her dry, shaved clam. I stared at it for a dull moment and felt no sensation whatsoever. Freud was right: It's a funny looking thing to get so excited about. Without the proper context, it just looked generically mammalian.

"Yeah, yeah," I said, dismissively.

"This is what you want to see, right? This is what you're spending all your money on. So here you go—for free!"

"All right, all right," I said, looking off toward the stage, hoping she would put it away. "So if money wasn't an issue, what would you want to do with your life?"

The cheap glitter on her eyelids sparkled as she perked up, eager to nibble at the bait of my hypothetical question.

"I've always wanted to be a veterinarian," she said.

Don't they all?

"I know you think that's stupid," she quickly added.

I didn't, really.

She twirled a shock of split-ends in her index finger.

"Who knows," she said, "maybe I'll meet a rich, eighty-year-old divorcee with no kids who's waiting for a transplant."

And she laughed like it was the funniest thing she'd heard in months.

"There's always that," I said, encouraging her.

Then, as our conversation risked losing critical momentum, I realized once again that I'm the sort of person who is incapable of letting the downtrodden wallow in their misery without tossing them a compassionate question or two.

Thus, to placate my own conscience as much as anything, I gently probed the roots of her dissatisfaction.

"Are your parents married?" I asked her.

"Uh-uh."

"And do you get along with your dad?"

She shrugged.

"Okay, I guess," she said. "He's a bit weird."

"Really?"

She laughed nervously before fixing a stern look on me. "I don't have 'daddy issues,' if that's what you mean."

"I didn't say you did."

"Okay," she said.

"How old is he?"

"Not too old. Fifty-one maybe."

"And what does he do?"

A smile trembled on her lips as she looked off toward the bar. Evading my eyes, she responded, "He's a mortician."

I burst out laughing and was immediately soaked with guilt. I apologized profusely and then laughed some more.

I couldn't help it.

By and by we shook off the girls. Duce excused himself to the bathroom at one point, weaving his way through a labyrinth of cocktail tables and fake leather sofas, carefully inspecting each fairway divot, sculpted topiary, and waxed *mons pubis* he passed along the way. Grouse leaned back in his chair and sipped his poisonous drink.

"Are you going to tell Julianne you were here?" he asked.

"She doesn't want to know."

"That's probably true," he said.

"She might say she does, but if I told her, she'd ask me why I told her."

"Either that or why you came here."

"I was with you two degenerates. You guys forced me."

"At least you've got an alibi."

I leaned forward and rested my elbows on the table.

"It's like the saying goes," I said, "if a tree falls in the forest, and no one is there to hear it, does it make a sound?"

Grouse shook his head as he swigged the cocktail.

"That's a cheater's mantra," he said. "And whatever this is, it isn't cheating."

"That's right. This falls under our genetic overlap with the chimpanzees. We can't control this side of us. It's built into our hard-wiring, this tickling of our curiosity."

Grouse reached under the table, into his boot, and came up with the stainless steel flask, which he shook briskly from side-to-side to demonstrate how much we had lightened it. Then he picked up my glass of ginger ale and drank half of it, before refilling it with booze, the remainder of his flask.

"I've got another one in my other boot," he said.

I laughed but wasn't surprised.

"Have one more drink," he said, setting the fresh cocktail on a coaster in front of me.

I stared at it quizzically for a moment.

"One of us needs to drive home," I said.

"Last one, then."

"Yeah, all right. I can do that."

I hesitated as I reached for it.

"Maybe I'll share it with Duce," I said.

"That's fine. He doesn't have a gash between his legs—like you do."

"Unless you want to take a taxi."

"Nah, forget it. Tomorrow's better. Give it to Duce."

I tasted the drink to be a good sport.

"Let's get shitfaced tomorrow night," he said.

"That's the plan," I said, putting the glass back on the table.

"What about your woman?"

"She's game. She said she would, at least."

"I mean: Are you going to hump her?"

I laughed at the verb.

"Things are moving in that direction, but it obviously hasn't happened yet."

"Well, quit talking about it and do it. What the hell are you waiting for?"

I took another sip of whiskey and ginger ale, swishing it around my mouth before swallowing it, and then replied in an emphatically melodramatic tone: "The right moment."

"Jesus, man. What could be more romantic than Babyk's mansion? It's like one of those highfalutin B&Bs on Lake Minnetonka, full of hidden little nooks and crannies. You don't even have to pay for anything."

I laughed.

"You're right. It'll be perfect: drunk as fish, with steamy hot liquor breaths, semi-blacked out, groping each other under Mrs. Babyk's Egyptian combed-cotton sheets. I'm sure that's how Julianne always dreamed she would lose her virginity."

Grouse leaned back, surveying the glitter that was now shimmering down over one of the stages. His wooden gaze—he appeared to be inwardly wincing at each thumping beat of the music—suggested the venue was somehow failing him.

Then he turned toward me and said flatly, "Hump her."

"You shouldn't talk," I replied. "Your Christian-Buddhist morality-slut girlfriend hasn't exactly turned out to be the sexual messiah either. You've been together for two years and you're still stuck on third base."

"She found Christ!" Grouse protested.

"Really? Do you think Jesus is going nine inches deep in your girlfriend?"

"Somebody better be," he said. "And if it's the J-bus I'm okay with that."

He swilled the cocktail again and wiped his mouth on his shirtsleeve, before adding with a sigh: "As long as He doesn't mind that she's blowing me on the side."

When Duce returned from the toilet, he sat down along Sniffer's Row, where he promptly arranged a row of crisp five-dollar bills folded the long way on the stage in front of him, like popcorn for a family of ducks. From underneath a proscenium arch, a pair of hard-bodied tramps slithered out toward the bait.

Eyeing us in the mirror, Duce raised his eyebrows in sarcastic intrigue before returning his gaze to the showgirls.

One of the performers, clad only in a feather boa, had assumed the unholy position of a female wolf in heat. And if you knew anything at all about copulating wolves, you would know to keep your belt buckled. Looking at her, Duce squinted one eye, then the other, as if he was testing a theory. He scrutinized the girl as though her exposed orifice was a periscope through which he could inspect her adenoids.

Grouse and I were admiring Duce's tact when our waitress returned to ask if we wanted anything to eat. Grouse ordered for all three of us.

"I'm going to have the steak sandwich," he said. "And he's going to have the soft tacos," he added, nodding toward me. Then he pointed at Duce, who was engrossed in the stage show, and said, "And that pervert down there, who you might've seen outside the club earlier wearing fishnet stockings and a garter belt—bring him the corned beef."

Duce craned his neck around to look at us, and his face bore an expression like a wild-eyed kid at a science fair as he said, "How does she make it *pucker* like that?"

I excused myself before the food arrived. The men's room, with its black tiled floors and walls, black porcelain urinals, and low-wattage lighting, gave off a cheap-swanky air that one might be tempted to label "strip club elegance," although it was, in spite of the mighty effort, *not* an upscale aesthetic. Sidling up to the urinal, I chuckled as I realized that the big rectangular mirror alongside the main stage was only a mirror from the outside. From where I stood, with my fly unzipped, I could watch the naked dancers through a one-way window. Old Tuna could surprise you sometimes with his ingenuity.

On the other side of the glass, on one of the stage wings, two strippers were pantomiming teasing gestures as if they could see into the bathroom, but since they didn't know where I stood—or *if* I was even there—their sightlines and motions were hopelessly misaimed. They giggled to each other, as one made the "just a pinch" sign with her thumb and forefinger.

Standing at the urinal next to me, a silver-haired man in a Texas-shaped belt buckle and plaid shirt with "Billy Lloyd" stenciled on his chest glanced sideways in my direction and said, "The view's so good from here, it makes you want to slap your pappy." Now, I don't want to say old Tex was playing with himself, but it sure looked to me, out of the corner of my eye, like he was mimicking a fly fisherman's casting motion.

When he departed for the sink, he turned back a few times, not wanting to miss any part of the action. I glanced over my shoulder, and he gave me two thumbs up as though he was drawing pistols from a gun holster.

"Now all I need is some whiskey," he said. "You yanks sure are strange operating your titty bars without any hooch."

"We're teetotalers," I replied.

He chuckled dryly.

"Well, y'all are something, maybe even one of them."

I thought of Grouse.

"Try the guys sitting in King's Corner near the VIP stage," I suggested. "I'm pretty sure my buddy's got some booze he could spare in a boot flask."

"All right, now you're talking, boy," he said, flashing a warm smile and revealing a mouthful of Texas-sized, coffee-stained teeth.

Tex poked an index finger into the bathroom attendant's chest, just beneath his bowtie, and warned him: "And don't you say nothin' neither."

Old Tex dropped a dollar bill into the tip basket to secure the man's allegiance, and the door swung closed behind him.

I shook the last drops of piss from my dick, careful not to get any on my hands, and avoided the sink on my way out. I had a philosophy about restrooms at places like that: I don't touch anything, even the sink, if I don't have to. The attendant offered me a six-dollar breath mint, but I politely declined.

Outside the bathroom, I spotted a row of payphones down a quiet hallway behind a glass door and decided to call Julianne to see if she was back from the Bahamas. The phone rang seven times, but nobody answered. Then I called my parents and told them we were bowling. The burgundy-colored, flame-retardant carpet smelled like it hadn't been shampooed since the Twins last won the World Series.

I noticed at the end of the hall an original Pac-Man arcade game and couldn't resist the temptation. I popped in a quarter, raced away from all the ghosts, gobbled up the power pellets, and went on a kamikaze mission trying to devour Blinky, Inky, Pinky, and Clyde before inevitably going down in a blaze of glory on the first board. I was a reckless gamer like that.

When I re-entered Tuna's, a dark-skinned Thai girl with luscious, maroon-colored island nipples was dancing on Grouse's table. A trembling smile played at his lips, and even from halfway across the room I could see that his eyes were glazed over and vaguely out of focus—telltale signs that the booze was preparing mutiny against central command. When he saw me approaching, he broke into a gargantuan smile.

"Bo!" he shouted. "I've got the yellow fever *burning in my veins!*"

He looked up at the girl with a contorted, sloppy-faced expression and told her to spread her legs "like a budding yellow tulip." The way he gestured with his hands, he looked like a wino begging for Communion. "Show me the way to the banana kingdom!"

Head back, eyes screwed shut, he sang out: "*Yellow on the outside, white on the inside.*" The girl had stopped dancing, but Grouse didn't notice. "Let me see if it's true what they say, that they're all pink in the middle!"

"That is not appropriate!" the girl burst out, climbing down from the table and snapping up her lingerie. Her frantic pace drew the attention of nearby patrons, and within seconds, it seemed, the muscular goateed bouncer was dispatched in our direction, his hostile, gorilla-like gait suggesting he was eager to vindicate all those protein shakes.

"What's the problem, fellas?" he asked.

"That bitch stole my money," Grouse said.

"Hey, watch your mouth, buddy."

"Yeah? Tell her to take off her clothes and keep dancing."

Grouse's words slurred off his tongue, and I sensed things weren't going to end well. I calmly tried to convince him that she had danced his money's worth and that we ought to go home. I said we could stop somewhere on the way for booze. I suggested pancakes and bacon—*anything*.

"Hey man, let's just get out of here," I pleaded.

"Fuck off, Bo. This is between me and the woman—and now this asshole." He gestured vaguely toward the bouncer. "Wait a minute, where'd she go?"

"I think you guys better leave," the bouncer said.

Duce and I agreed, and we moved to defuse Grouse, setting our hands on his shoulders and gently steering him toward the exit. For a second, he relaxed under our grip and seemed willing to heed our command, but then he suddenly twisted free and shoved the bouncer in the chest, saying, "Go fuck yourself—*and your prison pussy!*"

It was no contest.

The bouncer's forearm chopped down like a padded guillotine on the back of Grouse's neck, practically folding him in half. The bouncer grabbed Grouse's arm and twisted him into immediate submission. Duce pleaded to speak with Tuna, but more bouncers had arrived, and we realized we wouldn't get a fair trial, and so we followed Grouse like white-flag soldiers, our hands in the air, so we wouldn't get roughed up ourselves.

Fortunately for Grouse, the bouncer didn't toss him face-first into the trash dumpster in the alley. On some instinctual level, Grouse must've realized that resistance of any type would have been met with an overwhelmingly disproportionate use of force. Outside the club, the bouncer gave Grouse a small push, sending him toppling to the pavement, and told him never to return. The door slammed shut.

"Yeah, we'll see about that," said Grouse, mostly to himself.

With considerable effort, he struggled to his feet, wiping his hands on his pants, and soon he was laughing so hard that his eyes watered: the excitement had made him temporarily lucid. To Grouse, being thrown out of a strip joint in such a dramatic fashion was an early gift to himself in old age, a story he could regale my future children with.

Somehow, only moments after it happened, he already seemed to appreciate the value in that.

The downtown streets were covered in brown slush and devoid of traffic as the witching hour drew nigh. Above the entrance to Tuna's place, neon lights blinked the word: "F-R-O-L-I-C-K-I-N-G," and I watched as a dirty cat plunged into the shadows of an alleyway, dragging away a fish skeleton.

As we walked toward the parking lot a few blocks away, we passed an old black panhandler who was holding an empty bowler hat upside down, begging for small change. He leaned forward on a hickory cane.

"Help!" he shouted in a frail voice, almost theatrically.

"Sorry," we replied, our heads down.

The old man sighed wearily.

On the next block, a bum in tattered old formal clothes was standing outside a convenience store, preaching to the booze-hounds, the unseasonably dressed females, and other late-night shoppers, peddlers, and passersby about the virtues of Christianity, about repentance, about how we could all be "saved" if only we "believed" in God's redeeming love.

"God's a pussy," Grouse said to the bum.

"And yet his son was a fisher of men!" the bum replied, beaming a joyful smile that glinted with a golden tooth.

At the parking ramp, we rode the elevator up to the seventh floor and passed through the glass double-doors into the garage, where a familiar voice called out from the far end, echoing in the vast empty space. It was Old Tex, dog paddling in a river of sour mash whiskey. "*Minna-stroter!*" he bellowed. "Thanks for the hooch, pal!" And with no small amount of satisfaction, I noticed that Tex was opening the passenger-side door of his rental car for a future veterinarian.

Reaching our parking space, Grouse unzipped his fly, set a hand against the cement wall to steady himself, and released a comically long piss, his legs wobbling as he spelled out his full name three and a half times in loopy cursive. Then he zipped his fly and tossed me the keys, saying, "Drive safely, asshole."

It was like piloting an unwieldy pontoon boat, steering the pickup truck down the narrow ramp, spiraling from one level to the next, remaining ever vigilant not to sideswipe any pillars. It was nearly midnight and the lot was mostly empty, but on the second floor a woman in a gray flannel pantsuit emerged from the Skyway carrying an open-topped box full of legal portfolios.

I tapped the brake, letting her cross the striped pedestrian path. There was only one other car on the floor, and I assumed it was hers. Grouse stared impatiently at the woman through the front windshield, shaking his head.

"Let's go, *fatty!*" he cried, with an emphasis on the epithet.

The word slung out like a poison-tipped arrow through the cracked-open passenger side window, and the woman's silent, horrified reaction was like a high-rise building in the split second between the controlled explosion and the collapse. Duce squirmed in the back seat, saying, "Oh, Jesus!" and I slithered down, trying to hide my face behind the seat belt.

"What?" Grouse said. "I'm encouraging her."

Using drunken logic, he reasoned he was doing the woman two favors: first, getting her to her car, and thus wherever she was going, faster, and second, motivating her to get in shape.

"She should thank me," he concluded.

I was grateful I couldn't see the woman's face in the rearview mirror as I sped down the final two levels.

When Grouse spoke again a few moments later, his words had turned to babble. His eyes were clenched shut, and he was vigorously rubbing his temples, as though he was finally aware that he was swimming upstream in the devil's juice.

"Dryer sheets," he muttered.

"What's that?"

"Fat chicks," Grouse said.

I laughed.

"What are you talking about?"

"Fat girls smell like dryer sheets," he mumbled.

He appeared to be on the verge of passing out.

"Melting butter," he said. "Melt like butter, fat girls."

"Oh yeah?"

I smiled at Duce in the rearview mirror.

"I climbed into the pigpen two years ago at summer camp, fooled around with a real heifer. She was disgustingly wet. Fat girls love it."

"They love what?"

"It."

"Who doesn't?"

That was Duce from the back seat.

"Fat girls *love* it. Always up for physical pleasure. Lots of 'em are smokers, ya know? Instant *gratification*." The last word came out as a garbled cluster of impossible syllables. "Like to eat, like to fuck. Like to smell like dryer sheets."

I idled the truck toward the cashier's booth with the parking ticket in my hand and the window down, but the attendant wasn't there and the gate was up, suggesting that we could leave without paying. I lowered my head, scanning the lot from end to end, and had already started coasting through the gate when I heard a door slam across the garage.

"Sir!" a voice called out. We were halfway out. "Please wait, one second!"

"Just go," Grouse said.

I tapped my foot on the brake.

"Leave," Grouse said. "Go."

The attendant bounded in easy, loping strides toward the

booth. I'd already stopped. Now, I leaned out the window and smiled. "Riding the can, huh?"

"Yeah." He returned a shy smile. "Emergency. So sorry."

"All right, no worries," I said.

I shifted the truck into reverse and eyed the side mirrors as I idled backward toward the booth. Then: *BANG!* The front tires exploded as they were impaled on one-way road spikes. Recognizing instantly what had happened, I slammed my fist on the steering wheel and shouted, "*God fucking damn it!*"

"Told you to go," Grouse said.

But there was no malice in his voice.

It was late by the time a mechanic arrived with a tow truck. He hitched up Grouse's vehicle and said he would haul it to another downtown garage, where they'd put new tires on it in the morning.

By that point, Grouse had regained his senses. He gave the guy twenty bucks, asking him to park it somewhere safe. The mechanic promised it would be in a secure garage overnight, and he told Grouse he could pick it up around lunchtime.

The three of us rode home in a taxi. Our plans to rip the "U" off the Titus Building would need to wait for another day.

In the warming house, Grouse took aim at a new victim.

"Hey, fat fucker," he said to Goldy Lindenheimer, our behemoth buddy. "I thought you were having dinner at Murray's tonight."

Goldy occupied a full corner of the room, resembling in his current posture a replica of Michelangelo's *Pieta*, albeit with a cardboard pizza box on his lap. He lifted the lid and retrieved a floppy slice, folding it in half as he ushered it down his throat like a sword-swallower at the circus. You almost expected to hear the sound of a wood-chipper.

"He said he wanted an appetizer," somebody replied.

The University of Minnesota's senior football captains had invited Goldy downtown that night to see how many twenty-four-ounce Silver Butter Knife steaks he could eat in one sitting. The Gophers were considering offering him a scholarship, and the dinner was a way for the upperclassmen to get to know him better—to "test drive" the team chemistry, so to speak.

Now, Goldy wiped his hands on his jeans and plucked a few fallen pepperonis off the cardboard lid.

"Jesus, Goldy!" said Grouse. "That's like jacking off before an orgy. You'd better be careful, or next summer you might be wearing a two-piece to the pool."

Goldy giggled, as he was prone to do, like a post-pubescent Pillsbury Dough Boy, and reached for another slice of pizza. He had a seemingly insatiable appetite, Goldy did, and I privately worried that he was sharing all those calories with a tapeworm or some other form of intestinal parasite.

The summer before our junior year, a group of our pals was shooting hoops on O'Leary's driveway when Goldy announced, "I'll bet I can eat four foot-long sandwiches in less than ten minutes." It was a bold claim, obviously, and so to inject some excitement into an otherwise lackluster afternoon Duce wagered a hundred dollars against the big man.

We brought a stopwatch to The American Hero, the aptly named sandwich shop near the high school, in case the contest came down to the tenth of a second. But Goldy didn't need fractions. In just over eight minutes, he devoured forty-eight inches of submarine sandwiches, loaded with cold cuts, cheeses, vegetables, and sauces. Watching the last two minutes tick past on the wall clock, he calmly snacked on a bag of Doritos chips.

Astonished, we asked him how the hell he did it. Goldy chuckled, licking the orange powder off his fingertips, and answered: "I don't chew."

After that, he couldn't find any takers when he bet us he could wrap his scrotum around a cue ball.

When Goldy stood up to discard his empty pizza box in the trash can, the basset hound eyed him warily from the floor. Gump Worsley had curled up near a furnace vent, positioning himself in such a way that nobody could sneak up on him and quickly tie his ears in a knot above his head. Goldy crouched down now and lovingly fondled those ears, and the dog's face twisted in all kinds of agreeable contortions.

"In another life, he was probably a beagle that wore heavy earrings," said Goldy, punctuating his joke with hearty laughter.

Our behemoth buddy had been offered a walk-on spot at UCLA, where he'd attended a summer camp two years earlier. The football coaches there had already doled out scholarships to three blue-chip linemen, but they promised Goldy admission to the school's competitive undergraduate film program, where he could take screenwriting classes and "compete" his way into a scholarship. But he'd have to pay his own way at first—and maybe for the whole four years.

As a junior, Goldy had penned a ten-minute play called "The Urban Hermit," which won a national drama award and stoked his interest in writing as a potential career. The play was a character study, more or less, about a middle-aged recluse living in New York City who spent his nights wandering quiet side streets and poking his head into avant-garde art galleries, while delivering what amounted to a runaway monologue on the joys of liberation.

Dr. Bloom, the protagonist and sole character in the one-man play, was a crisis-line phone counselor by day, talking people down from the ledge, so to speak, and at night he was a cigar-puffing loner in Gotham. The judges praised the play as a "daring, ambitious work" that grappled with "mature subject matter," and the rest of us were mostly just impressed by Goldy's powerful imagination.

The football recruiting process had been unpredictable for him. The summer before our senior year, he was hounded after like a sorority virgin, as football coaches and university boosters regularly landed in Minneapolis to meet with him and his parents. They spoke paternally of joining the Notre Dame tradition, or becoming part of the Penn State family, or how many games Michigan would play on national TV.

Of course, Goldy must have realized at some point that their strategy with him, much like nailing the elusive Pi Phi, was more about the sale than the settlement. Coaches sold their programs first, pocketing commitments from the most highly sought-after blue-chip athletes, and then worried about securing bench depth, which, if we're being honest, included players like Goldy. High school kids and their families, most experiencing the process for the first time, were naturally flattered by all the attention but never quite knew where they stood.

One week, Goldy would receive a phone call from a head coach or offensive line coach, asking how his summer workouts were going, or if he saw the news about the new players' lounge in East Lansing. The next week, that coach might not call and Goldy would never hear from him again. The following week, another team might not call, and so on. Before long, Goldy was entertaining possible full-ride scholarships with only three schools: New Mexico, Connecticut, and Minnesota.

The Gophers were the only respectable football name in the bunch, historically at least, and Goldy had privately told me he was considering bagging his scholarship pursuits altogether and accepting the UCLA offer.

Early in the recruiting process, I had asked him hypothetically whether he would rather play for Miami, which regularly contended for a national title but where he'd likely sit on the bench for four years, or for Minnesota, where he could play a more impactful role but whose squad would probably only see the Rose Bowl on television.

"Miami," he said, giving it no thought. "They pay more."

I stepped over Goldy's outstretched legs and squeezed onto a spot on the bench next to him. Both of my legs together were about as wide as one of his—and his baggy jeans looked like they were cut from about a mile of indigo-dyed denim. A layer of baby fat still covered his boyish face, but a square jaw had begun to emerge underneath it, giving him a handsome, more angular definition. With his ink-black hair and big round eyes, he looked like a young Rodney Dangerfield playing the role of James

Bond. Shaking hands with him—gripping one of his capacious palms—was like clutching a sack of bananas.

"What's going on, pal?" I said.

"Nothing, Swilly."

He'd called me "Swilly" for years. I never knew why, but I always took it affectionately.

"How'd your article turn out?" he asked.

"Fine, I think. I quoted you twice."

"Yeah? What'd I say?"

Goldy had granted me creative license on all of his newspaper quotes as long as I didn't jeopardize his scholarship prospects. Better judgment had reigned on at least one occasion, when I wanted to write an article about him building PVC-pipe potato launchers in his garage and selling them to the neighborhood kids. I argued it was a story about entrepreneurship. Goldy didn't think "arms dealer" was a label he wanted to carry into his senior season.

The potato bazookas, as Grouse called them, proved to be a gateway weapon, as the thrill of firing spud mortars quickly gave way to discussions of where we could buy an actual pellet gun. Within days, a group of us was paddling out onto the creek in O'Leary's canoe with a loaded gun, looking for trespassing ducks worthy of the death penalty.

Goldy refused to shoot. I fired high on purpose.

When Grouse popped a mallard in the wing, guilt washed over the rest of us, and we promptly circled the canoe back toward shore, vowing never to hunt for anything except turkey sandwiches again. Grouse implored us to return to the wounded animal.

"We've got to shoot it in the head," he insisted. "We can't just leave it there."

The rest of us couldn't be convinced. The sight of the tormented animal was more than we could stomach. We dragged the canoe onto the grass and hurried toward O'Leary's garage, resisting the urge to glance over our shoulders at the helpless bird flapping its wings among the cattails.

"You're a bunch of pussies," said Grouse, as he ventured out to do the dirty business himself.

Anyway, Goldy wasn't an arms dealer.

This may come as a surprise to some readers, but *Solstice*, our school's esteemed student publication, was not a "newspaper of record." My sports column, The Eleven-Dollar Thrill, ran down the left-hand side of the back page beside my school portrait from eighth grade, when I had long, curly hair like a natural afro and orthodontic braces on my teeth.

One nice thing about working for the student newspaper was that we published only twice each quarter, meaning games would sometimes be a month old before we went to press—and by that point, of course, hardly anybody would remember what had transpired on the field.

So I had a habit of fictionalizing quotes and occasionally making up sources altogether. Tito Bandito, the fabled mosquito hunter, and Ira Emderzokzov, the Belarusian foreign exchange student, were both my inventions. Genester Odell Jefferson, the super-freak all-sport varsity athlete from Lindbergh High, was real, but I credited him with fictional heroics in bogus events like the sidearm javelin and hundred-yard moonwalk.

For four years, I had immortalized Goldy's athletic battles with Genester in the school newspaper. Their gridiron clashes, I wrote, offered one possible answer to the age-old question of what happens when an unstoppable object collides with an immovable one: it was like watching an irate sumo wrestler in a shoving match with a clawless grizzly bear.

Genester stood six-foot-six ducking under a doorframe, and he'd still weigh three hundred pounds if you pumped him full of helium. The popular anecdote, circulated in the masturbatory local prep sports press, was that G.O. had been ejected from an all-you-can-eat dinner buffet for eating too many chicken wings. Apparently, he'd eaten more than twelve dozen before they tossed him out.

G.O.'s dad originally hailed from southern California, where he was a part-time nightclub bouncer and part-time stand-up comic and starving actor, but now he worked as a cab driver in Minneapolis. And yes, the joke had already been made that Genester weighed more than a cab *full* of starving actors, plus their luggage.

Like Goldy, G.O. was a photo-finish recruit for the Golden Gophers, but he had also already received full-ride offers from Iowa and Purdue.

At our high school, where "diversity" basically meant a handful of adopted Koreans, Genester was a real novelty. We had picked his name off the basketball roster in ninth grade, thinking it sounded funny, and chanted it during an entire second half. In a packed community center gym, Lindbergh was trailing badly late in the game when Genester pulled up and lobbed a three-point jump shot from way outside the arc.

The ball rattled around the rim and fell in, and G.O. raced over to the base of our student section, planting his toes hard against the out-of-bounds line, like he was going to salute us, and hoisted both of his arms into the air, the middle finger on each hand extended.

We erupted into rousing chants of "*Three-point, G.O.! Three-point, G.O.!*" The ball was already at the other end of the court, but G.O. flashed a wide, amiable grin as he conducted our student band with his birds as batons. He was a good sport, we concluded.

I'd interviewed him our junior year after a game at Lindbergh's home court in which he'd picked up an effortless triple-double. He boasted, as he worked a toothpick in his gums, about his "jackhammer" inside game and "feather-touch" jump shot. He was putting on a show for me, I realized.

When I told him it sounded like he's the complete package, Genester beamed a genial smile and said, "*Sheeit.* I'm tall, dark, and something short of handsome—but two out of three ain't bad, I guess. Heh-heh."

Then I tested him to see how far he'd take the joking.

"Tell me, G.O. Who has finesse like you?" I asked him.

"Nobody," he replied, shaking his head.

"And who has your agility? Who crosses over like you?"

"Ain't no one else, man," he said, smiling puckishly.

"Okay, G.O.," I said to him, loading the next question with obvious emphasis. "So, why do *you* think you're the most dominant player in the Metro Lakes Conference?"

A sly grin emanated in his eyes—maybe *he* was testing *me*, I thought for a moment—and he chuckled in his deep baritone as his whole face lit up.

"Because I'm *black*," he replied. Then he playfully socked me on the arm, collapsing into more giggles and stumbling off balance against the hallway lockers. "You can print it, Scoop!"

He howled peals of laughter.

"Because *I'm black*!" he shouted.

Neither of them did much laughing, however, when they squared off against one another in competition. Then they both turned into a couple of three-hundred-plus-pound roosters, sans razors, congenitally hard-wired for aggression.

In late September, I'd covered their last high school football game against each other at our home field. I wasn't on deadline that afternoon, but I had arrived early at the stadium because I loved the atmosphere of fall: the cold wet grass, the crisp air, and the fragrance of impending winter.

I ignored the mighty privilege of "Press Parking," which would have delivered me about two blocks closer to the stadium, and pointed my car down a quiet, tree-lined residential street, employing a game-day strategy my old man called FIFO Event Parking—"First in, first out"—the term having been borrowed from an accounting class he'd once attended in Toledo, Ohio.

Three sophomore girls from our high school appeared to have the same idea, and they walked past me, casually linking arms at the elbow, as I pulled my car alongside the curb.

Several blocks from the stadium, you could already hear bass drums preparing for faux-war and trumpets loosening up on the school fight song. A middle-aged man in a hooded sweatshirt and jeans was raking golden-brown leaves into neat little piles on his front lawn. He'd already rolled up his sleeves, and his wool cap no longer covered his ears.

The gusty, concrete-colored autumn day was as crisp as a fifty-dollar bill, and the wind had shaken loose an abundance of leaves from the trees, giving the man no shortage of labor.

As the girls strolled past him, the man paused, leaning on his rake, and in his wistful, steely-eyed glare it occurred to me that he was perhaps undressing the girls in his mind. When I walked past him, he nodded at me, yielding a conspiratorial grin, before continuing his yard work with what seemed to me like deflated determination.

Trailing the girls, I admired the slender denim contours of their backsides. All three of them wore green sweatshirts, our school color, and one wrapped herself in a gold-colored fleece blanket. They screamed as they raced across the street near the community center, dodging game traffic, while giggling in a bulletproof fifteen-year-old girl kind of way.

I got stuck at the curb, waiting for an opening in the steady procession of homecoming convertibles, police cars, and school busses, and the girls disappeared toward the ticket booth.

I walked across the crowded parking lot to the end-zone gate, where I presented my press credentials to nobody before continuing down onto the track to watch our offense run dummy plays against a skeleton defense.

Coach Kurzeka was lined up at middle linebacker, wearing a hooded sweatshirt and mesh shorts, with a whistle around his neck. He barked commands at Peter O'Leary, our quarterback.

"Fake the handoff, Peter!" he shouted. "Or you're going to get your dick knocked in the dirt!"

He blew the whistle and they ran the play again.

I had spoken with Coach Kurzeka earlier in the week. As interviews went, his were always a piece of work. When Coach Kurzeka spoke to the press, he would say things like, "Now if only we could find a way to trade for someone like Genester Jefferson, who has all the athletic ability… and the Lindbergh defense, especially in short yardage, is capable of causing so much… but the thing about *scheming* against a player like Genester is that you have to consider that even if he takes off an offensive or defensive series now and then, you've got to find ways to disrupt the other… and with Goldy Lindenheimer, who is now reaping some rewards for all his, you know… he's bound to be a good football player!"

And I would be scribbling as fast as I could in my steno pad, crossing out every half-completed thought, and end up quoting the only sentence that made any sense: "He's bound to be a good football player."

It was trite and didn't really say anything, but I couldn't return from an interview like that without a single usable quote. Fogey would skewer me.

At the far end of the field, Genester stood out from the rest of their squad like a swollen lymph node. Calling out cadences in Lindbergh High's jumping jack routine, he sounded like an army drill sergeant disgusted by a pitiful new class of recruits.

"Come on!" Genester barked. "Come fucking on!"

Five, six, seven, eight…

A cold, thin drizzle began to fall like needles.

Fans gradually filed into the rain-slicked aluminum bleachers on both sides of the field, wrapping themselves in soggy blankets and ducking underneath orange ponchos. And yet somehow the only way you knew it was raining was to watch the precipitation in the floodlights: it appeared to hang there like fishing line from the sky.

Our band warmed up playing popular Hollywood movie songs, but every time they got about twenty seconds into one they would muddle it up so bad the conductor made them start again from the top. I always admired how the bandies viewed their game-day performances. Their motto, slathered in black paint on the wall in their practice hall, was this: "It's not a Football game with a band concert at halftime… It's a Band Concert, with two football halves on either side!"

This perspective, to bookend their role in the evening, was obviously clever, but it wasn't until later that I realized how both were necessary parts of the same whole.

Looking back, my only real regret about the marching band is that I never gave chase to any of the adorable ones, like the chick who sold her French horn our senior year for a pair of breast implants or the girl who could play a four-minute clarinet solo without taking a breath.

Someone told me she could breathe through her ears.

After finishing their warm-ups, our team retreated down to the community center locker room, a low-ceilinged, windowless crypt that had doubled as a nuclear fallout shelter in the 1950s and still smelled like Churchill's war room. Jake Stroops, a former all-state running back and absolute pistol of a guy, who had graduated three years earlier, limped beside me down the cement stairs to the "Mighty Bison Cave." Coach Kurzeka had asked Jake to deliver a pregame pep talk to the boys.

After the players funneled into the locker room, Jake and I lingered in the empty hallway under a pale fluorescent bulb that seemed to be flickering in Morse code. He reached into a pocket inside his leather bomber jacket and pulled out two airline-sized bottles of Kentucky bourbon.

He held one out for me, but I declined it with a hesitant, regretful grimace. He shrugged and unscrewed the tiny caps, before gulping down their liquid contents in succession.

Then he grinned at me with slit eyes and said:

"I'm a method actor. I haze best as a drunken Southern redneck."

When we were freshmen, Jake had orchestrated our high school's annual hazing ritual known as "Tape Fest," in which the seniors kidnapped the newest underclassmen and drove us out to a scum-covered pond someplace and duct-taped us to birch trees. They proceeded to dump buckets of week-old beer vomit and tobacco spit on us and pelted us with raw eggs. For reasons I never understood, Jake targeted Duce Babyk for special abuse, tying his hands to the opposite poles on a pond dock and slinging eggs at his crotch from point-blank range.

Evidently, Jake hadn't forgotten either.

"Is Babyk still queen of the pikers?" he said.

I stammered a reply: "He's... ah—"

"Naw, I'm teasing. He's a good boy, Duce Babyk."

The locker room door flung open, and Elliott Sturgeon, the rat-faced student manager, stumbled out, wrestling with a black canvas equipment bag that was hanging heavily from his shoulder. Elliott's eyes brightened when he saw the famous alumnus standing there, and with an eager grin he said to him, "Hey, Jake, how's college and shit?"

Jake Stroops laughed. Yeah, it was fine, he said.

Elliott spat a loogie onto the tiled floor and smeared it with the underside of his boot. I caught a whiff of his stale-smelling clothes: he stunk like a cup of cold coffee with a cigarette butt floating in it. He dropped the equipment bag onto the floor, sighing in relief, and motioned us into the locker room. Inside, players were pacing like zoo animals and nervously chewing on their mouthpieces. I heard whispers, the sound of a fist popping against plastic shoulder pads, and then, in a far corner of the room, a door slammed. "Okay, gentlemen, gather around. Jake Stroops, where are you, buddy?"

Coach Kurzeka was assembling his troops.

Jake made his way to the center of a half-circle and reached into the back pocket of his corduroy pants, removing a pouch of loose-leaf chewing tobacco. He stuffed a thick wad into his inner cheek and wiped his hands on his thighs, as his jaw went to work in determined figure-eights. The old wall clock buzzed as the minute hand reached for its next position.

Jake leaned over and expelled a gob of cherry-red saliva into a silver metal drinking fountain.

"I asked Jake here to speak to you guys tonight because he

knows a thing or two about big games," Coach Kurzeka began. "You want someone to imitate? I'll tell you what. When Jake carried the football, he was like a rhinoceros going downhill on roller skates. On defense, he roamed like a hungry baboon. I've never coached a tougher bag of nails in all my years, and I guess that means he's worth listening to. Jake, buddy, what say you? What does it take to be a winner?"

Coach Kurzeka stuffed a manila folder into his armpit and nodded at the graduate. Jake inhaled sharply through his nose, his nostrils flaring, and then furrowed his brow on the exhale, making him look just plain mad.

"All right now, listen up, you slap dicks," Jake growled, the whiskey evidently having raised the temperature in his vital organs. He wobbled slightly on his axis as his chest heaved with manufactured intensity. But then, unexpectedly, he whistled a sigh, holding his theatrical anger in check, and smiled wistfully, before continuing in an almost Texas drawl:

"Lust of the world, boys, and grown men *full of envy!* These are interesting times we live in, for sure: when decrepit and haunted old perverts like yours truly, whose football career died three years ago on this very field, are made to pursue vicarious pleasures through the physical heroics of youth. It was my turn then, and now it's yours, and I'm just here dry-humping my buried dreams."

His eyes fell to the floor and his babble tapered out. Silence filled the stuffy room, a buzzing silence, and several players gyrated in place, releasing nervous energy. Jake jingled the keys in his pant pocket. He appeared to be chewing his thoughts like he chewed his tobacco.

"*Haul ass, slap dicks!*" he shouted, finally.

A few players startled.

"Stir the *qi*, boys," he went on, drawling again. "When you look back on tonight with the perspective of a few more years, you will be surprised—nay, *shocked*—how you remember this experience. I mean, there are fathers up there in the stands who *still* dream at night of ramming into the end zone—I kid you not. They haven't woken up with a reliable hard-on in years, but sweet Nancy Reagan, the thought of Friday night lights sends goose bumps chasing up their thighs."

Jake's face was flushed red now.

"But sadly for us horny old goats, it's a one-way street to the slaughterhouse. You can't turn the truck around and do it again. And in that sense, of course, the joke's on us."

He paused to let out a raw, sinister cackle.

"But there's the rub, fellas, because soon the joke will be on you, too, and this whole episode will haunt you forever, like teenage ghost pussy—otherwise known as the pussy you left on the table in your prime-time youth. Tonight is your one and only chance for tonight. Forty-eight minutes till you're drinking forty ounces of malt liquor to unwind after the game. Forty-eight, two, forties. If you need motivation, remember this: Before I blew out my knee during the homecoming game, I used to be you… and you… and you. And now I'm just another self-flagellating geriatric who jerks off at night thinking about catching the winning pass and sniffing a pom girl's undies."

Jake grinned self-consciously, as though he hoped he'd remember that line tomorrow.

"All I'm saying is this," he added. "Do your best. Enjoy yourselves. Have some goddamn fun out there. Forty-eight minutes passes quicker than you'd think. I'd give my right nut to dance under those lights again. Man, if I could climb back into my uniform, you'd better believe I would. Hell, I'd even give you faggots a run for your money chasing pussy after the game. Except you, Babyk, since I know you prefer cock."

Jake grinned spitefully at Duce, who was staring blank-faced at his shoelaces.

"O'Leary, put the ball between the numbers," Jake said flatly. "Running backs, pound the holes. Linemen, hit your man. Defense, make them hurt. It's a simple game."

Jake picked at his crotch and lurched toward a verdict.

"One final thing I'd be remiss not to say—and I apologize

it assumes the form of a threat—but if you take this experience tonight for granted, or dog it even on a single play, or you look like you're not enjoying yourself, I've got just one thing to say to you: *To hell with you.* If you can't appreciate this, you don't deserve anything that follows in life."

He looked sideways.

"How's that, Coach?" he said.

Coach Kurzeka slapped a clipboard with his open palm.

"You heard him, Mighty Bison! Let's get 'em!" he shouted.

Seventy guys in cleats, two-by-two, stomped out of the old bomb shelter up the stairs and across the asphalt to the field entrance. I followed at the very end, trailing behind the coaching staff in their green-on-green warm-ups. The band cued for the fight song, and our guys went pouring onto the field, bursting through a paper banner that read "Feed 'em Cherries!" and splitting two rows of cheerleaders, who were hopping up and down, kicking their little legs in the air. The stands on our side of the field broke into a rousing chorus of our school song, "Mighty Bison, Mighty Bison, Live Long and Prosper."

Before our team's first offensive play of the game, Genester crouched down into a three-point stance at right defensive end and snarled like an angry Rottweiler while he clawed at the grass with his fingertips. "Here I come, you jive ass turkey!" he barked across the line of scrimmage at Peter O'Leary, our quarterback. "It's gonna be like gettin' hit by the *city bus!*"

Peter took the snap, and G.O. burst off the line like a Spanish fighting bull, muscling his way inside Goldy's block, and charging across the soggy turf into our backfield, where he toppled our halfback, fullback, and quarterback in a collective heap, with the easy force of a wrecking ball smashing through dry wall.

He stood over the group, wiped his hands clean like he'd seen on ESPN, and did a little Koko B. Ware dance, flapping his arms like a bird of paradise. Maybe the referee couldn't see the giant smile behind G.O.'s mouthpiece because he threw a yellow flag, calling "unsportsmanlike conduct."

The penalty resulted in an automatic first down. Players on both sides, including our trio that had been toppled, snickered at Genester's antics—but Goldy just stood there clutching his facemask with both hands, his chest heaving.

Coach Kurzeka called timeout and motioned Goldy over to the sideline. "Forget about it, son," he said. "Shake it off. I'm coming back at your side again to see what you're made of, so I hope your chinstrap is buckled tight. It's time to play some smash-mouth, Goldy. Come on now. You've got this guy."

Coach smacked Goldy's ass with his clipboard, sending him back to the huddle, and the next play was an off-tackle run at Goldy's side of the field, a confidence call meant to show him he hadn't lost any faith in him.

When the ball was snapped, our behemoth buddy grunted so loudly you could hear him from the sideline as he knocked Genester off the line of scrimmage into an outside linebacker, clearing out both players, while Duce carried the ball for a fifteen-yard gain.

The following play went to the same side again, and Goldy manhandled G.O. again. Our sideline went ecstatic. Four plays later—each off Goldy's rear end as he blasted angrily forward—O'Leary scored on an option-keeper, and we were up 7-0.

When Lindbergh got the ball and formed a huddle, their coach pointed a finger at Genester and then punched his closed fist into the palm of his other hand. Their first offensive play, and every play that followed, Lindbergh ran the ball at G.O.'s side of the field—toward Goldy on defense—every time on the ground, every fraction of a yard scratched and clawed for.

To make a long story short, the whole first half played out like this—in trench warfare, if you will, waged essentially between the two young men. The coaches on both sides evidently wanted to see what happened when a pair of heavyweights took turns slugging each other in the jaw. Even after both defenses caught on to the one-dimensional strategy and players began cheating to that side of the field, the coaches would call them off, hollering, "Don't cheat!

Cover the *wide* side!"

The battle of attrition wore on.

Both teams scored points. Both defenses held. The football was rammed at Goldy Lindenheimer's side of the field, then at Genester Jefferson's. Momentum swung back and forth like a three-hundred-pound pendulum. The behemoths were gasping for air—you could see their massive frames expanding from the sideline—and their uniforms were streaked with mud and grass. Before each down, the two boys hobbled to the line of scrimmage with grim determination.

Late in the second quarter, worn down by this brutal, unrelenting test of resilience and durability, Goldy came limping off the field, hobbling gingerly on his right side. Our medical trainer rushed over to him on the bench and asked him where he was hurt. Goldy sat there looking off vaguely toward the field, his eyes the eyes of an ancient mariner gazing out to sea, and he replied almost stoically: "In the right knee."

His chinstrap remained buttoned, his mouthguard firmly in place, and he clutched his facemask with both hands while the trainer prodded various parts of his injured leg, inquiring about the pain.

"How's this?" the trainer asked him.

"Yeah," Goldy said. "I'm—" He exhaled loudly. Taking a deep breath, he tried again: "I am—" But he trailed off again, chuckling as he finished a sentence he apparently hadn't intended to say: "I am, therefore I think." His face screwed up in a curious expression, and he shook his head, slobbering on his mouthpiece. "What I mean is, I'm okay, I think."

The trainer offered Goldy a hand, but he stood up using his own power.

Our team had called a timeout, during which a sophomore wearing a Zorro mask and baby diaper had dashed out onto the field and was dodging security officials, extending the duration of our sideline huddle.

Coach Kurzeka cast an indifferent glance at the scene before he leaned down to O'Leary and said: "I think we ought to punt the ball, Peter. We can't let this kid return it—he's too quick. Coffin corner. Dump it inside the fifteen, if you can."

Lindbergh had a lightning-fast bantamweight defensive back who doubled as their punt returner. He led the state in punt return yards and touchdowns, and was an all-state sprinter on their track team. In the rain, he would be slicker than a greased pig—and considerably nimbler.

Goldy set a hefty paw on Coach Kurzeka's shoulder. It was fourth down and two, and we were just over Lindbergh's side of midfield. Our guys were leading the game 21-17, and there were fifteen seconds remaining before halftime. Goldy insisted his leg was fine and urged Coach to run another offensive play to set up a possible field-goal attempt or one last toss into the end zone. O'Leary concurred, and Coach Kurzeka reluctantly assented.

O'Leary broke the huddle and set the line. He took the snap, faked a handoff to Duce Babyk, who slammed into a blitzing linebacker, and rolled out to his right, looking to throw the ball. On the line of scrimmage, Goldy dug in firmly on his damaged leg, fending off Genester's rabid attack.

O'Leary cocked his arm and let fly a perfect pass toward the sideline, to our wide receiver Dave Crooksten, but the wet ball squirted off Dave's fingertips and fluttered into the outstretched arms of the bantamweight defensive back.

Now, with time running out and a different-colored uniform controlling the ball, there was a sudden role reversal, as the bantamweight played a last-second game of "Smear the Queer" with our offense-turned-defense.

After slipping a couple of arm tackles, the tap-dancing cornerback looked like he was ready to take it back seventy yards to our end zone. He was much too quick for our guys on the torn-up field—much too slippery in the rain. But then he committed the cardinal rookie mistake of seeking refuge one too many times in lateral territory. After pirouetting around a would-be tackler, he instantaneously hit full stride, like only bantamweight athletes can do, traveling East-West without any sense of his impending collision with our over-the-road tractor-trailer known as Goldy Lindenheimer, who was doing full-throttle downwind.

Goldy smashed the poor bantamweight flush across the chest, sending a violent thump echoing off the end-zone scoreboard. I've always thought that sports crowds produce a fairly consistent sound, even when their decibel outputs are rapidly increasing or decreasing, but when Goldy changed the bantamweight's direction in a crushing instant, the steady audio track hit a tic, like a record scratch, followed by a collective gasp.

The ball carrier was laid out for all of halftime, as he whimpered and drooled and begged for his ribcage to realign itself; and I knew what Miss Fogey would splash as the headline over my story: "Behemoth Buries Bantamweight: Lindenheimer Levels Littleman," Fogey being a huge fan of alliteration.

When the teams disappeared for halftime, I lingered on the sidelines waiting for our homecoming court to promenade down the fifty-yard-line and the Mighty Bisonettes to shake their booties. Gazing into the bleachers, scanning the crowd to kill a few minutes, I fixed my eyes on Mr. Lindenheimer as he cautiously descended the rain-slicked stairs.

A former All-America tight end at the University of Wisconsin, and briefly a Green Bay Packer, he lumbered now like an arthritic Saint Bernard. He preferred sitting by himself in the stands, away from Mrs. Lindenheimer, whose limited understanding of the game essentially restricted her to two cheers: "Get him! Get him! Get him!" when we were on defense and "Get it! Get it! Get it!" when we were on offense.

Goldy had two younger sisters, Samantha and Sarah, who were in ninth and tenth grade, respectively, and whom Peter O'Leary jokingly referred to as the "Sugar Nipple Twins." They usually sat with their mother at the games, stuffing their faces with hot dogs and pink saltwater taffy.

I walked out to the hard sponge track near midfield, where

Heather Flynn, dressed in her cheerleading uniform, stopped me with a frown. "Console me, Billiam," she wept in faux-sobs, wrapping her arms around me. "I'm so upset."

"What's the matter?"

"Oh, I'm just *so* stupid," she sighed. "I'm *so* dumb. I wore *white*-ribbon laces in my all-white canvas cheerleading shoes when all the other girls remembered to wear *green*-ribbon laces in their all-white canvas cheerleading shoes, this being the homecoming game and all."

"I just forgot," she added with a sniffle, in a voice that managed to sound both despondent and horny. "And no one remembered to bring extra green ribbons."

Heather puffed her lower lip while she twisted the buttons on my jacket. I'm fairly certain she was in heat. She played her role as "class slut" faithfully, making no secret of the fact that she liked to bang like the Fourth of July. She'd always shown that proclivity, in fact. After puberty hit, at some point in late elementary school, Heather would stub her cunt on the edge of boys' desks while she flirted with us. It was a short road from there to fellatio—and the rest is history.

Now, I looked past her, toward the other cheerleaders, who were similarly dressed in impossibly soft white cashmere sweaters and kelly-green headbands. They were milling around near the bleachers, cuddling hot chocolate and brushing the salt off their warm pretzels. A few smiled at me, apparently curious whether Heather would catch me in her sticky trap.

"Can you give me a ride," said Heather, pausing just long enough to be suggestive, "to Clancy's after the game?"

"I'd love to but I'm planning to walk there with everyone else and come back later for my car."

Heather's gaze flitted between my eyes and my mouth as I spoke, while a smirk trembled on her lips as though she was silently mimicking my words.

"Okay," she said. "I can ride with someone else, or I guess I could walk there, too."

Frankly, I enjoyed the long stroll after our home games from the stadium to the all-night pancake house. I considered it a rite of fall and genuinely looked forward to it.

Taking leave of Heather, I wandered to the far end of our sideline, where three freshmen players now in their street clothes were sneaking glances at the pom squad—and at one girl in particular, the plumpish Shelly Finch, who despite blatantly advertising her willingness to play commitment-free "three-hole Monty" nonetheless had trouble finding dates.

You see, in order to be considered a troll Shelly would've needed to be significantly better looking. Indeed, there can be few more painfully assigned reputations in our world than that of the high school slut who can't find any takers.

Shelly and Heather were like yin-and-yang in this department.

Eavesdropping on a conversation between the freshmen guys, I heard one say to another, "But would you hump her if no one found out?"

"If *no one* found out?"

"Yeah."

"Man, I'd hump *anyone*, if no one found out."

I smiled, reaching for my steno pad to document the exchange. The verb "hump" was enjoying a renaissance after a TI-84 calculator game called "Who Would You Hump?" began circulating in study halls. The premise was simple: two girls' names were displayed side-by-side, and you were asked to pick which one was more "humpable." In the game's code, girls had been surreptitiously ranked from one to ninety-nine, and if you picked the right girl—the more desirable one, according to the game's programmer—you were rewarded with accolades like: "Now, that's taking the skin boat to tuna town!" If you chose poorly, a crude animation depicted castration by guillotine.

The game deeply offended some girls (upon realizing that she'd been ranked No. 99, Shelly fled home the day it reached the masses), while others found themselves privately flattered. The vice principal had launched an investigation into who was responsible for creating the game, but the culprit remained at large. We all had our theories, of course. And like I said, the term "hump" had roared back into vogue.

The freshman's response echoed in my head like a good punch line: "Man, I'd hump *anyone*, if no one found out."

Yeah, me too. I shook my head and chuckled.

Wandering closer to the bleachers, I spotted among a group of freshmen girls standing in the front row a pair of familiar crystal-blue eyes peering out at me from a narrow slit between a gray fleece cap and a neck gaiter. It took me a moment to place them. When I realized they belonged to my next-door neighbor's babysitter, whom I had known vaguely for several years, I smiled and approached her with a sort of half-shimmy as I sang out: "*Hello, little miss Julianne!*"

But rather than embarrassing her in front of her friends, as I had intended, I felt my own face turn red, and so I promptly changed tact and tried this: "It isn't that cold out here, is it?"

She pulled down the neck gaiter, which had been covering her nose and mouth, and replied: "It is. It's *free-zing!*" And she drew out the long "e" in a childish, funny way, giggling riotously and coyly diverting her eyes.

On a sweltering afternoon that summer, I'd pulled my car into the driveway at home as a swarm of whooping and hollering elementary school kids, their faces slathered in neon war paint, burst through the evergreen bushes armed with water balloons and squirt guns. Julianne, holding the tiniest tot on her hip, lobbed a balloon about ten feet over my head before laughing helplessly and ordering a retreat—which occurred only after a half-dozen other kids had thoroughly drenched me.

At the football stadium, I said to her: "You look like an Eskimo."

"Thank you," she replied, with a reflexive curtsy.

"Are you enjoying the game?"

"I think it's… uh, very—" she said, sniffling, "cold and rainy."

"Oh, come on. It's not that bad."

"Okay," she said. "More like cold and misty."

"Yeah, I'd say it's like a *fine sleet*."

"Be careful your lenses don't get wet," she said.

"Lens, singular," I said, glancing down at the sturdy thirty-five-millimeter camera hanging from a strap around my neck. "I've only got one." And then, interpreting her advice as an invitation of sorts, I removed the lens cap and pointed my little soul-stealer at her and her friends, saying, "I'll put you in the school paper. On a count of three."

Obligingly, the girls wrapped their arms around each other, tilting their heads slightly to one side, cutely mimicking a fashion-magazine pose, and slowly parted their lips to smile.

"One..."

I pressed the shutter button.

"Hey!" the girls cried. "We weren't ready!"

"Sorry, sorry. One more then."

They quickly re-arranged themselves and beamed instant-ready smiles, dubious of another quick count. They wouldn't fall for *that* trick again.

"One... two... three."

I paused, looking at Julianne in the viewfinder. She had removed her fleece cap and shaken loose her tangled golden hair. *Was she smiling at me, or was it my imagination?* Her eyes retained all the innocent, radiant sparkle of a much younger girl, and yet, I reminded myself, she was officially part of my "peer group" now, as a fellow high school student, a simple fact that somehow seemed difficult to comprehend.

I snapped the photo and said, "I'll make you girls famous."

"We'd love to be famous," replied Julianne, "but mostly we just want to see our picture in the newspaper."

"Okay." I laughed. "I'll see to it that that happens."

I was shooting in black-and-white film since *Solstice* hadn't evolved to colored print runs, and I didn't own any proper lenses, so my "action" shots would necessarily consist of team huddles on the sideline, players loosening up, coaches shouting—that sort of thing. I also intended to lobby for at least one "fan shot," and I figured three adorable freshmen girls in the drizzling rain would be an easy sell to the stoner guys who worked in layout.

At midfield, our high school marching band struck up a regal anthem heralding the arrival of the homecoming king and queen, and it sounded to me like a retarded version of "Hail to the Chief."Tuxedoed attendants on either side of the royal couple held umbrellas over their heads, even though the rain had pretty much ceased by that point.

"She's so pretty," Julianne fawned as the queen sauntered toward our sideline, waving a white-gloved hand at the crowd. "Oh, I want to be homecoming queen someday!"

Before I could think of a witty reply, another *Solstice* staffer, our photographer Veronica Hunter, raced up frantically from the sideline, out of breath.

"Hey, I need to ask you a huge favor," she said. "My battery just died and I haven't photographed the king and queen. Could you shoot them while they're still on the field?"

"Sure, I can do that," I said. "Yes ma'am."

I bid farewell to the freshmen girls with a hasty, duty-calls shrug, but after a few hurried steps in the other direction I spun around, eager to prolong the conversation a moment longer, and said to Julianne:

"I'll file the negatives in the photo cabinet in the newspaper office. Three years from now you might learn the glass slipper fits, and they can run your picture in a 'then and now' spread."

She smiled a confused smile and I dashed off.

The demolition derby continued as the second half got underway and the two behemoths resumed smashing into each other on every down. Their short-range collisions produced the same cracking sound as a pair of big horn sheep butting skulls; and the other linemen looked like fledgling young imitators in comparison. On offense, one behemoth would lunge for the other's knees, or batter him with open palms, or deploy a vicious forearm-elbow to the throat, while the other desperately fought to repel the attack, seeking an opening through which he might be able to maul the ball carrier.

And meanwhile, the coaches sent the football on the ground on practically every offensive play toward the two big men, who continued to line up opposite one another.

When we scored a touchdown early in the third quarter on a long, bruising drive, Goldy came trotting off the field, wiping dirt and sweat from his eyes. I noticed he had been cut on the bridge of his nose, that two of his knuckles on each hand were bound in muddy white tape, and that he had put on a bionic-looking knee brace at halftime. His face looked like a coal miner's after a lengthy stint down the shaft. Saturday was reserved for ice packs and movie rentals, no doubt.

But then, abruptly—and inexplicably—midway through the third quarter, the coaches on both sides abandoned this one-dimensional strategy. It was as though they had colluded on the decision. Suddenly, our offense ran the ball *away* from Genester's side on every down, no matter where he lined up, and Lindbergh went nowhere near Goldy Lindenheimer.

If G.O. lined up left, we went right. If he lined up in the middle, we pitched out wide. They did the same to Goldy. It was an uncompromising reversal that had no bearing on where their own offensive giant stood along the line of scrimmage.

The big men, huffing and puffing and, until that point, vital contributors, were now visibly frustrated as they chased the ball carrier always from a distance. Goldy cursed late in the third quarter when he came shuffling off the field after an extra point, having obviously relished the last-man-standing element to the ground battle. He and G.O. must have been especially disheartened since word had leaked out at halftime that University of Minnesota scouts were in attendance at the game. But neither player made another defensive tackle.

Our team won the contest, 42-38, ironically on a long pass

as time expired.

What other choice did I have? I penned my column on the trench warfare waged between the two boys, culminating in what I metaphorically overwrote as a prizefight pitting a heavyweight slugger against a glass-jawed bantamweight.

I ignored the final stretch of the game, after the offensive strategies shifted, figuring that Goldy deserved a heroic gridiron send-off without any footnotes.

The rain had subsided and a herd of us was slowly moving, like a migration of fearless wildebeest, along a murky highway frontage road toward the bright lights of the all-night pancake house about a half-mile up ahead. At one point, the road veered sharply away from the highway and tacked alongside the country club golf course, and it was here, in the denser shadows, that I found myself surrounded by unfamiliar voices. But it wasn't too long before I was playfully knuckled on the shoulder by a petite female form I couldn't immediately distinguish.

"Hi, choir boy."

The voice giggled. It was Julianne.

Eyeing the silhouette of an aluminum can in her hand, I said to her, teasingly, "I didn't know they changed the laws so that fourteen-year-olds could drink beer now."

"Fifteen. It's my birthday today."

"Well, how about that? I guess you deserve it then."

She wrinkled her nose and confided: "It tastes awful." And then she brought the can to her lips, cringing as she swallowed. Another freshman walked past with an outstretched arm, and Julianne handed him the beer, evidently happy to be rid of it.

"Are you going to Clancy's?" Julianne asked me.

"Oh, is that where we're going?" I said, feigning surprise. "Because I thought maybe we were going to ten o'clock Mass at Our Lady of Mercy."

She giggled again and pretended to stumble off balance into me. I stepped sideways, and she caught herself on my arm.

"Hey!" she cried, as she regained her footing. "You're supposed to catch me."

"I'm sorry. I didn't know the rules. Try it again."

The next time, I moved out of the way completely and Julianne nearly went tumbling to the wet grass, but at the last moment I reached for her, pulling her upright. When she stopped laughing—the giggles escaping through her lips sounded like so many chattering monkeys—she punched me again flirtatiously on the arm.

"How much did you drink?" I asked her.

"Four—"

"Four beers?"

"No, four sips!"

I laughed. "*Four* whole sips?"

"Shut up! They were big sips."

"I'm sure they were," I said.

Julianne bumped into me again, but this time more tenderly, and then she sort of remained there, pressed against me, arm to arm, shoulder to shoulder, so that I could feel her body's warmth through our clothing. Neither of us said anything for a few moments, and I wondered whether she was enjoying our shared silence as much as I was. But then she was the one who broke it.

"This is the sixth hole," she said, pointing past a chain-link fence that was covered with perennial vines. "And that's the tee box for No. 7 over there. We live on the eighth hole. It's a par-three over a small lake with a beautiful little geyser. You can see it from our kitchen window."

"I know it, actually. I play here sometimes."

"Really? My house is the one with the trampoline."

"Oh yeah? I'm pretty sure I know it. Do you play golf?"

"Sort of," she said. "I play putt-putt."

I laughed. "Are you any good?"

"I'm okay, but my sister could be a professional. The last time we played she made a hole-in-one on the nineteenth hole at the mall and won a voucher for a free round."

"That's pretty good. We should play sometime."

"Okay, I'll try to steal her coupon," she said with a giggle. Then, as though it suddenly dawned on her that she'd just been asked on a date, she smiled nervously and quickly added, "Anyway, I should find my friends, but I'll see you later, okay?"

And she disappeared into the crowd behind us.

I arrived at the pancake house by myself. The scene in the entryway was a restaurant manager's worst nightmare: throngs of drunk and stoned high school kids staggering into fake potted palms, plundering the Wishing Well full of children's toys, and gazing slack-jawed into the refrigerated pie case.

I weaved my way through the crowded diner to one of the deep-seated vinyl booths in the old smoking section, where Grouse and Henry were ordering from the waitress. I asked for a small stack of buttermilk pancakes and a side of crispy-chewy bacon, and then slipped off to the restroom.

The urinal was one of those narrow, one-man deals wedged between the toilet stall and a tiled wall, and as I stood there relieving myself, browsing the graffiti on the walls, something peculiar caught my attention in the open space between the floor and the partition: one too many pairs of feet! Even more intriguingly, one pair belonged to an inverted set of legs—and the kicker was that I was staring at the all-white canvas cheerleading shoes with those god-forsaken *white-ribbon laces*!

Biting my lip, lest I spoil my discovery with an outburst of audible laughter, I flushed the urinal and quietly tiptoed out of the bathroom. Nobody saw the creeping grin on my face as I speed-walked back to our table.

"He'll be there next fall, I'm telling you," Henry was saying to Grouse as I slid into the booth. "I'd put money on it. He'll get an offer, and he'll make the traveling squad."

"That's horse shit," Grouse said. "There's no way he'll be ready by then."

I interjected: "Grouse is right. *Horse shit.*"

"I can practically guarantee you he won't play even a single down in the Horseshoe next year," Grouse said.

I gathered they were discussing Goldy's odds of playing for the Gophers in a road game the coming autumn at Ohio State, whose stadium was nicknamed "The Horseshoe."

I interjected again, this time with laughter: "That's what I'm trying to tell you guys."

But they continued to talk past me.

"Maybe he'd see action if somebody got hurt—but that's a big *maybe*—and it assumes they don't redshirt him," Grouse said. "But there's no way he'll be on the starting lineup, or even the immediate depth chart, in the Big Ten as a freshman unless they start pumping him full of growth hormones tomorrow."

"She wasn't moaning at all," I said, grinning. "Which was the most surprising thing. She was completely silent."

Bingo. That got their attention. Goldy's football prospects quickly toppled by the wayside as I told them about the primal scene I'd (more or less) witnessed in the men's room. For high school gossip, it was about as juicy as it came.

"Who's the guy?" Grouse asked.

"Well, that's the ten-thousand-dollar question, isn't it?" I responded. "I have no clue."

Our necks bobbed and craned like swans as we each tried to gain a clearer sightline to the bathroom. Even for dignified, well-reared young men like ourselves, the suspense was overpowering. We each whispered the story in confidence to one or two other people sitting near us, making them promise not to repeat it, and of course it spread like a brush fire until finally it was like being at a surprise party, with everybody waiting for the unsuspecting stars to make their red-carpet arrival.

They came out separately to avoid drawing attention to themselves. Heather appeared first. We roared our applause, clinking our silverware against our water glasses like we were at a wedding reception. It was too bad nobody had a kazoo. Heather blushed and put her hands over her face, but behind the feeble shield she giggled sportingly, taking it in good form.

When Boy Wonder came stomping around the corner, wiping his hands on his corduroy pants and wearing an expression like he'd just finished writing a bluebook essay, the clapping wouldn't have stopped quicker if it had been one of our fathers who emerged from the bathroom. No, we definitely weren't prepared to see Jake Stroops, Class of 1995, as the story's protagonist. None of us knew Jake very well, other than his violent temper on the football field, and so our applause awkwardly and abruptly wobbled to a halt. Jake eased into a mischievous grin as he sat down at a table near us.

"Right between the numbers, huh, Jake?" I said, quoting from his pre-game speech. "You were pounding the hole all right, just like the old days."

"Yeah, yeah." Jake laughed. "Same, same but different."

The ruckus caused by our hoots and hollers, not to mention the continued arrival of more inebriated young patrons, clearly unnerved the restaurant's night manager, whom I watched from across the room as he convened an impromptu huddle with his waitresses around the hostess desk.

The majority of their customers were silver-haired regulars out for a low-impact Friday night. But with the football team starting to arrive, sober though they were, the under-eighteen population was set to multiply, threatening potential mutiny against the established geriatric order.

Among the new arrivals was Goldy Lindenheimer, who sat by himself in a booth adjacent to ours and ordered his trademark "Lindenheimer 37," which consisted of two "Dirty Dozens," a "Super Eight," and five extra blueberry pancakes.

"The police are in the parking lot," he told us, spreading the window blinds with his colossal fingers and peering outside. "On my way in, I heard them say they're waiting for another box of breathalyzers before they knock down the doors."

It was a short journey: the police station was across the street. Grouse's eyes registered mild alarm as he glanced across the table at Henry. The two of them had been nipping Irish whiskey from Grouse's boot flask.

They had offered me some but I declined, the upstanding citizen that I was and a member of the working press. But I thought of sweet little Julianne and how tragic it would be if she were to run afoul of the law at so tender an age.

"We should get out of here," Grouse said to Henry. "You want to do a runner on the food?"

"Yeah. Let's go."

"I'll join you guys," I said, putting a ten-dollar bill under a bottle of maple syrup to cover my order. "But let me rescue someone on the way out."

"Who's that?" Henry asked.

"My neighbor's babysitter," I said, enjoying his predictable reaction. "She's a freshman and was drinking beer on the way over here. I'll be her guardian angel and steer her out of harm's way."

"Nice… She'll owe you one," said Henry, wiggling his eyebrows to underscore his lecherous intents.

"Let's just consider it today's gift to youth," I said.

As those two calmly bee-lined for the exit, I detoured behind a long rectangular table where a church group was bowing their heads in prayer, giving thanks for their ham and cheese omelets and French toast sticks. Julianne and her friends were sitting in a window booth in the non-smoking section, and she blushed in a look of semi-panic when she realized I was approaching her.

"Can you come here for a second?" I said to her.

She stood up hesitantly and followed me into the aisle. As I quietly explained what was happening, the open-mouthed look of consternation on her face was priceless.

She relayed the news to her friends in an urgent whisper, and they promptly called for their bill. Her friends were heading in the opposite direction, I heard them say, and so I offered Julianne a ride if she wanted to flee with us. She accepted.

Grouse's girlfriend Ally Rawai emerged from the bathroom just as we reached the lobby, a fortuitous coincidence of timing, and our determined pace caught her attention. Ally offered a friendly smile to Julianne, but, in the split-second that elapsed as her eyes traveled to meet mine, her expression transformed into one of polite but distrustful curiosity.

Grouse didn't let her dwell on her concerns.

"Woman," he said, opening the door. "Let's go."

"Where are we going?" Ally asked.

"Yeah, where are we going?" Julianne said.

"Don't ask," I said. "It ruins the surprise."

Three cops were standing behind the opened trunk of a patrol car in a "Senior Citizens" parking space near the front door, but they ignored us as we crept along the shrubbery-lined pathway toward the far aisle where Grouse had parked his truck. He wheeled out another exit, on the opposite corner of the lot, and Julianne exhaled loudly in relief once we were a safe distance down the road and didn't see flashing lights.

"Oh, my gosh!" she said. "I could have been in so much trouble. Thank you guys for rescuing me."

"Well, I'm not sure your three sips would've set off any alarm bells," I said.

"Four sips!"

I laughed. "Sorry, that's right. Four sips."

"I could feel it," she said, emphatically.

"I'm sure you could."

She playfully hit my knee.

"Anyway, I'm glad you told me. I could've been arrested."

"Yeah, well, contrary to what some people in this city seem to believe, underage drinking is not the abomination of the Western world," I said.

"But you're right," I added. "Not getting caught is better than getting caught."

"You should be a philosopher," said Grouse, eyeing me in the rearview mirror.

Ally yawned audibly, registering her view on the subject. She was a non-drinker on religious grounds, but her yawn also indicated that the night was rapidly approaching its terminal station. I knew that Grouse would want to drive her home—and that he would drop off Henry on the way there—and so I decided to press my luck with Julianne, whom I'd taken a fast shine to.

I figured it was a textbook case of "strike while the irons are hot." If we dropped Julianne off at her front door, I knew I wouldn't talk to her again that night, and since I tended to be a "telephone coward," I suddenly feared we might not cross paths again socially for some time.

In a whisper, I said to her, "I need to pick up my car at the community center, so what if I walk you home across the golf course and then cut back over to the stadium? It's a nice night for a stroll now that the rain's stopped."

"Sure, that sounds good," she replied. "Let's walk."

To Grouse, I said, "Why don't you drop us off at the country club?"

As I spoke, my leg touched against Julianne's, and she set her hand softly on my knee but didn't look sideways at me or say anything. Ally turned around and flashed a wide, ambiguous smile that I thought could be interpreted in one of two ways: "They might be a cute couple" or "*Sheesh!* Bill is creepy!"

I was rooting for the former.

When we reached the country club's parking lot, Grouse flipped on the cab light as Ally opened the door to let us out. After we'd climbed down, I'm pretty sure Julianne saw Grouse as he indiscreetly tried to get my attention, while jamming his index finger into his closed fist and rolling his eyes in mock ecstasy. Ally smiled embarrassedly, shaking her head, and then patted Julianne on the back as she hugged her goodnight. I waved at the truck as they drove off.

The wet gravel on the cart path crunched underneath our shoes as we ventured deeper into the golf course, walking down a gradually sloping hill in front of the first tee box and between two rows of bony oak trees that divided the No. 1 fairway from the driving range. The cool night air was still heavy with moisture, and in the shaggy, wet grass on either side of us damp leaves, raked into giant piles over a recent weekend, looked like Indian burial mounds in the shadows.

Julianne broke a short spell of silence when she said, "I saw an owl out here last summer."

"Really?"

"Yeah, it was one of the most beautiful things I've ever seen in my life. It stood on one of these branches and twisted its neck around, one hundred and eighty degrees, and stared at my dad and sisters and me with bright yellow eyes."

"That's incredible."

"It was a great horned owl, my dad said. It watched us for about seven seconds before it flew away. It had a huge, majestic wingspan. We saw it just before sundown."

"I've never seen an owl in the wild. I'd love to see one."

"I still think about that one all the time. I wonder if it lives out here. I mean, it must live somewhere near here. Or maybe over at Mud Lake?"

"Yeah, I wonder what it was doing here," I said.

"Probably looking for mice."

"Here?"

"Or fish, I don't know."

"Do owls eat fish?" I wondered aloud.

"Maybe," she said. "What do I look like, a biologist?" She giggled.

"Are there even fish in these ponds?" I asked.

"Well, there are frogs and turtles."

"Yeah, so?"

"So there must be fish."

"Really? I don't know."

A vast blue tarp covered the putting surface on the first hole, and a makeshift green had been spray-painted on the fairway in front of it. An ordinary yellow flagstick was planted in the cup. I briefly recalled a late-October morning in eighth grade when

Grouse and I had skipped school to play golf in the bitter cold. We had worn long black pea coats and herringbone derby caps, and we'd played exactly one hole—the first—before we quit because our fingers had vibrated like tuning forks when we struck our long irons. We went back to Grouse's house and ordered pizzas.

"Do you know how they could make golf more interesting?" Julianne said.

"How's that?"

"Put more animals on the course. Like, they should turn it into a wildlife preserve."

I smiled, considering the idea.

"Not a bad suggestion," I said.

"Don't you think it would be more exciting to play golf with chimpanzees and reindeer and Shetland ponies walking around, grazing in the long grass?"

I laughed.

"Sure, and why not bobcats and lynx and pumas?" I said. "That would be even better—especially if they didn't eat for a few days."

"No, that's too much. I hate cats. I have a cat, and I absolutely loathe her. She's completely evil."

Good girl, I thought, inwardly grinning.

"I saw a TV show once about a golf course in Indonesia that has these wild monkeys all over the place, in the fairways and swinging from the trees," I said.

She beamed. "I love monkeys!"

"Well, these monkeys are an ornery bunch of thieves, it sounds like."

"What?" she said, horrified. "Like winged monkeys?"

"No, no. Crab-eating macaques. Apparently they'll swipe the sunglasses off your face, or steal your golf club out of your hands, or ransack your bag and run off with all your tees and cigars."

"They sound awful. I hate them already," she said, giggling again.

"Well, I don't think you need to worry too much about them unless they sneak onto a boat or jailbreak one of our zoos."

The second hole was a shapeless, boring par-three whose

sole reason for existence, I always assumed, was the tree nursery that was planted behind its tee box along the fence. We followed the cart path as it cut diagonally in front of the ladies' tees.

"What about those Japanese snow monkeys that spend all winter soaking in the hot springs? I love those monkeys. I'd love to own a family of them as pets," Julianne said.

"Now, there's an idea: the club should import a few dozen snow monkeys and populate the golf course with them. Cross-country skiers in the snowy months would turn out in droves with their cameras," I said.

"But," I added, after considering it a moment longer, "if we brought all those animals here, don't you think they might eventually start chasing people's balls and annoy the golfers?"

"That's what would make it more fun, I think. Because right now golf is sort of lame. It could be like a new sport."

"And when the golfers inevitably get frustrated, then what? Golf-meets-hunting? *Adios*, snow monkeys? Like a practical version of the biathlon?"

"What's that?"

"That's the Winter Olympic sport where the Swedes and Russkies, mostly, cross-country ski until they nearly puke and then shoot a rifle at a miniscule target one hundred sixty feet away. It's the sporting world's oddest marriage of skills."

"My dad says the same thing about golf. He says driving and putting should be two different sports."

I laughed. "He's probably right."

"My favorite Winter Olympic sport is curling," Julianne said. "It's like a glamorous version of shuffleboard on ice. I like it because it seems like everyone has a chance. It gives me hope that I'm not too old to dream about being an Olympian."

"Even my grandparents could probably be in the Olympics if they started getting serious about curling," she added.

Our conversation that evening, like so many others that followed in the days and weeks ahead, was full of these sorts of pleasant little meanderings and musings. I wouldn't say they were "child-like," because they weren't exactly that, but they were somehow full of a similar sense of buoyancy and wonder—and touched by the same untainted curiosity.

When I left Julianne at her backyard gate, we could see her mother in the window standing at the kitchen sink, but she couldn't see us, apparently, because of the way the interior light reflected off the glass. It must have caused Mrs. Caswell no small surprise then, or concern, when her newly fifteen-year-old daughter entered the house through the lower-level back door out of the pitch darkness of the golf course.

Meanwhile, I snuck off into the shadows, as enigmatic as an owl.

A fist banged three times on the warming house door and the early drunks went piling into the bathroom. Andy Morton, the rink attendant, glanced up from his physics textbook with an expression of mildly amused curiosity, seemingly aware that the only thing at risk in the event of a SWAT-style police bust was his part-time, underpaying night job.

O'Leary fish-hooked the snuff out of his lower register and slung it in the direction of the trash can. Then he stood up and pushed open the door. The floodlights above the hockey rink cast a glittering halo around our visitor, as the ice and snow behind him sparkled like a fancy chandelier. A gust of cold air wafted into the room what appeared to be the apparition of a Chinese restaurant delivery boy: it was an entrance worthy of Botticelli's *Venus* or Dickens' Ghost of Christmas Present.

In one of his bare hands, the delivery boy clutched a white plastic bag emblazoned with red dragon prints and heavily styl-ized Oriental lettering. His nostrils emitted a frosty puff as he continued squinting hard against the cold.

"I have order for Dudley Dawson," he announced, blinking his wet eyes. "Peking chicken, two scoop. Moon Palace beef, one scoop. Egg loll. Chimp fry lice, one scoop."

He was reading from the receipt slip stapled to the bag. The restaurant was called China, China Fast Food. They charged by the scoop. It was the best Chinese eatery in town, according to a recent poll. On their storefront, a neon sign advertised in glowing red cursive: "We Delivery," and the mangled grammar, we all felt, gave the place an air of authenticity.

The cover of their delivery menu featured a caricature of a smiling Chinese chef with a scythe in one hand and a bulging-eyed chicken in the other. Stitched across the chest of the chef's white double-breasted jacket was the name: "Egg Roll Man."

As Grouse stepped forward to claim his feast, he reached into his back pocket for his wallet. "I'm a real glutton ordering this many scoops, isn't that right, Egg Roll Man?"

"Ah, yes," the boy replied. "I sink so."

He seemed grateful, anyway, for a "yes-or-no" question. Grouse untied the origami knot of the plastic bag and peered inside. Then, with the thundering, theatrical delivery of a revivalist preacher, he added, as a way of toying with our guest: "Gluttonous... and a winebibber, and a friend of publicans and sinners. You know that, don't you, Egg Roll Man? I am *the very worst kind* of sinner!"

Peering out from underneath a knitted wool cap that was pulled down low over his eyes, the driver smiled cheerfully, as though genuinely entertained, but tendered no reply.

"Want some whiskey, Egg Roll Man?" Grouse asked him.

The delivery boy laughed nervously.

"Okay," he replied.

"Really?"

"Yes, really. But sorry, I cannot."

More laughter.

"How about a dip?" Grouse said.

The driver cocked his head, the way a dog does when you call its name in falsetto.

"Again, please?"

"Chewing tobacco," said Grouse, pulling a tin of Copenhagen from his front pocket and showing the label.

The delivery boy beamed a smile as he quickly responded: "I

sink not. No, no, I'm sure not."

We all laughed with him this time.

"Never mind, Egg Roll Man. Chopsticks in the bag?"

"Yes and spork."

"A spork?"

"Yes. It's good for you, I think."

"Okay, well. That's everything then."

We thanked Egg Roll Man and wished him a happy and prosperous Solar New Year. Grouse invited him to Duce's party, but he told us he had more deliveries to make.

"My god, you're like damned old Santa Claus," said Grouse with a smirk, which Egg Roll Man reciprocated. "Well, if I order more food later, I'll insist that you personally deliver it."

The driver smiled again as he turned toward the door, before returning like an apparition into the frosty, snow-blown night.

Grouse reached into the plastic bag and pulled out a fortune cookie wrapped in cellophane, which he lobbed across the room at Goldy Lindenheimer, who tore off the plastic packaging and put the whole cookie into his mouth, pulverizing it in about four chomps with his molars before swallowing it.

"I guess he'll read his fortune on the way out," O'Leary joked.

Grouse always ate his fortune cookie first, before the rest of his meal, believing that was the only way to guarantee a positive outcome. A "real Chinaman" had taught him that secret, he once told us. Now, holding the tiny paper scroll in his fingertips, he read aloud to the room: "You will spend the rest of your days searching for these."

A look of caustic disappointment drew across his face, but it was quickly replaced by a sly grin.

"That's not a fortune," Grouse said. "That's a riddle. Those sneaky little bastards."

He proceeded to spear the chicken and beef chunks with one of the chopsticks, eating as though off the tip of a blade, and then used the same utensil to rake shrimp fried rice from the oyster pail directly into his mouth. But before he could finish his meal, someone issued a call to begin our boot hockey game, and the room suddenly came alive with the sounds of rustling winter jackets, heavy boots trudging across the floor, and wooden hockey sticks clattering against hard surfaces.

Outside, the sight of the two glistening silver kegs on the back of Grouse's pickup truck set hearts aflutter. Henry Beach climbed up onto the bed and mounted one of the steely drums, pretending to hump it like a dog. After basking in the requisite laughter, he rocked it back toward the tailgate. Other guys had entered the cab and were rummaging through the liquor boxes, fondling the inventory.

"Hey, Goldy," said Henry. "How about a little help?"

With his bare hands, our behemoth buddy snatched the fifteen-gallon keg off the truck bed, lugged it across a patch of flattened snow, and set it down onto the ice, where he pushed it like a blocking sled into the hockey rink. It took a group of three guys, then, to hoist it over the sideboards at the red line and half-bury it in the snow on the other side.

"God's ice chest!" Grouse declared.

The snowfall had temporarily stopped, but a shaggy carpet still covered the ice, and so half a dozen guys with shovels began stomping back and forth across the rink, clearing it.

In the summertime, we'd have been standing in deep right-center at Cornelius Field, about three hundred feet from the backstop—well beyond the range of most Little League sluggers but surely at a distance they dreamed about. To the left of home plate, from our vantage point, was the Cornelius Elementary School playground, with its old-fashioned wooden jungle gym and tire swing, and beyond that loomed the formidable, afore-mentioned sledding hill, which was studded with birch trees.

Earlier that afternoon, as on most non-school days in the snowy months, legions of squinty-eyed kids, bundled like marsh-mallows, had piled onto toboggans and sat cross-legged on plastic saucers, and gone buzzing down the slippery slopes in a wintry pageant straight out of Norman Rockwell.

The classic joke was that Minnesota gave you nine months of frostbitten misery followed by three months of lousy snowshoeing and constant highway repair.

Rational minds fairly wondered why the emigrating Swedes and Norwegians, when given a second chance, didn't lay claim to Key West or some other beachfront paradise along the Gulf Coast. It said something about our mentalities up there—and maybe even about our relationship toward suffering.

Peter O'Leary retrieved a battered old tennis ball off the floorboard of Grouse's truck and side-armed it into the hockey rink, skipping it like a flat stone. Gump Worsley went bounding after it. Now, basset hounds aren't generally regarded for their superior athleticism, but in this instance I noticed Gump Worsley was moving pretty damn fast.

Unfortunately for him, it wasn't until he'd nearly reached the ball that the thought seemed to occur to him that he ought to consider slowing down. But hitting the brakes while moving top speed on the ice proved to be a futile endeavor, much like trying to claw one's way up a waterslide. The dog backpedaled, churning his legs in cartoon fashion, before slamming face-first into the sideboards. And then—embarrassed, I guess—he lost interest in the ball and retreated, leaving O'Leary to chase after it with his hockey stick.

Watching the episode, Andy Morton and I shared a laugh.

"How about it, chief?" I said. "A date at the Minneapolis Woman's Club."

"Ha! I know," he replied. "The old girl called me twice today to confirm."

With my hockey stick, I flung an ice chunk against the warming house wall, shattering it into a thousand pieces. Morty snapped shut the front of his insulated jacket and added: "I've got some news for her. And you too, for that matter. I think she's going to choke on her quiche Lorraine when she hears it."

I eyed him quizzically.

"What's that?" I said.

He grinned, evading my eyes.

"Well, I was going to make you wait until Tuesday, but I'll save you the suspense. It's quite a change of plans, but it'll be sweet if it pans out. I formally asked Harvard for a deferral so I can move to Calcutta after graduation with J.D."

John David Palmer, Morty's best friend, had already been admitted to the selective pre-med programs at Johns Hopkins and Georgetown when he announced that he instead planned to move to India to study with holy men and guide the impoverished and destitute toward more dignified deaths.

John David wore a bushy Charles Manson-style beard and had a slick, banker's-style comb-across haircut. He was the very definition of an eccentric intellectual.

"Damn, so you're giving Cambridge a pass?" I said.

Morty shrugged. "Next year, maybe two. We'll have to see what happens with this thing."

I impersonated Miss Fogey's curmudgeonly voice when she was on the offensive: "*Well, kid. You know how I feel: Boston is over bred and under fed.*"

Morty grinned.

"To be fair," he replied, "I don't think the vast majority of Indians are over fed either. But if Harvard is willing to give me a pass, I'd be foolish not to take it."

"What would you do over there?" I asked him.

"That's the easy part. I'll ride the old trains and photograph all the ancient Mughal palaces and colonial ruins and forts. I'll study Hindi and maybe try to write a novel. I'll get stoned on hashish and go listen to the sitar. At night, I'll wade into the chaos of Calcutta's streets, and on long weekends I'll escape to the mountains of Darjeeling for tea and poetry. You don't need much imagination to keep busy in India, as I understand it."

Morty had obviously calculated he could still sail through Harvard, and eventually law school, and someday earn all the money he ever wanted, and yet an experience like the one he was proposing would be worth more than money, in a sense, and wouldn't do anything to derail those plans anyway. It was the ultimate win-win, in other words.

"Well, if you write a novel, just remember what the old girl says," I said. Then, impersonating Miss Fogey again, I added: "*Nothing stares harder than a blank page.*"

Morty giggled and said in the same crotchety voice: "*Write pregnant sentences, sweet pea.*"

For the next hour or so, we all chased after the battered old tennis ball like so many eager basset hounds, while we played a friendly game of boot hockey, the beloved Minnesota winter pastime. We had tapped the keg at center ice and would pause from time-to-time to refill our plastic cups. There was something timeless, I thought, something ineffable even, about a group of young pals being engaged like that in a spirited but ultimately meaningless contest underneath the bright lights on an otherwise cold, dark winter night.

Later, we were sitting on the sideboards taking a breather, listening to another snowfall—it sounded like sleigh bells quivering in the distance—when Goldy's mom's old beater of a car came skidding down the icy path toward the warming house.

Those of us who were drinking beer sunk our plastic cups into the snow banks to conceal them, but it was a purely reflexive gesture since Mrs. Lindenheimer was not at all the sort of mother who was concerned about such things. We hopped down to the ice and followed Goldy to her car.

His mom manually lowered the driver's side window as she saw us approaching. "Tonight's a big night, huh, Sid?" she said with a big smile, before licking her thumb and leaning out the window to wipe crusted pizza sauce off Goldy's chin. "I had a dream last night you'd get an offer to be a Golden Gopher."

Anika Lindenheimer was an aging Woodstock hippie who put tremendous stock in the soothsaying powers of her dreams. A few summers earlier, during middle school, our friends had spent a night camping in tents in Goldy's backyard, and in the morning his mom cooked us buckwheat pancakes in the kitchen and told us about her obsessive pursuit of "lucid dreaming."

Her single greatest desire in life, she said, was to meditate alongside the infamous Vietnam War-era monk Thich Quang Duc in a dream state.

When she succeeded, our junior year, she got a colorful tattoo on her back of the monk and herself seated side-by-side in self-immolation. She also had a tattoo above her left breast of the Buddha being crucified. It was Peter O'Leary, a confirmed Catholic, who finally asked her, "So what's your religion, Mrs. Lindenheimer?"

She winked at Peter but didn't reply.

"Because it seems like some of those might be sacrilegious emblems," he added.

Goldy's mom chuckled, her jowls shaking like a bowl of refrigerated custard.

"I'm a Beyondarian," she said, enigmatically. "I believe in the hum."

"The what?" Peter said.

"If you can master an understanding of time, the past and the future become *literally* the same thing. And at their spatial intersection, there's a marvelous, intoxicating sound like a celestial hum—like a tuning fork that's been ringing for a trillion years. I believe in the unsurpassed potential of that."

And how does a sixteen-year-old respond to such an assertion? I suppose by asking, "Huh?" but then I don't think any of us really wanted to pursue the matter further.

"There's a real poetry," Mrs. Lindenheimer said outside the warming house, "an almost cosmic sense of justice in thinking that Sid might play college football for the Gophers."

"One might even be tempted to suggest it's a self-fulfilling prophecy," she added, with chuckles of delight. It was a notion that evidently titillated her to no end.

Goldy's real name, on his birth certificate, was "Sidney," but no one called him Sidney anymore, or even Sid, except his parents and maybe some teachers at school when they wanted to discipline him. Most of us had known him only as "Goldy" ever since we were about nine years old and he started bearing an uncanny resemblance to the grinning cartoon University of Minnesota mascot, that cheeky-faced rodent.

His dad, Raul Lindenheimer, had played one season for the Green Bay Packers on their practice squad, and had used his meager signing bonus to buy a lakefront cabin in Iyowassca, in northern Wisconsin. The family spent most of their summer weekends there, and sometimes, on the four-hour drive from the Twin Cities, Mrs. Lindenheimer would break long silences to issue bizarre musings like this: "You know, Sid, an hour from now we'll be an hour from the lake."

Then after another half-hour of quietude, she might say: "Say, Sid, I was just wondering: What time of day do you feel most creative?"

And there was the time she spotted a stray white hair on Goldy's head and remarked: "You know what they call that, Sid? They call that premature gray."

"Thanks, master of the obvious," Goldy replied dryly.

"I prefer master of the oblivion," she said, with laughter.

Which is all to say—what, exactly? That Mrs. Lindenheimer was a strange and peculiar breed, like most of our mothers? Or that she believed it had been foretold that her son would remain in Minneapolis for college, donning the maroon and gold on Saturdays, and validating her impression of herself as a gifted clairvoyant?

Goldy contracted his mighty frame as he squeezed into the vehicle's front seat. Bunched forward, he looked like a friendly gorilla inside a toy car. He flashed a thumbs-up through the frost-covered windshield and said, "I'll catch you fellas later at Palazzo Babyk. Be sure to save me some leftovers." We still had no idea what was being served for the main course.

◆ ◆ ◆

Duce Babyk arrived shortly thereafter in a black armored Lincoln Town Car with bulletproof windows. It was a gift from his "rich uncle," the savings trust fund he always referred to so fondly, and the anti-ballistic package was meant to thwart those nefarious thugs and terrorists who might otherwise wish him harm. The same generous benefactor had also bought for Duce his waterskiing boat at the lake cabin and his collection of ridiculously expensive wristwatches.

Duce was talking on the car phone as he powered down the tinted passenger side window.

"Listen, smart guy," he said, touching the dashboard-lighter to the back end of a cigarette. "The quantity-level limit isn't in the milligrams. It's in the tabs. Insurance will cover ten pills a month, so get the hundred-milligram tabs and I'll break them into quarters."

Following an impatient pause, Duce exhaled smoke through his nose and shook his head, adding, "This isn't rocket science, Wilkie. Use your brain."

Eddie Wilkinson was his dad's accountant and unofficial family *consigliore*. The two might have been discussing any of a number of pills Duce was meant to ingest each day on doctor's orders. Duce's stepmom had diagnosed him with Attention Deficit Disorder, along with a host of other spurious behavioral ailments, and the doctor just went ahead and wrote the scripts. But it was ironic, in a way, since the only time I ever saw Duce self-administer the controlled-dose amphetamines was when he crushed them into a powder and snorted them up his nose, or swallowed them with a shot of vodka.

Now, he pressed mute on the car phone and said to the group of us massed around his car: "Why do people insist on making shit harder than it needs to be?"

To which Elliott Sturgeon, who was riding shotgun with a cigarette smoldering in his own fingers, added with a nod: "You've got to maximize the minimum."

Soon after Duce arrived in Minnesota in eighth grade, he told us about his abiding philosophy in life, which he called "Maximize the minimum," also known as a strategy for getting the absolute *most* out of the absolute *least* amount of work.

He illustrated the concept initially with an example: "Picture four people carrying a canoe above their heads. I'm the one who appears to be straining with his part but who, in fact, is barely touching a finger to the bottom of the boat."

It meant working *just* hard enough not to get fired.

On the inside cover of Duce's science-class notebook, Andy Morton had scribbled the following words in jest as a further testament to "maximize the minimum":

Dominik Babyk, Jr.'s scientific rules of order:
1. Plot the data points.
2. Draw the lines connecting the points.
3. If time permits, conduct the experiment.

One bright Saturday morning the previous spring, Duce had elevated his credo to far more ambitious proportions. He'd arrived at the high school with a blistering hangover and, after popping a couple of aspirin, sat down and aced his SAT college entrance exam. The preparation had gone back years, he confided to me, saying, "It takes patience to tunnel into the Ivies."

When we were in ninth grade, it turned out, Duce's dad had planted Eddie Wilkinson as a volunteer proctor at the high school on exam day. Soon, Eddie was volunteering as an usher at school plays and concerts, and had become a "visible pillar of the community." A couple of years later, when we were sitting for the exam ourselves, he was a veteran administrator and friendly with all the high school guidance counselors.

Well, the test isn't exactly guarded like a roving collection of Gauguins. They show up in plain cardboard shipping boxes at the high school a few days before they're administered. Eddie happened to be there to sign for them. He photocopied one of the exams while the other office staff were at lunch and brought it home for Duce, who took it to his math tutor and to an English professor his father knew at the university, telling them it was a "practice test" that he needed their help with.

On test day, Eddie pulled Duce out of the exam room for "private supervision" in the school library, where Duce used a fresh No. 2 pencil to code the pre-recorded answers onto a scanner sheet and turn in a perfect score. Now, he was possibly Yale-bound and full of shit.

Of course, he was smart enough not to tell anyone else about his crooked scheme because he knew our pals would ask too many probing questions, make too many daring requests, and otherwise threaten to screw up everything for everybody—especially himself.

And maximize the minimum had bagged its biggest fish yet.

The snow was still prancing down when Duce ended his phone call. In the back seat of his car, Heather and her band of randy reprobates were sitting three abreast, in identical rabbit-fur coats, their heady perfumes mingling with the fragrant calfskin interior and sharp, musty aroma of cigarette smoke.

Leaning forward from the middle seat, Heather was practically resting her chin on Elliott's shoulder as she gave a little toss of her head.

"Do you guys like my haircut?" she asked.

No one answered, and so she reached awkwardly over Elliott's lap and poked Grouse on the arm through the open passenger side window.

"What?" he said, annoyed.

"Do you like my haircut, Ryan?"

It was an easy question, one that required only a mechanical response, but he hesitated for a moment, as if trying to determine what he *really* thought, before replying uncertainly: "I mean, I don't dislike it."

She crossed her arms, making a sound like "*humph!*" and slumped back onto her seat, her insecurity on full display.

"Don't worry, baby. I like your hair," said Duce, eyeing her in the rearview mirror.

And her sulky frown gave way to an expression of horny semi-satisfaction.

Henry Beach, approaching the car, ejected a gob of tobacco juice onto the snowy path.

"Hey Babyk, thanks for calling me back last night," he said.

"Yeah, sorry about that," said Duce, with casual insincerity.

"How did you feel this morning?" I asked Duce.

"About as good as could be hoped, I suppose. I woke up with scrambled porn on the tube."

I laughed.

"Where did you guys go?" Henry said.

"We went bowling," I said.

"Fucking liars," he scoffed, trudging off toward the rink.

"Hey man," Duce said to Grouse. "You get the loot?"

"It's in the truck. One keg is buried at center ice."

"All right!" said Duce, rapping the steering wheel in mini-celebration. "So let's meet at drop-point Charlie at eight pm?"

Near the warming house entrance, O'Leary bent down and scooped up a handful of fresh snow, molding it into a perfectly round snowball, and then cocked his arm as if he intended to sling it at Duce's car.

"*Don't even fucking think about it!*" Duce shouted out the passenger side window.

Then Duce pointed a long finger at Henry, who was now almost at the hockey rink, and O'Leary pivoted like a shortstop fielding a hot ground ball and whipped the snowball across the distance on a rope, plunking Henry between the shoulder blades and nearly knocking him to the ice.

"You bastard *prick*!" Henry shouted after he had recovered his footing. "I bet you liked jerking off the priest!"

"Hey Pete, twenty dollars says you can't do it again!" Duce hollered with a smile.

O'Leary crouched down and packed another big snowball, which he immediately fired at Henry, again with incredible accuracy. It was tracking for the middle of Henry's chest, but at the last moment Henry held up an open hand, like a stoic wizard, blocking the incoming mortar with his palm.

Now, Henry reached down and armed himself, packing his *own goddamn snowball.* From nearly twice the distance, he hurled it as straight as an arrow, right through the car's open passenger side window, smashing Duce in the face, and exploding into slush all over the dashboard and interior.

"*Bull's-eye!*" Henry shouted. "Don't fucking mess with me tonight, Babyk!"

It took the rest of us nearly fifteen minutes of relentless persuasion to convince Duce not to disinvite Henry from the party. Alas, the two parted ways—not exactly sworn enemies but hardly the best of friends.

The sage sat cross-legged underneath a sacred fig tree, tallying a rosary of teakwood beads. There were one hundred and eight beads on the string, and he counted them as he prayed, again and again. In a flowering bougainvillea not far from where he sat, a bird sang a joyful, effervescent tune: it was springtime! Turning toward the sound with a smirk glinting in his eyes, the old monk softly remarked: "It's all gallows humor in retrospect."

II.

WHEN THE HEATING VENTS finally began to exhale warm air, Grouse peeled off his buckskin choppers and dialed his girlfriend's number on the speakerphone. It rang three times before her dad picked up, and the gruff sound of Mr. Rawai's voice seemed to catch my buddy by surprise. Instinctively, Grouse flexed his cremaster muscle, hiking up his spermatic cords, as he asked in a pitched, almost falsetto voice if he could speak with Ally. Mr. Rawai called out to his daughter, who must have been upstairs.

"I am having the hardest time finding something to wear," was how Ally answered the phone. "I've already tried on four sweaters and three pairs of leggings. Oh my *gosh!*"

When frustrated, Ally was one of those inordinately devout non-denominational Christians who substituted "gosh" for the phonetically similar "god," believing, with some amount of faith, that two consonants might represent the difference between eternal hellfire and a world filled with flutes and candy canes.

"What should I wear, baby?" she asked.

"I don't know," Grouse replied absently, fiddling with the radio dial. "Wear something slutty. That shouldn't be a problem for you."

Click.

Only it wasn't Ally who had hung up the phone. It was her father setting down the other line. A look of exasperated disbelief washed over Grouse's face as he cast a long sideways glance in my direction. But then, just as quickly, his expression softened, and a hellish twinkle arose in his eyes, as though it was *precisely* the outcome he'd been expecting. With a diabolical grin, he silently mouthed to me the words: "Creepy Ryan."

Grouse's perverted alter ego had first "hijacked" my buddy, or been blamed for it, at a birthday party in Ally's basement during middle school. "Creepy Ryan," the alibi went, had found an old plastic children's doll in a storage closet and proceeded to scrawl pubic hair onto its flat-fronted crotch with a brown magic marker. He then wrapped the doll's little legs around his face and chewed like Cookie Monster on the faux genitals ("num, num, num!"), while his audience of fourteen-year-old sexual neophytes roared their approval.

Mrs. Rawai, meanwhile, had slipped downstairs with more pretzels and root beer, and, as you could imagine, she wasn't nearly as amused by the young boy's antics. Of course, it was vintage Grouse Boozer, since the harder we all laughed at Mrs. Rawai's horrified reactions, the more frantically "Creepy Ryan" gobbled on the doll's plastic crotch, riled up by the excitement of his peers yet unaware of who had joined them.

It took plenty of coaxing when he started dating Ally a few years later to convince her parents he wasn't the sort of guy who lurked in the hallways of elementary schools wearing a trench coat and high heels.

After the doll episode was dismissed—"forgiven but not forgotten," as Mr. Rawai put it—another one took its place. It was the summer after our sophomore year and we'd just finished swimming in Ally's pool and were toweling off in her kitchen while she made sandwiches for her parents' sundowner cocktail party. Without asking for permission, Grouse reached for a slice of tuna on wheat, chomped off a corner, and returned the tooth-marred section—which now looked like a cartoon depiction of a shark-bitten surfboard—back to the serving tray.

"Ryan!" Ally squealed. "Don't eat my sandwiches!"

Grouse laughed, and the two of us sauntered barefoot out the front door, across the grassy lawn to our separate cars. It was a gorgeous summer day—a bright blue sky over a throbbing symphony of yard sprinklers—and as I sunk my key into the driver's side door, Grouse called out to me from his truck, squinting into the late-afternoon sun.

"You know something, Bo?" he said, his face twisted in a curious expression. "Pussy doesn't taste a thing like tuna fish."

And by the time the words left his lips, it was too late. Somehow instinctively aware of our fate—experience had taught us well—we turned our heads simultaneously toward the driveway, where a figure that was previously just outside our peripheral vision—Mr. Rawai, hosing down his convertible in a bright blue swimsuit and white T-shirt—was staring right at us.

On the speakerphone, Grouse asked, "Do you think he heard that?"

"Probably," Ally said dismissively, "but he already knows you're a pervert."

Grouse nodded in tepid surrender.

"So when are you coming to pick me up?" she said.

"I need to go home and change into some dry socks and make sure Jack hasn't flat-lined in this cold front or run out of provisions—which means I need to make sure he's got enough canned food and cigars to see him through until morning. Then I'll drop off the dog, and then we'll be there. Give us an hour."

"You won't bring him to the party?"

"I wanted to, but Duce worried he might piss on the rugs."

You could practically hear her smile, the sound of glossed lips coming unstuck.

"I meant Jack," she said.

Ally constantly worried about whether Grouse's seventy-seven-year-old grandfather, Granddaddy Jack, who lived alone, had a sufficiently engaging social calendar.

"I thought you meant the dog." Grouse laughed, obviously pleased with his little joke.

"Hell, maybe Jack would piss on the floors, too. I don't know," he added. "No, Jack told me he plans to stay home and pray for an early thaw. And Gump Worsley is grounded."

Ally giggled. "Grounded for what?"

Grouse glanced over his shoulder at the slumbering hound, which was piled up like laundry on the back seat. The dog perked its fleshy ears, dealing a blow to Creationists, and Grouse replied, "For being too goddamn good looking."

Then, as though he was suddenly tired of the conversation, he added: "Okay, woman, sort out your wardrobe, it's not that difficult. We'll be there when we get there."

"Okay," said Ally cheerfully. "I'll slip into some Daisy Dukes and gladiator shoes and tell my dad it was your idea. Buh-bye!"

Grouse shifted his pickup truck into four-wheel drive and powered up the frozen embankment to the elementary school parking lot, where Duce Babyk's reinforced sedan was idling at the far end with its rear bumper backed against a snow bank. We sat there for a moment watching as Duce revved the engine a few times and then stomped on the accelerator, shooting down the ice-covered asphalt. Halfway across the lot, he yanked the emergency brake, sending the car into high-velocity loop-de-loops and at one point nearly clipping a street lamp. After the car spun to a halt, Grouse pulled his truck alongside them and rolled down his window.

The female passengers in the back seat of Duce's car were flopped all over the place, laughing hysterically, their cocktails and glowing cigarettes held aloft to mitigate burns and spillage. Duce was wearing calfskin driving gloves and aviator sunglasses, and he clenched a filtered cigarette between his molars in a way that gave him a maniacal grin.

Pulling one of the leather gloves taut against his fingertips, he called over to us, raspy-voiced: "You've gotta stress test her every once in a while to make sure she's up for an *all-nighter*. You never know—there could be a real emergency someday."

He took off his sunglasses and winked at us; then he put up the windows and shifted into gear, readying another run.

The stress test was part of a "widely applicable pre-emptive consumer defense theory" Duce had formulated at sixteen when he got his first car and went shopping for a stereo. In the sound-proof booth at the strip-mall audio store, he cranked up the bass speakers so loud that the thick glass walls shook, producing a dull, throbbing pain in my testicles. Over the godless rumble, Duce tried to explain his theory.

"The main thing is: I don't like quitters," he said, nearly shouting. "I demand a fairly heroic effort from all my toys and appliances, especially if I'm paying top dollar. Anything less and I feel like I'm being swindled."

He proceeded to blow out a half-dozen models before settling on a seemingly indestructible configuration of sub-woofers, speakers, and amplifier.

Leaving Duce to spin doughnuts in the parking lot, Grouse turned out onto the main school road, past a row of one-story ramblers with nativity scenes and reindeer glowing in their front yards. I found a pair of blue-blocker sunglasses on the dashboard and put them on. They made the neighborhood look like an old daguerreotype photo.

The empty streets were as slick as wet, flat-bottom boots, and thick snowflakes fell like little meteors through the truck's headlights. The heating vents rattled, straining against the bitter cold, and out of the corner of my eye I could see Gump Worsley slowly filling with air and slowly deflating.

Suddenly, the dog choked on a prodigiously tough snore and bolted upright, succumbing to a brief but ferocious sneezing fit. When it ended, he sat dazed for a moment, staring out through the front windshield, apparently waiting for an answer. When none came, he settled back down to his winter dreams.

Ally had hung a holy Catholic rosary from the truck's rearview mirror, and, despite Grouse's deep ambivalence toward organized religion, he had felt the need to counterbalance the gesture—a counterbalance for the sake of counterbalance—so he had glued onto the dashboard a bronze Buddhist monk figurine seated in meditation posture facing the road. The overall spiritual aesthetic called to mind so many Third World taxicabs.

On the stereo, a Texas country and blues musician—and former penitentiary inmate—named Earl E. Easter was singing about a death-row prisoner's last meal request:

> *Gimme a side of crispy bacon*
> *Cut from a three-legged kangaroo,*
> *And the boiled egg of a snowy owl*
> *Floatin' in some champagne stew.*
>
> *How about some ice cream as a sweet*
> *Pumped from a college girly's teat?*
> *Lord, I'm hungry—feed me, feed me*
> *Before you strap me to the seat!*

For as long as I'd known him, which was basically forever, Grouse had been listening to old country music, reasoning, as we grew older and he became capable of such explanations, that if it kept long-haul truckers from getting lonely while rolling down endless stretches of blacktop, sleeping in faraway truck stops, and getting sucked off by soulless lot lizards, then god damn, it was good enough for him, too.

Grouse had privately told me that his secret dream in life was to punt on college, get his commercial driver's license, and spend a few years working as an over-the-road truck driver, piloting long-haul routes anywhere between, say, New Orleans and Anchorage.

To follow through on the idea, he had said more recently,

would satisfy a longtime curiosity that had only grown stronger as he became more convinced that college nowadays was a "cliché" anyway, with panty raids and beer trophies the stuff of today's high school kids. I remember asking Grouse what he found so intriguing about the trucker's lifestyle, and, giving it practically no thought, he'd replied, "The independence."

"Independence is king, Bo," he said. "I mean total social freedom. Other people can't help but screw it up. They don't mean to, I suppose, but that's just the way it is."

And then he philosophized: "I think some people ought to pass through our orbit in life, and vice versa, without either party feeling the need to spin a 'lifelong friendship' out of it, which is another of college's great clichés. I already have all-time friends—like you. Maybe I want to mingle with a different crowd for a while and cast them away. They can cast me away, too. That's fine. They won't dance at my wedding, and I won't carry their casket at their funeral."

Then he said: "Bo, some people dream of visiting the Orient's holiest temples or climbing the seven summits or seeing the Mona Lisa at dawn, but I'm beginning to think I might seek my transformation elsewhere, like at out-of-the-way coffee and doughnut shops in northern Alberta. And if that doesn't pan out, I can always get my college degree and move to China and be a businessman like everybody else."

"It's like the great Marvin Tiller once said: 'I want to disappear for a while. I think that would be fascinating,'" he concluded.

I remember joking to him that the psychological root of his fantasy was probably nothing more than a subconscious desire to screw a whole bunch of small-town Dairy Queen girls. He just looked at me funny and replied, "Subconscious?"

But I had to admit that Grouse had the temperament for that sort of lifestyle. He suffered no seasonal allergies, no winter flues, no bouts of debilitating sentimentality. He never complained about the weather. On long car rides, he never had to piss. He was never lonely, as far as I knew. And I never saw him throw a tantrum, not even once, not even as a toddler. That just wasn't ever his style.

As he told me about his dream, I somehow knew that he would follow through with it, even if just for a year or two, and that premonition, as I digested what it meant, filled me with an almost god-like sense of possibility. Not "god-like" in my ability to predict a friend's fate but in what struck me then, for the first time, as the god-like power of reinvention, which I had never properly considered before. Now two of my friends were throwing curveballs at their lives.

Grouse eased off the accelerator as he approached a red light, lowering his head to survey all three directions before coasting through the empty intersection. I thought nothing of it, his running the red light. What would be the point of stopping under those circumstances? Life was sometimes about maintaining momentum.

I ought to point out that Grouse didn't have parents. Well, that's not entirely true. We all have parents. He *had* parents, I should say, but by the time we reached high school, he didn't have them any longer. And to explain how he'd arrived at that juncture, sleeping in an empty sugar hogshead, so to speak, and dreaming of becoming a goddamn truck driver of all things, I need to trace his life back to Christmas Eve four years earlier, when the gods of fate turned his domestic world upside-down.

As tradition dictated in those days, the Boozers had joined our family for Christmas Eve dinner—and not only Grouse's parents, Kenny and Diane, but also his Granddaddy Jack and Grandma Lillian, along with Ken Boozer's business partner, Mr. Zhu, who had flown into town from Shanghai with his young girlfriend, the affable Miss Hu. My parents played sporting Christmas hosts, and I ought to mention here that Grouse was an only child and that my older brother Andy was studying economics in London for a semester and didn't come home for the holidays.

That afternoon, we had all gone to Holy Virgin Lutheran Church, where God the Creator himself, a seven-foot-tall deity-among-men cloaked in a white robe, had blessed us with the deliverance of the good word. The Christ child, he said, born in a manger, had brought peace and salvation to us all, so long as we believed, as Grouse put it, "the tales invented by fanatical savages living in a time before flushing toilets and penicillin."

Even from the twentieth row, where we were seated, you couldn't help but notice that Pastor Cummings, who gave the sermon, had a deep, serious face that glowed like metal from the pulpit, hair as white as snow, and hands I'd seen somewhere before. Indeed, Michelangelo might have carved those very hands out of Carrara marble.

When I was seven or eight years old, I'd stopped praying to the god in the clouds and instead began directing my incantations to Pastor Cummings, figuring that the great and powerful Old Testament God was at best a middleman for the head of our church.

During the sermon, the pastor's droning voice whispered through the dim chamber of pews, into the overflow room downstairs, and across the public radio airwaves, preaching the same message he'd preached last year and the year before that, something about the "incarnation, as word becomes flesh" and the "coming of the Christ child." I'd heard the speech so many times that I nodded off, waiting for the choir to tickle me awake through song and the offering plates to zigzag through the pews.

Hark! A new record at twenty-eight minutes, the bells tolled three times, and Pastor Cummings drew the silver chalice to his lips, sipping a final time of Christ's merlot. Then we were off to retrieve our car from the Christian Scientist parking lot across the street, where a humbug note under our windshield-wiper kindly requested that Holy Virgin congregants refrain from using their parking spaces in the future.

When we arrived back at our house, Grouse and I headed straight downstairs with a backpack full of "video games" he'd brought from home. In fact, he had smuggled a half-dozen cans of Pig's Eye Lager, which he'd pilfered from his old man's office refrigerator in the weeks leading up to the holidays. We shot eight-ball for an hour or so in the basement, sipping our suds, and when we finally rejoined the party upstairs the others were well into the Christmas Scotch and nobody even remotely suspected that we were enjoying a warm beer buzz.

The stage was set with all the magic of the season. Burl Ives caroled from the stereo speakers, the fireplace rippled and danced, and the tree was primped for the occasion, strewn with colored lights and bubblers and family ornaments with years of personal affection.

Outside the house, white lights like distant stars dotted the hedges and crabapple tree, the backyard fence and patio railings, the wreaths and the garage. My dad had christened his holiday display *Aurora Borealis* following the annual stringing of the lights over Thanksgiving weekend. He railed against those blinking, twinkling, dizzying colored lights that some neighbors used in their yards and about which my dad liked to complain: "They make you want to regurgitate."

In the living room, Miss Hu knelt on the carpet in front of the balsam fir, hanging from its sinewy limbs a collection of elegant silk ornaments she had brought from the Orient. Sitting on an armchair near the fireplace, Diane Boozer flipped through the glossy pages of a mail-order fashion catalogue.

Granddaddy Jack and Grandma Lillian were nestled on the red-striped love seat, smoking cigarettes and drinking peppermint tea, laughing insouciantly as they reminisced about a Christmas past when they were still "young birds," as they called themselves, and Lillian had given Jack a cushioned toilet seat as a holiday present.

"What kind of a gift—?" Jack chuckled, unable to complete the question.

Lillian's cheeks flushed candy-pink, but no explanation would come to her. Even after all those years, the story still made her blush. Finally she threw up her arms, crying in defeated laughter: "Well, I didn't know what to get you!"

Grouse's dad and my old man were in the kitchen making gravy for the bird, and occasionally their vociferous banter filled the whole house.

"Slow down, Artie! Don't stir so much!" cried Mr. Boozer. "Nobody likes their gravy without a few lumps in it!"

"Oh, bite my ass!" my dad replied.

Mr. Zhu was pacing on the cordless telephone in the den, talking with a factory manager in northern China. As he barked commands, he thrust an index finger into the air, and, at one point, Mr. Boozer, who spoke a bit of Mandarin, entered the living room to translate for us. "Mr. Zhu said, 'I don't care if a hundred cats snuck into the containers. We don't have time to unload them. We will give them the cats as New Year gifts.'"

At times, the conversation fell silent, and we all listened to the yuletide music, the crackling dry wood in the fireplace, and the cars slushing past in the street.

It was during one of these quieter moments that Mrs. Boozer, glancing over the top of her catalogue, reproached Miss Hu in a sharply condescending tone.

"No, Miss Hu," she said, bitingly. "You're putting *way* too many ornaments on that branch. Here, give it to me."

She sounded like the bitch captain of the cheerleading team trying to teach a special education class how to tie their shoes. Mrs. Boozer sighed derisively as she reached for the ornament and set it on another branch, while Miss Hu slinked away to the sofa.

Grouse had always bristled at his mother's prevailing sense of self-importance. She could be a precious, thin-skinned cook, a hot-tempered country club tennis player, and humorless as an advice giver. Over the years, Grouse had learned to rebel by adopting an attitude of constant and casual indifference, even mockery, toward anything he felt she embraced with undue reverence. Ultimately, his mindset blossomed into a wholesale rejection of "society's nauseating tendency toward self-righteousness," as he termed it.

Mrs. Boozer was a part-time yoga teacher, one of those paradoxically edgy Zen people who always seem to be the first ones to come unglued. Judging by photographs I'd seen of her from her glory days as a small-town Ohio debutante, it was easy to guess what had motivated Mr. Boozer during their courtship.

She was an olive-skinned vixen in her youth, with sensual, smoldering eyes and witch-black hair. Strange to say it, but she was sexy as hell—although her thorny side had almost certainly made her less fun in middle age.

When she scolded Miss Hu about the Christmas tree ornaments, Grouse drew in a sharp breath, as if preparing to condemn her, but before he could say anything Mr. Zhu poked his head into the living room with a gentle grin and announced: "I believe the goose is cooked."

We were all gathered around the rectangular table carving away at our turkey, hollowing out our mashed potatoes, and chomping noisily on our buttered corn when my dad entered the candle-lit dining room, the last to serve himself—we had left him flecks of dark meat to scrape off the carcass—and said, "Please, everybody, go ahead and start."

The rest of us were half-finished.

"Wait!" my mom said. "I almost forgot. We haven't said grace. We need to give thanks for this wonderful celebration with friends. Miss Hu, will you say the blessing for us?"

Miss Hu's gaze immediately dropped to her plate, and she began nervously rearranging green beans with her steak knife. She produced a limp smile, quietly mumbled what I interpreted as a death wish against my mother, then stuttered an opening, took a hard pause, and finally confessed in a tiny, shattered voice: "I'm too nervous."

So Ken Boozer said, "Mister Zhu will say grace."

And Mr. Zhu blessed our meal with this: "Dear silver-haired man in the sky, thank you for making us smarter and more resourceful than these farm animals. We are happy to eat them tonight. The honestness of our friendship is a bountiful blessing, and Miss Hu and I are very pleased to be here, even though the weather sucks."

He glanced across the table at Grouse.

"Is that right," asked Mr. Zhu. "Sucks?"

Grouse nodded.

And Mr. Zhu concluded: "Oh, Jesus, please deliver Ryan to me in Shanghai so we can introduce him to a beautiful Chinese lady who will teach him honky tanky. Amen."

"Amen!"

Mr. Zhu raised a brandy snifter that was three-quarters full of Scotch and swirled it in his fingertips. With a baby-faced grin, he added as a postscript: "When Ryan comes to visit me in China, I will take him to become a man." Mr. Zhu knocked down a belt of whisky, suppressing an obvious recoil. "He will learn how to drink *baijiu* rice wine, and he will learn how to make love with an Oriental woman."

Mr. Zhu wiped his glistening lips with the forearm of his cashmere sweater and added, "Chinese women are the best teachers, you know."

The room rippled in laughter, and Miss Hu covered her mouth with her napkin, masking embarrassed giggles. Mr. Zhu smiled the way most people do when they pass gas in public but don't want to take credit for it—the way some old Chinese men smile when they see a really good magic trick for the first time.

"Well, what do you think, Ryan?" said Mr. Zhu.

Grouse stuck his fork into a slab of turkey and looked up.

"Can Bill go, too?" he said.

Laughter again spilled forth from everybody at the table—everyone except his mother, whose gaze remained as cold as the canned cranberries on her salad plate. Then Kenny jerked his chair back, his face reddening in mock outrage as he stood up. Gesturing with both hands, he built to a thundering crescendo, saying: "*Oh really*, Mister Zhu? You want to take my boy to the *massage parlor*? Do you *really* think so? Over my DEAD BODY!"

The words poured out breathlessly in half-laughs.

"No, no, Kenny," said Mr. Zhu, with a wave of his hand. "Ryan is like my own son—you know that. I would never take him to such a lowly place. You have my word. I will take him to the karaoke and mate him with a true white leopard."

Granddaddy Jack, sitting at the opposite end of the table, tapped the growing ash off his cigarette, took another drag, and said, "Speaking of pair bonding, Mister Zhu, why don't you teach him about salted ox penis? That might be a good place to start. It's supposed to make a man virile and cunning, isn't that right?"

Mr. Zhu gazed over the top of his spectacles at Grouse and whispered: "Don't listen to these buffoons, Ryan. They think that meatloaf and tater tots are sophisticated cuisine. Yellow people like you and me can safely ignore their bullshit."

Jack pressed on, telling us that salted ox penis was so popular in mainland Chinese restaurants that whenever he and Kenny had ordered it on their business trips—out of curiosity, he insisted—the chef would always send his regrets. Alas, the kitchens couldn't keep it in stock.

"Delicacy, huh?" Jack said. "Ryan, it looks how you'd think it would look. I've seen it on a picture menu. But don't worry: if you decide you like it, I won't tell anyone."

Mr. Zhu raised a finger in protest.

"Ox penis makes you *very smart*, Ryan," he said.

Ken Boozer roared in savage laughter.

"Look out, Ryan!" he cried. "They're thinking people now!"

Seizing the conch shell, Kenny told us about other "thinking people" he had encountered in China, like the street hawker who'd sold him a kite after "fiercely negotiating for upwards of an hour over the equivalent of about twenty-four cents." The vendor finally agreed to sell the kite at a slight discount, and Kenny briefly indulged his warm internal feelings of triumph.

But no sooner had he taken hold of his new possession than waves of suspicion flooded through him.

"The hawker grinned at me like a Disney villain," said Mr. Boozer, "and asked if I'd like to buy some string."

They were stories we had heard before.

"You were outsmarted, Kenny," said Mr. Zhu, with a satisfied grin.

"That's true. He was awfully clever. I'll grant him that—a reminder that even the King Pin needs to remain on his toes at all times. But they aren't all so quick, are they, Mister Zhu, like those street kids who flocked to me afterward like pigeons, selling Chinese finger-traps."

"Two for one dollar! Two for one dollar!" they hollered.

"How about five for two dollars and seventy-five cents?" Kenny asked them.

The group briefly paused, exchanging glances.

Then: "No! Two for one dollar!"

Mr. Zhu wiped his face with the palm of his hand, staring dully at Mr. Boozer.

"You're such a pain in the ass, Kenny."

Ken Boozer and Mr. Zhu had first gone into business together in the early 1980s, shortly after the Chinese government began allowing foreign investment in the country. Their maiden venture involved the sale of "invisible" dog fences that were manufactured at one of Mr. Zhu's mainland factories. The concept was simple: a dog owner marked a six-point boundary in his yard using special transmitter stakes, and if the dog passed through any two consecutive points, a "minor" electrical charge would "gently emit" in the dog's collar, "kindly reminding your beloved pet where he or she isn't allowed to go."

The product didn't work quite as advertised. Within days of reaching American stores, the fence electrocuted to death more than a dozen dogs. Mr. Boozer telephoned Mr. Zhu in a rage, screaming at him about the lawsuits that were piling up in his attorney's office. When Kenny finished lambasting his business partner, the line fell silent, and then tiny, childlike giggles began escaping from Mr. Zhu's end of the line.

"Oh, Kenny," he moaned. "We must have used the wrong voltage. *Oh no!*"

And Mr. Zhu let forth peals of belly laughter.

"This guy is nuts," Kenny later recalled thinking. "He's on the other end of the phone laughing like a lunatic. Meanwhile, I've got dead animals all over the place!"

But Mr. Zhu proved to be a loyal partner, realizing perhaps that vast fortunes could be made "making stuff" for Americans. He must have sensed that Kenny was a good horse to bet on, too, since he covered half the costs of untangling the lawsuits and then helped bankroll Mr. Boozer as they embarked on their next endeavor together in household ladders, wheelbarrows, and garden carts—nothing with live wires, Grouse's dad had insisted.

Now, Mr. Boozer was readying another incendiary tale—that much was obvious watching him as he swilled aggressively from his frosted pint glass—when his wife pushed back her chair, sprung to her feet, and flung her napkin onto her dinner plate, crying, "That's enough, Ken! You're making an absolute fool of yourself. *You're drunk…* as usual!"

The venom and conviction in her voice—the combination and degree of both—suggested that her emotional fuse had been lit weeks, months, or perhaps even years earlier. Yet the situation momentarily teetered on uncertainty. *Might a light remark reel it in?* The room throbbed with a palpable, nervous silence, like a distant hum, as the stereo hit a pause between tracks. Then Mr. Boozer set his wild, Picasso-like eyes on his wife and sneered:

"That's right. I'm drunk on life, *you bitch*."

I remember looking around the table to gauge whether anyone else had seen this confrontation coming. Judging by the plunge in Granddaddy Jack's throat, as he nearly swallowed his cigarette, and watching as Lillian breathlessly placed a hand across her chest, I guessed not. Creatures most definitely were not stirring—they were *damn right* about that!

Bing Crosby filled the itchy void, crooning from the stereo in his cheery voice, imploring us to "*Have a holly jolly Christmas!*" and the timing could only have been worse if a band of cherub-faced carolers had rung the doorbell.

What happened next makes me laugh, even now. It was one

of those rare instances in life when you have an opportunity to watch a non-genetic character trait being passed from one generation to the next, a moment of purely "learned" behavior. As if that final epithet—the "you bitch"—wasn't enough, Mr. Boozer pressed forward, like I have seen Grouse do so many times since, delivering a "clincher" that was the equivalent to shooting a deer in the head twice.

"You know," said Ken Boozer, "the only reason I married you in the first place was because I got tired of doing my own laundry after college, you *nut job!*"

Miss Hu gasped and I think nearly fainted.

The evidently well-rehearsed performance was marital discord at its purest, the sort of dramatic public unraveling that, had it not been his own parents, Grouse surely would have egged on with jeers and sarcastic play-by-play. Mrs. Boozer, in a climactic flourish, yanked off her diamond wedding ring and tossed it into the living room, one-hopping it off the carpeted floor into the roaring fireplace.

As Grouse watched all of this unfold, I noticed a slight but clearly detectable smirk emanating in his eyes, a look of wry amusement, and I was secretly heartened to know that his philosophical outlook stood on principle and that his habitual laughing off of melodrama and melodramatic people could withstand such an overtly personal test.

Curiously, I also noticed a sliver of a grin on Mr. Zhu's face—although he was watching neither Mr. Boozer nor Mrs. Boozer, but Grouse.

"I'm done with you," Diane Boozer fumed. "You *pig!*" It was the worst she could say. Storming into the front hallway, she hobbled into her shoes and wrestled into her fur coat before stomping out the door. Grouse never rose from his seat, but he did lean slightly forward for a better view through the living room window as his mother backed her black Audi out of the snowy driveway and sped away.

And that was that.

◆ ◆ ◆

Grouse didn't talk much about the separation. The way he saw it, his parents both got what they wanted, as simple as that, and to victimize himself over their split, he felt, would be to embrace a "loser's mentality." But he did say he resented that his mom gradually came to lump *him* into her list of grievances. She interpreted Grouse's stubborn non-participation in the household's dramas as a lack of support *for her*, or worse, as openly antagonistic, when all he really wanted, he told me, was to watch college hockey on TV without the constant bickering and bitching in the background.

Things went swiftly downhill between Kenny and Diane. The ink hadn't dried on their divorce papers when Grouse's mom came home one day and announced that she'd met a born-again Christian named Seth in her divorce therapy group and planned to move out West with him, to Santa Fe, to start a new life together. She never even mentioned child custody. Grouse later said only this of his mother's sudden departure: "It was a hell of a lot easier than if they'd forced me to make a decision."

Time marched on.

Grouse and his dad remained in the great big orange brick house on White Oaks Boulevard. My family lived a six-iron away, a high fade over majestic elms and a grassy traffic triangle that had served as home field, when we were kids, to epic, nine-inning, one-on-one baseball games between the two of us.

As a youngster, Grouse had the squinty eyes and toothy grin of early Theodore Roosevelt, the nasally pubescent voice of Mike Teevee, and the half-sidearm knuckleball delivery of the legendary Hoyt Wilhelm—a fearful combination to face as a young batter.

But I digress…

Only months after Mrs. Boozer left in the spring of 1994 with a mini-trailer hitched to the back of her Audi, Grouse came home from school one afternoon and found his dad standing at the kitchen counter, hunched over, his fingers trembling as they carried bits of broken sugar cookies to his lips. Grouse thought he was witnessing a nervous breakdown and asked his dad what was the matter.

"I'm fine other than these damn convulsions," said Mr. Boozer, staring at his jittery fingertips. "I'm pretty sure it's just low blood sugar. Maybe I'll rest on the couch a minute."

Grouse telephoned my house, and my mom, out of an overabundance of caution, called 911. Before the paramedics arrived, Mr. Boozer endured a succession of violent grand mal seizures, and when they loaded him into the ambulance, his limbs still flailing, it was the only time in my life I ever saw Grouse cry. Something in Mr. Boozer's brain had gone haywire.

That something turned out to be a malignant brain tumor.

When he stabilized in the intensive care unit and the MRI uncovered an "abnormality" in his brain, we all gathered around him, a vision of bleak faces, as he sat up in his hospital bed and tried to rally the crowd.

Of his seizures, he deadpanned: "I felt like a walleye on the sidewalk."

We laughed uncomfortably.

"All hail Julius seizure," he joked. "Hell, I had no choice in the matter."

A day or two later, when the biopsy confirmed that "abnormality" was indeed a cruel euphemism for "cancer," Kenny vowed to soldier on and "pummel the little son of a bitch, one way or another, until he's destroyed."

Of course, the latter option—"another," as he so inelegantly put it—referred to the less desirable way of ridding one's body of a tumor. Either you snuff it out through radiation and chemotherapy, driving it into remission, or you die yourself, at which point the imperialist mass of cells invariably ceases to survive inside its host.

A grave-faced oncologist explained to Mr. Boozer that the average life expectancy for someone with this most aggressive form of primary brain tumor, a *glioblastoma multiforme*, was less than one year.

"That's a snappy name for a tumor," Mr. Boozer fired back. "Who the hell came up with that one?"

Despite living under the Grim Reaper's patient gaze, Mr.

Boozer maintained a defiant sense of humor. After one radiation treatment at the hospital, as Grouse and I were pushing him back to his room on a wheelchair, Mr. Boozer looked up over his shoulder and asked us, "Do you know how you can tell if it's a mole on your skin or if it's cancer?"

Grouse and I shook our heads.

"If you die, it was cancer," Mr. Boozer said.

Within months, he looked like a skeleton encased in a thin layer of Silly Putty. His face was purplish and swollen from the medications, and when he told jokes, as he occasionally still did, they felt perfunctory, as though he had made them only out of some long-forgotten habit. The humor had drained from his eyes.

The last time I saw him before he moved into the hospice, Mr. Boozer summoned a final bit of strength to offer some parting advice to Grouse and me.

"This thing is about to run its course, but I wanted to tell you guys something, for whatever it's worth," he said.

His coal black eyes remained impenetrable.

"Remember," he said, "the world's rotating cast of religious protagonists offers prescriptions for lemmings or cattle, or self-loathing repressed homosexuals, but not for intelligent, discerning, red-blooded young men like yourselves. All the meditation and prayer in the world never turned up a damn thing. It never has and it never will."

"A lot of people want to drive you out to a dirt road someplace in the middle of nowhere and leave you there in your bare feet," he said. "I'll save you the trouble and tell you the riddle doesn't have an answer. After the circus ends, the clowns take off their costumes and face paint and climb into their cars and drive home like everybody else."

He hung in there like an overmatched prizefighter for a few more weeks. The treatments had done nothing to slow the relentless growth of cancer cells. Mr. Boozer succumbed on August 12th, 1994, the day the baseball players went on strike. Grouse was fifteen years old.

The funeral was held at Holy Virgin. Grouse delivered the eulogy. At one point during his remarks, he paused, seeming to lose his place, and gazed out at the sea of mourners as a half-minute or more ticked past in silence. Then, as though he forgot about the microphone attached to the podium, he laughed softly and uttered almost imperceptibly under his breath, "What the hell is this?"

Diane Boozer flew to Minnesota for the funeral. She apologized to Grouse, sobbing, for the manner in which she'd left him, and practically begged him to move to New Mexico. They spoke in a quiet corner of the church's reception hall, surrounded by pink azalea bouquets. I watched as Grouse put his hands on his mom's shoulders and looked in her eyes. He told her he didn't hold any grudges—that that wasn't who he was—and he promised to visit her in Santa Fe.

After the funeral, Grouse moved into his grandparents' apartment building, into his own spacious, if slightly outmoded, two-bedroom unit down the hall. My parents had offered him my brother's old room, but Grouse knew that Jack and Lillian were reeling from the loss of their only son and thought they should grieve together as a family.

They sold the handsome orange brick colonial home on White Oaks Boulevard—"which is a shame because I could've thrown some Gatsbyian parties there," Grouse had said—and Granddaddy Jack helped my buddy settle into his new digs.

Despite those critics who worried that the isolation would be tortuous—and those who endlessly cursed Diane Boozer for "abandoning" her son—Grouse found the arrangement wholly satisfactory, maybe even therapeutic, and never missed a beat with his friends.

"It is what it is," he conceded to me once. "But I'll tell you this: it's a shitty is."

He hadn't been in his new apartment six months when Granddaddy Jack came knocking on the door one morning with the news that Lillian had passed away in her sleep. Gone to bed crying, he said, and died of a broken heart. Grouse accepted the news as though he'd woken up that morning expecting it.

He put a hand on his grandfather's shoulder and told him, "No worries, Jack. We're going to be all right."

Grouse turned into his apartment complex, navigating down a narrow, winding lane of white-frosted oak trees and faux-Victorian street lamps. The cluster of mid-rise, brown-brick buildings that emerged in the pine tree clearing up ahead looked through the darkening twilight like they were made out of gingerbread, their balcony lights festooned with colorful gum-drops, their chimneys built from tootsie rolls. It was nothing like the 1960s utilitarian aesthetic of the non-Christmas seasons. The scene before us now was dripping with charm, if you want to know the truth—just dripping with it.

The truck barely squeezed under the low concrete beams in the subterranean garage, and the antennas dinged against the hanging metal signs. The lot was sparsely filled with pontoon-shaped automobiles, powder blue Skylarks, and honey-colored ancient sedans—maybe even a few with rumble seats. Grouse's extended crew cab was surely the only vehicle down there with a "Goat Ropers Need Love, Too" bumper sticker.

Finding his parking space, Grouse killed the engine and leaned over to unlock the glove box. "Don't want to forget these babies," he said, taking out the wallet with the fake IDs.

"Nathaniel Wakefield Hooper" was the all-American name we'd bestowed upon our flawless bundle of false identification, which included a Minnesota state driver's license, a valid credit card (which we were smart enough never to use), and a U.S. social security card, all of which could be traced back to legitimacy in the form of a notarized Hennepin County birth certificate dated 1976.

My image appeared on the license, although Grouse had used it that afternoon on the Indian Reservation. Admittedly, sharing the world's most foolproof ID wasn't a genius idea, but Grouse and I could pass for brothers, and Lucky Star Liquors already knew him on a first-name basis as "Nate."

Our operation had turned cavalier only after we'd been through several heart-palpitating early missions. We stored the wallet at Grouse's apartment for safekeeping.

Actually, how we came into possession of the IDs is a story worth recording. During the summers, we worked in Boozer's warehouse performing menial sweat labor: unloading shipping containers from China, drag-racing forklifts, and chain-smoking Marlboro Reds on the dock.

We wore polyester shirts with our nicknames stenciled in ovals above the chest pockets. Grouse's read "Booze," mine said "Bo," and Duce wore one that said "#2". (Duce worked there once a week when he didn't have tennis lessons.)

Our colleagues were a good-humored bunch of dudes who were always shrink-wrapping somebody else's lunch cooler as a gag or switching off the bathroom lights on him. They taught us all about the state's prison work release program, the area lakes with the biggest muskies, the best northern snowmobile trails, and other curious stuff—like how spark plugs work.

Our supervisor, Terry Wade Gilmore, was a twenty-nine-year-old shipping clerk with a crimped mullet and comb-over hairstyle who would squeeze a load onto the top pallet rack with the forklift, crack a smile, wink, and say something witty like "I squeezed it in by a cunt hair," meaning he'd fit it just beneath the ceiling.

Whenever he couldn't find a pallet we had prepared for shipment, Terry Wade would complain that we didn't take inventory often enough. And as far as I knew, he was the only supervisor ever to fail his own drug test. That led to the "two strikes" policy.

One afternoon, when we were downtown for a hardware show, Terry Wade, who was driving the company van, spotted a long-legged girl in fishnet stockings and high heels strutting past on the sidewalk. He rapped the horn with the palm of his hand and declared: "Now there's a skirt!"

Grouse, craning his neck for a second look over his shoulder, said, "Terry Wade, that's a bearded transvestite!"

But it was good, physical, heart-pumping work and occasionally even memorable, such as, for instance, when we found a severed human finger in a shipping container from China.

One morning on a cigarette break, Terry Wade boasted to us about a buddy of his who had recently been hired as a secretary in a local hospital maternity ward's records office.

"Shit," Terry Wade said to us, "I bet he could get you guys a birth certificate if the money was right."

He was always ending sentences like that: "…if the money was right."

"Why the hell would we want that?" one of us asked.

Terry Wade snickered at our naïveté.

"Well, for one thing," he replied, "you could get yourself a driver's license that says you're old enough to buy beers."

And he released one of his Goofy-like chortles.

Grouse, Duce, and I exchanged calculating glances.

"Are you serious?" Duce said.

"Scout's honor," said Terry Wade, holding up three fingers. "You just bring an original birth certificate to the DMV and fill out an application. They'll make you take a driving test, I think. That's it. I know a guy's little brother that did it."

That was another thing he always said: "I know a guy…"

We deliberated on it. Terry Wade's only precondition was that he didn't want Grouse's face on the driver's license, since Terry Wade didn't want trouble with the boss's family if things somehow backfired. So, a few weeks later, Grouse drove me to the nearest DMV, and he drank instant coffee and watched *Tom and Jerry* re-runs while I breezed through my road test, aced the vision exam, and signed the carbon triplicate forms.

Six weeks later, Nate Hooper, a registered voter (and organ donor to boot, God bless his heart), received his Class D driver's license in the mail at Grouse's apartment. And suddenly we had access to all the beer and liquor we could handle.

We slammed our doors shut, and the echoes reverberated throughout the mostly empty garage. Grouse had parked his truck between Granddaddy Jack's antique Cadillac—a white Coupe de Ville he'd won on a Las Vegas slot machine in the early '80s—and a do-it-yourself car wash stall; and it was so humid down there in the underground garage, even now, in the dead of winter, that you could have doffed your shirt to wash the car, if such a desire struck you. As it were, I simply unzipped my jacket and pawed off my toboggan hat as we trudged behind the basset hound toward the elevator.

On the second floor, the elevator doors creaked open to a dimly lit reception area that was furnished with yellow, pilled-fabric chairs and sofas that reeked of mothballs and mildew. Old-fashioned sconces with orange filaments glowed so faintly on the walls they seemed better suited to a carnival spook house. Gump Worsley nosed his way down a dark, dank corridor, around a corner, to Grouse's door. Grouse sunk his key into the lock, and the dog nosed his way in, into the blackness.

A single control panel brought up all the lights in the apartment, illuminating a recessed living room that was crowded with a pair of overstuffed leather armchairs, an Empire style sofa, and an eclectic assortment of old table and floor lamps, along with other remnants of Grouse's childhood home. An unopened envelope from the high school containing his second-quarter report card had been slipped underneath the door.

Grouse padded down the hallway to his bedroom, where he removed the fake IDs from the wallet and put them into an envelope, which he slid inside the cover of a King James Bible. Then he placed the holy book between dog-eared paperbacks by F. Scott Fitzgerald and Ernest Hemingway on the bookshelf, and it was meant to be a joke, I think: "G" for God.

Grouse was by no means a literature aficionado. He once said all he cared to know about books he'd learned from Miss Fogey: that Jake Barnes had a limp dick, Hester Prynne had trouble keeping her thighs together, Charles Dodgson's other pen name was Humbert Humbert, and Billy Budd was not a paralyzing strain of Elliott Sturgeon's infamous creeper weed. Grouse often referred to bookshelves in other people's homes as "display cases for trophy skulls."

His appreciation of classical music mirrored his opinions on books. He said that Bugs Bunny had rescued Grieg, that Prokofiev deserved whatever pussy he got, and that even a grown man could weep himself senseless if he were locked inside a dark room alone and forced to listen to Gorecki's 3rd Symphony. And Grouse once said that getting sucked off to the opening chords of Vivaldi's *Four Seasons* was "almost comically melodramatic."

Art, like religion, was a vicarious pleasure for Grouse, something that diluted, rather than enhanced, one's experience of life—if only because it wasn't the "real ticket."

Now he opened his sock drawer and pulled out another tin of snuff, shaking it in that peculiar wrist-snapping motion of dip users, his index finger thumping against the broad side as he packed the tobacco along one edge. Then he dragged his thumbnail across the label to open it. After he had secured a pinch in his gums, he licked the stray flecks off his lips and held the tin out toward me.

"No, thanks." I laughed.

I'd tried snuff once during middle school. I remember the tobacco coming loose in my mouth and floating freely over my tongue and inner cheeks. I must have gutted some of the tainted saliva, too, because I remember overheating—I distinctly remember that part.

Grouse enjoys telling people how I ended up in my backyard making snow angels in my boxer shorts. I don't recall that exactly, but I do remember heaving sideways as forcefully as I could, trying to project my vomit beyond the side of my face.

"A drink for the road?" he said.

Grouse looked like he'd been socked in the lower lip.

"Sure," I said. "But I need to use your phone first."

I dialed Julianne's number on the cordless and wandered into the kitchen, where Gump Worsley had convened underneath the dog food drawer. Eventually, he would start growling, doing a fairly decent impression of the dishwasher. The dog spent ninety-five percent of his idle time in two places: one was in the kitchen, near his next meal, and the other was in the living room, where he would spend whole afternoons crawling from sunbeam to sunbeam, waking up every thirty minutes in shadows, confused and slightly perturbed, only to slowly peel himself off the rug, like a running back pulling himself up off the artificial turf after a hard tackle.

There were worse things than a lazy dog's life.

When Julianne answered the phone, I breathed heavily into the mouthpiece. "What are you wearing?" I said in a husky, deliberately creepy voice.

"Um, nothing but a bra and underwear. But can you wait to rape me until after I blow-dry my hair?"

I couldn't suppress my laughter.

Giggles came from the other end of the phone, too.

"We'll pick you up in forty-five minutes," I said.

"Okay, I'll hurry and put some clothes on."

"Or don't. What you're wearing now sounds nice."

"Underwear and a bath towel?"

"Sure, why not?"

"You wish," she said. "Okay, I need to hurry or I won't be ready in time. I'll see you soon, Billy."

"Smooch."

"Yeah, you too."

"*You too?*"

I feigned injured pride, but she had already hung up the phone. Grouse entered the kitchen in his bare feet.

"On second thought," he said, "let's wait to cocktail until we get to Babyk's. I need to stop at Jack's on the way out to make sure he didn't forget to feed the goldfish."

Grouse was wearing a barn jacket over a checkered flannel shirt and long-sleeved Henley, and he sat down on the linoleum floor to pull on a pair of wool socks. He paused in this seated position to wag a finger at his dog. "No girls in the house while I'm gone, Bubba. Do you understand me?"

Gump Worsley stared back with droopy, dispassionate eyes,

but then, hedging his bets, apparently, in case Grouse had said something about beef sticks (a deaf dog could never be sure), the basset hound struggled to his stumpy paws and began ambling toward his owner. With each step, the dog's toenails sounded like he was plopping down small steel chains, while his wet rubber nose sniffed the floor expectantly. Grouse reached out and kneaded the dog's fleshy, oversized ears.

"That's right, you're a good boy," Grouse said to him. "But remember: if you misbehave while I'm gone, I'm going to use your ears to mop the floor tomorrow."

We walked in without knocking. Granddaddy Jack was in the living room, putting golf balls across the Oriental rug into an overturned highball glass in front of the fireplace. A pile of slow-roasting logs, charred and shriveled on the dog-iron grates, popped like a dud firework when we entered the room, sending a limp burst of sparks scrambling up the flue. Jack held the putter like a cane, like an old vaudeville actor handling his prop, leaning on it in such a way that he appeared ready to break into song at any moment. And then he did.

"*Hello, boys!*" he sang, releasing a grin.

If you didn't know any better, your first reaction to seeing Jack's breezy attire on such a dreadfully cold winter evening might have been to phone up the local old folks' home and book him a room in the lockdown ward. But then again Jack had practically invented the all-seasons "fishing dock" look, comprised of short-sleeved plaid shirts, khaki shorts, and weathered old boat shoes, with no socks. He was chewing on a golf tee.

During the winter months, Jack kept the thermostat in his apartment set at a balmy eighty-two degrees. The fireplace only added "set decoration," he liked to say, something to divert his attention from the otherwise depressing fact that it would be another four months—at least—before he could open the porch screens and listen to the birds sing. Any birds out there tonight would have their little legs in the air.

"Have a seat, boys," Jack said. "Can I get you something to drink?"

"I'll have a Glenlivet on the rocks," I said.

"Yeah, I'll bet you would," he replied, disappearing around a corner into the kitchen. In an elevated voice, he called back: "On the other hand, fortifying yourselves against this Inuit cold front wouldn't be such a bad idea."

The room momentarily fell silent, but it was soon filled by the haunting, incongruous sound of northern Minnesota loon calls emanating from the stereo speakers. It was an odd choice of audio accompaniment, I thought, for night putting alone in an otherwise quiet apartment. As Grouse and I listened to the native birdsong, a creeping grin spread across his face.

"I prefer honking geese," he said, "but I guess that's music for another season."

Jack's living room looked like a country club men's lounge with its collection of tartan wool blankets, vintage lampshades, and hickory-shafted golf clubs screwed to the walls. In one corner of the room stood a literally timeless grandfather clock, which told the correct time only twice a day, at 2:30 a.m. and p.m. On those rare instances when Jack still entertained, he would joke to his guests that it was always time for "the Chinese guy to see the dentist." If the line met with a blank stare, as it often did, Jack would squint his eyes and say in a cartoonish Far Eastern accent, "When his *tooth hurty*."

On the rusticated stone ledge above the fireplace stood a framed black-and-white photograph of Granddaddy Jack in a tuxedo, shaking hands with President Ronald Reagan at a re-election fundraiser in downtown Minneapolis in 1983. Jack's eyes were closed.

"I blinked," he'd explained once with a shrug.

When Jack smiled, crow's feet formed alongside his eyes. Two decades spent as a "winter bird" in Florida had given him a waxy, permanent sort of tan, and it wasn't until he flashed his warm smile—with his sunken, slit-like eyes that twinkled and his clownish steel wool eyebrows—that you fully grasped the magnitude of his kind-hearted demeanor.

He had re-entered the living room carrying a silver tray bearing a pot of freshly brewed coffee, a small plate with shortbread on it, three ceramic mugs, and a plastic, seven-day pill canister. "What are you boys doing tonight? Any plans?"

"I think Duce is having a small party," Grouse said.

"That sounds promising. Are you bringing dates?"

He poured coffee into the mugs.

"We'll pick up Ally and Julianne on our way there, but we wanted to stop here first to make sure you hadn't snuck off to warmer climes."

Jack smiled gamely.

"I considered it," he said.

Then he added, "You're a couple of lucky bucks, you know that? Girls like those."

Grouse leaned back on the sofa, clasping his fingers behind his head. "Actually," he said with a sigh, "I'd say they're a couple of lucky ladies."

Jack brushed aside the sarcasm with a flip of his hand. "Let me ask you this: did you clean your truck?"

Grouse smiled guiltily, and I reached for a piece of shortbread. The coffee had quickly helped to blunt the mild beer-drunk I'd felt after the boot hockey game. Nothing straightens the ship quite like an injection of hot black coffee.

"I don't think it's a problem, Jack," said Grouse.

Granddaddy Jack crossed one of his bony, flamingo-like legs over his lap and cautiously sipped his coffee.

"Well, remember," he said. "When I was your age, I once had a date with an absolute doll. I'm talking curls and dimples and simply adorable. As I escorted her down the driveway, I said to her, 'I'm sorry, I didn't clean out my car.' And she looked up at me with a sort of frown, produced this haughty little snort, and said, with delicate reproach: 'Well, obviously you weren't sorry enough to do something about it.'"

Jack chuckled at the memory and then let it pass.

"So what are your parents doing tonight?" he asked me.

"When I left home, my dad had just snuggled into an argyle sweater and plunked down onto the sofa with a grilled sirloin to watch a *This Old House* marathon. My mom was riding shotgun. I don't think she had the remote control."

"He's got the right idea, old Artie—a man who appreciates the finer things in life. If it ever stops snowing, I might drop by unexpectedly and say hello to them."

They would enjoy that, I said.

Jack glanced down at his outfit. "Of course, I'll have to change into some 'real people' clothes first." He sipped his coffee with a contemplative gaze. "And I hope I've got enough anti-freeze in the car."

Jack chuckled at his joke and raked his fingernails through his silvery hair.

"On the other hand," he said, "I thought maybe I'd invite Gump Worsley over to play gin rummy. He rarely wins, and so I like to keep him in the rotation."

Jack reached for the plastic, seven-day pill canister on the tray, flipped open the compartment marked "Sunday," and shook out a colorful assortment of capsules and tablets, briefly inspecting each one as though verifying it was indeed part of the proper mix, and then he swallowed down the whole fistful with a gulp of coffee.

His grimace transformed into a grin as he looked up at us and said: "They call it better living through chemistry."

"But if you think that's frightening, listen to this," he added. "The other morning I woke up and saw a piece of dental floss floating in the toilet bowl. For a moment, I was terrified, thinking it was a tapeworm I couldn't remember passing during the night. You can put it on your calendars, boys: old age. It'll give you something to look forward to."

Granddaddy Jack was a product of the World War II generation, and he watched over Grouse with a sort of casual indifference, believing that kids will be kids and that men can raise themselves. Jack didn't care much about curfews or test scores or unsupervised female companionship, and so Grouse lived a mostly hassle-free existence, liberated from the normal burdens and limitations associated with middle-stage adolescence. If he wanted to keep a bottle of Irish whiskey in the liquor cabinet, or stay awake until 3 a.m. watching *Cheers* re-runs on a school night, no one would tell him not to.

During the summertime, Grouse would often smoke Cuban cigars—which Mr. Zhu muled past the customs inspectors—or a Missouri Meerschaum on his balcony overlooking the woods, occasionally taking aim at the squirrels and other varmint with his pellet gun. Jack would usually drop by, shake a cigarette out of a soft pack, or gnaw on a cheap stogie, and the two would chat like old pals until it was time for bed.

It was during these sundown summits that Jack sought to elevate the young man's character by sharing with him what he considered to be his eternal grandfatherly wisdom.

"The only place you don't want a front-row seat is at a parole hearing," Jack once told his grandson, pausing to watch the cigarette smoke curl in front of his face. Then, having properly considered it, he added: "Or at a funeral."

Another time, he'd said, "There's no skill in telling a good joke. It's rescuing yourself from a bad one that requires talent."

He would sometimes preach: "Life is tolerable, even at its very worst, if you can learn how to laugh at yourself in the third person. One enjoys life the most, it seems, when he is wearing horse-blinders for the bullshit."

And when it came to dispensing advice, Jack returned to the same stock phrase for any and all forms of adversity. "Keep punching, kid," he would say with a growl.

During these sessions, Jack would also relate stories about his own grandfather, Grouse's great-great grandfather, Shipley O'Boozer, who had landed in rural Pennsylvania fresh off the boat from County Kerry.

"He was a nice guy, they say, when he wasn't drinking," Jack said. "Which, of course, turned out to be never."

"Old Shipley fled Ireland because he killed a man he caught cheating in a card game," Jack added. "He brought his whole family with him to the New World, and one of his sons—my dad—eventually took the bloodline halfway across the continent to Minnesota. Lord still wonders why."

And tales of Ken Boozer's escapades were never in short supply:

"Your father was a wild man, Ryan. He probably never told you about the time he cold-cocked a guy at Dugan's Bar & Grill for lipping off to your mother. He didn't hesitate an instant before he threw the punch. That's what the police officer told me when I posted bail. He was an all-timer, that boy. I mean his soul glowed white hot.

"But he had an extraordinary wit and a keen way of seeing things. I'll never forget the postcard he sent Lillian and me after his business started booming around 1990. He wrote, 'China is undergoing economic growth on an *intimidating* scale—it's like watching a woman give birth to a three-year-old.'"

Kenny had first visited Asia in 1983, hitching a ride on a factory tour with a group of manufacturer's representatives out of Pittsburgh. At the time, Kenny was a hardware rep himself, selling garage-door openers, trash compactors, and that sort of thing. Granddaddy Jack had groomed him for the business.

For decades, Jack owned a hardware store at 33rd Street and Normandy Avenue, near the old streetcar line. We used to visit it as kids. It smelled like greasy bolts and sawdust, mingled with the heavenly aroma of Joyce's doughnut bakery next door. During the Korean War, Jack had operated a bullet factory.

After Kenny died, Jack became caretaker of the lucrative manufacturing business.

"Mister Zhu has things on cruise control in China," Jack would say. "I'm only babysitting it until this guy"—nodding at Grouse—"decides whether he wants to take the reins. If not, I vote we sell the damn thing and go to Disney World."

During the winter months, the two relocated their chats to a pair of wingback chairs in Jack's living room, where grandfather and grandson would sip warm brandy, eat honey-roasted peanuts out of a crystal candy dish, and argue over whose turn it was to toss another log onto the fire.

Indoors, Jack was less likely to spark up a cigarette.

He had attempted to quit smoking several times after Grouse's father died, and mostly he did all right. The day Grouse moved into the building, Jack sat outside by the swimming pool, vowing to smoke his "last-ever pack of heaters," lighting each one with the burning ember of the previous. He finished the pack convinced that his lungs held enough tar in reserve that he could call upon it during a future craving, even if he never smoked another butt in his life.

The problem, he discovered, the hurdle that trips so many quitting smokers—and which manifested itself in his constant fidgeting—was the simple habit of it all. Jack wasn't a spearmint gum sort of guy. So he filled the void by smoking cigars, hoping they would cut down the frequency of his habit. He would pull a "little dandy" out of his glass humidor and use it to "fend off the gnats" on the balcony.

But he soon realized that the acrid pong would follow him back into the living room and, unless he took a bath before changing into his pajamas, back into his bed sheets, too. So he compromised again, resolving to chew on the bastards like an old army sergeant.

He still cheated now and then with cigarettes, but, well, everyone needs a guilty pleasure, he would say. His apartment never quite aired itself of the stale tobacco stench that had worked its way into the sofa fabrics and window curtains over the many years he spent as a multiple-packs-a-day smoker.

When Jack and Lillian used to leave my parents' house after a dinner party, leaving behind an ashtray full of stubbed-out Winstons, I remember my mom rushing me upstairs to shampoo my hair in the bathroom sink. Then she'd set little bowls full of vinegar throughout the living room. Somehow, it was supposed to lift the stink out of the wallpaper.

After Jack "quit" smoking cigarettes, I mentioned the remedy to him, and now coffee mugs half-full of apple-cider vinegar were scattered all over his apartment like mousetraps. I hesitated to tell him this, but the sour aroma of the vinegar, mixed with the old tobacco stink, made his place smell like an upstate VFW after an Easter-egg dye.

Jack presently began gnawing on a thick Cohiba.

I picked up his old blade putter and rapped a golf ball toward the highball glass. It pinged off the rim.

"How's your golf game these days, Jack?"

He shrugged.

"Consistent," he said. "Consistently shitty."

"You need to play with orange balls in this weather."

"Isn't that the truth?"

When the snow eventually melted and the fairways thawed, sometime in mid-June, Jack would golf nine holes a day with a group who called themselves The Ancient Lads, even though his playing partners were at least a decade younger than he was. The rest of the year, the same guys played poker most afternoons in the country club's men's lounge.

"I've been spending too much time at the club lately," Jack told us. "It's never a good sign when the bartender sees you coming and frowns, saying, 'You again?'"

"And how's your magic act?"

"You mean ladling beef barley soup?" he replied.

Twice a month, Jack dressed up as a clown—a regular Bernard Buffet—to perform magic tricks at a local nursing home, or "funeral home," as Grouse called it. We'd tagged along to the Naegeli Center countless times over the years, and I never failed to be horrified, even as I grew older, by the zombie-like invalids wandering the hallways who bumped into the walls and artificial potted palms and blurted out fearful, childlike mutterings like, "*I don't wanna go!*"

In the mid-1980s, Jack would smoke cigarettes during his clown act, since in those days you could still smoke in nursing homes. It was a memorable dichotomy and one of my earliest visual memories: Jack wearing white face-paint, a red-ball nose, and a curly red wig, with a smoldering cigarette hanging limply from his painted-on smile. Only Ken Shapiro in *The Groove Tube* had ever done it better.

The upside to performing in a nursing home, Jack liked to say, was that you didn't need a vast arsenal of tricks. His longtime go-to crowd-pleaser was an obvious sleight of hand in which he "magically transformed" a pigeon into a plastic egg. If you stood behind him, where you could watch the exchange take place, the gimmick was plainly infantile. But you had to remember that half the audience had Alzheimer's and the other half had glaucoma. One elderly woman with severe dementia liked to sit in the front row in her wedding dress.

At a recent show Grouse and I had attended, Jack held the stuffed pigeon out in front of him, allowing the audience, most of whom sat on wheelchairs, many of whom who were drooling on their bibs, to inspect it for themselves. Then in a clumsy, convoluted motion, he swapped the props behind the podium and held up the egg for the audience.

"*Whoa!*" the lady in the wedding dress gasped. "How'd he do that?"

"He turned the pigeon into an egg!" another exclaimed.

An angry old codger in the second row scowled. "Pigeons don't lay eggs," he grumbled, raising an interesting debate. Jack was momentarily flummoxed. He scratched behind his ear: *But pigeons must lay eggs.* Alas, he decided it was time to unveil a new trick. He'd finally worn out the pigeon act, he thought with some sadness. But before he could try out "The Vanishing Rolex," the old codger with the droopy jowls and jaw like a marionette's pounded his fist on the table.

"Okay, enough," he commanded. "Laugh, clown!"

Jack reached for the antique wooden bellows on the marble floor beside the fireplace and pumped it a few times into the hearth, trying to revive the small, dimly glowing shards of wood that had fallen through the iron grates. With each puff of air, the chips momentarily flared up a brilliant shade of orange, but when the stack of charred and shriveled logs above them failed to reignite, Jack shrugged, semi-defeated, and hung the bellows from a Christmas-stocking hook on the underside of the mantel.

"Forget it," he said, mostly to himself.

Then he turned toward us and added:

"So, this morning I was at the grocery store buying a few things—bananas and cereal and what-not—and when I went out to the parking lot I couldn't find my damn car. I searched all over the place. Eventually, I had to go back inside and ask one of the bag boys to help me look for it. Of course, he found it right away, just around the corner from the entrance, by the loading dock. I felt like a complete fool."

"But then, as he was walking away," Jack added, "I heard him remark to his manager that I ought to consider moving into one of those minimum-security geriatric prisons, like where I do my clown show. For Christ's sake, I thought, the whole city is turning into a parking lot. I'm surprised it doesn't happen more often. It feels like a house of mirrors sometimes."

"Plus," he continued, "when you get to be my age it hardly matters anymore, and searching for your car seems like a perfectly good sport. If there's an upside to growing older, it's that you don't need to worry as much about being too busy."

Jack's eyebrows did a little dance, and he added: "So put it on your calendars, boys: old age. It'll give you something to look forward to."

In my periphery, I felt Grouse resisting the urge to look over at me, and so I quickly diverted the conversation, reaching for a glossy magazine on the coffee table. It was a spectator guide from the 1980 Masters golf tournament.

Flipping through its aging, sticky pages, I seized on a two-page spread showing patrons thronged around the green at the par-three sixteenth. One guy in particular stood out wearing a blazing orange-checkered, high-collared shirt. He had a fierce, vintage-1970s horseshoe mustache.

"Whoa!" I said, holding up the page for Jack and Grouse to see. "Look at this guy."

Jack took the bait.

"I'll tell you what," he said, ignoring my observation. "They were among the best four days of my entire life. The fairways are a shade of green like—I don't know even how to describe them. Like they make you want to carpet your bedroom in Bermuda grass. Your dad told me that if he'd had a daughter, he would have named her Augusta. Honest to god, you need to experience that place once in your life with your own eyes, golf fan or not."

Jack and Kenny had flown down to Georgia that year with members' badges courtesy of a large Southern retailer that was expanding its operations in the Midwest. The badges gained the Boozers access inside the ropes on Augusta National's fabled clubhouse lawn, where they sat near the old hackberry and oak trees, and nibbled on pimento sandwiches and peach cobbler, listening to the roars and watching the golfers come in.

"I'll never forget hiking out to the glorious twelfth on Sunday and watching Seve Ballesteros knock his ball into the drink. He did it again on thirteen. But, of course, he hung on to become the youngest champion since Nicklaus—the youngest until this latest superhuman came along and lapped the field last spring."

Grouse was still fixated on the guy's facial hair in the glossy spectator guide.

"Do you remember when Henry tried to grow a *mustache*?" he said, pronouncing it "moose-stash." Grouse stroked his upper lip with his thumb and forefinger.

"It looked like rat fur," I said. "The problem with Henry is that he's just not very handsome. I mean, he's got a face like a catfish. It's a face only a mother could love."

"Yeah," Jack sighed, "and even she—"

He allowed the silence to taper off into a punch line. Poor Henry couldn't escape it—even from our *grandparents*.

"When I grow a mustache, I look like a starving porn star," Grouse said.

A dyspeptic scowl drew across Jack's face. "We won't ask how you know what that looks like."

"It looks like eyebrows for my lips."

"I always thought you looked like Van Gogh's *Zouavre*," I told him.

"I was hoping you might say early Teddy Roosevelt."

There wasn't much to say about my own facial hair, which amounted to a few straggling patches of whiskers on my jaw.

"Well, if you boys admire illustrious mustaches," Jack said, "you ought to have seen the ruffians who sold me this firewood. They came door-to-door selling it in bundles about a month ago, and each of these fellows looked like Rollie Fingers."

The diversion satisfactorily accomplished, and the topic evidently exhausted, Grouse steered the conversation toward the nearest off-ramp, setting down his empty coffee cup with a noisy clink, before sighing and rising from the couch.

"We should get going," he said.

"All right, let me walk you boys out," Jack said. "All this talk about golf and I'm liable to be broken-hearted when I wake up tomorrow and there's another foot of snow on the ground. I knew I should have taken up ballroom dance."

Jack disappeared again into the kitchen. I could hear him setting the dishes in the sink and running the faucet. When he returned, he was carrying a brown paper grocery bag, which smelled like old banana peels and damp coffee filters. It bulged with a week's worth of newspapers.

"Would you mind tossing this into the incinerator on your way out?" he said.

"Looks like some good fish wrap there," I joked.

"Yeah, well, if they're using it for fish wrap now, I feel sorry for the fish."

And he chuckled.

The floor mat outside Jack's door was wet with the melted snow we had trudged into the building. His galoshes sat neatly side by side. As I stepped into my boots, I regretted not bringing another pair of dry socks. Grouse bent down and laced up his scuffed brown leather shit-kickers.

Jack set a hand on Grouse's shoulder.

"You treat those girls like princesses," he said.

"We will," I replied.

"And don't drink too much if you're driving home," Jack added. Grouse took the fifth, tendering no reply.

"Have a good night, gentlemen," Jack said.

And we walked out.

I called my house on the speakerphone in Grouse's truck. My dad answered.

"Hello, may I speak with Bob Vila please?" I said.

My dad sniffed a laugh.

"He's not here right now," he replied. "He's outside with Norm building a three-season porch. Could I give him a message?"

"Just checking in, dad."

"All right, good. What are you doing, pal?"

"Nothing," I said. "Nobody lost any teeth or toes playing boot hockey, but Henry complained that he thought he had dicksicle, so we quit after only an hour."

"Dicksicle?"

"You've had it?"

"Very mature, pal. Well, you're right about one thing: it's colder than a rat's ass out there, and I still need to go outside and put the cover back on the grill. So I guess that's what passes for excitement around here. What are your plans?"

"We're heading to Julianne's now. After that it's anybody's guess. But if anything exciting comes up, I'll be sure to let you know."

"All right, then. Just in case, I'll go upstairs and polish my dancing shoes."

I smiled.

"So, anyway—" my dad said after a brief pause. "I'm thinking about changing my ring name to 'Sterling Golden.' What do you think?"

"It has a nice sound."

"I think so, too. Plus, it's back in circulation, so I figured I might claim it off waivers."

"Are you going to watch the rasslin' tonight?"

"Bollea versus Borden."

"Hogan Sting."

"It's going to be epic."

"Epic theater."

"Speaking of which," my dad said, "what do you suppose are the odds that Fezziwig's daughters are played by sprightly men in drag this year?"

"I'd say around fifty-fifty, if recent history is any guide."

"Well, we'll find out soon enough. The matinee starts at one-thirty. Shall we do waffles and bacon at eleven? Shaved and showered by ten-thirty? Does that sound all right?"

"That sounds perfect."

"All right, pal," he said. "Thanks for the call."

In the background, I could hear my mom saying, "Tell Billy I love him."

My dad said: "Your mother says she doesn't remember who you are."

"Okay, thanks." I laughed. "I love you guys."

"Be good, pal."

We hung up.

Earlier that night, in our cozy den at home, I'd watched as my old man carved into a charcoal-grilled sirloin and buttered popover, and it brought to mind a dinner he and I had shared a month or so earlier, just the two of us, at Murray's Steakhouse downtown, where my dad had ordered his beef "rare," as usual.

"Okay, sir," the waiter said. "That's a cool pink center. Is that how you like it done?"

To which my dad replied: "Actually, I'd prefer if you brought it over on a leash, but whatever you said is fine."

The waiter laughed out loud, and my dad wet his lips on the Glenlivet. Steakhouse waiters are always such good old boys at heart. The waiter turned and moved in brisk strides toward the kitchen, but he paused briefly at the last booth, leaning down to whisper to the old-timer eating his dinner alone: "You know they're going to check your pockets on the way out, so don't try to steal any of our silverware."

The gray-haired customer fumbled a few starts, in tangled laughter, before calling after the waiter: "Oh, fuck you, Charlie."

But the waiter had already disappeared into the kitchen.

Some fathers and sons rack up major league ballparks. My dad and I had pledged to eat at every prime steakhouse in the Twin Cities before I left for college. Murray's put us over the halfway mark—and we had reservations the next weekend at Sgt. Slaughter's Chop House, which served their T-bone steaks with little American flags stuck into them on toothpicks.

At home, my dad set his steak knife onto his plate beside a strip of pink beef, took a sip of Scotch, and said, "Stay home with me tonight, pal?"

"I'd love to, but I told my friends I would go out."

"I know. Did I ever tell you about the girl in my elementary school class whose mom threw a birthday party for her and nobody came?"

Just as he finished asking the question, headlights beamed through the den window, illuminating a row of hardcover books and leather-bound encyclopedias on the oak-paneled bookshelf. O'Leary's car had climbed the driveway.

"No, I don't think so," I said, standing up and pulling on my jacket. "What happened?"

My dad cleared his throat.

"Her name was Janey Duchovny," he said. "She lived up the street from us. We must've been eleven years old. I remember her parents tied helium balloons to the railings outside their front door. She and her mom waited for the other kids to arrive, I suppose, and at some point her mom must have said to her, 'I guess they're not coming,' and Janey went upstairs and changed into her pajamas and got ready for bed."

The ice cubes in my dad's glass jingled as he put the drink to his lips. I blinked the front stoop light to let O'Leary know I was coming.

"I don't get it. What happened?" I said.

My dad stared blankly at the TV, which was on mute.

"To be continued," I said. "I've got to run."

"All right," my dad said, emerging from his brief reverie. "Have a fun night, pal."

And my mom, echoing that timeless parental advice for teenagers, called after me: "And don't do anything stupid!"

Julianne lived in a five-bedroom white brick colonial home on Schiller Lane. It was a timeless and enchanting little mansion, like something you might find replicated inside a snow globe. The naked birch trees out front looked like giant Dalmatian legs sticking up through the cottony snow, and electric holiday candles were blazing in each of the upstairs windows, including in the dormer windows on the wood-shingled roof. On the ground floor, a great big tinsel tree glittered in a bay window.

The year before Julianne was born, her father had mounted an old-fashioned, white-wooden basketball hoop over the two-car garage, envisioning himself grooming a future all-conference varsity point guard on the flagstone driveway. But when he and Mrs. Caswell ushered into the world one baby girl after another—four girls in total—his three-point dreams gradually faded away, even as the old hoop remained.

When the family's fourth daughter, Katrina, was born, even the obstetrician joked about needing a second mortgage to pay for all those weddings, which prompted Mr. Caswell to quip: "I'll only have two rules for my girls. First: no leather pants. And second: elope, elope, elope."

He'd delivered the line with a wink, I was told.

Mrs. Caswell greeted me at the side door. As I stepped out of my boots in the mudroom, touching my snow-crusted socks to the heated wooden floors, I nearly groaned out loud in pleasure: *Sweet Jesus, heated wooden floors!* I felt like a dog curled up beside a furnace vent, and I could have stood there all night warming my toes, but Mrs. Caswell invited me into the living room while Julianne finished getting ready upstairs.

Leading me through the kitchen, where a heady aroma of cinnamon sticks and cloves filled the air from a simmering pot on the stovetop, Mrs. Caswell asked if we could stay for dinner. "We're having veal and pumpkin pie," she said, temptingly.

The pie was cooling on a rack on the counter.

"I'd love to, but I think we're meeting some other friends for dinner," I replied vaguely.

Hearing a newcomer's voice, Rosebud, the family's gregarious golden retriever, nosed her way out of the walk-in pantry, storming across the shiny hardwood floor to thrust her snout into my crotch. For what it's worth, I considered it a positive omen for the night. I leaned down to scratch Rosebud's ears. She was smiling, I think.

"Did you have a nice trip, Mrs. Caswell?"

"Oh, it was phenomenal, Billy. Have you ever been to the Bahamas?"

"No, I haven't. But I've heard it's beautiful."

"It is *so* picturesque. Here, look at this—"

Off the breakfast bar, she picked up a framed black-and-white photograph of her husband and held it up for me. It captured him shirtless on the back of a sport fishing boat, the veins on his muscular forearms popping as he reeled in a giant tarpon off the coast of Bimini. On the horizon loomed a pair of small, palm-fringed islands.

"It's a late Christmas gift for Ted," she told me. "There's another one we took with an underwater camera while we were scuba diving in shallow water near an old shipwreck. It's wrapped underneath the tree in the living room."

There were people with less charmed lives, I thought.

"Could I get you something to drink, Billy? Would you like a glass of juice?"

"Sure, what do you have?"

"We have apple, grape, pineapple, and pear juice."

"That's quite a selection."

Mrs. Caswell shrugged like it was nothing new to her.

"That's what you get when you have four daughters who don't agree on anything," she said.

"I'll have a glass of apple juice," I said. "That sounds perfect, actually."

Which was true: the thought of a cold glass of apple juice, after the beer and coffee—and a burst of strenuous exercise—suddenly sounded irresistibly quenching.

"Where are the girls now?" I asked.

"They're outside in the hot tub."

"Ah, nice. There's nothing like it on a snowy winter night."

"Isn't that the truth?" said Mrs. Caswell, practically nibbling on her wine glass.

If I had been any less naïve, I might have detected in her quick penetrating gaze and husky-soft voice a hint of cautious flirtation, or maybe that's only my recollection now, with the hindsight of so many years and the blurring of so many other details. Memory, like anticipation, can be a horny beast.

In their backyard, the Caswells had planted four billowing lilac trees, one for each daughter, along the side fence. In the summers, Julianne and her sisters would bounce on the trampoline, or suntan on it, while golfers hit their tee shots on the par-three eighth hole at Thorpe Country Club, just beyond their backyard fence. After sundown, when the golfers retired to the clubhouse for burgers and iced tea, Mr. Caswell would chip balls from the grassy part of his lawn toward the green.

Incidentally, my dad had recorded the only hole-in-one of his golfing career—albeit with an asterisk—on the eighth hole that summer. He'd bladed a seven-iron low over the water, and the ball skipped through the sand trap in front of the green, ramped off the lip, and dropped a few feet from the pin before trickling in. The asterisk was that he had topped his first tee shot into the water.

Handing me a tall glass of juice, Mrs. Caswell ordered "Rosie" back into her closet and then led me through a swinging white wooden door into the living room, where she announced my arrival. Another couple was sitting on the sofa with Mr. Caswell, and they all glanced up as we entered the room.

"Bill, I'd like you to meet Dr. Richard Miller and his wife Suzanne," she said.

Dr. Miller stood up and we shook hands.

"Hi Bill, I'm Richard. My wife Suzanne."

"Hello, Dr. Miller. Mrs. Miller. Nice to meet you."

"Hi, pleasure," said Mrs. Miller, taking my hand in her bejeweled fingers.

"We weren't sure the Millers could join us tonight since Dr. Miller is on-call at the hospital," explained Mrs. Caswell. "He enjoys the seldom predictable but always exciting life of an in-demand cardiac surgeon at Riverside Hospital."

Dr. Miller half-smiled, apparently unsure whether the description was intended as flattery or straight commentary.

"The operative word there is 'enjoys,'" he said.

I laughed politely.

Mr. Caswell also rose to shake my hand.

"Hello, Bill. How are things?"

Julianne's dad was always courteous toward me but rarely warm—if that makes sense. Born and raised in Charleston, South Carolina, he still spoke with a polite Southern accent, and somehow, I thought, he even *looked* vaguely South Carolinian. He was tall, graceful, and perennially tan-skinned. He worked for a medical device maker that sold fake tickers, and the dinner with the Millers, I gathered, was an intersection of business and pleasure.

"Things are good," I replied. "Well, except that we got clobbered by Beltrami last night, which was sort of heart-breaking, but which happens, I guess."

I shrugged casually, hoping to leave it at that.

"It sure does, sometimes," Mr. Caswell said.

"Bill plays on the varsity hockey team at Westfield," his wife explained.

"Is that right?" Dr. Miller squinted another quizzical half-smile. "Say, is Rupert Kincaid still the medical trainer there?"

"That's right, he sure is," I said. "He stitched up my chin last season." I tilted my head back, hoping the lamplight would kiss off the tiny scar in such a way that it would appear more gruesome. "He told me that when the North Stars used to get stitches on the bench, they wouldn't even miss a shift."

Dr. Miller chuckled heartily.

"That's probably true," he said. "Those are some tough guys. Rupert was a resident at the hospital a few years ago, and he and I were friendly at the time."

"He's a great guy," I added. "He gave me all the Novocain I could handle. I couldn't eat for a week without spilling food down my chin, but I appreciated it. Stitches, and every other type of invasive medicine, make my stomach churn."

"Is that so?" Mrs. Caswell interjected. "Then you'll be glad you weren't at the middle school earlier this month. Dr. Miller showed Therese's class a video of open-heart surgery. One of the boys turned green in the face and lost his lunch behind his desk."

I laughed. "That sounds like something I would have done."

The others smiled politely.

"We hear you're going to see *A Christmas Carol* tomorrow?" Mrs. Caswell said.

"That's right," I replied. "It's an old tradition for my dad and me. We've been going to see it every year since I was about seven years old."

"Who's your favorite ghost?" asked Dr. Miller, grinning.

"Probably the one who snuffed out our car's engine the first year we saw it. When we parked before the show, my dad forgot to turn off the headlights, and later the engine wouldn't start. We waited two hours for someone to show up with jumper cables. That wasn't easy for a young kid on a school night."

"What's that—Dickens?" said Dr. Miller, jesting.

"Well, that or the car battery being dead as a doornail."

Suddenly, I was gripped by the intense prelude to a sneeze and I pinched my nostrils hoping I could suppress it. I was deathly allergic to the Caswell's cat, a one-eyed human society adoptee they had playfully named "Winky." Within minutes of entering their home, I could usually feel the cat's dander, as it inflamed my nasal passages and made my tear ducts gush. Now, at the first itchy twinges, I looked up and saw Winky across the living room, glowering at me from behind a grand piano leg.

Then, inexplicably, the urge to sneeze receded, but I didn't have a chance to explain my contorted facial expression because Dr. Miller embarked on another line of questioning. "We hear you're going to Madison in the fall. That's a terrific school and, as I understand it, a real party town." He winked fraternally at me. "What do you plan to study there?"

"I'm hoping to major in art history," I said.

"Interesting," Dr. Miller said.

"Well, isn't that fun," added Mrs. Miller.

The others nodded but didn't say anything.

Not that it should have surprised me, but I was somewhat disheartened to learn that my age, however indirectly, had come up as a topic of conversation before I got there. I knew it couldn't have been easy for Mr. Caswell when his eldest daughter, at fifteen, brought home a seventeen-year-old senior as her first high school boyfriend. It doesn't take much imagination to realize how much suffering that could inflict upon a man. Multiplying it by four—taking his other daughters into account—seemed downright cruel.

Fortunately, I was rescued from the harsh glare of the inquisitor's lights as Julianne came bounding down the polished wooden staircase, singing out a cheerful "*Hi-lo!*" as she descended. She was wearing a white turtleneck and snug blue jeans, and she had a white cashmere sweater draped over her elbow. Julianne had tiny hips and a pouty little butt: her petite frame didn't show even a hint of an hourglass figure. And her face was the same color palette as a

Neapolitan ice cream treat: Caribbean bronze skin, gleaming white teeth, bubble-gum-pink gums.

Stealing a glance at her still-ripening chest, I couldn't help but ask myself whether a future doctoral thesis might be residing in there somewhere underneath her turtleneck: "If we all have nipples, why are yours so breathtaking?"

Julianne stopped in front of the hallway mirror and traced her eyes with a dark-colored makeup pencil she had concealed in one of her hands.

"I wish you guys could stay for dinner, Jules," Mrs. Caswell pleaded.

Julianne raised her eyebrows at me and puckered her lips in a cute, questioning gaze. I responded like a lousy mime trying to convey my willingness.

"I don't think we have time," replied Julianne, her face morphing into a girlish frown. Then, studying her reflection in the mirror, she batted her eyelashes slowly, like languid butterfly wings, before doing a little sideways prance into the living room. She exchanged pleasantries with her parents' guests, and with me, and then she turned to her mom and said: "Can I give dad his gift?"

"Shouldn't we wait until your sisters are here?"

"Hmm, okay, but I was hoping he could open it while I'm still home."

Julianne's voice seemed to lose about a decade in maturity when she spoke to her mother.

"Yeah, okay, that's fine. Give him the one under the tree," Mrs. Caswell instructed.

Julianne did as she was told, and her father, upon receiving the gift, tore off its newspaper-comics wrapping paper and slid the large framed photograph onto his lap, briefly inspecting it before holding it up for the rest of us to see. The picture showed all six Caswells in the sea—two in scuba gear, four in fins and snorkels—before a sunken cargo ship. The old vessel on the sandy ocean floor made for a beautiful, almost haunting backdrop.

The photo would be a fine addition to the other gorgeous Caswell imagery in the living room. There was the picture at Lake

Itasca of the girls crossing the headwaters in their bathing suits; at Fair Hills Resort, playing croquet on the lawn; on a beach in Naples, Florida at sundown, standing underneath palm trees that looked like silhouettes of exploding fireworks; and on the old-fashioned pony carousel at the Minnesota State Fair.

Julianne and her dad immediately set about searching for a spot on one of the walls to hang the new photo, but the prime real estate, it seemed, was already taken. Mrs. Caswell and Mrs. Miller retreated into a corner of the sectional sofa, sipping their wine and nodding thoughtfully at one another.

Dr. Miller cast a quick, bored look around the room, glancing first at the gas fireplace, then at the cat, which was licking its paws, and finally, with practically theatrical disgust, at the glass of apple juice I was holding.

"I know why you're leaving," he said. "It's the veal, isn't it?"

He was deadpanning.

I liked people who deadpanned.

"Yeah, you might be right," I said, playing along. "How did you know?"

"Let's call it a hunch."

His eyebrows screwed together in a look of earnest consternation as he added: "So what do you prefer: chicken?"

"Yeah, chicken. Or turkey. Mostly chicken."

"Factory farm fowl," he said, carefully enunciating each syllable, as though the alliteration somehow produced a secret, deeper meaning. "You might be on to something."

I shrugged. "Not from Hong Kong, of course."

"Of course," he quickly rejoined, before adding in a conspiratorial whisper, "but you know what I say: If heaven is governed by chickens, we're all fucked."

"Which is why I eat chicken almost exclusively," I said. "I'm betting against them. Some might say I'm betting the farm."

"Interesting strategy. And how do you feel about other land animals?"

"How do I feel about eating them?"

"Yeah."

"I like the occasional filet mignon or Sunday bacon as much as the next guy."

"And fish? Would you stay tonight if they were serving beer-battered walleye?"

"To be perfectly honest, Dr. Miller, the menu isn't really the problem. But you're right. I'm not a big fish eater. Not freshwater anyway."

"So, what: deep blue? The cold-water dwellers?"

"Maybe. It helps if they're rich in Omega-3s."

"That's vital stuff. Say, let me ask you, Bill: Are you an angler? Do you ever go fishing?"

"Not really."

"Really? Never?"

"Let's call it rarely."

The truth was that I'd been fishing only twice in my life. Once, we'd set sail on Babyk's speedboat on Crystal Lake with a case of beers in a foam ice chest, but either the muskies weren't biting or we had gotten so drunk we forgot to bait the hooks, because the fishing was altogether unprofitable. At sundown, after most of the other boats had gone in, I was relieving myself off the stern, and, being funny, I pretended to lose my balance and toppled into the lake. As I splashed to the surface, Duce throttled the boat off toward shore, leaving me treading water, monkey drunk, in the middle of the melted glacier.

For a moment, I feared I was a goner, doomed to oblivion in a patch of lakebed seaweed, but Grouse had dived in, too, and he was less drunk. Somehow Grouse was always less drunk at critical moments like these. He put an arm around my shoulder, clutching a beer in his free hand, and kicked like mad to keep us both afloat. When Duce circled back, laughing hysterically, and saw my panicked red eyes, I think he lost a lot of respect for me. The two of them teased me mercilessly once we were back onshore—and ever since.

My other fishing experience involved the three of us again, but this time we'd gone ice fishing in northern Minnesota near Duce's cabin. A half-mile out onto the frozen lake, whole streets and neighborhoods had been plowed out of the snow, and were populated with heated little shacks replete with kitchenettes and bunk beds, all so that grown men could bore holes into the thick ice and drop fishing lures down into the cold water, hoping to surprise a walleye or northern pike with the prospect of an easy meal and yank it up to the surface—and, with any luck, straight into a pre-buttered, sizzling-hot frying pan.

Early in the evening the bell in our hut jingled, alerting us to a nibble, and Grouse jerked the reel so eagerly that the hook ripped off the line, descending into a watery grave. The bait-shop owner on shore had turned off her lights after giving us the room key and roadmap, making it clear she was closing for the night. She hadn't seemed entertained when Grouse checked in wearing a three-holed balaclava.

With our only fishing lure gone, Grouse stood grimly over the ice hole, measuring our loss. Unless we drove into town, we couldn't get another hook until morning—and none of us had thought to bring a tackle box. Meanwhile, Grouse tipped a bottle of Kentucky bourbon so that it splashed down into the hole, and as he did so, he sang: "*I'm a-gone do me some muskie grapplin'*."

Turning toward us, he said in the exaggeratedly devout tone of a Lutheran minister, "Come ye after me, and I will make you to become fishers of fish."

Then, slipping into a parody of a bumbling, earnest Southerner, he added: "What I'm a-gone do is, when he comes up for a nip of this 'ere whiskey, I'm a-gone grab the little *sum-bitch* by his throat and choke the livin' daylights out of him."

Alas, the muskie grappling wasn't profitable either: none surfaced for a nip of the hooch. We debated driving to a nearby Indian casino to play blackjack, but Grouse reiterated his vehement opposition to gambling. He never liked his odds, he said. As we weighed our other options, Grouse pulled a thick Cohiba out of his backpack, struck a match against a splintered wooden ceiling beam, and set fire to the stogie.

Leaning back on his bunk bed, he proceeded to blow smoke rings up toward the exposed insulation, which looked like pink cotton candy, and our sleeping quarters soon filled with a gauzy cigar-smoke haze that made our eyes water like the arcade room at Bunny's Bar & Grill.

By the time Duce and I sparked up our own cigars, you could hardly see across the room; and not long after that, we faced a legitimate predicament: do we open the door and risk freezing to death while we sleep or endure the choking stench of so much vile cigar smoke?

Grouse suddenly bolted upright on the top bunk.

"I know! Let's bomb the old Eskimo speedway," he said.

Duce grunted noncommittally, lying on his back on the lower bunk, with a cigar sticking up from his mouth. He looked like a caricature of an old railroad tramp.

"You didn't see the signs on the way here for the Inuit 500 Raceway? This is the home track!" Grouse said.

He plucked stray tobacco flecks from his tongue with his fingertips.

Duce ashed his cigar on the floor.

"What the hell are you talking about?" he said.

Grouse swung his legs over the bunk and pounced down to the floor, landing with a hollow thud, and when he jerked open the squeaky door plumes of smoke were sucked out into the night. Duce and I listened to Grouse's boots crunching across the packed snow, and then we heard the click of his truck door being opened. By the time we'd both struggled into our own boots and jackets and stepped outside, Grouse was in the driver's seat with the window rolled down.

"*Gentlemen,*" he said in a rare whisper, "*start your goddamn engines.*"

Duce and I climbed into Grouse's truck, and he leapt off the starting line, full speed down an icy straightaway. But he leaned too hard into the first turn, with ill-advised velocity, and spun out into a snowdrift. We spent the next half-hour digging the wheels out with an ice scraper, and by the time we returned to the shack, frozen through to our vital organs, we were dog-tired. The last thing I recall from the night was Grouse pissing down the ice hole. I passed out while he was still mid-stream.

Mrs. Caswell offered me a slice of Spanish sheep cheese smeared with fig jam. The group had reconvened on the wide sectional sofa, sitting shoulder-to-shoulder around a low glass coffee table whose centerpiece was a decorative wicker basket full of wooden apples. I could practically hear Grouse imploring me to hurry up, so I resolved not to linger too much longer in conversation.

"You have a birthday coming up, don't you, Bill?" asked Mrs. Caswell.

"That's right. January 6th."

The cheese was delicious.

Julianne snorted a laugh.

"What?" I said.

The fig jam was the kicker.

"Nothing," she said. "It's just that... well, never mind."

She snorted again and continued giggling.

"What?" I repeated.

It really was better than the sum of its parts.

"I guess that makes you a New Year's baby," she said.

I directed my gaze to the Persian rug on the floor, briefly admiring its lovely teardrop motif while I stalled my response. Chewing slowly and deliberately on the cheese and jam, I mulled the appropriateness of correcting her in the present company.

"What's that?" I finally said.

"I mean, you were born just after January 1st. Isn't that what they say about people born that time of year—that you're a *New Year's baby?*"

She was trying to tease me.

"Jules, sweetheart," said Mrs. Caswell with gentle pity.

But Julianne obviously didn't follow.

"Actually," I said, yielding impulsively to the devil on my left shoulder, "I was conceived sometime in late spring. A New Year's baby, if I'm not mistaken, is one who was conceived on New Year's Eve."

I immediately regretted saying it.

Julianne's mouth fell open in a caricature of surprise as she recognized the peril of her misstatement and the mathematical impact of her own September 26th birthday. She swallowed hard, digesting what the numbers told her: that, counting nine months in reverse, *she* was possibly the New Year's baby.

"Oh, no. Oh my gosh," she muttered.

She looked at her mother, part-pleadingly, part-accusingly.

"Please tell me I wasn't conceived in some dirty, vacant coat room after too much champagne," she said. "That you and dad just couldn't wait to get home—or at least to the car."

I should have said nothing, changed topics, and fled the premises, but it was too late.

Julianne snorted another nervous laugh, and by the look on her face I could tell she was trapped in that awkward teenage emotional space between embarrassment and disgust. She was still cringing at the thought of that dubious copulation when her mother, in a sunny voice, full of only too much confidence, said, "No need to worry, Jules. You weren't conceived on New Year's at all—I can promise you that."

Now, I'm not sure what's more upsetting to a young person fresh out of puberty: the realization that his or her parents at some vague point in the past enjoyed having sex together, or knowing they could still recall *specific instances* of having sex, recalling some episodes with such clarity as to be able to place the actual moment of one's conception.

When I was eleven and learned where babies came from, I remember marching home from school one day and teasing my dad for having had sex with my mom enough times (twice) to produce my brother and me. My dad gave what I later realized was a clever reply, saying they only did it once but that he benefited from "time-release sperm."

The image I conjured up when envisioning my fifty-year-old parents in the sack bordered on inappropriate, maybe even obscene. To witness the Caswells in the primal scene, on the other hand, well now… Even after four pregnancies, Mrs. Caswell remained lithe and lean, with sun-kissed legs and vivacious blue eyes that belied her thirty-some-odd years.

But I knew the damage was done, and also, regrettably, that I couldn't prevent myself from my next remark, and so I just grinned at Julianne as I said teasingly: "Your parents did it *four* times?"

"Eww! I can't think about it."

She slumped forward, pressing her palms to her eyes as she pretended to brood. It was a wonderfully cute little drama, a poignantly girlish performance that won sympathetic smiles all around—all except from her dad, who, I noticed with growing concern, refused to muster even a token courtesy grin.

"Don't worry, Jules," said Mrs. Caswell. "We only did it twice. Therese and Katrina were delivered by stork, just like most babies."

It was at this point in the conversation that Mr. Caswell silently stood up from his chair. He didn't look at me or even turn in my direction as he said in his typically sober but polite tone, "Please follow me, Bill. I want to show you something in the kitchen before you leave."

He managed a glance that ricocheted off my forehead.

I rose from the sofa and Julianne stood up, too.

"No, darling. I want to speak with Bill alone for a minute," Mr. Caswell said.

It was Duce, I think, who once joked that talking with a girl's father one-on-one was a bit like screwing the girl when she's wearing bug spray: You could never be quite as direct as you wanted to be and you always sort of held your breath. But I had earned this conversation—there was no doubt there. The instant I made the "New Year's baby" comment, I regretted it. It was a dumb thing to say in that sort of company.

As I followed Mr. Caswell out of the room, Julianne flashed a tender smile at her dad that I interpreted as a signal of her loyalty to him and also—though in a distinctly secondary role—as a plea for whatever mercy was available on my behalf. I followed him through the swinging white wooden door into the kitchen, where we were alone with the veal and pumpkin pie.

He continued straight across the room to the granite countertop, where he picked up a *meat thermometer*—no, I'm not joking—which he held above his head, reading the temperature in the ceiling light. And he was standing like that, with his back to me, studying the long, sharp, probe-shaped instrument when he said in a calm, emotionless voice:

"You know, Bill, I think you're a good kid. I like you."

He set the thermometer down onto the counter, and I felt oddly relieved.

"But all fathers have similar protective instincts for their daughters," he continued. "And I guess you know where I'm headed with this."

"Yes, I understand."

Initially, I'd worried that he wasn't looking me in the eyes, but I regretted it as soon as he did. His gaze smoldered with the same thousand-foot intensity as a silverback gorilla's, and my eyes automatically retreated to the floor. But then, mindful of appearing weak, I quickly adjusted my posture, straightening my spine and forcing my shoulders back, hoping to convey a semi-reciprocal measure of manliness and maturity.

"You're welcome to take my daughter out, Bill, provided you treat her with utmost respect and return her to my house by a decent hour. Those are my rules. Now, I don't want for us to have this conversation again, so I'll only say it once."

He drew in a sharp breath.

"I think this goes without saying, but I want to make it abundantly clear to you. If you ever step out of bounds with my daughter, Bill, and I hear of it, I promise you one thing."

Leveling a steely gaze at me, he added:

"I will cut… it… off."

He spoke the last three words in an even, bloodless tone, with enormous gravity, lest I somehow miss his point. I nodded grimly, half-expecting him to yield a smirk. When he didn't, I had to bite the inside of my lip to keep from laughing, as my internal audio mechanism replayed his warning in my mind. (Mr. Caswell could have no idea that our friends would soon be endlessly parroting his speech as jocular threats to one another.)

"I understand," I replied.

He nodded, indicating we were done, and gestured toward the door. As we re-entered the living room, Mrs. Caswell and Julianne looked up expectantly. They appeared to be relieved by the brevity of our conversation and perhaps by the fact that I hadn't been Irish-whipped into the china cabinet.

Our exit was mostly a blur due to my adrenaline surge. Julianne and I exchanged goodbyes with the Millers. "See you later, Billy," said Dr. Miller, like an old friend. We left through the kitchen, moving swiftly and silently toward the mudroom.

When we stepped outside onto the driveway, the cold air was deliciously refreshing, and I put my arm around Julianne's waist. She looked up at me hesitantly, searching my eyes, and asked if I was okay. I eased into a smile and told her it had been "a fairly standard protective father speech."

"More importantly," I said. "Are you ready to party?"

Her eyes twinkled. "I can't wait."

"Good. Me, too."

"I'm *sooo* excited!" she softly cheered.

"Be careful," I warned her. "If you get too drunk, I'll take advantage of you."

She squeezed her body against mine and looked up with a coquettish grin.

"Do you promise?" she said.

A congregation of our pals was gathered on the parking lot outside Saint John the Evangelist's church, milling around in knee-deep tire tracks in the snow and stooped like Quasimodo against the cold. A handful sucked gloomily on cigarettes, a few hurled wet snowballs up at the darkened floodlights, and many more were ensconced in idling cars, worshipping the dashboard heaters. In an adjacent row, another group of vehicles—the "decoys," if you will—belonged to those pious souls who had left town before Christmas on a mission trip to Tijuana, where they were now digging outhouses in the dirt and hammering together wood-framed abodes for the "less fortunate."

When Grouse killed his truck's engine, the cab instantly began to cool, and I was surprised, as always, by how quickly a vehicle's interior heat dissipated in the winter months when its motor stopped running. Warmth turned lukewarm, which begat a sudden, windless chill—all within about thirty seconds.

We had picked up Ally, and she climbed down now from Grouse's truck onto a lane of flattened snow wearing black leather high-heel boots and a hip-hugging corduroy skirt. The porcelain skin of her honey-colored legs was exposed between the two. She was dressed like she was ready to go barhopping in Lan Kwai Fon, like she was up for anything.

Ally was three-quarters Hong Kong Chinese and one-quarter colonial imperialist. Her maternal grandfather had been a blonde-haired British banker. Ally had these exotic, horny eyes that could back you into a puddle six inches deep, but then her gaze would fall, or she'd blush, and momentarily you felt like she was secretly in love with you but too shy to say it.

Ally was a guilty-pleasure Christian shrouded in a Buddhist's mystique and, if you thought about it, a genetic case of reverse imperialism—of the Chinese standing their ground. Her parents had met in the United States during graduate school and never left, and Ally was as American as chop suey.

Turning his palms up toward the sky, Grouse called out for "a brief supplication," and although nobody gathered around him, he prayed like a preacher in the public square, saying, "Oh Lord, with thine blessing, thy flock yearns to grow holy-spiritually shitfaced tonight!" He grabbed a beer can out of Sangwich's hand and turned it upside-down to "pour some out in Jeebus's name," but the can was empty. Ally socked him on the arm.

"Serves you right for being so selfish," she said.

"For Christ's sake, woman, tell me a prayer that isn't."

Grouse had once pressed Ally on her Christian faith, saying, "Give me one reason you think Jesus is the Son of God." No response could stump him, he declared. Ally answered, "Because I really, *really* want to believe it." And he was stumped. "Of course, in some ways the idiocy of faith is its strongest validation," he said. "But, then again, it's also an indication of the sort of mindset you're dealing with."

Grouse joked that he enjoyed going to church because it was "cheaper than the Guthrie." Few situations in life offered more reliable laughs, he said, than watching little old ladies take Communion directly from the priest's hand. When he demonstrated what he meant, his tongue slopped all over his lower lip, recalling nothing of grandmotherly devotion to Christ—more like cunnilingus after a Novocain injection.

In my early teens, I'd gone through a brief religious phase when it became fashionable, but now I hated myself for having ever been religious in the same way I hated myself for having ever danced the Macarena. However, lately I tended to agree with Andy Morton, who said: "The giant leap isn't from atheism to theism but from theism to Christianity." Which left me as a believer of sorts, I guess—just less an assembly-line version of one. I was a believer in the Great Unknown.

After my conversion to this particular brand of heathenism, I uttered to Ally that most banal of conciliations: "I respect your beliefs." Duce overheard me and said, "What the hell does that mean? 'I think you're full of shit, but I won't hold it against you?'" Yeah, I guess that's what I was saying.

"I couldn't possibly believe in any fiction," Duce said. "Give me a philosophy. I'll take Buddhism any day of the week, minus all that bullshit about non-attachment."

To which Grouse responded, "To hell with religion *and* philosophy. Tell a few dirty jokes and live a few good goddamn stories—that's what I say. Philosophy is nothing but gymnastics for quadriplegics."

Indeed, Grouse's reply to Socrates might have been that most lives are not worth examining.

As long as we're keeping score: Peter O'Leary was a classic insurance-policy Christian, or, as Morty called it, "a nervous atheist." And Goldy Lindenheimer was president of the high school's Fellowship of Christian Athletes, although his mother was a mystic-animist-spiritualist and his father was Jewish.

Go figure.

A pair of windowless, steel-sided commercial vans turned into the parking lot at the far end, switched off their headlights, and droned down the aisle toward us, before crunching to a halt on the packed snow behind Grouse's truck. On the side of each van, in elegant red cursive, a logo read: "Bambino's Fine Italian & Catering." Duce Babyk drove the van in front, Henry Beach the one in back.

"All right, bitches, transfer the loot, let's go," Duce barked, his arm out the window, an unlit cigarette twirling in his fingers. "Let's get this show on the road."

On his stereo, a choir was singing "Joy to the World" as the beer kegs and liquor boxes were promptly relocated to the back of the "raper vans," as they were more affectionately known.

Amid the rustle of winter jackets and considerable grunting and groaning, our friends piled into the back of the vehicles, too, stuffing them like so many sardines. But still not everybody would fit, and so Julianne and I hung back, along with Grouse and Ally and a few others, waiting for the last shuttle to return. A handful of impatient pilgrims set off on foot through the snowy woods in the direction of Babyk Manor.

Silence descended on our decimated population, and I thought of golden hand-bells ringing in an empty cathedral, of eternal solitude and a kind of musical, mystical stillness. Even in the gauzy darkness,

I could see that Julianne's nose had turned bright red at the tip, like Lady Elaine Fairchilde's, and she kept sniffling as though she was allergic to the cold.

"You're so tan," I said. "Like a graham cracker."

She giggled her contagious giggle.

"Is that good?" she asked.

"It's the best."

She blushed.

"I laid out by the pool every day," she said.

"Did you go in the ocean?"

"Sometimes, but I was afraid of the sharks and jellyfish. A girl at our hotel got stung on the beach last month. But I wasn't worried when we went snorkeling, because they said sharks don't like the taste of wetsuits and flippers."

I laughed, wrapping my arms around her, and told her I'd missed her.

"Oh, I missed you, too, baby," she said, pressing her face into my scarf. Looking up, she added, "But only you. I didn't miss this weather at all. I can't believe yesterday I was wearing a bikini on the beach. Now my toes are like frozen baby carrots. It's so unfair."

I laughed again.

"Just pretend it's beach sand," I said.

Her eyes widened.

"I have an idea!" she exclaimed. "Let's build a snow castle tomorrow. When this is finally done, there's going to be so much snow on the ground."

"That's a great idea. We can make the world's biggest snow castle on the eighth tee box at the country club."

"It'll be like our first date!"

The first night we'd hung out, after the football game, after the unsavory incident I witnessed in the men's restroom, and after I walked Julianne home across the golf course, I joked to her about building sand castles for the morning golfers in the sand traps. In some ways, now that I thought about it, snow was a better medium—it was more *magical.*

"Was Santa Claus good to you?" I asked Julianne.

Jesus, when did I start sounding like my mother? I wondered to myself.

"So good," she said. "My sisters and I got new sundresses and swimsuits, and we got to try so many new things. I rode a horse on the beach and went deep-sea fishing—but I didn't catch anything—and I ate a lobster and went snorkeling on the coral reefs and saw a seahorse."

"You went snuggling with who?"

She giggled, being a good sport.

"Oh, and I snuck a naughty gift for you in my luggage," she said. "I think you're going to like it: Caribbean lingerie."

"Nice." I laughed. "Sounds sexy."

"It's a coconut bra," she said, with more laughter.

She added, "But I got you a real Christmas gift, too."

"Oh, yeah?"

"Do you want it?"

"Sure."

"Now?"

"Yeah, now."

"You can't wait?"

"No, I want it now, damn it," I said, laughing.

"I'm going to make you wait."

I shrugged helplessly.

"Okay, I'll give it to you now," she said.

She reached into her goose-down jacket and pulled out a small box, about the size of a deck of playing cards, which she'd wrapped in magazine paper and prettied with a small white bow. I slid my finger under the Scotch tape and pulled out a brown leather cuff-link box. I lifted its tiny latch and inside found three delicate seashells she had collected from the beach—perfect little seashells on a bed of sugary white sand.

"I got you the Bahamas," she said, and I was overcome with feelings of warmth and gratitude. Sentimentality was practically dribbling down my thigh.

In choosing my gift for her, I'd heeded my dad's timeless advice that memories frequently make the best presents, partly because they can't be thrown away during an argument. I'd got her tickets to the circus, which was coming to the Civic Center in a few weeks. Julianne had told me that she always wanted to see an acrobat be fired out of a cannon. When she opened the silver envelope and saw what I'd bought for her, she covered my face and neck in dry kisses. "Oh, you're so sweet, so sweet, so sweet!" she swooned. "My ice castle prince!"

The old gray stone church was draped in shadows, save for the heavy pinewood entrance door and its knocker, which were glowing dimly under a solitary yellow lamp. On the church's rusticated sidewall, the stained glass windows looked oily and opaque in the darkness. Snow banks piled up like dirty lamb's wool alongside the unshoveled walkways. The steeple had grown taller in a recent renovation, I noticed, stretching ever heavenward in what was, it seemed, a literal display of holy prosperity.

"I read in the *Star Tribune* they installed a new pipe organ that can be heard all the way in North Minneapolis," I said.

Grouse and Ally had joined us, and the four of us were huddled together in the same posture, more or less, with our shoulders hunched and our chins tucked down, while we rocked back and forth like strung-out addicts, exhaling plumes of frost with each breath into our cupped hands.

"It's *very* loud," Ally agreed. "And it's huge. It takes up a whole wall inside the church. I played a recital here a few months ago, and they had to run my violin through the speakers just to be heard over the organ accompaniment. But the acoustics *are* beautiful."

"They had better be," said Grouse. "They paid enough for them."

Ally was college-bound as a violinist, on a scholarship to New York University. She and Julianne sat next to each other in the high school orchestra, and they were friendly if not exactly friends. Julianne had a quiet talent for the string instrument but practically zero ambition beyond the occasional transitory pleasures of making music.

"I haven't practiced at all over break," Julianne confessed outside the church. "Our holiday concert was so morbid I felt like I needed to decompress. Seriously, who listens to that sort of music except serial killers who live in little cabins in the woods? I bought a ukulele on the beach just to cleanse my palette."

"That's so cool!" said Ally. "Are you any good?"

"I'm terrible." Julianne giggled. "But it's so much fun, and it was surprisingly easy to learn how to play."

"I sort of liked the concert," said Grouse. "Especially those songs with the three French horns and all that creepy plucking of strings. What's not to like?"

I'd attended the show at the high school theater with him. The experimental songs he was referring to were a bit avant-garde for my taste, but I enjoyed the wintry minimalist pieces by the Polish and Estonian composers. That said, I am a traditionalist at heart and felt a bit short-sold by the conspicuous absence of holiday season classics.

"Whatever happened to *The Nutcracker Suite*?" I asked. "Nobody plays that one anymore? I always thought that was a Christmas-time standard."

"It's offensive," Grouse said. "Just remember: Christmas is offensive."

"The spring show is usually less depressing," Ally said. "I hope that's the case this year anyway. Fewer cello dirges, more flutes and piccolos and soaring violins."

Sidestepping the orchestra shoptalk, I told them I wanted to wander over and inspect the church's stained glass windows more carefully. I'd passed the building countless times over the years but never stopped to study them properly. I knew the artwork dated to the mid-1930s and had been executed by a then-well-known British painter who saw in the rise of the Third Reich signs of impending religious apocalypse. He dealt in grim subject matter, I remembered reading.

Taking a giant, lunging step into the snow, I hummed to myself the classic rock tune that began with the shouted line, "*Jeremiah was a bullfrog!*" and when I stopped singing, after the three-step guitar riff, the silence instantly deepened.

It was a couple more steps to the wall where the stained glass panels were set. Among the scenes I immediately recognized was one from the Book of Revelation, in which the Whore of Babylon rides a seven-headed beast ("And the woman was arrayed in purple and scarlet color, and decked with gold and precious stones and pearls, having a golden cup in her hand full of abominations and filthiness of her fornication.").

Another showed a tyrannical Herod with his sword drawn in Bethlehem. A third was Mater Dolorosa, the sobbing virgin. They were grisly, depressing choices, I thought, even by Catholic standards. And yet, there was something reassuring in their familiarity, an old-shoe comfort derived simply from being part of such a long-shared mythology.

Indeed, it felt almost transcendent to be standing there in the waist-deep snow, shrouded in semi-darkness, gazing at the ancient subjects in colorful painted glasswork on a century-old stone building. It wasn't all that dissimilar, I thought, from stargazing in northern Minnesota on a moonless summer night. Both pointed in the direction of the Great Unknown.

I retraced my footprints as I stepped backward out of the snow in reverse slow motion, carefully locating each of the crusted, boot-shaped pockets I had formed on my way in. At the sidewalk, I turned and saw Julianne waving her arms over her head, alerting me that the van had returned, and I trotted back in double time, quickly forgetting about the artwork.

As the others piled into the van's rear, I stomped my feet and brushed the snow off my jeans while wondering how it was, scientifically, that automobile exhaust smelled thicker in the frozen air—like you could taste it on your tongue. It was an indelible winter scent, just as chlorine was a summer one.

Henry shouted out the open driver's side window that the

passenger seat was vacant, and so I raced around the front of the van to claim it. Fastening my seatbelt, I luxuriated in the dry, sauna-like heat that was pouring out of the dashboard.

Later that night or the following morning, one or two of our pals would gather up all the empty liquor bottles and "party trash" from Babyk's house and stuff it into black plastic leaf bags, which they'd toss into the dumpster behind the church. Like the van shuttles, the off-site waste removal was part of our grand strategy for maintaining anonymity, leaving no trace of what we'd done. As I've said, in the suburban hinterlands where we dwelled the underage consumption of alcohol and tobacco were seen as the great abominations of the Western world, and so we did our best to conceal our sins.

Henry was wearing oversized black ski gloves, snow pants, and a white T-shirt emblazoned with a fluttering Old Glory and spirited typeface that read: "Babyk for President." Duce had successfully campaigned for student council president that spring. Initially, he'd planned to run for treasurer—"Why would I want to be president? The treasurer handles the cash, right?"—but I had convinced him to seek the top spot by dangling the allure of "wholesale ownership" in front of him.

As Duce's campaign manager, however, I knew we needed to avoid reminding our constituency that in ninth grade, under his stewardship—then as treasurer—a few thousand dollars in the Freshmen Fund had inexplicably disappeared one day after he and I finished counting it. We didn't steal a nickel, but that wasn't the point: the heist had occurred *on his watch*. We'd tallied the cash, rubber-banded it in bundles of tens and twenties, and handed it to Ms. Gibson, the school secretary, who locked it in a metal toolbox, which itself was secured inside a vault in the main office. We watched her load the toolbox into the vault.

What happened, Duce surmised, was that the secretary and the vice principal—a middle-aged, hot-for-teacher disciplinarian named Dr. Korkian—had nabbed the loot so they could buy a few things for themselves. The circumstantial evidence was tenuous at best, but Duce insisted that his theory had merit. Dr. Korkian got breast implants, he suggested, and Ms. Gibson went on a weeks-long alcohol bender.

"Women's tits don't grow like that in their fifties," he said, "and have you ever seen Ms. Gibson more irritable?"

Three years passed in the meantime, and Duce the wily politician was banking on our classmates having forgotten the incident—or simply accepting his "tits and booze" alibi.

On the last day of the campaign season, a student assembly was held in the school's gymnasium. Those candidates who had already finished delivering their speeches were sitting on metal folding chairs to one side of the podium when Principal Vaughn announced into the microphone: "Our next speaker is Dominik Babyk, Jr., who is seeking the office of president."

Dressed in a charcoal-colored pinstripe suit, with his black hair gelled back, Duce strode across the stage like a veteran of the Chicago politburo. The gymnasium was silent except for the distinct sound of leather wingtips moving across a basketball court. At the podium, he reached into his jacket pocket for his notes, which he unfolded on the lectern in front of him, and when he finally spoke his tone was so solemn I assumed he was being sarcastic.

"My fellow classmates," he began, "I stand before you today with an important proposition. And I ask you to listen carefully to what I have to say because my plan differs substantially from the one being pitched by the other candidates and endorsed by Principal Vaughn."

He cleared his throat.

"I want you to consider something of grave consequence and utmost seriousness. I want you to ask yourself the following question: Who among us, in the waning days of the twentieth century, is willing to turn a blind eye to *genocide?*"

He sharply enunciated the last word, clipping the final syllable, causing the question to gather force, as sudden silences in large gatherings tend to do. Muffled laughter shook pockets of the crowd, but Duce remained absolutely stolid as he answered his own question.

"Most of us are, sadly," he said, with a shrug. "It happens way over there, right? We're powerless. It's okay—I get that. But what I really want to know is *how* can we submit that it's beyond our control?"

He unhooked the microphone from the lectern and began pacing in front of it.

"Let me ask another question. If a teacher at this school was flogging his students with a bullwhip, would we expect an outcry? If a teacher stabbed a pupil with a knife, would we just cover our ears and hope the problem went away? What if it happened down the highway at Lindbergh? Would we still ignore it then? Because I'm fairly certain we would not."

He held the microphone cord in a loop in his free hand.

"So, let me ask you this: How far away does a problem need to be for us to say, 'There's nothing I can do about it. It's too far away. My resistance means nothing.'"

He dropped the snake of cord onto the ground and held up an index finger.

"Of course, the attitude of one person might not change anything, and that's my point. If we cared—if we *all* collectively decided: 'No, this is unacceptable,' and demanded action from our government—starting with our local representatives—surely we hold the power to enact that sort of change. That's what our democracy promises us anyway."

Now, let me say this about the atmosphere in the gym: it was obvious that nobody in the crowd had any idea where Duce was headed with his meandering philosophical musing or what it had to do with the office of student council president, but they seemed willing to give him a chance to explain himself.

"But therein lies our dirty little secret," Duce said softly.

"We don't care," he added. "The vast majority of us look away. We pretend not to see the misery and starvation and bloodshed in Africa, in the Middle East, in Asia. We ignore it and go about our daily lives, blissfully unaware, as if we can satisfy our rotten, shame-filled consciences by clinging to false notions of ignorance and powerlessness."

He looked down at the floor. His speech, until this point, was far too sincere for the administration to step in, but I did notice some eyes flitting nervously among the faculty. Duce continued staring down at his polished shoes as a half-minute or so ticked past in silence. The audience was presumably meant to be contemplating the hypocrisy of their compassion.

But then, in a tone that felt like blossoming hope—as though the idea struck him spontaneously—he added, "But you know what? In some ways, it's *liberating* to recognize our true nature, since it absolves us of the heavy burden of being guilt-soaked, God-fearing members of a quote-unquote 'just' society."

"And so, some of us overcompensate," he went on. "We do things—artificially, I'd suggest—to make ourselves feel better about this hidden selfishness. We might volunteer at a soup kitchen, for example. Yet even then, when we peel back the layers of this supposedly selfless good deed, we can often see how hollow the intentions behind it really are."

"Take a lawyer who volunteers in a soup kitchen," he said. "Everyone knows that a lawyer's time is worth far more in cold hard cash than in his ability to ladle clam chowder. So why does he do it? Why put on the hairnet? I say it's because *he* wants to feel the reward of his good deed. It is for *himself*!"

A girl's voice from somewhere in the crowd interrupted him. "Just because you don't care—"

Here, Duce smirked, his stoic pose lapsing for the first time.

"Few of us care, actually," Duce responded. "If we cared, there would be no need for this discussion. But, fine, you want other examples? Consider the carnivores who deny the horrors of the slaughterhouse, or the fathers and brothers who lust after pornography but ignore the humanity of the girls they feast upon. Consider the failure of our current system to deny Pol Pot, Idi Amin, and other murderous tyrants. Hell, consider all the people who will drown this year in monsoon floods in South Asia. And let's be honest, why does Principal Vaughn care so much about helping educate an impoverished Central American kid he's never met?"

"Because it's the *right thing to do*?" Duce added skeptically. "On whose account? I think it's self-righteous. No offense, but I think the reason Mr. Vaughn wants to do it is for *his* own sake, for the publicity our school will receive, to see his photograph in the newspaper, and not for the sake of some Spanish-speaking kid living near the Equator who can't hit a curveball."

That set the audience grumbling. Duce held up a hand and nodded, indicating he was ready to arrive at his point.

"I suggest we simply acknowledge these facts. I say we pay damages to a sentient beast that was *already* wronged by one of our own hands. Some of you know what I'm talking about. I'm referring, of course, to the noble Sichuan takin, that defenseless mortal, which was on the receiving end of a snowball thrown during German Day at the Zoo."

Duce looked down at me and winked. In a twist, he'd given sudden—but still cryptic—meaning to the esoteric campaign posters in the school hallways stamped "Babyk '97."

One sign outlined the animal's scientific classification: "Animalia–Chordata–Mammalia–Cetartiodatyla–Artiodactyla–Bovidae–Caprinae–Budorcas–B. taxicolor."

Another read: "Free Takin Rides for Freshmen and Bulimics." That sign was accompanied by a crude illustration of a saddled animal. (Note: As far as I know, the gold-fleeced takin does not enjoy a reputation as a fine riding animal.) Another depicted a zoo poster describing the takin as a "most unusual animal": with cow-like legs, a flat goat's tail, gnu-like horns, and moose-shaped nose. "Was it designed by a committee?" it asked. In whiteout, Duce scrawled: "No, it too was designed by God!"

Facing an increasingly hostile assembly, Duce raised his voice, saying: "As your student body president, I say we sponsor this extraordinary mammal. Buy it or lease it or whatever the hell you do with it—" he laughed now, aware of the growing chorus of democratic opinion rising up against him. "I propose we bring this golden wonder to the verdant grasslands of our high school's courtyard for all of us to venerate and admire."

He slammed the podium with his fist for theatric effect.

"I say: forget about educating people on the other side of the planet! Let the weak vie for themselves! And let us be reminded of their weakness every day through the symbol of the majestic Sichuan takin as it grazes in our courtyard."

He was thundering to a finish.

"Let Mr. Vaughn grin for the cameras and congratulate himself in the mirror. If you need a reason to feel guilty, consider this: Without our financial support, the *magnificent* creature I propose rescuing could be mercilessly slaughtered and turned into takin burgers!"

Half the crowd broke into raucous laughter and applause, the other half into jeers, boos, and furled brows. Grouse buried his face in his hands, cracking up. I stood and applauded diplomatically. Miss Fogey later decried the speech as "pseudo-Nietzschian bullshit." Alas, Duce had changed the tenor of the debate, meaning, among other things, that the Sichuan takin would at last receive its due.

Postscript: After applying pressure in all the right social channels, Duce won the election by a hair, and, despite protests from Principal Vaughn and others, he was sworn in as president of the student body. All we ever saw of the takin was a lousy plaque from the zoo's sponsorship board, but Duce did order a few hundred screen-printed T-shirts that read "Takin' our Time," which we wore one evening to a tailgate in the high school parking lot, where we barbequed venison, which Duce said was the closest thing he could find to Sichuan takin filets.

The apple, as they say, doesn't fall far from the tree—meaning it wouldn't take a team of White House speechwriters to determine where Duce had picked up the art of deceptive elocution. His father, Dominik Babyk, Sr., an old Chicago mafia hand who had relocated to Minneapolis to operate a franchise branch (more on that shortly), displayed similar oratorical skills at his divorce proceedings before leaving Illinois.

I never learned why Duce and his younger sister Adriana had been invited to attend their parents' divorce court hearings, but whatever the reason Duce always seemed to relish talking about the experience.

His dad, the story goes, was on the legal ropes—a huge moneymaker, tons at stake in terms of financial assets, etc.—and, how can we say, a somewhat blemished record when it came to marital fidelity.

The arguments before the judge, Duce told us, centered on these alleged "extracurricular activities." Of course, Duce put together that his dad had been caught "double dipping," or as his dad himself later described it: "outsourcing his sex life." His mom, bolstered by the recklessness with which her wealthy husband had carried on his affairs, was playing the alimony slot machine hard, with the feverish enthusiasm of a first-time Las Vegas high roller on a hot streak.

Facing a hostile interrogation from his soon-to-be-ex-wife's counsel, Mr. Babyk raised an open hand to the judge and proclaimed himself innocent of the charges that he'd had an extramarital affair.

"I am one-hundred percent guiltless, honest to our Lord," he swore.

Then, being facetious, or perhaps simply provocative, he volunteered the following: "Any suggestion that I quote-unquote 'cheated on my wife' should be considered admissible in these venerable chambers only if you're willing to take into account the very critical fact of my being held *hostage* at the time of the charge."

The skeptical judge glared over his glasses at Mr. Babyk.

"Hostage?" he said.

"You're damn straight," replied Mr. Babyk, stone-faced. "My genitals held me hostage."

Had the judge continued listening, he would have heard Dom Babyk's feeble attempt at eliciting fraternal empathy. "It was a classic case of your nuts sticking a bayonet into your spine and saying, 'March, motherfucker! You haven't got a choice!'"

He let out a raw cackle, before proceeding to forfeit a huge chunk of change in the settlement with Duce's mom—which, naturally, wasn't all that devastating for someone whose business card might as well have read: "Used furniture dealer."

On the surface, Dominik Babyk, Sr. owned a chain of pizza and pasta joints around town, but everybody knew that his real money came from organized crime. The restaurants just offered plausible cover for his more lucrative dealings.

We didn't have hard proof that Mr. Babyk was a mobster, but there was plenty of circumstantial evidence, beginning with the simple fact that he dressed *exactly* like a Hollywood Mafioso, in finely tailored three-piece wool suits and Borsalino fedoras.

He had a chauffeur who drove him around town in his own private limousine, and he frequently departed on short notice to classic gangster hideaways like Sicily, Atlantic City, the Greek islands, and elsewhere.

Plus, the math didn't add up. The pasta and pizza chain was moderately successful, as far as anyone could tell, but their family lived in a gargantuan marble estate full of priceless art, thousand-dollar whiskey decanters, custom-made furniture, and all the latest high-tech gizmos.

The home's basement, intriguingly, had hollow floorboards, suggesting there were levels *below* it—either for escape tunnels, we guessed, or maybe the disposal of corpses. We had asked Mr. Babyk once, in a moment of courage, about these suspicious floorboards in the laundry room, and he just smiled coyly and flipped the page of the *Wall Street Journal*.

Furthermore, Duce and his sister were strictly forbidden from spending time inside the restaurant offices, which seemed like a strange prohibition if the only thing the regional operating managers—Serge and Mikko—were doing was ordering more Wisconsin shredded mozzarella and canned tomato paste.

But the real smoking gun was an old Chicago *Sun-Times* article one of our classmates had dug up on microfiche in eighth grade shortly after Duce arrived at our school as the new kid. It told of an old-style gangster shootout in downtown Chicago, in a second-floor Italian restaurant on Monroe Street.

Half a dozen Italian and Eastern European criminals were gunned down in the incident, and the police had tied a number of them to a financial racket that operated bogus shadow companies for the mob. The damning evidence was a black-and-white photo on the jump page of Mr. Babyk in a trench coat, holding a pistol in the street. It honestly couldn't have been anyone else.

Which partly explained his sudden departure from Chicago and, later, his close ties to the financial brokerage community in Minneapolis.

We would often hear him on the phone, saying things like, "Uranium mines, molybdenum, coal-bed methane. I know a guy who can get us shares in low-risk, big-reward exploratory-phase companies. That's where we need to be stashing our loot until we get more inside tips on the small-caps."

We were almost certain that Mr. Babyk was doing laundry for the mob, and Duce never said anything to disavow the talk.

And about the divorce hearings, we could all laugh now. Duce's mom had remarried—her move to Minnesota was one impetus for the whole broken family to relocate there—and Mr. Babyk had climbed into the ring again with a two-time divorcee named Sharon Piltdown.

We all gave Mr. Babyk a proper roasting one night at the mansion, asking him what sort of respectable man brings his children to a divorce hearing.

Apparently, he'd swallowed down too much red wine, because he just shook his head and sighed.

"Boys," he said, "you know your primal urges are ruining your life when the gal you're cheating on your wife with gets upset with you for cheating on her with another gal."

Mr. Babyk treated Duce's pals like his own, and he always encouraged us to hang around the mansion. On the weekends, he would barbecue swordfish or rib-eye steaks for us, and he'd order all the heavyweight boxing fights on pay-per-view. In the summers, he would take us up to their gigantic lake house on Leech Lake.

And he seemed to enjoy sharing his life stories with us—the funny ones, that is, never the incriminating ones.

"So the nurse is asking me all these questions the other day during my health check," he'd told us recently, "about my bones and joints—and my sex life—and whether I'm a recreational drug taker and all that. And one of her questions was, 'Have you ever paid for sex?' I had to pause to think about it, because I'd never considered it in those terms, you know? After a few moments, I said to her, straight-faced, looking right into her eyes: 'Every fuckin' day of my life, baby!' and I howled, laughing. I still don't know if she got it.

"After I'd collected myself, I added, 'I mean, she's never made me pay for sex, so I know she isn't a prostitute.' But then, double-checking my logic, I thought: 'Unless, of course, she's keeping a *tab*!'"

He grinned with all the arrogance of a sixteenth-century pope as our friends broke into cackles of delight.

The lucky woman toward whom this affection was directed was Sharon Babyk, formerly Sharon Piltdown in a previous marriage, a forty-five-year-old frosted blonde from the Minnesota Iron Range who looked, some said, like she'd been "ridden hard and put away wet."

Indeed, the hulking, glittering jewels that Mr. Babyk put on his wife's knuckles appeared to be having the same effect as those golden neck rings worn by the hill-tribe women in parts of Southeast Asia: Sharon's fingers were unquestionably becoming longer.

I've been told that stepmothers are fair targets for criticism, and so, for the record, I'll add that it looked like she paid for her breast implants with a coupon. They loomed on her chest like the obscenely large fake udders conjured up by a thirteen-year-old boy during a shower wank.

Not that I disliked her. I hardly knew her. Duce complained frequently about his stepmother, but that was *his* gripe, not mine. I figured, what's not to like about a woman who has herself "surgically re-virginized" as an anniversary gift to her third husband?

But life, I'm afraid, had never been the same for Sharon after she achieved that towering apex of success in 1969, winning top honors at the Minnesota State Fair, where she was crowned "Princess Kay of the Milky Way" and had her likeness carved out of a gigantic slab of butter.

If you don't know what that looks like, I suggest you seek out an image of Bernini's bust of Constanza Bonarelli. All State Fair butter sculptures, I suspect, have aspired to Bernini's genius.

"Honey, in my generation, a 'go-getter' was a girl who wanted to be an airline stewardess," said Mr. Babyk, teasing her in front of us. "But look at you. You're a real princess."

And she sat there blushing like a dope.

Dom and Sharon had left town Saturday morning before our hockey game and weren't due back until after New Year's, which would give Duce and his sister plenty of time to shake the rugs and hunt down any rogue cigarette butts that might have been pitched into one of Sharon's Ming dynasty vases.

The couple had flown down to Kirsten Springs, Florida to celebrate their third anniversary at a waterfront cottage that belonged to Sharon's extended family. It was a rare conciliation Mr. Babyk made to her, staying at the decidedly middle-class cottage when he probably could have afforded to buy the whole neighborhood. It was his idea of chivalry, I suppose.

When the cat's away, the kittens will play. And we were off for some merrymaking at the vacated residence.

Worried that Julianne might be freezing her little woo-hoo in the cargo hold, I cranked up the dashboard heaters to "full blast" and re-positioned the vents so they would blow the warm air back between the front seats in her general direction. I looked over my shoulder and saw her sitting cross-legged on the floor with Ally, giggling. Knowing she was enjoying herself gave me an almost paternal feeling of contentment.

Grouse was standing back there like he was on a surfboard, touching his fingers to the ceiling for support. At a bend in the snowy road, Henry glanced in the rearview mirror and tapped the accelerator, sending the van into a controlled fishtail, and Grouse went toppling onto the people seated on the floor.

Henry was steering with one hand on the wheel. In his other hand, he clutched an empty pop can that he was using as a spitter. He stared straight ahead as he drove, not looking down even when he spit his juice into the can. A plastic cup full of beer was in the cup holder, and he reached for it twice on the way to Babyk's, enjoying a greedy swig both times.

"You've got your game face on, huh, Henry?" I said.

"Mmm-hmm," he replied.

A pair of rusticated stone pillars marked the entrance to Rolling Evergreens, and Henry turned the van into the upscale residential neighborhood that was home to local stock-option-jackpot chief executives, prime-time pro athletes, extreme blue bloods, and, apparently, at least one Chicago mafia don, who, at present, was slurping fresh oysters on the Gulf Coast while his children, unbeknownst to him, kicked open the doors to his house for an evening of reckless good fun and debauchery.

We wended past expansive snow-capped lawns and fairy-tale mansions: the streets were a wonderland of modern castles in every architectural style, from stately Georgia red bricks to sprawling Tudor estates and ultra-modern houses straight out of *Miami Vice*. Some had private tennis courts and outdoor pools, others had detached "guest cabins" as large as ordinary homes, and a few even had heated underground garages.

It was the sort of place that made you viscerally envious, putting the Biblical commandment "Thou shalt not covet" to a strenuous test. It was like joyriding through purgatory.

But something about the neighborhood also bothered me, and it was this: the homes there all appeared to have had their Christmas lights professionally strung. And there was something unforgivable about that, I thought, something profoundly un-American. But onward we went all the same, sucked in by the tractor-beam party vibes that were emanating from somewhere deep inside Babyk Manor.

The sage returned to his cave with a trembling flame, groping his way through the darkened chamber, over rock and ash and bone, to a far corner where he sat down and propped his back against the limestone wall. He picked up a charcoal pencil off the ground and studied it for a moment. Then, balancing a hide-bound notebook on his knees, he scrawled in childlike cursive on a smudged empty page: "Some thoughts with no special meaning except that they came from me for you to think about in the days ahead."

III.

FLANKED BY TOWERING spruce trees and sculpted hedges, the hulking white stone palatial estate known as Babyk Manor leaned down on four mammoth Doric pillars carved out of marble. It was as solid as a brick shit-house, a nod to the glory of ancient Greece herself, with every window offering a museum's peek into the privileged world of material excess. It was also par for the course, as they say, in the upscale neighborhood, meaning the neighbors didn't eat off of food stamps either.

The house occupied the widest portion of a quiet cul-de-sac, extending across what were previously two adjacent lots. The Babyks had bought the lesser mansions for a small fortune in 1992 and torn them down to erect their own personal Xanadu. No, it wasn't really *that* grand, but it was still somehow, in its own way, equally monstrous in scale and proportion—although maybe that was simply owing to its address in the heart of greater American suburbia.

Small floodlights beamed up from the lawn, through melted pockets of snow, illuminating the residence in a dramatic glow, like the Lincoln Memorial at night. As the van climbed the semi-circular driveway, I leaned over my shoulder and whispered to Julianne that the home's cockeyed interior lighting—a single lamp here, an overhead bulb there, several totally darkened windows—was a dead giveaway that the master of the house was away. If Sharon Babyk were in town, the dissymmetry alone would have given her a panic attack.

The human cargo exited through the rear door, one after another like a carload of clowns, and massed under the portico over Babyk's front entrance. It wasn't exactly an Army Ranger night drop behind enemy lines, but our stealth operation would be successful, we figured, as long as the rich old bitch across the street didn't catch a glimpse of us while putting her dirty dishes in the sink.

The "shuttles" helped us avoid putting too many cars on the street or driveway, both of which would be obvious tip-offs to snoopy neighbors or idle policemen that area youth were gathering under potentially disreputable circumstances.

Waiting with the others to gain entry, I admired, as I often did, the glowing stone fountain beneath the driveway arch that depicted a naked young boy riding a chariot being pulled by a pod of pink Yangtze River dolphins. The smirking cherub held the reins in one hand and his tiny pecker in the other, as he urinated off the front end of the vessel—pissing into the wind, so to speak. Mr. Babyk had explained the significance once, but the details now escape me. I remember it being sleazily poetic.

Adriana Babyk greeted us at the front door wearing a tiara and stiletto heels.

"Hi!" She had swung open the door with one arm and was balancing a tray of mimosas in the other, laughing. "Welcome to our humble abode. Here, take a drink."

I waved mine off politely, as did Julianne. Grouse took two and gulped them down in succession. The others collected their sparkling fizzy orange drinks, and we meandered into the vestibule, where a pile of shoes had begun to accumulate against the wall like a burgeoning termite mound.

"Please, come in," said Adriana, her honey-brown legs slithering down from a snug black cocktail dress. Not that I was looking, but I didn't see any underwear lines. Or, put another way: it didn't look like she was planning to shovel any snow that night.

We had slipped past our host's younger sister and unloaded our shoes onto the pile of footwear when Ally sheepishly confided to Julianne: "She's a total whore."

Julianne smiled appreciatively but didn't respond.

"*Jesus!*" Grouse cried. "You say it so condescendingly."

Ally put a reflexive finger to her lips, giggling, as Adriana slid past with an empty drink tray.

Even to an amateur art historian like me it was obvious the Babyk's reception hall borrowed generously from Lorenzo de Medici's interior decorator. The foyer was filled with neo-classical marble statues and busts, oil paintings of old monarchs and noblemen, even an upright display of medieval knight's armor. Nodding toward one of the statues, I joked to Julianne that history frowns on noses and penises.

She giggled.

A commotion lured us through the formal dining room, where a table was set for twelve, into the kitchen, where a group of guys was huddled around the breakfast bar, shouting at one another as they played cards. An iced tea pitcher was filled to the brim with keg beer, and a motley collection of shot glasses stood armed and ready off to the side, near a partially drained tequila bottle. Someone slapped down his cards and the table roared, erupting in a torrent of laughter and insults, while the losing side was ordered to guzzle their beers.

Taped to the stainless steel refrigerator door was a note from Sharon Babyk requesting that Duce and Adriana be on their best behavior—"No parties!" was underlined twice—and to call Eddie Wilkinson in the event of an emergency.

Ally nudged past me searching for a non-alcoholic beverage in the fridge and settled on a jar of organic apple cider. Grouse had quickly procured a beer and given himself a foam mustache. He handed me a plastic cup with lukewarm brew flowing over the sides. Adriana walked past our little group and noticed that Julianne was empty-handed.

"Here," she said, reaching for a glass of red wine on the countertop that appeared to be unclaimed and handing it to Julianne. "This is yours now. Cheers."

Julianne smiled gratefully as she brought the goblet to her mouth.

"Mmm," she said, wetting her upper lip. "It's like Communion."

I chuckled and said, "This is the blood of the covenant. Drink ye all of it."

Adriana grinned sideways at me.

Then Ally held up her glass of cider and said, "Here's a toast to all of us—"

We raised our drinks.

"To our very special friends," Ally added, letting her gaze fall on each of us in turn, "who know each other well, including our deepest flaws, but who love us all the same—"

"Jesus Christ!" Grouse exclaimed.

"Yes," said Ally, breaking into laughter. "And to him, too!"

The rest of us laughed and clinked glasses, enjoying a long, appreciative swallow as we celebrated that the night's big dance was finally underway.

After finishing his van duties, our gracious host had retired to private quarters and was yet to make an official appearance at the party, we were told, and so the girls, Grouse, and I formed a little search party, setting off four abreast down a grand, teak-floored corridor in pursuit of him. On the walls hung decorative swordfish and sailfish that were gloriously frozen in the act of tearing at baited hooks, and at the far end of the hallway a stuffed grizzly bear stood upright on its hind legs with a plasticized salmon in its mouth. The décor gave the impression that the Babyks were avid outdoorsmen, but that simply wasn't the case. No, these were the trophies of actual hunters and fishermen, and, of course, skilled taxidermists, and the Babyks merely aspired to be tastemakers.

At the house's rear, we mounted a glossy wooden staircase with an ornate Persian runner to the second floor, where we found Duce down another hallway in the high-ceilinged library. He was wearing a plush white bathrobe, standing behind a vast mahogany desk, and thumbing his way anxiously through a disheveled pile of papers. Heather and her church pals were across the room, lounging on a wide mohair sofa, toasting their toes on an ottoman before a cavernous stone fireplace that could only be described as "Rockefeller-esque."

Duce told us rather petulantly that he had "misplaced" his college application essays, which he had typed during his week-long suspension from school, and that he had neglected to save the files on his computer.

"God damn it," he said, briefly scanning the documents one at a time before tossing each back onto the heap. "Son of a cunt!"

The church girls giggled at his adventuresome language. Duce had a reputation among our friends for being careless, often leaving those important things, like car keys, wallets, and college-entrance essays, in easily forgettable places where they might only turn up again at inopportune times—or not at all.

"You'd lose your dick if it wasn't attached," Grouse told him now.

Duce nodded reluctantly.

"Yeah, but not in my own fucking house," he said.

Then he straightened up, being careful not to let his robe come untied.

"Well, it doesn't matter," he said. "They were lousy anyway. Next time, I'm going to save myself the headache and pay someone at the *Star & Sickle* to ghostwrite them for me."

He added, "I mean, how the hell are you supposed to write an essay about your educational and career ambitions when your only real passions in life are violent video games and European pornography?"

"That's the thing," Grouse said. "It's all how you spin it."

The church girls laughed again, and Duce seized upon their levity.

"What, tell the admissions committee that studying German has helped me understand the dialogue in my imported smut videos? Tell them about my Bavarian pen pal, Jens Kroeger, who keeps phoning me up in the middle of the night to hum the opening bars of The Nutcracker Suite March before quickly hanging up? Show them I'm a quote-unquote 'man of the world' and humanize myself that way?"

(Most of his international mail-order adult videos were from the Netherlands, but no matter.)

The three of us had suffered through German language classes together since eighth grade, and it had become something of a running joke among us. Incidentally, we'd ended up enrolled in German only because we'd skipped school on registration day and by the next morning all the Spanish and French classes were full. After five years of German, straight A's, all any of us could say was, "*Ich habe Scheiss in meine Hose*" and "*Frau Hopf, ihr Kartoffelsalat ist ausgezeichnet.*"

Our junior year, we had taken the standardized National German Exam, and our classmates each pooled twenty dollars in a winner-take-all bet to see who could legitimately earn the highest score. I won with a mark in the eighth percentile. Grouse finished in the fifth; Duce the third. And our pal Rajwan Bajwa, who hailed from that great bastion of German scholarship— Calcutta, India—scored in the "zeroeth" percentile, meaning that one hundred percent of the students nationwide who took the exam performed better than he did.

I gave Raj his twenty-dollar ante back.

"Well," Duce sighed, conceding the search, "let's not let it ruin our night."

And with that, he flashed a defiant grin and crouched down underneath the desk, before coming up with a bottle of *baijiu* Chinese rice wine.

"Holy hell!" Grouse exclaimed.

"Anybody want to jump into the deep end?" Duce said.

"What is it?" Julianne asked.

"It's Chairman Mao's truth serum," I told her.

Mr. Zhu had sent Grouse a bottle of *baijiu* as a Christmas gift a few years earlier, and we had gotten absolutely ham-boned on it one night at Grouse's apartment. I would describe what it was like being drunk on *baijiu*, but I can't remember anything except for vague snippets of mildly belligerent and wholly unintelligible conversation. Most of the evening was simply erased from the hard drive. I recall awakening the next morning to the sound of a bubble popping and the irrepressible urge to vomit.

Somehow, Grouse had acquired a second bottle—from Mr. Zhu, no doubt—which he'd in turn presented to Mr. Babyk as a "thank-you" gift for hosting us at their cabin over Fourth of July weekend. Duce's dad—wisely, perhaps—had stashed it under the desk, out of sight, possibly hoping he'd forget about it. Or maybe he was testing whether the nauseating liquor would mature. Who knows—it's possible that neglect over a long enough time period might ripen the spirit's top notes of dirty sweat-socks and mangy Chinese street dogs into something more agreeable to the olfactory senses.

"Wait, your dad doesn't want it?" said Grouse, with a touch of regret entering his voice. "Well, okay."

And he took hold of the bottle, whose peeling labels were covered in indecipherable Chinese characters.

"Shot glasses are in the kitchen," Duce told us. "I'm heading downstairs to change into my party duds, but make yourselves at home."

"You don't want a shot?" Grouse asked him.

"I do, I do," said Duce, cracking a smile as he added, "I *do*. I definitely want one… in a few minutes. I'll have it downstairs at the bar."

I grinned as Duce sidestepped out of the room.

The three debutantes silently got up and followed him.

"*Now is the time to drank!*" Grouse roared.

His whole face puckered as he swilled from the bottle.

"Hot damn, *that* shit is good!" he cried, after swallowing with tremendous effort.

He passed the bottle to me.

"*Ganbei!*" I chanted, pouring the devil's fiery ejaculate down my own throat.

I felt the cords on my neck bulge as my innards were set ablaze and my eyeballs glazed over. The *baijiu* tasted vaguely toxic, and I inexplicably yearned for a cold glass of buttermilk as a chaser. Alas, I reached for the next best thing: a mouthful of warm beer.

Julianne leaned over, sniffed the bottle, and pretended to gag.

"I take that to mean you don't want any?" I said.

She cringed, shaking her head, and stuck out her tongue.

"I'm fine with red wine for now," she said diplomatically.

The beer had already started doing its thing when the *baijiu* cannonballed into my stomach, and it wouldn't be long, I knew, before we were all polluted drunk, acting like our "real, unfiltered selves," which was how someone once described our personalities in a state of heavy inebriation. No, it wasn't the fluttering moths and blue gardens of West Egg but something far more lowbrow: a swift unraveling of decorum and a careening around tight corners at unsafe speeds as we hurtled toward a greasy state of social lubrication.

"How are you?" somebody might ask.

"Actually, I'm fairly well-lubricated," you might reply.

There always seemed to be a distinct moment when you first realized you were drunk, typically when you stood up to break the seal. The world suddenly felt different—somehow heavier but pleasurable—and you said things you wouldn't normally say ("Does anyone have a spatula? My scrotum is stuck to my thigh.") and did things you wouldn't normally do (like lean over and chew on your girlfriend's forearm for a laugh). Of course, we had been warned in health class that alcohol leads to failed inhibitions, but like most young people who imbibed we sort of considered that the whole point.

A traditional Irish bar with stained-glass liquor cabinets and intricate hand-carved woodwork stood in a dark corner of the sprawling basement. Mr. Babyk had bought an old pub on a whim a few years earlier on a golfing trip to County Kerry on the country's gusty Atlantic coast. He deconstructed its antique, main-room bar and shipped it over to the States on a boat. Then he refurbished the gutted interior in a modern style and sold the pub back to its original proprietor for a relatively steep loss: "the price of owning rarity," he'd said. The reassembled bar in Babyk's basement, with its dim lighting and scarred, dark wood, retained much of its old-world charm, even in the upscale surroundings of its new home.

Much of the alcohol Grouse had bought earlier that afternoon on the Indian Reservation was now prominently displayed behind the bar so that nobody would be tempted to nip into Mr. Babyk's collection of rare, hundred-year-old Scotch whiskys. Twinkling blue fairy lights were strung around the back-wall mirror above our booze stash as a sort of blinking advertisement for it.

Our parties in the past had typically been "each man for himself" as far as alcohol was concerned, meaning if you could pinch a few beers from your parents' refrigerator then that was your haul for the night. If you could score a half-bottle of rum, that was even better. The practice naturally led to hoarding, to the same sort of behavior squirrels exhibit as winter approaches. We would hide our loot in the unlikeliest of places, the harder to find the better, which always seemed like a brilliant idea when the night was young but foolish several days later when the host's parents—by then, back in town—went to do their laundry and discovered three cans of Grain Belt Premium in the dryer. Tonight's party would be an experiment in "adult-style" sharing, or as Morty might call it, "A bid to end the tiresome practice of the have-nots cadging drinks all night."

Henry Beach had slipped a dark blue apron over his T-shirt and was standing behind the bar mixing cocktails. Occasionally, he would wipe off the countertop with a wet rag or replenish ice cubes in people's drinks. A small crew had taken up position on the bar stools in front of him.

"Hey, ugly," Duce said to Henry. "I should've hired a crew of midgets in tuxedos to walk around carrying silver trays so we wouldn't have to look at your ugly mug all night."

Henry smiled as he polished a pint glass with another rag. Sometimes he seemed to enjoy being razzed.

"Don't you think that would be sort of belittling?" I said.

Ignoring my joke, Duce turned toward me and said: "Bo, wait until you see what I've got outside. You're going to die laughing—it's so precious."

He stood up and indicated for me to follow him.

Near the sliding glass door, which opened to the patio, he noticed some fresh red wine spots on the cream-colored carpet. He dabbed them with the toe of his sock in a half-hearted attempt to wipe them away, but the peeved look in his eyes suggested that he knew the task would later require more strenuous effort.

"I'm serious about those midgets," he said, stepping into a pair of patio loafers as I did the same. "Remind me next time we throw a party." Then he slid open the door, drawing in a gust of frosty air, and added, mostly to himself: "God damn it," as though it had been a truly splendid idea.

Steam vapors hovered over the heated swimming pool, which glowed a radiant shade of aqua green, and as I stepped outside I immediately saw what he wanted to show me. In a corner of the patio, boxed in by a pair of snow-covered hedges, a pig roast was slowly rotating over a low flame. I sensed that Duce was eagerly awaiting my reaction, and I managed to laugh sportingly. He joined me, evidently satisfied by my response.

"Pretty good, huh?" he said.

"Classic Duce Babyk," I replied.

A portable outdoor heater spit out a bluish flame, like a jet engine, warming a vast section of the patio, and as we moved past it the fire nearly singed off my leg hair through my pants. Most of the cement deck was snowless, and trickles of water were dribbling toward the drains at the edges of the pool.

Duce used a carving knife and long fork to separate a hunk of flesh from the swine's flank.

"You want some?" he asked me, biting the meat off the tip of the blade.

"Yeah, man. I'm famished."

With his fingers, Duce pulled a chunk of slightly charred meat off the blade and handed it to me. "You're going to love this. It's fucking incredible."

I put it in my mouth and instantly agreed: it was tender, moist, and delicious. "God damn, that's good," I said, chewing hesitantly because it was still hot.

"Wait until Queenie gets here," Duce said. "I can't wait to see her face."

"She's going to slap you."

Duce smirked. He was proud of himself.

"By the way," I said, changing subjects, "you missed a hell of a pep rally last week. Did you know our adapted floor hockey team has the state's all-time leading scorer?"

Duce dug a crumpled soft-pack out of his front pocket, tapped out a cigarette, and stuffed it between his lips. He patted his pockets in search of a lighter and eyed me inquisitively, as though urging me to continue.

"They presented our team with the championship trophy, and the kid stood up and waved to the crowd with this giant, shit-eating grin on his face. It was the first time anyone had ever seen him. He's a freshman, I think, at Lindbergh. You know how these Special Ed teams are always made up of kids from different districts? Anyway, the funny thing is that he looked as normal as they come—no different than you or me."

"That handsome, huh?"

"I mean he didn't look like he was mentally or physically stunted in any way," I said.

Duce spit on the patio. "So what's the deal?"

"Yeah, so I went to see Mrs. Calhoun in the athletic office, and she told me to close the door and then made me promise I wouldn't write about it in the newspaper. I have no journalism ethics, so of course I agreed without hesitation. And she told me the kid is *color blind!*"

Duce tilted his head back in a caricature of good humor.

"Are you serious?" he said.

"We've got a kid on our mentally disabled floor hockey team who scores about a dozen goals a game before they run up the white flag, and his only handicap is that he can't tell the difference between certain shades of blue and green. Apparently, he exploited some loophole in the rules, and the state high school league wants to keep it quiet out of embarrassment."

"That's fucking priceless," Duce said with more laughter. "I wish I would've thought of that."

Before long, the patio door slid open and Queenie poked her head out. She was wearing a thick pea coat, and her neck was wrapped in a long, chunky-knit scarf that was colorfully patterned like a string of Tibetan prayer flags. Spotting Duce and me near the swine roast, she cocked her head, drawing in a sharp breath.

"You're a heel, Duce. Murdering a pig like this to get a rise out of me," she said.

Duce returned a vulpine grin, as though he'd been anticipating the conversation with delight. "That's funny, Queenie, I thought we were at *my* house."

"And besides," he added, "I didn't kill him. I paid a butcher to do it."

Queenie smiled nervously, her arms forming teapot handles on her hips. She knew it took courage to confront Duce like this and risk facing his scorn, but she had obviously been wounded by his practical joke, if you could call it that, and felt he had crossed an unspoken personal line.

"You're a dog," she said. "You're a street dog with no regard for anyone but yourself. You just need a fire hydrant to piss on and a vagrant to scratch behind your ears."

"Are you done?"

"And you're full of fleas," she added.

Duce grinned insincerely, spreading his arms as though he wanted a hug. It was a buffoonish gesture, and it managed to crack Queenie's tough outer shell, causing her to yield a radiant, almost pitying smile, as she appeared to grasp at last the profound deafness of her audience. Her rebuke had almost certainly inflicted less damage in actuality than when she had rehearsed the lines in her mind on her way downstairs.

"I'm not denying what you say, Queenie," said Duce. "I've never claimed to be a saint."

He stepped forward, putting his hands on her shoulders.

"Don't," she said, snorting an anxious laugh. She must've known it would be futile, registering her disapproval in this way, but a determined inner voice urged her on.

"Pigs are smarter than dogs," she pointed out.

"Well, maybe next time we can have a dog roast," he said.

Queenie's fragile smile went limp.

Duce continued, "You know how they kill them, don't you?"

She frowned.

He leaned in and whispered, "I'll give you a hint: they don't sneak up behind them and put a bullet in the back of their heads when they're not looking."

"Why are you such a jerk?"

"You know why I'm such a jerk?" replied Duce, his voice rising. "Because I was kicked in the shins in kindergarten for coloring a zebra pink." At this he released a brutish, masculine cackle. "That's a true story," he added, looking at me.

It was also true that their friendship had always been like this. When they first met the summer they both moved to Minnesota, Duce had tossed Queenie into Minnehaha Creek. Although that telling of the story makes Grouse and me sound like non-accomplices, which is a stretched truth. In fact, all three of us—*at Duce's insistence*—had carried Queenie by arms and kicking legs across the neighborhood and, on a count of three, hurled her into a murky, scum-covered section of the creek, where as younger boys we had netted out small crawfish and snails. It wasn't exactly our favorite swimming hole.

Years later, reminiscing about old times, I asked Duce, "What could she *possibly* have done to deserve being thrown into the creek like that?"

Without a moment's hesitation, he replied, "I don't know, but she must have deserved it. Otherwise we wouldn't have done it."

On the patio, he sliced another hunk of meat from the pig's carcass. "Anyway, Queenie, I'm not in the mood for your harassment tonight," he said. "I got plenty of that from my stepmom on the phone."

I gave Queenie a sympathetic look. "For what it's worth, he's having a lousy day. Mr. Perfect Score lost his college-application essays, and now he's suffering from writer's block."

Queenie chewed on her lower lip.

"Oh, you poor thing. You're really so unfortunate," she said.

"Yeah," Duce said. "Well, they weren't exactly inspired by greatness. I think I need a better line of attack. You know those ridiculous, open-ended questions: 'Tell us about yourself and why you think you would be a good fit with our university?' The only proper response to an essay topic like that is to feed them *more* bullshit."

Queenie shifted the weight on her feet.

"Have you read any good books lately?" she asked. "That's always a clever way to sidestep a question like that, while letting you preemptively conceal what an illiterate dumb-ass you are."

Ignoring the jibe but sensing possibilities in her suggestion, Duce said he had, in fact, read one such thought-provoking book over Thanksgiving weekend. It was called *African Genesis*, and it'd been written a half-century earlier by a New York City dramatist, who suggested that all modern humans—and not just Goldy Lindenheimer—descended from a line of hairless, weapon-wielding killer apes that fought their way off the central African plains swinging antelope femurs like baseball bats.

The weapon gave birth to the species, the author posited, and not the other way around.

The dramatist had also colorfully spelled out the biological premise underlining our everyday struggle, Duce said, namely that aggression leads to territory (or money); territory (money) leads to status; status leads to power; and power leads to pussy. It was a simple equation, Duce said, half-suppressing a grin.

"It's the only correlation in God's nature you need to know," he added, before paraphrasing further. "Cunning leads to cash, and cash leads to coochie."

Queenie frowned like a disappointed aunt.

"Duce, you don't want a girl to like you just because you're rich," she said.

"Sure, I do. Why not?"

"Because it's not right. To have someone want you only for your money?"

"So what?"

"It's not right," she said again, groping for a more rational explanation.

"What's not right about it?"

"I mean, someone should love you *for you*—because of who you are."

"That's ridiculous. Why?"

"Because… I don't know. Because there's fulfillment in it, I guess."

"Okay, well, let me put it this way: Your dog only loves you because you feed him twice a day, but you don't pretend it's a bad thing to have a dog."

It was a point he'd evidently been contemplating.

"Whatever, Duce. You're just trying to get me riled up." She laughed. "And, of course, it's working, as usual."

Duce wasn't finished.

"It explains why I'm so aggressive," he said.

Queenie aimed to head him off.

"Naw, I think, deep down, you're a softy," she said.

"Not true. I'm aggressive because I want lots of dough."

"Oh, yeah?" she said, indulging him now.

"Tons of dough. Piles of it. I need it."

"Why is that?"

"I want to make sure I've got enough stashed away so that no matter what happens in my life—if my old man goes belly up financially, or whatever, or if I get indicted over a funny banking deal—that I'll always have enough cash squirreled away some-where to be able to afford an occasional blowjob."

Queenie snorted another laugh.

"What are you doing *buying* blowjobs, Duce?" she asked.

"The better question, Queenie, is what are y'all doing giving them away for free?"

His eyes sunk into his face as he beamed at his self-assured brilliance, squinting into a cloud of cigarette smoke. The laughter might have been a fine reward, I thought, but it brought him no closer to a suitable essay topic. Privately, he later told me that he hoped to earn a hockey scholarship to an Ivy League school, like Yale or Dartmouth, which would allow him to sidestep having to write the essay at all. Maximize the minimum—there you go.

Grouse was holding court at the bar when we went back inside. "There's nothing worse than that, huh?" he said, sipping from his beer. "I used to call it the morning wood march."

He stood up to demonstrate, thrusting his shoulders forward and sticking his rear end out. Then, maintaining an erect posture, he strode briskly forward, as though into a stiff wind. He looked like he was mimicking the stereotypical gait of a 1950s insurance salesman in old Hollywood films. "*Hiya, mom!*" he said in character, saluting with a wave of his hand. "*I'm just goin' to take a leak!*"

Everybody laughed.

The gang sitting at the bar had expanded. Henry nodded at me, inquiring whether I wanted another beer.

"Give me a gin and pineapple juice," I said, feeling hopeful.

Henry asked Grouse if he needed a refill. Grouse held up a plastic cup three-quarters full of beer with his right hand and then reached across the bar with his other hand and seized a tumbler half-full of whisky. He turned to Henry with a satisfied smile, hoisting a drink in each hand.

"Good thing you're not an octopus," Duce said.

"*The king drinks!*" Grouse bellowed.

The rest of us saluted and roared Viking cheers.

"So, when is Goldy coming?" asked Grouse after the crowd quieted down. "I wonder if he got any better idea of whether the Gophers are planning to offer him a scholarship."

Nobody had heard anything, but Grouse wasn't ready to relinquish the spotlight, and so he segued into a well-worn tale about a time in middle school when he and Goldy were sitting in the back of the biology classroom at a lab station while Miss Peterson lectured about owl pellets. Suddenly, a panicked look seized Goldy's face, widening his eyes and forcing him to speak out of the corner of his mouth.

"Dammit, Boozer," he whispered, urgently. "I had two egg-salad sandwiches for lunch, and I really need to rip one."

"Go ahead," Grouse whispered back, reassuringly. "I'll take credit for it."

"Are you serious?"

"Yeah."

Goldy winced. "Do you swear?"

"Sure, no problem. She'll probably blame me anyway."

"All right. Thanks, man. I definitely owe you one."

"Don't mention it."

Then, bracing himself against the lab station, Goldy slowly shifted his weight to one side, tilting ever so slightly, appearing virtually immobile, as he produced a sound like a long, wet rag being torn. He later dubbed it "The Foghorn." The whole class immediately spun around, bursting into spontaneous laughter, and Miss Peterson halted her lecture mid-sentence. She might have even dropped the chalk.

Grouse rocketed to his feet and plugged his nose in theatrical disgust, crying as he backed away, "Oh my god, Lindenheimer! That's disgusting!"

Miss Peterson pointed a long index finger toward the door, ordering Goldy out of the room, and he trudged, downtrodden and double-crossed, toward the exit.

"Ho, ho, ho!" Grouse laughed. "Whoa, Goldy!"

The bar crowd at Babyk's house laughed appreciatively. No one appreciates that type of puerile humor quite like drunken high school students. And Grouse was rarely in short supply of stories that fit the bill.

The party gathered pace as newcomers continued to arrive in droves: slender foxes with winter tans, dirtballs clutching six packs, starry-eyed nymphets, athletes of all stripes, gun-shy under-classmen, and hordes of people I only vaguely recognized or had never seen before. These were the late-arrivals, the stragglers who had missed the van shuttles. But everyone was welcome, Adriana reassured them at the door, as long as they didn't park their cars in the driveway or cul-de-sac and as long as they weren't "filthy, backstabbing whores" who had defiled her good name behind her back, she added with a laugh.

Judging by the swirl of bodies moving through the house, I guessed there were around one hundred fifty people there at the night's peak, although I'd give that estimate a wide margin for error because I'd made it after a second shot of *baijiu*.

At one point, O'Leary appeared at the bottom of the basement stairs with his girlfriend Sandra Flanagan, who was wearing a mink coat and puffing furiously on a menthol cigarette. "I'm *wasss-ted!*" she hissed, tapping her ash into the nearest Ming dynasty vase.

Peter and Sandra both hailed from "good Catholic stock," meaning they were born into families with so many brothers and sisters that they needed to use a panoramic camera lens to shoot their annual Christmas card photos. Peter was the oldest of six, Sandra the youngest of seven, and each had countless aunts, uncles, and cousins.

Sandra had learned early in life that she needed to speak loudly if she wanted to be heard. Consequently, she reminded you of the argumentative talk-show host whose microphone is always turned up a few notches louder than his guest's. If the other person tried to return fire, using a similar tactic, Sandra would squint her beady little eyes and stick out her tongue, making a noise like: "*Naaaggghh!*" And she would punctuate it with throaty laughter—an unexpectedly endearing sound that somehow left you no choice but to laugh along with her.

Over the years, her vocal cords—due to the smoking and squawking, both—had strained to the point that she seemed to have developed a permanently raspy voice.

Sandra was a ubiquitous party girl who could work a room like a golden retriever puppy. One minute, you'd be downstairs overhearing her cigarette-stained voice jabbering away over the music, and by the time you climbed the stairs, you'd find her propped on the kitchen countertop, gulping white wine, laughing hoarsely with a new group of people.

When I envisioned Sandra's apartment in college, I saw a place strewn with bras and overflowing ashtrays, and a dining-room table that consisted of an ironing board spread across two empty keg shells.

But while Sandra was a lush, Peter wholly abstained, and nobody quite understood his steadfast refusal to drink alcohol. Some said that he believed too literally in the athlete's code of conduct. Others said he feared God held a dim view of those willing to endure tequila hangovers. As close as they were in so many ways, Sandra and Peter traveled on starkly different roads to letting loose.

"Hey, barkeep," O'Leary said to Henry. "How about a soda water and lime?"

"Coming right up," Henry said. "You want a Jolly Rancher to suck on with that?"

"Pour a splash of gin in it!" Sandra cried. "Make him live a little, Henry!"

"If you do," Peter warned him, "I'll make you wear it."

Henry set the virgin cocktail on the bar, sans Jolly Rancher, and O'Leary leaned over and sniffed it. Satisfied, he took a sip. But a few moments later, when he briefly turned the other way, Henry dumped in a jigger of vodka, directing a surreptitious wink at Sandra. The next time O'Leary drank from it his face immediately soured in recognition.

Henry bolted like a jackrabbit from behind the bar, and O'Leary caught him near the pool table, where he locked him in a full nelson. Henry resisted mightily, causing the pair to whirl around the room attached to one another.

"Oh, no you don't," Henry said when they had stopped spinning, his lanky arms now flailing above his head like a marionette's. He chuckled feebly at his lack of options.

"Or what?" Peter said.

Henry's face was purple with struggle. They were both breathing heavily.

"I'm flying, Jack!" said Henry, with desperate laughter.

He bent forward, thrusting his rear end out, and forcing O'Leary into a similar posture. They looked like a pair of copulating apes, but Peter held on tight.

"Uh-oh," Henry said. "I think I'm beginning to like it."

Then he lifted a foot and tapped O'Leary's crotch with his heel. At this potentially dangerous escalation, O'Leary released his captive, and Henry quickly turned and drove his shoulder into Peter's midsection. The momentum carried the two clear across the room, and just as Peter was about to fall backward he spun around and they both went toppling into a large cardboard box that was set against the wall, crushing the top half and smashing whatever "fragile contents" were inside.

Their horseplay abruptly ceased, and O'Leary peeled the tape off the box and peered inside, surveying the damage. It was a new droplet chandelier that Duce's stepmom apparently wasn't sure she wanted to keep. A few pendants had come dislodged and three arms were bent. The damage would be neither cheap to fix nor easy to explain.

Duce and I had been talking while the guys tussled. He'd sipped his vodka-soda and hadn't protested, but I detected an irritated glow in his eyes. When the two went crashing into the box, he cast a boiling glare at O'Leary like he was sizing him up for cement overshoes, but that flash of anger quickly subsided as Peter flushed pale with regret and apologized.

"Don't worry, it's not your fault, man," Duce told him. "Well, actually, it is your fault, but you know what I mean."

Peter and Henry found a roll of packing tape in the laundry room and used it to re-seal the cardboard box, which they then pushed behind the bar, out of further harm's way.

"Maybe tell them it came like that?" someone suggested. "Or blame the delivery crew? Or why not just deny it?"

In his own mental calculations, however, Duce had likely figured that his family's "credit" at The Galleria, accumulated through a sufficient number of big-ticket purchases over the years, would ensure that the damages would be written off as a "cost of doing business." But in the panic that briefly ensued after the incident, Sandra said: "It's a good thing Duce doesn't give a shit about anything, because if he did this would almost certainly be the kind of thing he'd give a shit about."

My ex-girlfriend Jessica Miles arrived with her new beau, Porter Ginchquim-Highman IV, of the venerable Ginchquim-Highmans, an old money Minneapolis family whose paternal great-grandfather, Porter Ginchquim, Sr., a prosperous flour miller, had been hyphenated by a railroad tycoon's daughter, Sylvia Highman, at the turn of the century. The family hadn't sweated many credit card bills over the decades. Porter lived up the street from Duce in a house that looked like a replica of Mount Vernon.

"*Hola!*" Porter sang out as he entered the basement, spreading his arms to dispense friendly hugs to some of the girls. He was wearing a pink button-down shirt tucked into designer jeans, and the jeans, I suspected, he laundered at the dry cleaners. Porter was "country club handsome," meaning he was tall, athletic, and square-jawed, with wavy golden-brown hair and a haughty little mouth that seemed to express perpetual condescension, even when he wanted to smile good-naturedly.

As a younger adolescent, Porter had practically begged his parents to send him to a prestigious all-boys prep school out East, somewhere he could wear a crested blazer and repp tie to class each day, somewhere he fancied himself standing defiantly on his chair in class and proclaiming, "O captain, my captain!" But they told him he'd be better off as a "big fish in a small pond" in Minnesota, and so they enrolled him at the private William Henry Harrison Academy, which was the academic equivalent to bumper bowling.

While Andy Morton and the rest of us slugged it out in the public school system, competing against not a hand-selected few from the Lucky Sperm Club but hundreds of eager scholastic beavers, all elbowing past one another vying for valedictorian, Porter was privately tutored at ninety bucks an hour and graded alongside the coddled chosen ones whose penalty for half-assed term papers was an A-minus.

Porter was immensely proud of his reputation as a "rabble-rouser" at Harrison, and he once told us, practically gagging on his laughter: "My junior year, I got two demerits in one day. It was *extremely* hysterical."

He described funny movies as "effing hilarious." He drank piña coladas on spring break. On the tennis court, if you served the ball into the net, he would raise an index finger and call "short." But worst of all was that he was in a running club at Harrison and liked to quip: "We call ourselves a *drinking* club with a *running* problem," which he almost couldn't spit out past all the titters and barely suppressed squeals.

Porter had recently announced that Amherst College in Massachusetts was his "back-up" school. He was fond of these sorts of chest-puffing proclamations.

"Ideally, I'd like to go to Brown," he would say and pause, waiting for everyone around him to be sufficiently impressed. They were all interchangeable: "I'm hoping to go to Vanderbilt, which I hear is really a work-hard, play-hard kind of school."

Wherever he went, I was certain he would rush a fraternity that hosted wine and cheese parties on Friday nights and whose brothers would wear sport coats and pastel-colored polo shirts to the football games and chant "overrated" when Vanderbilt took a three-point lead over No. 10 Georgia in the first quarter.

To be honest, I didn't mind that Porter was humping my ex-girlfriend. Somebody was going to step into that role, and at least Porter was someone I had fun ridiculing. In Babyk's basement, he extended his hand toward me and smiled.

"Henning," he said, as we shook hands.

"How's it going, Porter?"

"Terrific," he said. "You?"

"Yeah, same here," I said.

Then, in a voice loud enough for everyone around us to hear, I added in a sarcastically reassuring tone: "No, seriously, Porter. I know a lot of straight guys who wear bright pink shirts."

To which he boomed a hearty chuckle, deflecting my slander and perhaps inferring that he'd just zipped up his pants after the ride over with my ex-girlfriend. To be fair, he wasn't a bad guy, and I appreciated that he took my ribbing in stride—and that sometimes he even dished it back.

He turned to Grouse. "Hey, Bruce. How's it going?"

And Porter let out another thick belt of staccato laughter.

But that was a funny reference, actually.

On the first day of seventh grade, our math teacher Mrs. Potamus was calling out attendance and jotting down our nicknames in a notebook. She called out "William Henning?" and I replied, "I go by Bill." She called out "Katherine Fink?" and she said, "I go by Katie." She called out "Ryan Boozer?" and he said, "I go by Bruce." Our classmates squirmed in their seats, biting the insides of their lips to stifle giggles—some of us nearly to the point of drawing blood—as Mrs. Potamus penciled the name into her little book. Thenceforth, she knew Grouse as "Bruce."

Grouse would raise a hand in class and say, "Mrs. Potamus, lard ass say what?"

She'd glare over the top of her glasses at him. "Pardon me, Bruce?"

"Lard ass say pardon me, Mrs. Potamus," he would say.

"What do you want, Bruce?"

We were all squirrely, misbehaving little rapscallions at that awkward age, but no one was less well-behaved in school than Ryan Boozer, and so when Mr. and Mrs. Boozer turned up for parent-teacher conferences in late October, Mrs. Potamus greeted them with a bulging dossier of all the disciplinary actions she'd taken against their son that semester.

"You ought to know," she began frankly, "we are having some serious behavior issues with Bruce in class. He is an intelligent and capable young boy, as you well know—and I *do* want him to succeed, of course—but Bruce's personal conduct can be awfully childish at times."

And as Mrs. Potamus went on detailing Grouse's rascally antics, Mr. and Mrs. Boozer sat there quietly, eyebrows half-cocked, wondering to themselves, "*Who the hell is Bruce?*"

"Ultimately, it's up to *Bruce* to determine what kind of student *Bruce* wants to be," Mrs. Potamus concluded in an unwitting parody of the whole situation.

By that point, Grouse's parents both realized what had happened and didn't want to embarrass poor Mrs. Potamus by informing her she was the victim of a juvenile prank, and so "Bruce" remained enrolled in seventh grade algebra for the remainder of the year. Mr. Boozer gave Grouse a stern talking-to at home that night, but Grouse told me later his dad couldn't suppress the creeping smirk on his face as he scolded him.

"I'm good, Porter," replied Grouse. "How the hell are you?"

"I'm *en fuego*," Porter said. "As usual."

"Yeah?" said Grouse. "That sounds pretty gay."

But I don't think Porter heard the last part because Grouse had mumbled it.

The crowd moved past, and I welcomed Jessica with a half-hug. "Why did you bring that limp wrist?"

"He's not a limp wrist."

"Well, why did you bring him?"

"Why did you bring a twelve-year-old?"

Fair point, I thought.

"He doesn't even go to our school."

"So what? He's friends with Duce."

"Plus," she added. "Your girlfriend doesn't have any friends here."

"Well, yeah. Except for Ally."

The dig was intentional.

"Ally only talks with her because she feels sorry for her," Jessica replied. "I'm sure she'd rather be hanging out with *our* friends," she added, being a bitch.

For whatever it's worth, Jessica struck me in hindsight as the kind of girl whose life would peak shortly after she graduated from college, maybe even at the very instant she flashed her tits on Bourbon Street as the crowd finished counting backward from three. From that moment, amidst the roars and popping flashbulbs, it would all be permanently downhill for her. She'd marry some over-the-hill sugar daddy, squeeze out four or five bratty kids, embark on a series of unnecessary plastic surgeries, and blush whenever she looked in the mirror at night, wondering if an image of her bare breasts was circulating somewhere in the netherworld.

She and I had dated for nearly two years, from mid-freshman year to the summer before junior year, and we had been in love, more or less. For the first time since puberty, I'd felt truly and supremely content, in the way only a young man receiving steady hand-jobs for the first time in life can feel.

Jessica had a way of smiling intimately at me with her eyes when she wanted to let me know she was "feeling frisky." Her dark eyes gave off a devilish glint. It was a look that drove me wild with excitement.

Alas, this charming attribute turned out to be her greatest liability, for I didn't realize that, even though I was the only one receiving hand-jobs, she went around giving practically everybody the intimate look. It seemed only a matter of weeks between my noticing of this fact and the unraveling of our romance. She and Porter hooked up one weekend on a camping trip our friends had organized in northern Wisconsin. I couldn't attend because I was at a cousin's wedding, but when I heard through the grapevine what had happened, I entered a period of profound regret and stabbing jealousy.

It led to the lowest moment of my life. I couldn't sleep for weeks. Tormented by the loss of my first love, I would lie awake in bed at night envisioning the two of them alone in a tent, sharing a sleeping bag. Something about man's ancient reverence for chaste brides is hard-wired in so many of us. The negative feelings gnawed at the core of my being, and I found it impossible to rationalize them away.

One night the pain turned unbearable, and so I tied a long telephone cord around a doorknob in my bedroom, strung it up over the chin-up bar, and fixed a noose around my neck. Even now, I don't know how serious I was about the attempt, but I remember being surprised that I had allowed things to progress that far. As I knelt there quietly sobbing, trying not to wake my parents, I suddenly saw myself in a wall mirror and laughed out loud. Have you ever noticed that it's nearly impossible to watch yourself cry for longer than a few seconds?

I told myself: "Quit being such a fucking drama queen."

And at that, I untied the cord, plugged it back into the phone, and went to bed. "What's the cosmic impact of a suicide anyway?" I wondered.

I spent most of junior year in psychiatric counseling.

◆ ◆ ◆

Under admittedly devious pretenses, I lured Julianne down a long, soft-carpeted hallway toward Duce's bedroom suite at the far end of one of the basement wings, where the party sounds grew so muffled it was like they were buried underneath six feet of fresh dirt. Taped to the door outside Duce's room was a poem he had written for English class our junior year. It was graded "A+" with enthusiastic praise written in the margins: "Such rich imagery… So evocative… Brilliant!" In fact, it was the lyrics to a Dream Theater song, "Pull Me Under," which Duce had submitted as his own work.

"Duce is a *poet*?" asked Julianne incredulously.

"Sort of," I said.

"I never would have guessed."

"Well, he isn't John Milton."

And I left it at that. It didn't seem honorable for me, as his friend, to expose what I considered to be relatively minor deceptions. We're all entitled to our little charades, I thought.

As we entered Duce's room, I flicked on the overhead lights. Painted on the wall above the bed's headboard was a mural of James "Buster" Douglas standing over a floored Mike Tyson in Tokyo in 1990. The look in Buster's eyes was pure shock: Tyson wasn't back; he was *on his back.*

On an adjacent wall was a framed, game-worn Minnesota North Stars jersey, No. 17, which had belonged to Basil McRae, one of the sport's all-time great pugilists. Basil had signed the jersey: "To my old pal, Duce Babyk. Keep your fists up, -Basil McRae." And on a wall opposite that hung a promotional film poster for *Natural Born Killers,* showing Woody Harrelson with a skinned head and a pair of mirrored tea shades.

All things considered, it was a fairly ordinary eighteen-year-old American male's bedroom, with discarded clothes on the floor, a stereo system flanked by bulky speakers, a lava lamp on the bedside table, and piles of *Sports Illustrated* magazine everywhere. Duce's working desk was an architect's drafting table, and when the mini-blinds were opened he could see the swimming pool from a stationary bike in the corner.

Julianne reached for a framed photograph atop a four-drawer metal filing cabinet. The picture showed Duce and his dad in suits and ties, seated in a tall-backed booth at the Green Mill Cocktail Lounge in Chicago, listening to jazz. Duce was eleven at the time and looked like a handsome young film star. His old man, donning a gray fedora, looked dangerous and debonair. It was the last photograph that had been taken of Duce during his Chicago years, he'd told me.

I moved closer to Julianne and slid my arms around her waist, pressing my nose into her hair, inhaling the rich herbal fragrance of her shampoo. She eased into my embrace, setting the photograph back onto the cabinet and placing a soft hand on mine. I kissed her cheek and nuzzled her more suggestively.

"In Duce's bedroom?" she whispered doubtfully.

"What about on the sheepskin rug?" I said with a smile.

She giggled. "It *does* look soft."

"Come here."

She turned around and kissed me on the mouth—eagerly but, alas, briefly—and then batted open her eyes, before saying, "Not now," while touching an index finger to my lips.

Practically on cue, the doorknob twisted and Grouse barged into the room in stride. Catching us in semi-embrace, he paused, flashing an impish grin, and said, "Please, don't let me interrupt your little moment. I just wanted to grab something and I'll be on my way."

Julianne reflexively stepped backward.

"Or there's a camcorder in here somewhere if you want me to film you. It might be a nice keepsake of your first time."

Julianne blushed.

"I'm looking for a movie," said Grouse, excusing himself past Julianne to rummage in the bottom drawer of the filing cabinet, behind actual files. "I know it's in here somewhere. Ah, yes... Here it is, in the old secret hiding place: *Stiff Competition*, an all-time classic. This belongs in the National Film Registry. We're going to watch it in the movie room if you guys want to join us. Maybe you could study it for pointers."

Our pals had enjoyed a funny habit of late: watching old adult movies from the 1970s and early '80s and fast-forwarding through the sex scenes. The ham-handed plots offered a genuine source of entertainment, we all thought, and, in many cases, the vintage porno flicks elicited more laughter than the regressive mass-market comedies being peddled by Hollywood. It wasn't so much the porn stars' senses of humor that won us over but the earnestness of their performances under such patently absurd circumstances. It was similar to professional wrestling in that way.

"Sure, we're coming," I said. "I wanted Julianne to see this end of the castle dungeon—the host's quarters—as it were."

"Please, no hurry," Grouse said. "I'll feel bad if I've interrupted your budding romance. Sing a song or two. Finish what you started. I'm sure Duce will be glad to know you chose his bedroom out of the fifty-six other rooms in the house."

I laughed as Grouse shut the door behind himself.

A half-dozen of us had piled onto the sectional sofa like hamsters and were gaping wide-eyed at the big-screen TV, as we watched the X-rated movie about an illicit underground blowjob competition—a high-stakes suck-off syndicate, if you will—in which a pair of tornado-tongued dynamos raced to see who could bring their Tito to completion first. It was practically art-house cinema.

In the film's opening scene, a distinguished looking older gentleman in a tuxedo is riding in the back of a limousine with a horny-eyed young blonde. They arrive at a seedy, low-rent office building, where a group of unsavory punters encircles two pairs of contestants, barking out their wagers, and shaking grubby dollar bills in the air. The blonde turns to her companion and says, "Aren't you going to bet?" And with a haughty air, the tuxedoed man replies, "I'm into it *purely* for the sport."

"Can we watch something that's not porn?" Ally said. "I want to watch *Titanic*."

Julianne's face brightened at the suggestion, but I noticed that whenever Grouse fast-forwarded through the hardcore "love" scenes, her eyes remained glued to the screen, flitting back and forth as though she was speed-reading.

Overruled, Ally nevertheless became a fully engaged participant, even going so far as to venture a comment during the movie's obligatory lesbian scene: "I've never understood why boys get so excited by the sight of girls making out with each other." Turning toward Grouse, she asked, "Would you really be turned on if I fooled around with another girl?"

"Absolutely," he said, giving it no thought.

"You wouldn't consider it cheating?"

"No way."

"Really?"

"Here's the deal," Grouse explained. "If you hooked up with another girl it wouldn't be cheating as long as you told *me* about it before you told anyone else."

Ally giggled. "What's the logic behind that?"

"I don't know, but that's how it goes."

"What if I hooked up with another boy?"

"Obviously, that would be cheating."

Ally leaned over and patted my forearm.

"Even if I hooked up with Bill?" she said.

Her smile was kittenish and demure.

"Well, Bill is like my brother. You know that. I'd give him the shirt off my back."

"So it would be all right, then?"

Julianne eyed me with a slippery grin.

"Go for it," Grouse said.

"No offense, Ally," I put in, embarking on a monstrous untruth, "but I wouldn't touch you with a thirty-nine-and-a-half-foot pole."

"Wait, how is that 'no offense'?" she replied with embarrassed laughter.

And she directed an inscrutable smile at me.

"The truth, woman," said Grouse, "is that if we were having some *ménage e trois*, as I've suggested, cheating wouldn't be an issue. It would all be in the open."

"Great. So—you, me, and Duce then?"

"I'm talking about two girls."

She laughed. "I am not going to have a threesome with you and another girl."

"So tell me," Grouse pressed ahead, "which do you prefer: shaft or jewels?"

"Ryan! I can't believe you'd want to hook up with another girl!"

"Baby, I'm giving you first choice!"

A wandering eye, meanwhile, had lured Julianne's attention back to the television screen. "And why are boys so fascinated by boobs?" she mused aloud.

"Because we're all yearning to get back to our Oedipal teat," replied Grouse. "That's what Freud says anyway, and I sort of agree with him."

"Man, who didn't like having his braces tightened as a thirteen-year-old?" I said.

"For the love of God!" said Grouse. "When that girl would ask me to turn my head, all I could think was, 'I'll bet this is as close as I ever get to sucking this woman's tits.'"

Ally slugged him on the shoulder.

"Ugghh," she grunted, "do we have to watch this?"

Grouse stuffed the remote control down his pants and folded his arms across his chest, beaming a satisfied grin.

A few minutes later, when interest in the movie inevitably waned, Grouse began to casually probe the cracks between the sofa cushions with one of his hands. His eyes widened as he fished up a pair of red lace underwear.

"Holy hell!" He laughed.

"Adriana's latest study date," I said.

Grouse lobbed the tangled underwear at Henry, who pulled them over his head like a helmet, eliciting boisterous laughter from the rest of us. Then Henry tossed a kernel of popcorn into the air and snatched it in his open mouth like a circus seal—after pulling aside the panty's crotch at the last moment! We all cheered. He was on a roll, and so he plunged his car key into a beer can and snapped the tab, guzzling all twelve ounces without spilling a drop. He let out a terrific belch just as Adriana happened past.

She eyed him donning her knickers, with a mashed beer can in his hands, and we all figured it was curtains on Henry's lucky streak. But Adriana just burst out laughing, red-faced, and blew Henry a kiss!

Holy hell was right.

Shortly thereafter, with Adriana having fled the room in embarrassment, Henry got up and retrieved a videocassette from his duffel bag on the floor. He inserted it into the VCR, aimed the remote control at the machine, and pressed play, saying: "Elliott told me this afternoon that he rented *Faces of Death*, but who knows when he's going to get here—and I've got the next best thing. Wait until you see this."

A sepia-toned picture emerged from the static, showing a dingy old kickboxing stadium in Bangkok, Thailand, with low wooden rafters, overcrowded bleachers, and chicken-wire fence surrounding a gambling pit. Henry had visited Southeast Asia over the summer with his family. On the television screen, his camcorder zoomed in unsteadily on one of the corner men, who was puffing a cigarette while a dark-skinned young fighter in blue trunks—his lean, muscular frame glistening with Tiger balm—lowered his head, bowing to the turnbuckle.

"What's that guy doing, praying?" Grouse asked.

"Buddhists don't pray. I think he's talking to himself," said Henry.

"Buddhists don't pray?" I said.

"I don't know. Just watch the video," Henry said.

When the bell rang to start the first round, music whined out from a four-piece band, and the fighters slithered like cobras to the center of the ring, where they tested one another with cautious, half-speed kicks. Their intensity slowly ratcheted up as the round went on. I found myself leaning forward expectantly as the kicks grew stronger and the music more tightly strung. It was a sound conceived in a psych ward: like deranged bagpipes, tribal drums at a campfire, and the relentless tintinnabulation of bells. It wasn't so much Arabian Nights as Arabian Nightmare.

In the second round, the kid wearing blue shorts thumped a roundhouse kick off red corner's thigh, just above the knee, and one of blue's other corner men—his younger brother, going by appearances—led a flurry of quick hand claps to try to influence the judges.

Ally returned from the bathroom and saw that her real estate had diminished.

"Where should I sit?" she asked.

"Sit on my face," Grouse replied without looking up.

Ally lowered herself onto the sofa arm.

"Oh great," she said. "We've traded sex for violence."

The music turned downright neurotic in the third round as the fighters unleashed savage elbows and leaping, thrusting knees. The ancient sport was known as the Art of Eight Limbs, Henry told us. Later in the round, the referee separated the two fighters from a clutch, and they squared off in the center of the ring at what appeared to be a safe distance from one another. But then red suddenly whipped his rear leg around with such terrific velocity that blue never saw it coming.

Red's shin cracked against his opponent's cheekbone with such extraordinary force—it sounded like a baseball bat smashing a coconut—that I immediately assumed we'd just witnessed a death in the ring.

Ferocious cries rang out from the gambling pit as the kid in blue shorts collapsed to the canvas, utterly lifeless, his arms and legs splayed in a perfect X. Henry anticipated our reactions with an eager grin.

"Can you believe that shit?" he said, rewinding the tape so we could watch it again in slow motion. Even at that speed—even when you knew it was coming, frame-by-frame: "wait for it… wait for it… wait for it!"—you couldn't help but wince at the sudden and shocking violence of the impact.

Thai boxers were paid according to how their fights ended, Henry informed us, with losers supposedly paid "by the stitch." Knockouts promised a far more lucrative payout than a judge's decision, meaning the loser of this bout would be handsomely rewarded for his shiner. A pair of stadium officials pulled the semi-conscious fighter out of the ring by his ankles.

The thrill of witnessing such awesome brutality, however, quickly faded. Drunken adolescents, I suppose, can only muster so much empathy before springing back full-force into their sloppy self-obsessions. Ally had toppled onto the sofa behind Grouse, draping an arm around his waist, and now she shrieked in high-pitched laughter.

"*Stop it, Ryan!*" she cried.

"You are so old fashioned," he grumbled, shaking his head. "*So* old fashioned."

"Not now, baby," she whispered, blushing.

"I only wanted to place my hand betwixt your thighs."

"Baby," she said, lowering her whisper. "You can't touch my pussy right now."

"Hey!" he replied loudly. "Don't call it your pussy!"

He grinned.

"Call it *our* pussy," he insisted.

She rolled her eyes and forgave him the immature joke with a peck on the lips. But as she pulled away, her expression turned diagnostic. "What kind of mouthwash is that?"

"Pepto Bismol!" Grouse laughed.

"Gross, Ryan!" Ally squealed, fleeing the room.

Queenie entered with her script practically in hand.

"Does anybody know where Porter went?" she said.

"He's probably outside fagging around," Grouse said.

"Don't use that word," Queenie said.

Grouse knitted his eyebrows together.

"Really, the crusade is in our living rooms now?" he said.

"It's not nice," she said. "You know that."

"Well, if you can't call people fags anymore because the fags get offended, what about when you call someone annoying? Should we expect an outcry now from all the annoying people?"

Sandra interjected. "I think he's outside by the pool."

"Yeah," said Grouse, "that's what I said. He's probably outside by the pool—fagging around."

Queenie glanced at the TV and managed a grin. "You say he's outside 'fagging' around, but y'all are the ones watching greased-up young Thai boys having a go at each other."

And she reached for a large pillow on the sofa, holding it up to shield herself from a retaliation that failed to materialize.

Duce Babyk resembled a bull walrus corralling his mates as he ambled past the TV room linking arms with Heather and Chloe, while the blowjob queen Robyn Cook trailed in their immediate wake. It was a Hugh Hefner vision: the virile young man of wealth and station enjoying the full possession of his harem of horny harlots. And the girls were playfully assenting: *they knew the score*. Robyn raked her bright pink-painted fingernails down the length of Duce's back.

"Do you like that?" she purred.

"Oh, yeah," he replied, sarcastically.

They were putting on a show for us.

"What's your fantasy?" she asked him.

"A five-some," he answered.

Laughter shook the room.

"Come on," she said, pursuing a more serious response. "Do you want us to wear costumes? Would *that* turn you on? What if we dressed up in police uniforms?"

Duce squinted ponderingly for a moment and then replied: "Do you think you could dress up as altar boys?"

The girls tilted their heads back, issuing peals of open-mouthed, lustful laughter. Easy girls make terrific audiences.

"Wait!" Robyn exclaimed. "Have we forgotten all about tradition?"

And she commenced to hum the opening bars of the Star Spangled Banner, while the other girls tittered thrillingly. Duce flashed the audience a double thumbs-up and then set his hands on the girls' lower backs, just above their waistlines, as they continued their fateful march down the long hallway toward his bedroom.

"Whip 'em and ride 'em, Duce!" Queenie called after them, nibbling on her lower lip in a mischievous smile.

"*We've had this date from the beginning!*" Duce roared back.

It was probably a jealous observation on my part, but Chloe and Robyn looked to me, respectively, like Christina Aguilera with Down syndrome and Britney Spears with a repaired cleft palette. Sure, they were pretty enough girls, but each had her own fatal flaw. Robyn had "child-bearing" hips, sturdy thighs, and tits like Mr. Lindenheimer, and Chloe always smelled vaguely hospital-like to me.

Heather, on the other hand, was a legitimate seven, in my appraisal. She had a cute, girlish smile and a lanky frame, with these floppy, unhinged limbs that had a kind of "sexy puppet" quality to them, if that makes sense. Grouse had fooled around with her in ninth grade and afterward gloated that her "delicate little peach" was as "fragrant as petunias." The first time he "got there," in O'Leary's basement, after a group of us locked him and Heather in a closet for five minutes on a dare, he passed his forefingers around a circle of our pals so we could each take a whiff. Grouse was always considerate like that.

When the multitudes later found their way into her pants, he stole back the praise, claiming he'd turned her into a slut and slandering her as "a real panty-dropper."

An unfair stigma now attached itself to Heather, and I privately grieved that I hadn't stolen home when I had a chance. Before my relationship started with Julianne, I'd enjoyed many an extraction thinking about Heather's company. But, alas, I had "missed my turn," it appeared, and now she was "seeing" Duce. I could already envision myself as a doddering geriatric, rocking on my chair in the old folks' home, muttering, "Why didn't I? Why didn't I?" Pre-emptive regret is a strange emotion, and I seem to have been born with a keen sense of it.

Forty minutes or so after disappearing with the girls, Duce emerged from his lair, shirtless, with the drawstring on his sweatpants hastily tied and a cigarette drooping from his lips. I detected a temporary tattoo, a little raspberry, on the skin above his collarbone. He had apparently done well for himself.

"How'd it go?" I asked him.

He took a long, determined drag on the cigarette and held the smoke in his lungs for several seconds before replying in a fraternal whisper, through a dragon's breath of smoke: "*Coitus interruptus.*"

I laughed. "Who says chivalry's dead?"

Meanwhile, Elliott Sturgeon called from a payphone at city hall to say he had been inadvertently detained en route to the party. Apparently, he'd been howling down East 55th Street, a tempting straightaway that bisects Lake Cornelius (or "Swamp Cornelius," if you want to be more precise), doing eighty-eight miles an hour in a thirty-five-mile-an-hour zone.

When the cop pulled him over, Elliott, who had eaten a fistful of prescription amphetamines—doctor's orders—couldn't help from enthusiastically proclaiming to the officer: "One point twenty-one jigowatts! *Great Scott!*"

So Elliott wouldn't be joining us after all. His parents had promptly left home to bail their only son out of jail, no doubt leaving an ashtray full of smoldering cigarette butts on the kitchen table, and we quickly dispatched Henry to Elliott's house since the rest of us remained committed to ending the night with a ceremonial peace-pipe session. The front door of his house would be unlocked, Elliott had said on the phone, and we'd find a zip-lock bag full of "yard clippings" in a shoebox under his bed that he had prepared in advance just for such emergencies.

In our high school class, Elliott was voted "most likely to commune with Baba Fats on the mountaintop." He was perpetually seeking the perfect high, or, failing that, a strong chemical buzz, or, at a minimum, any discernible artificial change in his mood or perception.

During a discussion of Thoreau's "Civil Disobedience" in literature class that fall, Mr. Jenkins had smirked at Elliott and observed: "Mr. Sturgeon, your eyes are inexplicably bloodshot."

"I know. It's this dang hay fever," said Elliott, rubbing his eyes with his knuckles.

Another time, Mr. Jenkins paused during the middle of a lecture on Huckleberry Finn to remark matter-of-factly: "Mr. Sturgeon, your lip is inexplicably swollen."

Elliott surreptitiously ushered the tobacco plug down his throat with his tongue while trying not to gag. Turning pale, he asked Mr. Jenkins, "Could I use the bathroom?"

Mr. Jenkins grinned at him sportingly. "You betcha."

The banter between pupil and teacher routinely proceeded as such.

Now, it appeared poor Elliott would miss the party of the year.

As Henry sat on the tiled floor in the vestibule lacing up his sneakers, Duce's sister walked past, and Henry paused for a moment to look up at her. "Adriana, do you want to come with me to Elliott's house to pick up the grass?"

"Sure," she replied breezily with a cheerful smile, much to the surprise of those of us standing there—none more so than Henry. "But I'm not riding in that creepy van."

Henry laughed. "That van is a chick magnet! Come on!"

"That van is anything but a chick magnet," she answered. "We'll drive my car."

"Come on, it's full of candy!" he protested to deflating laughter.

And thus, the two of them, an unlikely pair, set off in Adriana's black Mercedes on what the rest of us dubbed a "humanitarian mission." They returned to the party before most people even knew they were missing.

I found myself in the kitchen with Ally and Julianne, who were scavenging in the refrigerator for something that might satisfy their sweet tooths. The girls emitted tiny shrieks of joy when they discovered an unopened sleeve of Girl Scout Cookies hiding behind a half-eaten box of apple pie.

"And the diet starts tomorrow!" Ally quipped as Julianne giggled.

Adriana, unbuttoning her black pea coat and draping it over the kitchen table, said, "Remember, nothing tastes as good as being thin feels."

She smiled wryly to let the girls know she was joking.

"I say nothing tastes as good as eating Thin Mints feels," Ally replied.

The three girls cracked up laughing.

"Actually, I totally agree," Adriana said. "But I tell myself I should moderate my sugar intake. Anyway, there's a dance party starting downstairs if you want to burn off the calories. I'll go outside and smoke a cigarette and meet you down there?"

"Sure," the girls replied.

Then Grouse passed through the kitchen with a fishing rod slung over his shoulder and a tackle box in his hand. Ally eyed him skeptically. "What are you doing, Ryan?"

"I'm going to drop a line in the koi fish pond in the parlor room."

"You're *what*?"

"That's right, I'm going to batter and deep fry a koi fish for dinner."

"No, you're not, Ryan," Ally said.

"What the hell gave you that idea?" I said, laughing.

"O'Leary bet me twenty dollars I wouldn't do it. But what's even better is he promised that if I hooked one out of the pond he would eat *sushi*!"

One thing about Grouse, I always thought, was that he could never be truly satisfied in the modern world because deep down he was a big-game hunter living in an era when it was no longer really possible to hunt big game. The territories for those animals had grown too restricted—and the human population too vast and technologically sophisticated—essentially rendering "the big hunt" unfair, a poser's farce, a preordained slaughter at the zoo.

I think Grouse genuinely regretted that he'd never be able to visit the African plains of the early twentieth century. It was easy for me to imagine him boarding an old propeller airplane in Tanganyika with a wildebeest skull in his carry-on luggage and a lion pelt in the hull.

Fishing, by comparison, was unsubstantial, and spectacularly so when factoring in modern sonar. It hadn't been a fair fight since the advent of the net, Grouse liked to say. He enjoyed it well enough, but the pursuit of r-species was only a minor thrill, he said, lacking the grandeur of an old-world bush hunt. And so, as with the koi fishing stunt—or our ice fishing trip—he treated it as a frivolity, as simply one more thing in the world that deserved to be openly mocked.

Fishing was to hunting, in Grouse's estimation, what the pigeon was to the silverback gorilla. *In fishing you're waiting for the bite; in hunting you're doing the bite.*

So off he went to hook a decorative koi fish out of an aquarium, more or less, while the rest of us headed downstairs to join the dance party in the basement.

An orgy of swirling, multicolored lights splashed down from an industrial lighting rack onto the dozen or so girls who crowded the checkerboard dance floor. Several of them pawed one another friskily as they cast playful, smoldering glares at the flat-footed boys standing along the periphery, evidently hoping to entice us to join them.

The most self-assured of these *femme fatales* was Adriana Babyk, who bounced lightly on her bare feet, twisting her slender hips, as her snug, spaghetti-strap black cocktail dress swayed like a young coconut palm.

As a general rule, my pals refrained from dancing until the penultimate upright stage of drunkenness—imminent blackout—and then we danced like the floor was on fire. That was true for all of us except Peter O'Leary, who, even sober, would prance around heedlessly, snapping his fingers, whirling his arms, turning into that rarest of merrymaking specimens: the heterosexual male who actually looks cool dancing.

We'd asked him once where he learned to groove like that, and he answered in a series of rhetorical questions: "Dancing is such a funny concept, no? I mean, it separates us from the animals, right? I wonder if it's accurate to say that humans became humans the first time a chimpanzee knowingly busted a move?" (I always thought it was the first time a chimpanzee broke wind and giggled.)

Now, a group of us huddled in the peanut gallery, looking on enviously as Peter improvised a high-octane two-step to a 1980s funk-soul tune, his arms flailing in front of his body while his feet tapped out a circuitous route on the floor.

"Hey, Peter!" Henry shouted over the throbbing bass notes as O'Leary spun by. "Did you ever accidentally slug yourself in the nuts while you were dancing?"

Adriana overheard the remark and burst out laughing, rewarding Henry with a flirtatious little butt shimmy and seductive smile. Ordinarily, Henry would miss obvious cues like these, but he'd evidently drunk just the right amount of liquor because he sidestepped toward her in a confident, rhythmic rejoinder, and as he did so, she beckoned him nearer with a curling index finger.

Meanwhile, Julianne was doing a one-two punch with her shoulders while I deployed my usual dance floor strategy of moving just enough that I wouldn't be accused of "not dancing," all the while not actually dancing. I glanced over at Henry and was surprised to see that he and Adriana had entered one another's orbit, so to speak.

The two of them were cautiously grinding their bodies together, and I could've sworn I heard her whisper into his ear: "This is happening for you tonight, Henry."

But her comment was drowned out by the music. His reply,

which I heard more clearly because he shouted it with a cupped hand beside his mouth, was: "That's great, as long as you don't have an uncle Guido who'll come after me later with a shotgun."

"Oh, my god!" Adriana shrieked. "How did you know? I do have an uncle Guido!"

Henry's dopey smile morphed into a fatalistic grimace.

"So, anyway, I have an uncle Gary," he quickly went on, evidently determining that his best strategy was to barrel forward with a non sequitur. "And he recently told me something, but I'm not sure what he meant. He said, 'Always remember when you're in a night club that a red flag under a black light is a white flag in broad daylight.'"

Adriana sipped her drink through a twisty straw and shook her head, partly as though she didn't understand what he meant either and partly as though she didn't care. When the song ended, and she no longer needed to shout, she said to Henry in ordinary volume: "Why didn't you come to our cabin over Fourth of July, Henry?"

Her proximity—and her tractor-beam gaze—boded well for him, I thought.

"I was there," he said, "but I had to leave early because I got attacked by a tick."

Adriana eyed him skeptically. "That's lame. You could've just pulled it out with a tweezers and poured some vodka on it."

"Yeah," he replied. "Well… um… this one was, uh… on my—"

He gazed down past his naval.

She snorted. "Oh my god!"

Regaining her composure, she asked, "How did *that* happen?"

"Well, you see, Grouse had borrowed my shorts earlier that afternoon when he went swimming in the lake, and he'd hung them on a tree branch to dry. And when I put them on later, I went commando-style because I'd gone swimming that day in my boxers."

"That's too much information, Henry," she said.

"Anyway, I discovered the little bugger while we were out

on the pontoon and immediately realized what had happened," he said.

Adriana was nibbling on her straw.

"Burrowed right into the skin," Henry said ruefully.

Adriana sought an off-ramp. "Do you know if it was a deer tick or a wood tick?"

Henry grinned slyly, and then went for it:

"Actually, I was hoping you could help me with that."

And thus, Henry re-wrote the greatest "clincher line" of all time. (The previous title-holder, incidentally, was Duce Babyk, who, after chatting up a mall slut one afternoon in the Southtown food court, worked up the nerve to say to her, "So, I've got four de-scrambled porno channels and a half-bottle of vodka back at my place. What do you say we go pick up some mixers?")

Henry didn't have long to savor his witty remark, however, because a new song came over the speakers that sent the room into giddy applause. It was the synthetic drums, juicy keyboards, and funky bass riff of Billy Ocean's hit "Caribbean Queen," and all eyes on the dance floor swept toward Adriana, who blushed and then beamed a smile, holding up her champagne flute in the universal gesture of "cheers!"

A year earlier, as a freshman, Adriana had won top prize in a "skin-to-win" contest in Acapulco after shimmying down to her undergarments—and then some. The final-round song was "Caribbean Queen," and the spring-break crowd roared as Adriana untied her black bikini top, letting her sprouting, tan-lined breasts pop out for the world to see. Even the nightclub's bouncers and military police were clapping in rhythm with the music and whistle-cheering. When Adriana was handed her trophy and complimentary "Roman Coke," her older brother (and chaperone, I might add) was outside on a beach chair, fooling around with a local girl.

Later, Duce laughed off concerns over what his sister had done, telling us in a mescal-drowned voice that a Mexican guy in a sombrero had approached him on the sun-lounger and said to him: "Hello, my friend. Would you like to marry my *seester*?"

The exaggerated pronunciation was the punch line.

Now, Adriana grabbed Henry's hand as she led him off the dance floor. "Come on, Hank," I heard her say. "Let's go make like Chinese New Year."

Henry glanced over his shoulder at me, his eyes bulging in disbelief, as the crowd cheered their departure.

A sultry R&B tune slowed things down on the dance floor, and I watched through the uneven darkness as Duce Babyk, freshly attired and hair-slicked following his tryst with the girls, paired off with Heather in back-to-back snowballs. She draped her arms around his neck, pressing her cheek against his shoulder, and it was hard to tell, the way she clung to him, whether she was sloppy drunk or just yielding to her post-coital affections. I rocked Julianne slowly in their direction, past other amorous couples, including, I was heartened to see, Robyn and Chloe, who were embracing each other.

When we were within earshot, we watched as Heather stepped back from Duce and gazed penetratingly into his eyes as she confessed: "I'm crazy about you."

"I know," Duce replied. "Me too, babe."

"You know I did that for you, right?"

He kissed her forehead.

"I know you did, babe. You're truly something else."

And he clasped her tight.

But Duce later told me privately that it was right then, after her naked declaration of feelings, that he "instantly and inexorably fell out of like with her."

Overhearing their exchange, Julianne looked up at me with a tremulous grin, but it turned playful when I squeezed her little derrière with both hands.

Then Grouse pushed through the crowd, sniffing at the air like a prairie dog and causing whatever romance still lingered on the dance floor to be promptly sucked up the proverbial chimney.

"Something stinks," he said, lifting an arm and sniffing one of his armpits. "Oh man, that smells ripe. Anyone want to step outside for some fresh air?"

With the music indicating another slow dance, several of us agreed it sounded like a capital idea, and Grouse led us out to the patio through the sliding glass door.

O'Leary was alone at the pig roast, carving thick slabs of meat onto an oversized ceramic platter while he took a break from the dance floor. As Julianne and I shuffled toward him, he nodded his head at a beautiful white frozen waterfall of a tree in a far corner of the backyard, and, adopting the pathetic, milksop voice of Elmer Fudd, he said, "I always wondered what happened to weeping widows du-wing win-tah."

I played along in a hushed tone. "Be vewy, vewy quiet. I'm hunting wabbits."

"It's weeping willow, not widow!" Julianne cried.

"Aw, shucks," said Peter, adding a feeble laugh, still in character.

"*Now, I say, boy!*" I continued as Foghorn Leghorn.

We could have gone on like that all night, through the whole Looney Tunes cast, but O'Leary had quietly set the platter down and begun tiptoeing past us with a finger to his lips. He had spotted prey: Grouse Boozer caught unawares, a beer bottle pressed to his mouth as he watched the steam rising from the emerald-lit swimming pool.

O'Leary stalked slowly at first and then suddenly lurched forward, thrusting his palms into Grouse's shoulder blades. As Grouse hit the water, he extended his left hand, the one holding the beer bottle, straight up into the air.

Through some lucky combination of the alcohol agreeing with him and the fact that he'd rescued the second half of his beer, Grouse surfaced with a smile on his face. "You bastard!" He laughed. Eyeing the bottle in his hand, he added, "Pretty good, huh?"

He set the bottle on the pool ledge and clumsily defrocked underwater, and then lobbed his soggy lump of clothes like a fat grenade toward the rest of us and climbed out of the pool.

Standing naked on the deck, he glanced down at himself and shook his head with a touch of mock shame.

"Can you believe this pitiful little thing?" he said. "It's not usually this shriveled, I swear."

The girls smirked as they stole furtive glances at his unit, but, politely, none let her jaw come unhinged.

"Christ," said Duce, "you're hung like a female hyena."

"I'm hung like a light switch," Grouse retorted. "Thank god it's always on."

"Ryan, your epidermis is showing," I said, echoing an old childhood taunt.

Grouse swigged his beer. "Well, if this isn't an invitation for a swim, I don't know what is."

And he frog-dived back into the pool.

O'Leary had promptly fled indoors seeking dry haven, and Ally turned to Julianne and said, "Come on, let's go put our bikinis on," and they disappeared through the sliding door, too.

As I pivoted to follow them, Grouse called out: "Get in, Bo, you pussy!"

But before I had a chance to respond, footsteps thundered in my periphery, and Duce Babyk, who had swiftly doffed his clothes, leaped high into the air over the pool, tucking his hairy limbs into a cannonball that sent tides of water plunging over the drainage grates. He surfaced, spit out a mouthful of pool water, and said in his best Scrooge McDuck impersonation: "Aye, I think I'll go for a swim in me money bin."

The excitement proved infectious. Heather and the church girls followed Duce's lead, stripping down to their colorful push-up bras and thong underwear before plugging their noses and pencil-jumping into the deep end. Then they quickly shed their undergarments, too, and tossed them onto the deck.

Not wanting to seem too puritanical, I took off my jeans and sweater and set them on a patio chair, but then I hesitated in my boxer shorts and bare feet. I was granted a temporary reprieve when Grouse hollered, "Hey, Bo, would you grab some beers and leave them by the pool?"

I dug three cans of moose piss out of a foam cooler near the pig roast and set them down beside the pool. Then I said to myself "to hell with it" and pulled off my boxer shorts, before dashing through the shadows and hurtling into the water.

Others had drifted outside, curious at the sudden frenzy, and many of them took off their clothes, too, before diving or jumping into the pool.

Queenie, never one to shy away from her "natural state," wasted no time in stripping down to her "industrial-strength panties," as Grouse called them, and then she peeled those off, too, revealing a muff as thick as if Gustave Courbet had painted it. Her voluptuous nude figure was clearly fashioned in the neo-classical tradition.

"*La maja desnuda!*" I bellowed, feigning extreme drunkenness from underneath the diving board.

To which Duce responded with a deep-chested "*Shamuuu!*" as his ape-like buttocks breached the surface of the hot tub at the opposite end of the pool.

When Julianne and Ally re-emerged on the pool deck, they were plainly stunned by the escalation that had transpired in their absence. The girls looked downright prude now, in their polka-dot bikinis, while the pool was filled with so many naked and partially naked bodies.

Queenie, with her heaving D-cups exposed, smiled at them and casually shrugged her shoulders before lowering herself into the water on the pool ladder.

"Bikinis?" I said, treading water. "That's not really in the spirit of things, girls. Why don't you take those off and hop in?"

"Um, I don't think so," Ally replied emphatically.

Julianne nodded in agreement, her arms akimbo. It was a defiant pose that belied an obvious inner fear that she might be pressed further on the matter. The girls made their way around the deck and stepped down cautiously into the hot tub.

The details turn a bit hazy around this point, but I remember climbing out of the pool, drunker than I thought I was, and walking butt naked to the edge of the diving board, where I tucked my genitals between my legs before whining in a childish voice: "Come on, you guys. Give it back."

Scattered laughter but not worth the gambit.

"Bo, you've got a tumor growing out the back side!" roared Duce, winning raucous laughter all around.

Julianne blushed and slid down deeper into the hot tub, wetting the rest of her hair. I swan-dived into the pool, swimming the length of it underwater and surfacing near Julianne. She reached over the tiled divider and tapped me on the shoulder, giggling silently as she held her bikini bottoms above the surface of the bubbling cauldron. I couldn't help but think of her furry little rabbit pelt down there stewing in a chlorine broth.

Even in our wildest fantasies, it was impossible to imagine this scene unfolding in the daytime, sober, in ordinary reality. In the summers, these same girls could be found lying in their bikinis at the far end of the country club swimming pool, rotating all afternoon like gas-station hot dogs.

They'd slather themselves in coconut oil and flip through glossy women's magazines while, every few minutes, another caddy on the golf course would wander curiously close to the brown picket fence, looking for a lost ball that he knew damn well was in the first cut of rough beside the fairway.

As far as gratuitous skin was concerned, the best the caddy could hope for was a slightly repositioned bikini strap to prevent an awkward tan line or maybe an extra bit of tit bulging out of its holster. But that was all. The "bits and pieces" were simply inconceivable—dream stuff resigned to one's imagination during a long, hot shower.

Lo and behold, Goldy received a scholarship offer!

He emerged on the pool deck while the rest of us were frolicking in the water and trudged in his baggy chinos and untucked dress shirt onto the diving board to deliver his good news. As he stood there on the plank, he shook crushed ice into his mouth from a University of Minnesota plastic souvenir cup and chomped it noisily with his molars.

"Coach Brown called me at home before I left for Murray's and formally made the offer. I told him I wanted to discuss it with my parents, but that I was probably going to accept it. So, yeah, it looks like I'm going to be a Golden Gopher," he said.

A small applause broke out.

"Oh, Goldy, I'm so happy for you I could cry," said Grouse, who was carving himself a light snack at the pig roast, dripping wet and nude in the shadows. "If I cry, will you drink a beer with me to celebrate?"

"I'll tell you what, Boozer. If you cry, yes, I'll drink a beer with you," Goldy responded.

Our behemoth buddy had never in his life taken even a sip of beer. He had never professed even the slightest curiosity in knowing what it tastes like. Therefore, a contest of sorts had begun, and for the rest of the night Grouse would fall silent at long intervals while a look of steely determination settled over his face—an expression that was like a grotesque parody of a Venetian tragedy mask—as he tried to will himself to tears.

"I haven't cried in years," Grouse said. "It's not as easy as you'd think."

"Well, keep trying," Goldy replied. "I'm thirsty tonight."

Genester Odell Jefferson had also been at the dinner, Goldy told us, and Coach Brown had informed G.O. that he too was receiving a scholarship offer to play offensive line.

"Which means Genester and I might be *teammates*, if you can believe it," said Goldy, shaking his head at the irony. "We might end up competing for the same position. Ha!"

"No kidding," I said. "Well, either way, that's a hell of an accomplishment and a real honor."

Watching the diving board flex under Goldy's tremendous weight reminded me of an Easter Sunday years earlier when my dad held me upside-down by the ankles at the country club swimming pool as a photo gag. I must have been about seven years old. We were dressed in our church clothes and had just finished brunch, and the diving board bent in a similar way under the weight of the two of us. As my dad doubled over, struggling with his grip, my neatly combed hair dipped into the pre-season pool water—which stunk like a shrimp farm—and my mom snapped a photo of us laughing, red-faced, before my dad reeled me up as quickly as he could.

Goldy put more spring into it now, bending his knees like he was on a trampoline, trying to launch someone to the moon. I thought he was going to snap it in half. He giggled like a fat kid on a sugar high but then regained his composure.

"So the offer is on the table," he said, "although I suppose it technically isn't official until I sign the papers in February." He looked down at me clinging to a sidewall in the pool as he added: "The jockey could still fall off the horse."

He was referring to an afternoon the prior summer when he and I nearly won a thousand dollars on a Pick Three wager at Canterbury Downs. Our long-shot horse in the second race had won by disqualification after the winning horse's jockey toppled off his mare on the final turn. We stood to make a veritable high-school fortune on a two-dollar bet, and our horse in the third race was practically a shoo-in at 7/4 odds minutes ahead of post time. We could hardly believe our luck.

I was already spending my loot as the ponies trotted out toward the starting gate. I couldn't decide between a big-screen TV for my bedroom and a new set of golf clubs. Then a voice crackled over the grandstand loudspeaker: "Ladies and gentlemen, there's a jockey change for Hold Your Pockets." That was our horse. "Please scratch Luis Quionez. Davie Hogan will now be riding the No. 4 horse," the announcer added.

"My god," Goldy moaned. "Look at that guy. He looks like my uncle Bernie."

Sure enough, old Davie was bulging out of his form-fitting neon silks—not exactly the flyweight munchkin we would have wished for in a last-minute jockey change. He looked like he should have been riding a Zamboni—not a thoroughbred horse.

After plodding out of the starting gate, Hold Your Pockets immediately fell to the bottom third of the pack and never threatened. When the other horses came thundering around the final bend, ours was trailing by a hopeless dozen or more lengths. And yet Goldy clung to the chain-link fence at the finish line, holding himself about a foot off the ground, as he waved our betting slip over his head, screaming: "Run, you *fat nag*! Run!"

Alas, Posse East Queso, at 18-1 odds, practically sauntered the final two furlongs to victory.

On the diving board, Goldy grabbed hold of his skull with both hands and twisted his neck, producing a sound like a heavy zipper coming unstuck as he cracked his vertebrae. I thought he was trying to tear it clean off.

"That's terrific news, Goldy," said Duce. "I mean—that's big-time D-1 ball."

"Thanks, Babyk."

"I'll come into town to watch you guys play, and you can introduce me to some of that fine Gopher tail on the sidelines."

Speaking of which: another pair of streakers now came dashing out from the house, their bare feet slapping against the pavement in quick, mincing steps, before both bodies went cartwheeling through the air into the pool. It was Henry and Adriana, basking in the warm afterglow of his cherry popping.

It was all quite a scene, frankly: all those naked and semi-naked bodies. But I repeat myself, I know. Partly I do so for my own reassurance, knowing that my traitorous memory had turned unforgivably hazy. I recall a group of guys in the hot tub badgering Jessica Miles, urging her to stand up and pull down her panties to prove she wasn't a fire crotch, while Porter sat on the edge in his boxer shorts, looking on uncomfortably.

"I'll tell you what," one of the guys persisted in that smug, cocksure way of a drunken high school alpha dog, "if you show us yours, Henry will show you his."

"I just saw Henry's!" she cried. "And I don't need to see it again!"

But, of course, she ultimately acquiesced, much to Porter's chagrin. Jessica stood up and peeled down her leopard-print undies just far enough to reveal an auburn-brown mat of pubes that were deemed by the attending jury to be "not all that fiery." The cheers she received were louder than the ones Goldy got when he announced he was getting a scholarship.

Good vibrations were in the air, it seemed, and I desired to rub the genie's lamp myself, so I pinched Julianne's rear end underwater. She turned around eel-like and wrapped me in a slippery embrace.

"Let's go inside," I whispered to her.

She leaned closer, as if to whisper something in reply, but instead just nibbled my ear lobe and said, "Okay, let's go."

I followed her up the pool ladder and through the sliding glass door into the house, where the music was still being blasted at full volume even though no one was on the dance floor.

While Julianne showered, I sat on the edge of the queen-sized bed in the guest room, admiring the regal, silver-and-gold, damask-patterned wallpaper and matching silk-covered throw pillows—such impeccable displays of good taste! But I also noticed, rather curiously, that the bedspread was rumpled on one side and not quite perfectly cornered. Finding this a bit odd—and sensing that more was possibly amiss—I inspected my surroundings more intently.

"I knew it!" I blurted out loud when I saw the torn-open condom wrapper in the trashcan. We were in the room Henry had used with Adriana, not twenty minutes earlier! Facing a moral dilemma, then, of whether or not I should divulge my findings to Julianne, I heeded the devil on my left shoulder as I took about nine handfuls of facial tissue off the bedside table and used them to conceal the evidence.

When Julianne emerged from the bathroom a few minutes later wrapped in a towel, her hair glistening wet, I said to her, "I want to rinse off the chlorine, too."

I had dried myself with a small hand towel, which I now clutched prudishly to my midsection as a fig leaf.

She waved me into the bathroom like a graceful matador, and as we traded places I noted to myself that if heaven indeed exists, one scent that will surely follow from this world is that of a bathroom after a beautiful girl showers in it.

I registered another subtle throb when I locked the door behind me and noticed Adriana's black cocktail dress carelessly discarded on the white-tiled floor. That throb doubled pace when I saw her bright pink bra—still warm, perhaps, I didn't check—resting atop a pile of dirty clothes in a white rattan laundry hamper. Men are like bloodhounds for these kinds of details.

Steam hung densely in the air when I finished my shower, and I wiped a layer of condensation off the mirror with my hand. Wrapping a towel around my waist, I decided—as one does in these situations—to examine the drawers and cabinets more thoroughly in case any other titillating objects were waiting to be discovered. Beneath the sink, I found a blood-pressure cuff and stethoscope, along with a half-dozen empty prescription pill bottles. The doorknob twisted and slammed into the dead bolt.

"One minute, babe," I said.

"Hurry up," her little voice replied.

I hung the stethoscope around my neck and studied myself in the damp mirror. When I opened the door I planned to say to her, "Doctor Humbert will see you now," but Julianne beat me to the punch line.

"Mister Hardwick!" she gasped.

(Kid always was ahead of her time.)

She was lying on her stomach on the bed, propped up on her elbows, her palms supporting her chin. She was, if I wanted to be poetic about it, a vision of succulence in its human form: a breathtaking little creature, half-wet, in snug jeans and a tank top with no bra. I said to myself: "Just seeing her there smiling like that makes me indescribably joyful."

As I approached her, she rolled onto her side and puffed out her belly, swelling it to fill her tight shirt, and, being funny, she asked me, "Do you think this is what I'll look like when I'm pregnant?"

I bent down and kissed her wet hair, inhaling the sweet apple fragrance of what was probably Adriana's shampoo.

"Something like that," I said.

I leaned over and switched off the bedside lamp, transforming our bodies into silhouettes, outlined by the faint light that was seeping under the bathroom door. I nuzzled Julianne's warm neck and briefly entertained what I knew even then was a sinful thought: that it was strangely pleasant, erotic even, as we pulled back the bedcovers, knowing that Adriana had been naked in those same sheets a short while earlier. The knowledge was both exhilarating and somehow intimidating.

Julianne and I began tuning our instruments ahead of the symphony, so to speak. She propped her little butt in the air so I could help her wriggle out of her jeans. With my eyes adjusted to the darkness, I could see that her underwear was patterned with cartoonish red butterflies and yellow daisies.

I pulled her shirt over her head and she slinked forward, stretching her hands to the far corners of the mattress, her hips writhing almost imperceptibly. Her back was a slender canvas of bronze silk. She had delicate shoulder blades, and just above her pouty little butt was the faintest trace of peach fuzz. I kissed the upper reaches of her back and neck, and then rolled her over, sunny-side up, and kissed her softly on the lips.

"Wait," she suddenly whispered, frowning in the darkness.

"What's that?" I said.

"I'm—I'm actually out of order," she said meekly.

"Really?" I said.

"Yeah, I'm *temporarily* unavailable. It's such bad timing, I know." And she giggled nervously.

Then, for the first time since we'd snuck away to the bedroom, I noticed the garbled party sounds coming from the far reaches of the basement. As we lied there in motionless embrace, the urgency of our passion dissipated like a pricked soap bubble.

"Actually, I just really want you to earn it," she said, trying to relieve some of the tension that had crept into the room. I laughed and pecked her on the cheek but didn't say anything. She lowered her head to my chest and left it there, her cold, damp hair draped over my bare skin. A couple of minutes later, as we both gazed up through the darkness toward the ceiling, Julianne asked, "If I got pregnant, would we get married?"

"If you got pregnant, I'd buy you a gift certificate to the abortion clinic," I joked.

"What?" she shrieked with offended laughter, and I could feel her smile go limp. "You wouldn't want to keep it?"

"What, as a souvenir?"

"Well, if that's how you feel, I don't think we should be doing this," she said, in her unfailingly sweet, girlish tone.

"We're not," I said, with a laugh.

"Do you hate me?" she asked.

I laughed again and kissed her on the forehead.

She ran an index finger down my chest.

"Of course not," I said. "Why would I hate you?"

"Because we can't do it tonight?"

She sat up, brushing her damp hair back around her ears.

"It doesn't really matter, babe," I said. "The timing isn't all that important. And I definitely don't hate you."

"Do you still like me?"

She had rephrased the question to sound like a four-year-old who had accidentally spilled grape juice on the carpet.

"Of course I still like you," I said, stroking her leg. "Just not as much as I did fifteen minutes ago."

She giggled and slammed me in the face with one of the silk-covered throw pillows. Then she rolled off the bed and began putting on her clothes. When we left the room a minute later, we heard the desperate sounds of overindulgence coming from a hallway bathroom. It was Sandra Flanagan praying to the commode. I peeked in through the cracked-open door. Peter was holding her hair up in a ponytail, rubbing her back, while Sandra kneeled on the floor.

Spotting me, Peter shrugged and said, "She's paying the tax for too much fun."

To which Sandra groaned, her head deep in the porcelain bowl, and bellowed, "*Soak the rich!*"

After a few more voluminous hurls, she produced the same empty sound a toilet makes when you flush it too soon before the tank re-fills. Apparently she had purged her stomach of its disagreeable abundance.

"*Ohhh!*" I heard her moaning as we walked away. "Now I've got hot pipes."

From upstairs came the vigorous sound of men singing: "*For He's a Jolly Good Fellow! For He's a Jolly Good Fellow! For He's a Jolly Good Fellow! Which Nobody Can Deny!*" It was an incongruous pairing: their ironic jubilation and my regret.

Julianne and I were drawn toward the sound of the merry voices, which we soon realized were coming from the kitchen. When we got there, the singing died and someone suggested it was time to set fire to the cannabis and summon the ganja gods: it was time to get high.

The living room curtains were drawn, the lamps were switched off, and the sleekly minimalist, overwhelmingly white interior was illuminated only by a small, decorative gas fireplace, whose faint, bluish-orange flames cast a sickly pallor over the faces in the room. A few people were sprawled on the angular white sofa and ottoman, and on the walnut-trimmed divan, while others reclined on the shaggy rug on their elbows or sat Indian-style on the swirled-marble floor in front of the fireplace. Two joints, rolled purely with marijuana, no tobacco, began to circulate in opposite directions: one clockwise, the other counterclockwise.

The joints would pause briefly at intervals and hiss, flaring up between a pair of lips, before continuing their roughly circular journeys around the room. The grass Henry and Adriana had brought back from Elliott's house was in a plain cardboard shoebox marked "The Grim Creeper" in black felt pen.

I couldn't see the hands on the golden clock on the mantel, but I hesitated to disrupt the meditative silence that now filled the room, so I said nothing. I guessed it was around ten o'clock. I had been stoned at my parents' house before, and I tended to be slightly paranoid there. I felt as though the dog looked at me funny, like he knew I was askew—not judging me so much as measuring, with his keen animal sense, whether I could still be trusted despite my demonic, bloodshot eyes.

My curfew was midnight, and I knew I wouldn't be home by then if I partook in the smoking session and waited for my head to fully clear. At the earliest, I figured I could be home by one o'clock, which would give me another three hours or so to travel full circle from mildly drunk to ravishingly high and back to moderate sobriety.

I thought of a trick I had once played on my mother when I got home at 1:30am and told her it was 11:30pm, knowing her night vision wasn't very good and that she would likely assume my dad's pillow was eclipsing the missing digit. It had worked, and I wondered if it might work again. As far as my dad was concerned, I was only too late if I brought in the newspaper with me. He seldom awoke when I came home.

Julianne had appealed to her young-at-heart mom for a "late curfew" and been granted one on the grounds that she not wake up the whole house—and especially her dad—when she came in.

As fate should have it, both joints reached Julianne at the same time, one from me and another from the opposite direction. I had taken a cautious, measured drag on the one, being careful not to fall comatose in the first round. When it came to getting high, I was admittedly a bantamweight.

Julianne shrugged amusedly as she found herself pinching a joint in each hand, and quiet laughter rippled through the room.

"Beginner's luck," Duce called out.

"How should I—?" she asked, looking at me.

"Here," I said, relieving her of one.

Julianne eyed me studiously as I flicked the lighter, took a cursory puff, and sent it on its way.

"Come on, take a big drag," Duce teased me. "You smoke like my grandmother."

I grinned silently across the room at him.

"Can you help me light it?" Julianne asked me.

She had never smoked anything before, even cigarettes, and so I held up the lighter for her and ignited it as she pinched the tightly rolled joint delicately in her fingertips.

Sitting in a white Chesterfield armchair opposite us, Duce instructed her: "Hold your breath, make a wish, count to three."

The tip flared as Julianne puffed on the joint. When she tried to inhale she hacked out a thick cloud of smoke but was undeterred, and on her next attempt her slender shoulders rose evenly as her lungs took in the smoke.

"Mmm," she said, pausing to regard the glowing end, which she held up in front of her face. "I like the way it smells."

Duce interjected again, this time in song: "*On your way to where the air... is... sweet!*"

The others remained silent.

In a deep, theatrical voice, he went on: "You'd better close your eyes, my child, in order to be better in tune with the infinite."

Julianne puffed more confidently on it now, taking another slow, steady drag before passing it along.

"Julianne," said Duce, "why does a sky fly a cloud?"

She gazed at him blankly through the lingering smoke and semi-darkness.

"I don't know," she said. "Why?"

"Why, why, why, why, why, why?" Duce replied. "I wonder why, too."

He tapered off into silence.

"Why don't you shut the hell up?" I said with a smile.

"I wonder why, too," he said, returning a grin. "Why, why, why, why, why, why."

Then he spoke no more: no more songs or riddles.

The first time I ever smoked pot was the summer before our junior year. Elliott had brought a glass pipe and zip-lock bag full of weed to the Fourth of July fireworks at Cornelius Hill. I'll never forget how the sensation of being stoned warped not only my perception of that evening but also managed to retroactively deflower my earlier childhood impressions of the holiday. Suddenly, the John Philip Sousa Memorial Band was laughably schmaltzy, the rah-rah patriotism seemed trumped up and forced, and the overall pomp felt childish and regressive.

After the fireworks ended, we crossed a pedestrian overpass to the other side of the highway, where Elliott had parked his car. I called "shotgun" once the car was in sight, but as soon as I went for the door, Duce lowered his shoulder and tackled me onto a grassy front lawn.

"Wait!" he cried.

"What?" I said, genuinely alarmed.

His eyes glowed with fear as he pinned me to the ground. I was stunned.

"Don't let the bugs in the car," he said.

Almost instantly, we both recognized the extreme foolishness of what he had said and buckled over in giggles. By the time we stopped laughing neither of us could remember if he'd meant it as a joke or if he had actually lost his mental bearings for a moment. But no sooner had we gotten into the car and set our course for the all-night pancake house than we spotted one of the proboscis-faced little bastards fluttering in the light cast by the passing street lamps.

Which led to a seemingly profound paradox: *Do we open the windows so it will fly out? But, if we do that, won't another one possibly fly in?*

The inimitable voice of Daffy Duck tugged me out of my reverie, as I traded one bizarre mental image for another. The sound emanated from a blaring television in another room. Daffy was saying, "Thanks for the sour persimmons, cousin."

But that moment was cut short too because Grouse howled in a far-off corridor: "*Usquebaugh!*" Then, still shouting, he added, "*I'm a-gone get me a Valley Tan!*"

Grouse had quit smoking pot a few months earlier after a "severely unpleasant episode" in which he took a "monstrous, fully committed" bong rip and "heard a flywheel snap" inside his head (his descriptors). He spent the next three hours staring, in dull terror, at a bull-moose rug on his kitchen floor, groaning pitifully to himself while incoherently muttering parts of Theodore Roosevelt's "Dare Mighty Things" speech.

In Babyk's living room, two fresh joints had begun circulating, one of which now reached Henry on the sofa. Adriana was sitting on the floor in front of him, leaning affectionately against his legs, and Duce leered at the newly romantic couple for a moment before addressing his younger sister's suitor in a mildly antagonistic tone: "How you doing, Henry? All good?"

The joint flared up as Henry toked on it, and he just sighed and shook his head, before replying in an incredulous, almost nostalgic tone through a heavy fog of marijuana smoke: "*Goddamn… motherfuckin'… paradise high.*"

And that about summed things up.

We continued smoking ourselves into virtual catatonia, passing all the familiar signposts. First came the insane giggles. It felt like we were on a bad television sit-com.

"Duce, you like getting high *too much!*" cried Queenie. "The last time we were all here, you got so stoned so fast that by the time the joint reached you the second time around the circle, you were already passed out."

"I was resting my eyes!" he protested.

(The studio audience laughs.)

"The problem is," he added, "you don't know the difference between sleeping and resting my eyes. This is resting my eyes."

(He closes his eyes and the audience roars in laughter.)

"Honey, are you taking the pot?"

A shrill, motherly voice has intruded on the scene.

(Cheers, more laughter from the audience: *it's Ma!*)

Actually, it was Henry doing an impersonation of Elliott Sturgeon's mother the time a group of us was smoking dope in Elliott's garage while his parents sat in the den watching network television. Henry had accidentally dropped the glass pipe on the ground, shattering it in a thousand pieces, and we'd been forced to improvise by smoking out of a crushed pop-can pricked with needle holes. When we went back inside, Mrs. Sturgeon took one look at us and burst into tears, accusing her son of "taking the pot," as she memorably phrased it.

"I think we ought to go see Jerry Garcia," Duce said.

"What?" one of the church girls said.

"We should go to Jerry's grocery," Duce repeated.

When I was stoned it sometimes felt like I was reading a book while someone in a nearby room was talking on the phone. Words were obviously being spoken, but what the hell did they mean? Even if I paid attention, all I heard were garbled sounds, like the grown-ups in Peanuts cartoons. I couldn't decipher the words even when I replayed the preceding five-second audio clip in my head. Pot turned me into a semi-retarded savage, in other words.

"How are we going to get there?" Robyn said.

"I'll drive," I said, standing up and doing some cross-body limbering exercises as part of my false sell. "It's not that far."

"No, you won't, Swilly," said Goldy, who was sitting in the room with us but hadn't smoked. "I'll drive you guys."

Hook, line, and sinker. It was like watching a largemouth bass impale one of its eyes on a fishhook. Goldy didn't have a driver's license, but that didn't matter. He considered it a "moral imperative" to chauffeur his stoned buddies to the grocery store so we could load up on all the major junk food groups. He was good like that.

We were all fairly Dondered and Blitzened by this point, as our merry little band of slant-eyed, cotton-mouthed miscreants tiptoed out the back door and across the heated asphalt driveway to a detached second garage. Duce tapped a security code onto a slender black keypad and the door rose. Then he pressed a button on his keychain and the taillights on the glossy black Suburban flashed and the horn gave a quick honk, indicating that the anti-theft system was disabled.

He tossed the keys to Goldy and we all filed into the belly of the three-quarter-ton beast, with Duce riding co-pilot.

When Goldy turned the ignition, the dashboard lit up like a spaceship's, a glowing panel of richly saturated neon indicators, and the stereo launched into a full-throated choral rendition of "Oh Come, All Ye Faithful." Duce jabbed a finger at the dial, irritably muttering something about "fucking Bethlehem," as he switched the radio to the classic rock station and turned down the volume. Then he dug a radar detector out of the glove box and plugged it into the cigarette lighter. The device struck me as a profound technological supermarvel, and I got tangled up in my thoughts considering what it all meant.

Ditto when we arrived at the grocery store and the glass entrance doors sensed our presence, sliding open noiselessly, and then slid shut again behind us. Our ape forebears appeared to be about a billion years in the rearview mirror.

Jerry's exuded all the small-town charm of an upstate mom-and-pop grocer, with handwritten signage advertising "Special Deals" in colorful bubble letters, with pumpkin-and-cream-colored checkerboard floors, and with a veritable profusion of holiday-season paraphernalia, such as mistletoe, tinsel, and cut-out cardboard snowflakes, which were hanging from the ceilings and mounted on displays.

Inside the store, we scattered in different directions.

Julianne, who had been silent on the ride over, grabbed my hand and pulled me down one of the center aisles, and I kept grinning to myself, imagining I was on that popular television game show I used to watch as a kid when I stayed home sick from school. I couldn't help but laugh out loud thinking of that cheery-voiced announcer describing our movements in play-by-play. Julianne led me straight to the non-prescription pharmaceutical aisle, where she found what she was looking for right away. (She would've been a great contestant on the show!)

She shook a tiny plastic bottle of Visine out of the box, tilted her head back, and let a couple of drops fall just above her eyebrows, practically on the middle of her forehead.

"There," she said, blinking her eyes, satisfied. "That's much better."

But her reprieve was short-lived, as her face suddenly seized up in a disagreeable pucker. Resist it though she did, she reared back and unleashed a terrific sneeze that knocked her back a few steps. She stood dazed for a moment, leaning against one of the shelves, bracing for potential aftershocks. After she'd steadied herself, she gestured with her thumb and forefinger to let me know she was okay.

"Whoa," I said. "I thought we were going to lose you."

She giggled softly.

But those giggles were like kindling underneath a campfire. She giggled harder and harder still, and it proved contagious. Soon, we were both convulsing in eyes-shut, tears-streaming-down-the-cheeks, open-mouthed guffaws, culminating in one of us "shhh"-ing the other, holding up a finger, then begging for a "time out," and punctuated all the while by more trembling, full-body laughter.

"Shhh! Baby, you're giving us away!" Julianne pleaded in an attempted whisper.

I managed to mute my laughter, but the throbbing pressure behind my eyes continued without mercy. We finally regained our composure after what felt like an eternity, and the episode concluded as I said to Julianne in my best solemn priest tone:

"Bless you, Julianne, for you have sneezed."

And those were the magic words, apparently, because the "giggles" instantly lifted and we returned our attention with all due sincerity to the original task at hand.

We stalked up and down the aisles, filling our basket with cheddar cheese puffs, whole-fat chocolate milk, gummy worms, and a jar of locally made pickles—something to arouse each of the vital taste buds. Julianne also tossed into our basket a loaf of impossibly white bread and a pack of American cheese singles. In the canned deli-meat aisle, I pointed to the tins of mystery meat on the shelves and joked: "Mama Cass ought to be careful around here. She choked to death on a pork-loaf sandwich, you know."

"Who's Mama Cass?"

"The Mamas and the Papas," I said.

"Oh," she said.

The name obviously didn't register, and I figured it wasn't worth delving into the legend of the lethal tinned-ham sandwich.

Indeed, the grocery store seemed to be a treacherous place. A wet-floor sign in the refrigerated section depicted the silhouette of a man in the midst of a tremendous fall. The poor bastard looked like he'd been pushed off a skyscraper.

"You'd better be careful," I said to Julianne. "Right now, it's slippery."

"Huh?"

"Right now, it's slippery... Right now *is* slippery."

I had repeated the phrase because I liked the way it sounded—it felt slippery coming off my tongue. In my mind I went on repeating it until I'd tied myself in another hopeless mental knot, which was unfortunate because I was suddenly convinced that I was on the cusp of a momentous philosophical revelation. It's funny how banalities can seem so profound when you're on the pot.

Shortly we found ourselves plunked down, cross-legged, on the tiled floor in the breakfast cereal aisle, where we were shoveling into our mouths fistfuls of Peanut Butter Cap'n Crunch, alternatively chomping noisily on the sweetened oat cereal and laughing in fits at something—but we couldn't remember what it was anymore.

Chloe entered the aisle. "Have you guys seen Robyn?" she

asked. She was holding a wax-paper bag with a glazed doughnut visible through a cellophane window. I heard the heavenly angels singing and trumpets blaring in another aisle, as I experienced a holy vision of those glistening, pillow-soft delicacies that had earned Jerry's bakery its stellar reputation.

"We can't forget doughnuts," I said to Julianne.

"I think she's in the freezer section," Julianne told Chloe.

Duce wheeled a cart into the aisle, but I was already on my feet with my hand extended, pulling Julianne up.

"We'll meet you in the checkout lane," I told Duce.

There's an old saying among doughnut connoisseurs that no doughnut could possibly taste as good as a doughnut shop smells. As scents go, the doughnut shop ranks right up there with the used bookstore, the wood-burning fireplace, and, indeed, the bathroom after a beautiful young girl showers in it.

Arriving at the bakery, I thought of dear Homer Price and his runaway doughnut machine. The book suddenly struck me as a form of pornography for children, but I quickly vanquished the thought, telling myself that it did nothing but encourage the corruption of youth and the perversion of innocence.

Using the plastic tongs, I selected two plump raised-glazed doughnuts from the bakery case and plopped them into a wax-paper bag. Julianne asked me for one powdered-sugar doughnut hole. *God, I loved that girl!*

We met Duce and the others in the checkout lane. Their cart was loaded in a towering pyramid that included five boxes of macaroni and cheese, a few cans of quick-bake cinnamon rolls, three frozen pizzas, two bags of tortilla chips, a Brower blueberry muffin, a jar of salsa, two pounds of hamburger beef, a dozen hamburger buns, one empty box of Peanut Butter Cap'n Crunch, two packs of smoked salmon, and a tub of raspberry cream cheese—and that was just what I could see on top.

The girl working the cash register went to our high school. Her name was Dorothy T. Holmes. She had shown up one afternoon at the student newspaper asking if she could write a "Miss Lonelyhearts" column, but Morty and Miss Fogey turned her down, saying they felt like she was merely trying to amuse *herself* with her application. For instance, she had insisted in the interview—adamantly insisted—on keeping the middle initial in her byline. A derisive smirk tugged at her lips each time she mentioned it. Her first column, she said, would offer advice to a sophomore girl whose parents had euthanized her cat while she was away at summer camp—and later told her the cat had cancer.

"My counsel will *ooze* with empathy," Dorothy said.

She was a textbook-case high school loner who clearly felt that the world's presiding social order was total bullshit. She wore too much dark eyeliner and had a pierced lip, and it was evident, judging by her slumping shoulders and sour gaze as we wheeled our cart into her aisle, that she considered us an unwelcome intrusion into an otherwise passable, if somewhat boring, night. Of course, what her reaction signaled in practical terms was that she was an ideal target: precisely the sort of person Duce enjoyed taking aim at.

As she listlessly slid the frozen pizzas across the barcode scanner, Duce leaned over the counter and recited a popular advertising slogan from the time: "It's not delivery, it's—"

"No, it's a goddamn Tombstone," she interjected flatly.

At this slightest of provocations, Duce's spine went erect. "You don't seem very happy," he said, plainly trying to goad her.

She studied him for a long, dull moment, as if deliberating an uppercut reply, but then just shook her head, refusing the gambit, and mumbled something under her breath, masking her obvious contempt behind a curtain of greasy black hair.

Julianne knew Dorothy from the high school orchestra and bid a quiet, friendly "hello," but either Dorothy didn't hear Julianne or she ignored her.

At the winter concert, Dorothy had performed a solo, "Taps," the military funeral dirge, on a brooding cello, and it was a powerful sight: she wore a willowy black dress and ankle-high army surplus boots, and she played her instrument like a coffin-maker saws wood. In the concert program, where students could write brief messages to their parents and teachers, or tell of their college plans, hers included only a single gloomy line: "Buzzards ought to fly north during winter."

Even more memorably, perhaps, Dorothy had attended our school's Halloween party that fall as "Cyanotic." It was a theme costume. She wore a blue sweatsuit and painted her exposed skin a faint, chalky blue and told everyone she'd died from autoerotic asphyxiation "while jerking off." It might have been funny if not for the fact that one of our classmates, her ex-boyfriend, it turned out, had died that way over the summer. Come to think of it, it was still funny, in a way.

"Ah, for Christ's sake, hang on a second," Duce said to her now, dashing off. He returned with an armload of ant-killer and sticky paper.

"You see, we're buying all these snacks," he explained, "and surely someone's going to drop some crumbs on the floor, luring those damn vermin into the house, and then my parents will know we threw a party."

"Right," Goldy said sarcastically. "Because there wouldn't be mice and ants in the house unless your drunk friends bought late-night snacks and dropped their crumbs on the floor. Smart thinking, Babyk. I see your point."

"Anyway," said Duce, ignoring Goldy's remarks. "You know what they say: *time to decrease the surplus population.* Is that really what they say?"

Dorothy could no longer contain herself. "Do you think the devil himself could conceive of a more gruesome way to kill a sentient being than with bait and sticky paper?"

"I bet he could if he tried," Duce replied.

"You think we ought to go for old-fashioned wire traps?" I butted in. "Would that be the more humanitarian option?"

Dorothy shook her head but didn't say anything else, and I regretted having inserted myself in the conversation.

"In case you're wondering," Duce said to Dorothy, "we're not drunk."

She strained to look more disinterested.

He leaned over the counter and whispered, "We're stoned." And with that, he seized a pack of jumbo batteries off the impulse rack and slammed them onto the conveyor belt.

"For the *old powerhouse dildo*," he said with gusto, as Chloe and Robyn burst into giggles.

I might have been the only one who heard Dorothy when she replied, again under her breath: "If you actually manage to catch a mouse with this thing, I'll bet none of you has the balls to put it out of its misery with a hammer."

Duce pulled his wallet out of his pocket and handed her a credit card. The rest of us offered to pay him for our share, but he brushed us off. "No, no," he said. "This one is on me."

Dorothy swiped his credit card.

The machine beeped.

She tried again.

It beeped again.

"Umm, I don't think your card is working," she said with a slight grin, enjoying the tiniest of pleasures in his misfortune.

"Here, let me see that—" said Duce, reaching for the card and inspecting it more closely. "Well, Jesus H. Christ, look-ee here. The damn thing expired last month!"

He handed me the card and said, "Don't say I never gave you anything, Bo."

I glanced at the card before putting it in my front pocket with my house keys, and Duce counted off eight crisp twenties and waited for his change. The rest of us hoisted the bulging paper grocery bags into our armpits like oversized footballs, and as we moved toward the exit Duce turned over his shoulder and called out to Dorothy: "Have a wonderful night, sweet tits."

In the parking lot we bumped into Andy Morton, who was still wearing the red insulated nylon jacket with "Rink

Attendant" stenciled on the back in white letters. He told us he was stopping into Jerry's to buy some microwave buttered popcorn to eat with the thermos full of eggnog Henry had given him at the warming house earlier, before heading home to watch "A Charlie Brown Christmas," which he had taped the previous week, and listen to old Chet Baker albums until he fell asleep.

"Is this beautiful or what?" exclaimed Morty, wild-eyed, gesturing at the fresh snowfall that half-buried a number of cars and glittered atop the lampposts like mounds of diamond dust.

"Absolutely," I said, with newfound appreciation that was undoubtedly enhanced by the ganja. "Nothing in the world is more lovely than a Minnesota snowstorm in December."

"That's right. It's the snowstorms in April that make you want to puke."

The car tracks in the parking lot had turned grayish-brown with sand and soot, and the crisp, frozen air was so thick with exhaust from the grocery store's pick-up lane that you could practically chew on it with your rear molars. But I kept those observations to myself.

"How was the party?" Morty asked.

Julianne gave a silent double thumbs-up.

"Ham-bone city," I replied.

He laughed.

"Were a lot of people there?"

"A lot of people *are* there," I said, correcting him. "It's still underway. We just came out for more provisions. We're pretty blazed, in case you couldn't tell."

Morty took another careful look at us and chuckled again. "Nice. I guess that would explain the surfeit of grocery bags."

"Exactly," I said. "And that's the first time in my life I've ever heard someone use that word in a sentence."

He shrugged.

"You're welcome to join us for a nightcap, Morty," said Duce, after dragging on a freshly lit cigarette. "I've heard you brew a heady moonshine, but you really ought to try some of my old man's fine aged whisky and a few tokes of Elliott Sturgeon's giggly, introspective private stash."

"That sounds terrific, actually, but I've been looking forward to watching this utterly depressing cartoon for months. And now that I've got the eggnog I think I'm going to cash in my chips and go home."

"Fair enough," said Duce. "Not a bad call, Morty."

Goldy pressed the sensor on the keychain, unlocking the Suburban's doors with a honk. And that was that. It was a brief but somehow meaningful exchange, I felt. Just after we had bid each other farewell, I spun around with one final remark.

"Tuesday... quiche Lorraine," I said to him. "Can't wait."

He smiled, holding up his right hand in a two-finger peace sign. "Likewise," he said, morphing into a soldier's salute. "God save the old girl."

Nobody said anything in the car for several minutes as we each pawed through our bags taking inventory. Mine was an embarrassment of riches. I felt like the kid who had conquered Halloween, and in my mind I crowed, "Take that, you nagging little trick. I'll whip you yet." But what came out of my mouth instead was: "*God fucking damn it*! I knew I should have bought a chocolate long john with sprinkles."

"Huh?" said Duce.

"Two raised-glazed doughnuts," I groused, crumpling part of the bag. "Lack of diversity is such an amateur mistake."

But redemption, which quickly followed, came with remembering that there's little satisfaction in eating just one doughnut. At least I'd had the foresight to buy a pair.

The windshield wipers squeaked as they brushed aside a layer of moist snowflakes, and Goldy eyed me in the rearview mirror as he said, "You know what they call that, Swilly? They call that buyer's remorse."

Even behind the wheel of such a preposterously large vehicle, Goldy looked like an elephant riding a tricycle.

"That's funny," said Duce. "I sometimes get that after I hook up with my girlfriend."

Everybody laughed, Chloe the hardest.

"Heather?" she said, with a blush.

"I'm joking," said Duce, directing a sly wink at me.

The car fishtailed when we turned off the main road into Rolling Evergreens. The neighborhood still hadn't been plowed. An out-of-town relative of mine once joked that Minnesotans are the only people in the world who need to use construction equipment to move their snow. I thought of that line as Old Leadfoot Lindy, being playful on the slick roads, stepped on the accelerator and jerked the wheel, intending, I think, to mildly accentuate the fishtail. What happened instead was he lost control, and we spun out in nauseating, high-speed rotations that made me lose my bearings for a moment. When we stopped spinning, I realized we were a quarter of the way up someone's snow-capped lawn.

"Julianne," said Goldy, with mild panic entering his voice. "Could you get out and give us a push?"

"Okay," she said, opening the door, which automatically triggered the dome light.

"I'm kidding, sweetheart," Goldy said.

So, Duce and I plunged into the knee-high wet powder and waded to the rear bumper. Our feet kept slipping underneath us as we pushed against the back of the monstrous vehicle with all our strength, inching it off the lawn toward the road.

On the home stretch, Goldy joked a few more times like he intended to yank the steering wheel again. His eyes flitted toward the mirror and he giggled, and I knew the temptation was real for him. Each time he did it, Duce barked savagely at him: "Goldy, quit *fucking* horsing around behind the wheel!"

Of course, Duce could have driven us himself. When he was stoned, he was the kind of thoughtful, selfless driver who would roll down his window two miles before a tollbooth.

No, having the chauffeur was a false show of propriety, although I'm not exactly sure for whose benefit. In the end, we arrived back at Babyk's house unscathed, which I guess justified Goldy's magnanimity—and maybe even his shenanigans.

By the time we returned to the party only a couple dozen people were still there, and most of them were gathered in the kitchen demanding sustenance. For laughs, Duce had put on an apron that depicted the torso of Michelangelo's *David*, from his muscular abdomen to his well-defined thighs, including, as a sort of visual punch line, the statue's little marble pecker. Duce had bought it from a street peddler outside the convent of San Marco in Florence. Presently, he stood over the gas stove, tending to a stew-pot full of macaroni and cheese—maybe three or four boxes worth, a full stick of butter per box—stirring the ersatz-cheesy glop with a long wooden spoon.

"Man, you need a hair net for your ass!" I joked. Duce was naked except for the apron. That was part of the gag.

Ignoring the remark, Duce patted his chest, where his shirt pocket would have been, and then reflexively patted his hips. Nothing. So he fixed the fresh spliff between his front teeth and turned on another gas cooktop, flicking the pilot lighter several times before leaning down and taking a few sharp puffs to ignite the far end. He nearly singed off his eyebrows in the process—a frightfully close call that made him bolt upright and cast a devilish grin at no one in particular.

I couldn't escape the impression we were in a television sit-com studio. I liked the metaphor, I'll admit, even though I was no longer high enough to actually believe it. Still, the kitchen felt like it was all stage props and klieg lights, and when I let my vision blur the lights melted into vertical and horizontal beams.

"Jesus Christ, it's hotter than Hades in here," said Duce as he hoisted the stew-pot with both hands and lugged it across to the breakfast bar, where he proceeded to ladle out macaroni and cheese to all comers, provided they retrieved their own bowls and silverware.

"It's like a stoner's soup kitchen," he joked.

Then Julianne set about making butter-fried grilled cheese sandwiches with her loaf of white bread. They were so delicious that orders began to come in, forcing her to churn them out three at a time on an oversized non-stick skillet.

"Can you make me one with a fried egg on top?" Grouse asked, rubbing his temples.

Normally indefatigable as a drinker, Grouse showed signs of imminent surrender. Slumping on a wooden armchair at the kitchen table, he periodically nodded off before suddenly jerking to life, presumably to ward off the dreaded spins. Single-handedly attempting to conquer a liter of Scotch whisky, plus countless beers and *baijiu* shots, would have that effect on most mortals.

Queenie put her hand on his head and lovingly scratched it.

"Good morning, sunshine," she cooed.

"Oh, lord Jesus," he replied in a voice full of ecstasy. "That is so nice. Your fingernails are like dildos for my head."

Queenie snorted a laugh and stopped massaging his scalp.

"No, no. Keep going," he implored. "I love it… *I love you.*"

She stood up, blushing embarrassedly.

"No, you don't, Ryan," she said.

"Yes, I do. *I love you.* Those are the three magic words that make them putty in my hands."

In his drunken fugue state, Grouse had ordered three dozen fried egg rolls from China, China Fast Food while we were at the grocery store, and a collection of grease-saturated bags was now scattered all over the kitchen.

When he had opened the front door to receive the delivery, Ally told us, Grouse had thundered, *"Egg rolls in the hands of a hungry mob!"* expecting to find Egg Roll Man. Alas, someone else brought the order, and Grouse, in his profound disappointment, came his closest all night to shedding real tears.

There was no chance all the egg rolls would be eaten—that wasn't even a question—but with so many ravenous appetites on display, one could be forgiven for wondering whether *all of us* were privately suffering from tapeworms.

"Who wants milk shakes, to fill in the cracks?" I joked.

The church girls had untwisted a pair of metal coat hangers and were using them to roast jumbo marshmallows over a low flame on the gas stove. They'd also bought graham crackers and chocolate bars to make "campfire" s'mores.

"Hey, quit trying to shanghai all the marshmallows," Henry complained as the church girls delicately charred their soft little sugar cubes.

"Hey Sandra, would you bum me a cigarette?" Porter said across the room.

Duce tilted his pack of Marlboro Lights toward him.

"No, thanks, man. I prefer menthols," replied Porter, with a shameless grin.

"No laxatives in these brownies, right, Babyk?" said Henry.

"I hope not," said Duce, who'd pushed aside his empty bowl of mac and cheese and was biting into a warm brownie, fresh out of the oven.

They were the chewiest goddamn brownies I'd ever eaten in my life, some kind of fudge-caramel swirl, and we all sat there for several minutes laboring like dogs eating heartworm pills in a clump of peanut butter. I felt like I'd be smacking at the roof of my mouth all night. Finally, I just ushered the damn thing down my throat with my tongue, like the Pit of Sarlacc.

"These aren't Elliott's secret recipe, are they?" Henry said. "No surprises later?"

"You're worried someone sprinkled pot in them?" I asked.

"I've had pot brownies before," Henry said. "I'm fine to eat one now. I just want to know what to expect."

Duce reached for another brownie.

"I'm doubling down, in case I get lucky," he said.

"Duce, didn't you give pot brownies to a Jehovah's Witness once who showed up proselytizing at your front door?" I said, not at all confident the story was true.

The room laughed.

"No one ever did that," said Goldy. "Giving pot brownies to

missionaries is a classic urban legend—sort of like the kid who wipes his ass with poison ivy when he's camping."

"Bullshit!" said Grouse, coming alive in his chair. "I knew a kid at Camp Lincoln who did that."

Peter O'Leary had quietly entered the kitchen carrying a portable fire extinguisher, which he suddenly deployed in the direction of Grouse's crotch, causing Grouse to spring off his chair like a cat at the sound of exploding firecrackers. The fire retardant splattered all over the walls and floor like imitation whipped cream.

Grouse was still hopping up and down as O'Leary fled the scene, along with most of the bystanders, who didn't want to be enlisted for the substantial cleanup effort. Grouse later said it didn't hurt as much as it simply shocked the hell out of him.

In the aftermath, Julianne and I found ourselves in the hallway outside the kitchen, where Porter was standing wobbly-legged with his hand against the wall. His sagging, watery eyes suggested he was maybe on the verge of regurgitation—and likely blacked out. Someone had drawn a pencil-thin moustache above his lips with a magic marker, or maybe he had drawn it himself trying to be funny.

"That cigarette did you no favors," I said to him.

He hiccupped.

"I'm undercover, Bo," he said, weaving slightly.

"You're undercover for what?" Julianne asked him.

"They haven't told me yet," Porter replied.

"Who are *they*?" Julianne said.

"Don't worry about it," he said, breaking into giggles.

With the great mystery left unexplained, Porter hobbled downstairs on those unreliable legs while Julianne went to the bathroom and I snuck into the kitchen for a glass of water. Alas, I was safe: Ally, Queenie, and a few other Good Samaritans appeared to have the wiping and mopping under control.

The basement was ravaged, with detritus everywhere: shot glasses coated with sticky remains, tumblers half-full of melted ice, soggy cocktail napkins, pulped limes, plundered cigarette packs, bowls of crusted cheese dip, and various other discarded mementos of the night. The checkerboard dance floor had also been abandoned, although the colorful lights continued rotating through a sequence of vibrant hues.

Porter stood off to one side of the dance floor in a cheap straw sombrero and woven shawl that Duce had brought back from Acapulco, and he glassily eyed the karaoke monitor as he sang "Nights in White Satin," the Moody Blues hit, into a cordless microphone. In his other hand, he jostled an orange-painted maraca.

Grouse listened for a moment to Porter's uneven crooning before he leaned in closer to Jessica and put a hand on her shoulder, saying to her in a cockeyed-drunk but warmly sentimental tone, with as much false sincerity as he could muster: "He has *such* a beautiful voice… it's *so* beautiful."

And Porter, despite being equally shitfaced, became self-conscious as he realized Grouse was talking about him. Porter quit singing, even as the background track played on, but then he gently swayed to the flute solo.

"I hope you don't mind that I'm wearing your poncho," Porter said into the microphone to Duce, who had entered the lower level still wearing the *David* apron.

Duce took a clipped drag off a cigarette and replied in a raspy, over-smoked voice: "It's not a poncho—it's a fucking *sarape*." He was holding a milk chocolate bar shaped like Han Solo encased in carbonite. It was a Christmas-stocking gift, he said, as he peeled down the wrapper and tinfoil, and bit off the head and hands in one go. Then, grimacing at the loud musical crescendo coming through the speakers, he motioned me away from the dance floor. Grouse wandered off in another direction.

"You've got to come over tomorrow," Duce said when we'd reached a quieter space. "We've got three smoking hot broads coming from Tuna's. Apparently, they'll scrub down the whole house, floor to ceiling—and *anything else* that needs a good polishing—and they do it all butt naked."

"Man, that's a tough one to miss," I said, being honest. "Unfortunately, I'll be at the Guthrie with my old man watching Ebenezer Scrooge find redemption."

"What good is that? You already know how it ends?"

"I know. I know."

"Ah, well. Tits are tits. You've seen them before, too."

"Sure, I know how *that* ends, but somehow it never gets old."

"There's always next time," he said.

We'd wandered into the billiards room, where Henry stood hunched over the cue ball, squinting as he measured his angle. He paused to glance up at us.

"When I'm high," he said, standing upright to chalk his cue, "I've got vision like the Terminator. I can *see* the geometry. It's like red graphs showing the precise strike-points. Pocketing the shot becomes a *mathematical* certainty."

He lowered himself over the cue ball again and proceeded to rap it forcefully into the nine-ball, which bounced off the rail six inches wide of his intended pocket and caromed off three other rails before coming to a rest.

"What's that, Henry?" I said.

"You can't win 'em all." He shrugged, laying the cue diagonally across the table among the scattered balls.

Four dope-eyed stowaways—underclassmen, all of them— were slumped on the big sofa in the TV room watching "The Wizard of Oz" synchronized with Pink Floyd's "Dark Side of the Moon." Duce and I entered the room just as Dorothy Gale stepped out of her Kansas house into Technicolor.

Our host moved swiftly to the CD player and hit "pause," and then used the remote control to switch the channel to an obscure satellite station that was broadcasting a Christian rock mega-concert from Waco, Texas. To the bitter groans that filled the room, Duce replied in a scolding tone: "Oh, come now. A bit of churchin' might do you heathens some good."

In a corner of the room, Henry began playing an original

Pac-Man arcade game, and the noisy "*Chomp! Chomp! Chomp!*" as Pac-Man weaved around the maze obviously grated on Duce, who directed a boiling glare at Henry.

"Hey, asshole, do you mind?" he said, gesturing toward the television. "A little bit of respect for the old lord and savior?"

But Henry was so absorbed by the game that he didn't hear him. Duce turned up the volume on the TV, but the Christian rock ballads were no match for the electronic beeping and siren-like sounds. God didn't stand a chance, frankly, and so at last Duce marched across the room and yanked the plug out of the wall.

"Hey, *fucker*!" Henry cried. "I was in the middle of my game, and I'd just eaten a power pellet!"

"*Party's over, boys!*" sneered Duce, in a comical impression of an irascible witch mother.

Indeed, the night was screeching toward its inevitable conclusion; that much was certain. I watched across the length of the basement as Porter staggered off the dance floor, his arm draped heavily over Jessica's shoulder, his lips puckered into a bottle of soda water. The karaoke music had been switched off.

"C'mon, Ports," she said. "We need to take you home."

They stumbled toward us.

"Okay," he replied, "but let me go to the bathroom first. I might need to puke for a little bit."

She smiled at me, as though pretending to be surprised. I'd come out of the TV room, into the billiards parlor.

"I'll wait for you upstairs by the front door," she told him.

An uneasy silence arose as Jessica and I found ourselves alone together for the first time in so many months. She picked up the orange-striped pool ball and rolled it the length of the table, nine feet, before catching it on the rebound with her fingertips. She did it twice more, rolling the ball a bit harder each time, and finally she turned to me and said: "Your hair—it's getting long."

"I know. I'm thinking about getting a perm."

She smiled.

"Can I ask you something: Does my breath smell?"

She stepped toward me with her mouth slightly ajar, softly exhaling toward my face. I tilted my head up, flaring my nostrils like a rainforest gorilla, and let my eyes roll back, pretending to fall unconscious. We both giggled. It was one of our old running jokes. Then I put my arm around her shoulder, friend-like, and she patted my waist with her hand.

"Don't give me the pat," I said.

"Well, don't give me the one-armed hug."

We laughed again and embraced more tenderly with both arms, giving each other a big, friendly squeeze.

"Good night, Jess," I said to her.

"Night, Billy," she replied.

With Porter occupying the main downstairs bathroom, and chaos still lingering in the kitchen, I decided on an unorthodox move: I would have my final piss of the night in the king's commode. I don't know why the idea struck me as such a novel and adventurous one. I guess it was just that the house's top floor, where Mr. and Mrs. Babyk kept their private quarters, had always been declared "strictly off limits," and those types of blanket prohibitions tended to make me curious. The fact that I'd never seen the master suite, up there in the bird's nest, suddenly struck me as a grave injustice.

He was, after all, a mafia don, and who wouldn't want to know how such a man lives?

The crowd of partygoers thinned as I wended my way up to the second level. From there to the third floor the house became a veritable ghost town. On the carpeted landing outside the master suite, a pair of gilded, ornamented doors resembling Ghiberti's baptistery gates were flanked by a pair of gleaming, golden Bodhisattvas mounted on museum stands. As I heaved open one of the doors, I was met by the pleasant smell of rich calf leather and expensive French perfume—the sort of heady aroma one might normally associate with a Louis Vuitton or Chanel boutique.

The bedroom was spacious but not obscenely so, although you could have played hide-and-seek in its walk-in closets. The furniture, also, was rather predictable: a designer chaise lounge and twin Barcelona chairs, with a low glass table between them. Merlot-colored velvet curtains encircled a four-poster, California king-sized bed, and the curtains were pulled back on one side. Through the opening I could see Sharon Babyk's cat, The Ninth Act, regarding me with glowing, alien eyes.

Sharon had brought exactly two material possessions into her marriage with Mr. Babyk. One was the grumpy, gray-coated British Shorthair she called "Barney" but everyone else knew as "The Ninth Act," and the other was the waterfront cottage in Kirsten Springs, Florida, where she and her husband were now vacationing. If you asked anyone else in the family what the cat's name was, I doubt they could have told you it was "Barney."

"It's not like a dog, where you call his name, or whistle, and he comes running," Mr. Babyk once explained. "This cat abides by his own whims. I mean—we never see the damn thing unless he's hungry. Or if we do see him, he'll be creeping across the far side of the room, like a ghost, and one of us will whisper, 'There goes The Ninth Act.'"

Unlike most domestic felines, Barney lacked the inborn natural reflexes to always land on his feet. You could hold the cat at shoulder-height above the sofa and drop him backside-first, and he wouldn't even try to spin around. The Babyks used this as sort of a parlor trick whenever they entertained guests. Barney would just bounce off the sofa cushion on his backside, casting an irritable glare all around, while Mr. Babyk wagged a finger at the dumbstruck cat and warned him that he had already wasted his first eight lives and ought to be more careful. It was the ninth act, the final inning. The nickname stuck.

Duce's stepmom had vowed to cast a bronze statue out of Barney after he died. She intended to place it in the living room beside the fireplace for all of eternity. She had *that* sort of attachment to her cat. She had kept it locked in the castle tower for years.

As I entered the bathroom, motion sensors triggered the overhead lights, and I told myself that determining whether a bathroom technically qualifies as "palatial" is at least partly a question of how much proper furniture is inside it. The Babyks' master bathroom had furniture in spades: a pair of lacquered wooden dressers, an antique, wrought-iron table, and two vanity chairs topped with needlepoint cushions.

There were, of course, his and her sinks. There were also, more surprisingly, I thought, his and her deep-soaking bathtubs and glassed-in shower stalls. A mosaic depicting the vast antlers of a northern Minnesota caribou stretched across the middle of the white-tiled floor, and on the walls between the mirrors hung a number of framed etchings, including one of the Flavian Amphitheatre and another of a young girl in a long black dress on an empty beach, sobbing into her palms. The title, in pencil, read: "*Ein Leben: Verlassen.*" At times like that, I wished I'd paid more attention in German class.

A framed photograph atop one of the dressers showed a considerably younger Mr. Babyk, dressed in a powder-blue suit and knitted navy-blue tie, leaning against an old car whose windows were soaped with the words: "Just Married." No bride could be seen, but I guessed maybe that was the point—that it was a keepsake from his first wedding, to Duce's mom, and that it possibly captured the finest moment of the day for him.

Then, as I began to regret my excursion into this restricted territory, with my findings more or less underwhelming and as expected, I discovered something that turned it all upside down in a crushing instant, simultaneously reducing all the mansion's stately poise and costly bric-a-brac, effectively, to meaningless rubble—to mere costume jewelry.

With dull curiosity, I opened one of the dresser drawers and peered inside, where I saw, with no effort made to conceal it, a framed newspaper clipping, yellowed with age, dated June 28, 1989, and a headline that read: "Local restaurateur nabs $13 million in largest-ever state lottery payout."

Beaming a ruddy, winsome smile, the same handsome man from the wedding picture, in the same handsome suit and tie, could be seen shaking hands with a man identified in the caption as "lottery commissioner Joseph Summers."

I read the article three times out of fear that my brain and eyes were deceiving me at that sodden and depraved hour of the night. Indeed, at that very moment, fact and fiction leapt toward the last empty chair, and I've been left to wonder ever since if anything in the world is actually what it seems.

Whenever Grouse switched his drink order to Bloody Marys it usually signaled that he had rebounded from the depths of his intoxication and regained control over some of his more basic faculties—like the ability to speak English in fully formed sentences. His eyes at this stage of the night generally took on a warm, Florida-sunset glow, and his mood turned gentle and almost reflective. From here on in, if experience held, he was the master of his own destiny.

And for what it's worth, I felt myself emerging, too, from the delicious fog of what Henry had called a "paradise high." The return of mental lucidity and the knowledge that a sleep-coma was coming soon felt like delicious, hard-earned rewards.

The last bastion of revelers, maybe fifteen or twenty of us, was holed up in the kitchen, listening to Grouse tell—or rather *re-tell*, as was more often the case—a story about the time he got expelled from school our sophomore year over what he deemed a "misunderstanding" in English composition class. The students had been assigned to write and illustrate their own children's books, and Grouse's submission had promptly earned him a summons to the principal's office.

Taking a small sip of his spicy tomato juice and vodka, he reminisced: "Principal Vaughn told me to sit down and he asked, 'Why are you enrolled in this course, Mr. Boozer? Because it seems like you have no interest whatsoever in literature, other than to mock it, and no clue about the boundaries of the craft.'

I told him, 'Sir, I never had any younger siblings, and I always *deeply* regretted having missed the opportunity to read some of my favorite stories to a little brother or sister.'"

The room chuckled at his gooey coating of sarcasm, and they kept snickering as he went on in an earnest, boyish tone:

"I said, 'Mr. Vaughn, the best-selling children's book *Everybody Poops* impacted me profoundly as a child. I swear, I was only acting in good faith when I wrote what I considered to be a post-pubescent installation in the series, titled *Don't Worry Kid, Monkeys Jack Off, Too*. I wanted to provide similar comforts to a new generation of young shower-tuggers.'"

The title was obviously the punch line, and by the time he tacked on the last bit the sound of high-pitched laughter and slapped thighs all but drowned it out.

Principal Vaughn expelled Grouse from school for three days, the paperwork noted, for his "*extremely* immature drawings of naked orangutans and other primates inappropriately touching themselves."

Grouse had labored painstakingly over those cartoons with crayons and colored pens, he said, and even after his expulsion he continued to insist: "The illustrations were pretty damn good. Now, I'm not going to say they were Caldecott-worthy, but they were *pretty damn good*."

"Is that true?" someone asked him in Duce's kitchen.

"Is what true?" he said.

"Do monkeys really jerk off?"

"Of course they do. Do you think I would make something like that up?"

"It's like the old joke," I said. "Do you know why dogs lick their balls?"

"*Because they can*," answered Peter O'Leary, providing the punch line.

"Yeah, yeah," O'Leary added, "but that's too obvious. What I want to know is this: Do you guys think masturbation is an admission, on some level, of latent homosexuality? I mean, okay, you look at magazine pictures of naked girls to reassure yourself, but you have to wonder: *part of me likes having a dick in my hand.*"

Laughter shook the kitchen.

"There goes my manhood," I said. "If we're heading down that road, then how about this philosophical musing, which seems especially timely tonight for sweet little Julianne. It's one I've pondered myself. If you found a sex tape of your parents from the moment you were conceived, would you watch it?"

Groans, more laughter, and a squeamish but short-lived debate ensued. When the room finally quieted down again, Goldy tossed in a more sober query, beyond the realm of human or primate sexuality: "Have you ever stopped to think how strange it is that sporting events are the only time in our lives that people get so excited they hop up and down, screaming as loud as they can, and hug total strangers? I mean, what the hell does that say about the rest of our lives?"

"What about rock concerts?" someone asked.

Goldy shook his head, loading salsa onto a tortilla chip.

"Not really," he said, putting the chip into his mouth and swallowing it in one bite. "Sports fans are *emotionally* invested in the outcome, whereas with music people cheer the moment. Nobody chants or cheers, or jeers opposing fans, in a parking lot after a concert. You could win the lottery and I doubt you'd act like you do at a football game. And to my mind, that ought to be the definition of psychotic."

"Dejected sports fans *would* make an interesting doctoral psychology thesis," I agreed.

More questions followed, steering the conversation even further from Grouse's *extremely inappropriate* children's book: Why don't guys think about their girlfriends more often when they masturbate? Why is it so far fetched to imagine a monkey owning a pet goldfish? If you double double-check something, how many times are you checking it? Why don't you ever see ants walking? What do you think the Macho Man was like out of character? When you light a candle and all the wax burns down, and eventually there's none left, where the hell did it all go? Do you think computers will outlive cockroaches? And why are my nightmares still narrated by Robert Stack?

At last, Queenie muscled her way into the conversation.

"Y'all have to see this," she said, unzipping a side pocket on her jacket and pulling out a re-sealable plastic sandwich bag, which she held up to the ceiling light. Inside was a paint chip, no bigger than a postage stamp, that she said she'd found on the floor underneath a Jackson Pollack painting at Chicago's Art Institute the previous week.

"It fell off a huge canvas titled *Greyed Rainbow*, which looks like a thickly textured, raised-relief globe that's been flattened out and dripped to the Himalayas," she explained.

"I mean, can you believe this?" she went on, eyeing the shard of dried paint. "It's incredible. It isn't *the same* anymore."

(I ought to note that a group of us privately agreed that we could envision Queenie fingering herself in college while looking at a Georgia O'Keefe painting.)

"What's not the same?" Henry asked.

"The painting," Queenie said, solemnly. "Because of this."

And she indicated her paint chip.

"Now, it'll never be like it was again," she added.

"Jesus Christ, how much did she smoke?" Duce said.

To which Queenie snorted an embarrassed giggle, as though suddenly aware of the melodramatic nature of her assertions. "Too much apparently," she said with another laugh before retreating down to the sofa to snuggle her paint chip.

"Just wait until the Chinese start dumping on canvases and marketing it as contemporary art," said Grouse. "They'll have no problem giving our boring hacks a run for their money."

And at that, I stood up, deciding it was as good a note as any to end the night on. As I did so, the cartilage in my knees cracked. I motioned across the room to Grouse, and the others, taking some primordial social cue, all decided to rise as well.

Then, as though the house lights in the theater had come

up, the evening's main drama was finished. But Henry, for one, wasn't ready for the night to conclude, and so he made one final attempt, in vain, to revive the spirit of the discussion.

"It's like the infidelity of *being*," he said, as people got up and searched for their car keys, filled water glasses, and shuffled toward the exits, "how you can lead an honest, faithful existence and still be treated unfairly."

He took a serious gulp from his beer and added: "Because life cheats even on its most loyal lover."

Then he shook his head and said, mostly to himself, "Why the hell is that?"

And O'Leary, who was standing behind Henry, put a hand on his shoulder and answered, in a voice meant to be genuinely comforting, I think: "Because, Henry. Just because."

Nobody added to those words, maybe because we were all physically and emotionally spent, or maybe because no one was listening. In any case, they marked the night's official end, but let it be sung upon high: "A good time was had by all."

The van shuttles, apparently, were only one way. When we left Babyk Manor, on foot, we trudged back to the church atop freshly plowed roads, but the shovels hadn't cut down to the bone, as they say, and so we walked on a crusted layer of packed frozen snow, which squeaked like hard styrofoam under our shoes. Back at the ranch, Duce, Heather, the church girls, Adriana, and Henry—newly refueled, ready for Round Two—had just poured more drinks and rolled fresh spliffs.

The rest of us needed to get home.

In Minnesota, in the dead of winter, the midnight hours had a strange, empty quality to them, as if the atmospheric layers that separated the upper sky from outer space had disappeared—as if the dimensions of our solitude had expanded.

Using his bare hands, Grouse scooped up a baseball-sized snowball from the roadside, and his voice filled the frozen silence as he boomed like a radio announcer: "*Sweet Music goes into his windup*—"He hurled the snowball at a stop-sign twenty feet away, but it went sailing past it, missing by a long shot, and plunged deep into the shadows beyond the glare of a corner streetlamp.

At the church parking lot, O'Leary offered to drive home the girls, Goldy, and a sleepy-eyed Sandra Flanagan, who all lived near his place, more or less, and Grouse said he'd drop me off at my house even though it was out of his way.

His truck's windshield and side windows were covered in frost, and he had left the scraper on the bed, where it was now buried under a pile of fresh snow. Neither of us was eager to dig it out, but then I remembered Duce's expired credit card in my pocket, and I used that to scrape off the frost on all four sides and the rearview mirrors.

It logically followed that the old truck's engine wouldn't start, but fortunately, again, O'Leary kept a set of jumper cables in his trunk. Goldy fixed them to the two vehicles' batteries, connecting them positive-positive, negative-negative, or whatever. It was funny: He couldn't legally drive a car, but he knew how to jump-start an engine, which in this case, I guess, was just as valuable and maybe more so. As the pit crew negotiated the popular mechanics, Julianne and I hugged goodnight and she made me promise I'd go to her house in the afternoon as soon as I got back from the Guthrie.

"Don't forget about our ice castle," she said.

"There's no way I'd miss it," I said, wrapping her in another hug and pecking her on her cold cheek.

We exchanged waves through the window as O'Leary sped off, his compact car jammed full of passengers.

As I climbed into Grouse's truck, I immediately regretted that I hadn't opted for the vehicle with a more advanced heating system. The interior surfaces were all cold to the touch, and we sat in the idling icebox for several long minutes before velvety, warm air finally started pouring out of the vents. Then Grouse promptly shifted the truck into gear and piloted us out of the deserted, darkened lot.

Waiting for the engine to warm was a solemn ritual where we came from, one that was typically observed in noble silence. After we'd partially thawed—after a moderate spell of quietude, in other words—Grouse said, "I think Ally's pissed off at me."

"Why's that?"

"She said I got too drunk."

"Well, gosh, she really went out on a limb there," I teased.

"I think she missed the point. The point of tonight was *precisely* to get too drunk."

"Yeah, maybe she was being overly sensitive. Maybe her radar is too finely tuned."

"Shit, you can't sneak anything past a woman who doesn't drink," he said.

I'd cupped my hands over the vents, and was trying to facilitate the blood flow in my fingertips.

"When I hooked that koi fish out of the pond, she chewed me out like you wouldn't believe," he went on. "I thought she was going to start throwing fishing lures at me. She didn't see the humor in it at all."

We both chuckled sort of grimly.

"I told her that I was going to bake it at four hundred degrees with some olive oil and paprika, and I've never seen her so mad. She was absolutely furious."

"What did she say?"

"She said koi fish are beautiful creatures and that we ought to admire them for their brilliant colors and for *the poetry of their motion*—she actually said that—and that only a selfish prick would do what I was doing for no good reason. She was so upset that I just tossed the fucking thing back into the water, bloody hook-gashes and all. I couldn't handle her outrage or her pity. It was one fish, for Christ's sake!"

We passed the police station and city hall, where most of the lights had been switched off, and I glanced at the analog clock on the truck's dashboard. It was 1:06am.

"But I will say, that was one of the best nights I've had in a long time," Grouse said. "I was completely soused."

"Yeah, that was a great night," I said. "It was worth whatever trouble it'll cause me when I get home after my curfew."

We crossed the old stone bridge over the creek falls, which were stilled by the ice and snow, and curled around a wide residential boulevard entering my neighborhood proper. Grouse turned onto Mallard Lane, which was lined on both sides by mature elms and stately oaks that towered over the road. In the summertime, the trees formed a narrow, winding passage—lush and leafy and shaded—like a remote stretch of a meandering upstate river. But now, barren of leaves, the naked branches just rattled in the cold air like so many frozen twigs.

The neighbors were all sleeping, warmly cocooned in their brick Tudors, stucco Mediterraneans, and three-story Colonial Revivals perched on elevated lawns. A few porch lights glowed, but mostly the windows were darkened and the upstairs shades were drawn, while heat vapors rose from the chimney vents like factory exhaust.

But this placid and charming little milieu—this picturesque scene of domestic wintertime tranquility—was upended by the sudden appearance of swirling red and blue lights at the bottom of the tunnel of elms. The lights were beating rhythmically against an old tree trunk—*thump, thump, thump, thump*—and spewing against the dull-gray snow banks.

When we reached the source of these lights and I jumped down from Grouse's truck onto the icy street, the frozen air clamped around my face like a steel mask. A team of paramedics was wheeling a stretcher over the snow-covered sidewalk from the front door of my house to the driveway, and I intercepted them just as they were preparing to load their passenger into the rear of the ambulance.

He gazed up at me with the fragile eyes of a very sick child and the resigned countenance of a wise old man. I tried to reassure him through my eyes that I knew what he needed me to say. I groped for the words but none came.

Finally, in a weak voice, he said to me, "It wasn't supposed to end this way." And after a brief pause, he added, "But maybe it's as good a time as any."

Then he winked at me. Or he didn't.

Even now, I don't know if he said any of that to me—or if he said anything at all. My memory of those moments is a kinetic blur: of scrambling medics and static-filled radio voices, of my frantic mother and those god-forsaken lights.

When one of the paramedics raised the defibrillator paddles above his head, Zeus-like, and brought them crashing down to deliver another bolt of lightning, I remember thinking I already knew the score—I knew how *this* game would end.

Then the ambulance raced away, with my mother in a squad car trailing desperately in its wake, and I slumped against the hood of Grouse's truck, pressing my cheek to the frozen metal, feeling as if my soul had just been hollowed out by an ice cream scoop. I would eventually cry until I couldn't cry anymore, until my tear ducts fired blanks, and I turned *emotionally impotent*—a condition even today I fear might be permanent.

As I stood there on the empty street, clutching the old pickup truck's side mirror to steady myself for a moment before we chased after the little parade, Grouse put a hand on my shoulder and squeezed it through my jacket. It was all he could say.

It was bright outside by the time my mom and I got home from the hospital. The early morning sunshine sparkled on the newly fallen snow, creating an almost blinding glare, but it did nothing to alleviate the bitter sub-zero temperatures. That was the paradox, I suppose, of cloudless winter days in Minnesota: they were often the coldest of them all.

Trudging into the house, bone-tired and brutally hungover, a mess of anguish and confusion, I retreated straight upstairs to my bedroom, where I lowered the window shades and climbed into my bed under a pile of heavy blankets.

Sleep was on its way like a falling anvil.

I knew the descent into slumber would be almost violent in its intensity, and so I fought to stave it off, even if just for a few more moments. I listened, gazing out numbly from my pillow, as a snowblower went to work on the neighbor's driveway—and the roaring white noise helped to calm my restless mind.

Dawn was filtering into the room and I could see a handful of old photographs tacked to a corkboard on the opposite wall, including a candid shot I'd always liked of Grouse and me as little kids in our house-league baseball uniforms. He was resting an arm on my shoulder and we were giggling at something off camera, and it was fitting, I thought now, as I lay there on the drowsy verge of oblivion: we were standing in front of the backstop at Cornelius Field.

And looming behind us in the distance, out there among the shaggy green grass and dandelions and fluffy seed heads in deep right-center field, the warming house was baking in the mid-summer sun.

www.ingramcontent.com/pod-product-compliance
Lightning Source LLC
Chambersburg PA
CBHW021110110726
47900CB00007B/2115